Jodi Taylor is the internationally bestselling author of over twenty five novels and more short stories than you can shake a stick at.

Her Chronicles of St Mary's series follows a bunch of disaster-prone individuals who investigate major historical events in contemporary time. Do NOT call it time travel! She is also the author of the Time Police books. Set in the same world as St Mary's, this spinoff charts the highs and lows of an all-powerful international organisation tasked with keeping the Timeline straight no matter what the cost. Efficient and disciplined, obviously they're nothing like St Mary's. Except when they are.

In 2024, *The Ballad of Smallhope and Pennyroyal* accidentally grew from a short story to a full-length novel, revealing the origin story of two beloved characters who feature in both series.

Jodi is also known for her gripping supernatural thrillers featuring the mysterious Elizabeth Cage, together with the enchanting Frogmorton Farm series – a fairy story for adults.

Born in Bristol and now living in Gloucester (facts both cities vigorously deny), she spent many years with her head somewhere else, much to the dismay of family, teachers and employers, before finally deciding to put all that daydreaming to good use and write a book.

By Jodi Taylor and available from Headline

THE BALLAD OF SMALLHOPE AND PENNYROYAL

TIME POLICE SERIES

DOING TIME   HARD TIME   SAVING TIME
ABOUT TIME   KILLING TIME

THE CHRONICLES OF ST MARY'S SERIES

JUST ONE DAMNED THING AFTER ANOTHER
A SYMPHONY OF ECHOES
A SECOND CHANCE
A TRAIL THROUGH TIME
NO TIME LIKE THE PAST
WHAT COULD POSSIBLY GO WRONG?
LIES, DAMNED LIES, AND HISTORY
AND THE REST IS HISTORY
AN ARGUMENTATION OF HISTORIANS
HOPE FOR THE BEST
PLAN FOR THE WORST
ANOTHER TIME, ANOTHER PLACE
A CATALOGUE OF CATASTROPHE
THE GOOD, THE BAD AND THE HISTORY

SHORT-STORY COLLECTIONS

THE LONG AND SHORT OF IT   LONG STORY SHORT
THE MOST WONDERFUL TIME OF THE YEAR

ELIZABETH CAGE NOVELS

WHITE SILENCE   DARK LIGHT
LONG SHADOWS   BAD MOON

FROGMORTON FARM SERIES

THE NOTHING GIRL   THE SOMETHING GIRL

A BACHELOR ESTABLISHMENT

BAD MOON

JODI TAYLOR

HEADLINE

First published in Great Britain in 2025 by
HEADLINE PUBLISHING GROUP LIMITED

1

Cataloguing in Publication Data is available from the British Library

Paperback ISBN 978 1 4722 8695 6

Typeset in Times New Roman by CC Book Production

Printed and bound in Great Britain by Clays Ltd, Elcograf S.p.A.

Headline's policy is to use papers that are natural, renewable and recyclable
products and made from wood grown in well-managed forests and other
controlled sources. The logging and manufacturing processes are expected
to conform to the environmental regulations of the country of origin.

HEADLINE PUBLISHING GROUP
An Hachette UK Company
Carmelite House
50 Victoria Embankment
London EC4Y 0DZ

The authorised representative in the EEA is Hachette Ireland,
8 Castlecourt Centre, Dublin 15, D15 XTP3, Ireland (email: info@hbgi.ie)

www.headline.co.uk
www.hachette.co.uk

PROLOGUE

I took my time getting out of bed. There was no rush. This day would almost certainly be a carbon copy of yesterday – and tomorrow wouldn't be much different, either. Nor the day after that. This seemed to be my life now – a few days of panic and terror and fighting for my life, followed by months of nothing happening at all. Literally nothing. Everyone else would drift off to new days, new experiences, new lives, but here I would sit, silent and still – widow of this parish, living alone in my pretty pink world in my pretty pink house, waiting for the next time the universe decided I should be frightened out of my wits. I've seen visions, ghosts, demons, evil trees, the dead. I've been threatened with death, incarceration, and sectioning under the act. I've been kidnapped. I've even been menaced by a red armchair.

I used to think all I wanted from life was just peace and quiet and to be left alone to enjoy it. Now, for some reason – something had changed. What had formerly been peace and quiet was in danger of turning into uneventful tedium. Day after day of unchanging nothingness.

I wasn't sure what might be different. I suspected it might be me, but I couldn't quite put my finger on it. It hovered in the back of my mind – tantalisingly out of reach. I knew it was there and I knew it was important but I just couldn't quite drag it out into the light.

I'd been puzzling over it for ages but nothing had stirred my memory, so I'd tried to tell myself it was only my imagination. And if it hadn't been for Michael Jones then I might easily have talked myself into believing just that. Everything in my life was exactly as it had been, except for him. Outwardly he was unchanged – unemotional, sarcastic, capable, kind. Inside, however . . .

No one can keep a secret from me. Whether they want to or not. You could be the best liar in the world but ten minutes with me and I know what you are. I can tell whether you're happy or sad, bored or interested, tired, angry, anxious, afraid, hiding something . . . *lying* . . . Whatever your state of mind – I know it. No – I can't read minds: I read people's colours.

Everyone has a colour. An aura, some people call it. When I was young, before I'd heard that word, I called it a colour. Along with its shape, its movement, its depth – your colour tells me all about you. And no, I don't like it any better than you do. It's not a gift – it's a curse. Do you want to know what people think of you? What people *really* think of you? Your best friend who's scheming behind your back? Your husband who fancies your neighbour? Your boss who's secretly taking credit for your work and despises you for it? The shop assistant who thinks you're too stupid to notice your change is wrong?

I try to filter it all out as best I can, in the same way other people automatically filter out the noises of a busy street, so that after a while they just don't hear them. That's what I try to do, but it doesn't always work. It certainly wasn't working now.

I'd spent years trying to hide my gift. Unsuccessfully, as

it turned out, because now here I was, on the verge of being employed – and by the government of all people – just because of this so-called gift. A gift they thought that, under certain circumstances, might prove useful to them. They hadn't actually detailed what those circumstances might be. I'd signed a very vaguely worded contract, together with the Official Secrets Act, and was on a retainer to some sort of government organisation – in the form of the very enigmatic Mary Bennet, together with her . . . what? Henchman? Employee? Spy? Security guard? I don't know. Pick any label – Michael Jones was all, some, any, and none of them.

I'd thought he and I were friends. There had even been one or two moments when I'd thought – I'd hoped – we were about to become more than friends. We were just hovering on the brink . . . and then something had happened last Christmas – the thing I couldn't quite remember.

We were both doing our best to carry on as normal. I had returned home and Jones himself was back at work. Perhaps that was where the problem lay. And there definitely was a problem. Because while he was actually doing a very good job of concealing whatever it was that was troubling him, unfortunately for him, I'm me, and no matter how carefully, how casually, how normally he tried to behave, there was no getting away from it. Something had happened. Something that danced just outside my memory, and now Michael Jones was . . . what? Worried? Wary? Suspicious?

None of those were quite the right words. The word I was looking for was . . . afraid. For some reason, Michael Jones was afraid.

Of me.

CHAPTER ONE

That was the first day I found blood on my front doorstep.

I'd heard my elderly neighbour, Colonel Barton, outside and had gone out to say hello because I hadn't seen him for a few days. Instead, I found him peering over the wrought-iron railings that separated my steps from his and frowning.

'Something nasty happened here, Mrs Cage.'

'Oh.' I stared down at the small puddle of sticky blood on the top step. A few smears on the lower steps indicated that something had either dragged itself down and, given the lack of body, escaped – or dragged itself up, which seemed unlikely, since I have four steps up to my front door and they're quite steep.

'A cat with its kill, I expect,' he said. 'Or possibly, given the location, an urban fox. Something brought you a gift in the night, anyway.'

'Perhaps it wasn't as dead as it thought it was,' I said confusingly. 'I'd like to think it got away.' And then, in an effort to introduce a slightly more cheerful note, 'Are you going out, Colonel? A lovely day if you are.'

'Mrs Barton and I,' he frowned heavily at the absent Mrs Barton, 'are attending an event at the tea rooms.'

'How lovely,' I said, because it was. Up until a few months ago, Mrs Barton wouldn't have been well enough even to leave the house, and now they were painting the town red at the tea rooms. 'A piano recital?'

'A private showing of Bram Stoker's *Dracula*. The latest version.'

'Oh,' I said, quite taken aback. The latest version was – or so I had read – full of blood and violence and nudity and sex and not in that order. That would teach me to stereotype the elderly. 'Well, that sounds very . . . pleasant.'

'It might well be,' he said grimly, 'but at this rate we are unlikely to find out.' He called through his open front door, 'Do get a move on, Dolly!'

Mrs Barton appeared, her delicate robin's-egg blue colour floating gently around her like gossamer in the breeze. 'Why are you booming at me, Arthur?'

Colonel Barton tapped his watch. 'We're going to be late.'

'No, we aren't, dear,' she said placidly. 'I know very well you always tell me things start thirty minutes earlier than they actually do. We have plenty of time yet. Oh, look, Elizabeth. Here comes one of your young men.'

Much as I would love to give the impression Rushford is simply dripping with young men belonging to me, sadly – no. Particularly not this one. This one belonged to someone else. Which didn't stop him turning up on my doorstep whenever it suited him, taking over my sofa and my TV, watching the latest episode of *Olympian Heights*, spending an hour discussing the finer plot points, scrounging fish and chips afterwards, and very often staying the night. On the sofa, of course. And he invariably brought his faithful companion, Nigel. A dog who made the dead smell good.

Iblis halted dramatically at the foot of my steps in full view

5

of the Bartons on one side and the respectable solicitors' firm on the other, together with everyone enjoying the sunshine on the green that afternoon. His silver colour streamed behind him like a banner. He flung his arms wide.

'It is I who appears before you. Iblis.'

The colonel snorted.

Mrs Barton beamed. She's a big fan of Iblis and frankly, if she wanted to celebrate her return to good health with a little flirting, then more power to her elbow. If I hadn't been acquainted with the somewhat scary love of Iblis's life, then I might flirt with him, too.

As always, he looked magnificent. A gentle breeze teased his long blond hair back off his shoulders. His T-shirt only emphasised his impressive physique. Everyone was staring at him, and he knew it. A couple of the younger solicitors were nearly falling out of the window. If Jones had been here, there would have been scowling and sarcasm.

Nigel, scenting food and drink, bundled himself up my steps and disappeared through the front door to make himself at home.

Extending a hand, Iblis helped Mrs Barton down her steps as carefully as if both they and she were made of fragile glass. Once safely at the bottom, he bowed extravagantly and kissed her hand, folded it gently and held it between his own. 'My heart rejoices in your presence.'

If she'd had one of those old-fashioned fans, she would have flirtatiously rapped him across the knuckles with it.

The colonel coughed and stumped down the steps, determinedly under his own steam. 'You're making us late, Dolly.'

'Alas, Venerable One, it is I, Iblis, who must bear the blame. My eyes were dazzled . . .'

6

'Ha,' said Colonel Barton. He's not terribly enthusiastic about being referred to as Venerable One. Offering his arm to Mrs Barton, he said formally, 'Good day to you, sir, Mrs Cage.'

The two of them set off down the path. The colonel's back was ramrod straight and it would have been a very impressive exit, if Mrs Barton hadn't ruined it by turning around and blowing Iblis a kiss.

He snatched it dramatically from the air and pressed it lovingly against his heart.

I said, 'Idiot,' and he laughed. I asked him why he was here.

'To visit the light of my life, my friend, the incomparable Elizabeth Cage.'

'And to watch *Olympian Heights* which starts in five minutes,' I said. 'It's the omnibus edition. Get a move on or you'll miss it.'

He peered at the top step. 'Is that blood?'

'Looks like it. The colonel thinks something came to a sticky end on my doorstep last night.'

'Mm,' he said, apparently losing interest. 'Is there beer?'

'Well, I don't have any. Jones might have left some in the fridge.'

'Good,' he said, closing the door behind him. 'It always tastes better when it's his.'

One hour and thirty minutes later, he switched off the TV, crushed the last can in his fist and turned to me, his eyes sparkling. 'Well, who'd have thought?'

'I know,' I said, equally excited. 'Who would have believed that Shady would turn out to be the missing triplet? After all these years. And that Danton knew all along. And that Mrs

Clapp the cleaner is actually Rosella's long-lost maiden aunt and knows the secret of the Mystery Room where Othello thought he'd buried the locket, which will prove he was the pilot whose flying accident killed Rachel's mother's cousin, who isn't actually dead after all.'

I had to pause to get my breath back.

'I'll put the kettle on,' I said, 'while you and Nigel get your head around things. Tea or coffee?'

There was a knock at the door.

We both knew that knock. Iblis stared at the three empty beer cans on the coffee table and then at me.

'He knows I don't like beer,' I said. 'You're on your own, I'm afraid. Unless you want to nip out of the back door now.'

'I am Iblis,' he said with dignity. 'International Man of Mystery. I do not nip out of back doors.'

'In that case,' I said, pulling out the mugs. 'Can you let him in?'

Jones stepped over the threshold, glaring at Iblis. 'There's blood on the step. Dare I hope it's yours?'

'Not this time,' said Iblis. 'Although even were I mortally wounded, I would still use my last strength to drag myself to the feet of Elizabeth Cage. My heart could not rest without one last glimpse of her exquisite beauty and—'

'Are you hungry?' I asked, because otherwise this could go on all night.

'Fish and chips,' he said, effortlessly diverting into more important areas than my exquisite beauty.

Jones was surveying the signs of our late afternoon debauch. From there, his gaze travelled to Nigel, stretched out in a patch of sunshine and displaying bits better left concealed. Or even

8

buried. Looking at the state of him – Nigel, I mean – I couldn't help worrying about the lower life forms currently abandoning ship to live long and prosper in my soft furnishings. Iblis assures me Nigel benefits from regular grooming and I'm not sure I believe a word of it. Except, as far as I know, the two of them still live with Melek and I couldn't see her allowing Nigel to shed his load all over her sofa. Not for one moment.

Jones hadn't finished. 'Was that my beer?'

'Good afternoon, Cage,' I said. 'Well, good evening, actually. How lovely to see you again. How are you? You're looking very well. In a moment I shall remember why I've come to see you, instead of carping on endlessly about blood and beer, and getting on your nerves.'

'You drank my beer?'

'Not me, buster.' I indicated a grinning Iblis. 'And I think Nigel had half a can as well.'

He turned to Iblis. 'You gave my beer to that . . .'

'The kettle's boiled,' I interrupted. 'Nigel and I are having tea. You two can look after yourselves.'

To add insult to injury, I tossed a digestive at Nigel, who snapped it out of the air without even opening his eyes. That dog had major skills.

I curled up on the sofa with my tea while Jones took himself into the little kitchen area on a beer hunt. My house is all open plan downstairs. The front door opens directly into – well, not a large room, but it's big enough for me. And the sun streams through the front window, from which I can see the castle opposite. And the green with its ponds, and the willow trees and the swans and ducks posing for tourist photos.

I love my room with its wooden floor, colourful rugs, and

9

bookcases. There's a small sofa and an armchair with a low table in between. Nothing matches, nothing's coordinated, but it's comfortable and quiet and mine.

The kitchen is at the rear and looks out over my tiny walled backyard. Downstairs there's a cellar that I use as a laundry room, and a flight of rickety and very narrow stairs winds up through the middle of the house to an upstairs landing. The single bedroom is off to the left and the bathroom to the right. Everywhere is bright and light and shining. Yes, I love my house and my house loves me. I can tell.

Jones was stamping around, pulling open cupboard doors and investigating the contents of the fridge.

'This fridge is empty.'

'Of beer, yes.'

'You drank it all?'

'Omnibus episode of *Olympian Heights*,' I said briefly. 'Why are you here?'

'What are you doing early next week, Cage?'

'Nothing,' I said, without even having to think about it.

'Fancy a trip out to the Sorensen Clinic?'

I regarded him warily. 'For the purposes of . . . ?'

'Sitting in on one of Sorensen's interviews. He's been given the all-clear to travel and they've brought him back to the clinic for the preliminaries. My boss thinks the change of scenery will do him good. Plus, of course, the clinic is the scene of his crimes, so he'll have a chance to mull over all the poor life choices he's made over the last two years or so. Ever since he met you, in fact.'

Dr Sorensen was the former director of the Sorensen Clinic, a very upmarket rehab clinic just outside Rushford where, ostensibly, the great and the good went to be listened to as they talked endlessly about how dreadful their lives were. In reality, that was just their cover and a very good one it was. Hiding behind its high profile, the clinic's true purpose was to provide a sanctuary – a refuge, perhaps – for people far more important than politicians and celebrities grappling with their latest public catastrophe. The clinic's main purpose was to take in burned-out members of the military, security people, those who were coming in from the cold and needed to be quietly debriefed, and those whose loyalties weren't quite as clear-cut as they should be and needed reminding. All these and more found a temporary home at the Sorensen Clinic, while that manipulative bastard – please excuse the language, but Dr Sorensen is really not a nice man – teased out their secrets and reported back to his masters.

My lovely husband, Ted, had worked there for some years as head of security, which is how Sorensen had crossed my path – deliberately, according to Jones. Sorensen used Ted to get to me. I don't know how he'd found out about me, but he had. He didn't know everything, but certainly enough to suspect I was far from what the world would describe as a boring 1950s housewife. He'd been trying to get his hands on me from the moment Ted had introduced us and I'd been trying to shift him out of my life ever since.

And then, around last Christmas, Sorensen had got himself mixed up in something very unpleasant indeed. Not only was a very dangerous drug – Ghost – being manufactured on the clinic's premises, but patients and staff had died in various unpleasant ways. Some were still missing and had never been found.

What role Ghost had played in all this was something Jones

and his colleagues were still trying to establish. With some difficulty, because everyone who had taken Ghost had died shortly afterwards. No one survived Ghost.

Except for me. I'd taken Ghost and lived. I had no idea why.

I knew that Ghost opened doors best left closed. Because what came through had not been the victims' longed-for loved ones as promised. Every single one of us carries our own demon around with us. It's always there, standing invisible at our shoulder, whispering silently in our ear. Most people are completely unaware of its presence – until they take Ghost. Ghost opens that door and their demon is suddenly visible to them.

From that moment on, it never leaves them. No matter how far and how fast they run, they're never able to shift it. They could run and run and run until they drop with exhaustion, but it's still there. Then, when they are too weak to defend themselves, the thing crouches on their chest and just . . . eats their life force. I'd seen it happen. I'd seen the demon tear at the victim's colour with clawed hands, ripping it to pieces, then cramming it into its mouth and gobbling it down. And when the victim's colour was all gone, then so was their life. I'd seen it happen almost right outside my own front door and I'd never forget it as long as I lived.

Sorensen had drugged me with Ghost and escaped in the confusion. I'm genuinely unsure what happened next – I know there were dead people everywhere, and I know that at some point something had stood behind me, but the details were becoming hazier and hazier as time passed, and these days it took a conscious effort from me to remember them at all.

I wasn't actually sure how much I *wanted* to remember, but I knew I'd been dragged from Jones's bedroom just as . . . well,

I'm not saying any more about that. I knew I'd been taken to the clinic. I knew Sorensen had drugged me. I know Mrs Painswick was there. I think she'd tried to help me and was killed because of that. I have a vague memory of being imprisoned in the basement and of overwhelming fear, but the next thing I clearly remember is being with Jones in hospital.

Jones himself had fought like a lion for me and taken a really bad beating. His left eye had been damaged. Possibly permanently. He was making light of it, but he had another physical coming up and his colour told me he was worried.

I watched his colour now as he worked his way around the kitchen, searching out the secret stash of beer he knew I'd have somewhere. His usual red-gold glow was muted. The red had darkened, almost to a crimson, and the gold – that lovely luminous golden colour that had lit up his bedroom like a firework display – was almost completely gone. The shape was different, as well. Less swirly – more solid. Like a shield. Because he was afraid of something, and I was pretty certain it was me.

I looked away and drank my tea.

'Aha.' He reached into a cupboard and pulled out two cans. Iblis sat up, eyes sparkling.

Jones threw him a look and sat down as far from Nigel as possible in such a small room. 'Hands off, you scrounging bastard.'

The scrounging bastard grinned irritatingly. 'You can buy more when we go out for food.'

I live at the top of a very steep hill in a little close which isn't accessible to vehicles. Other than the postman, no one would deliver up here. If Iblis wanted food, someone was going to have to go out and get it.

Jones groaned. 'Oh God, are you staying that long?'

Iblis grinned at me. 'All night, if my gracious hostess permits.'

I suspected Melek had chucked the pair of them out. Probably one of them had peed in the corner.

'Of course you can stay,' I said. 'We'll have something to eat and I'll make you and Nigel up a bed for the night. What would you like?'

'Fish and chips,' he said again.

'Indian,' said Jones.

I stood up. 'That's fish and chips then.'

'No, it's not,' said Jones indignantly. 'How do you work that out?'

'Two to one.'

'The scruffy mongrel doesn't get a vote. Nor the dog, neither.'

'We'll have Chinese then,' I said. 'A diplomatic compromise because I'm hungry and I want to eat this side of midnight. And what were you saying about Sorensen?'

'We've been given the all-clear at last. To begin his debriefing.'

'I thought he was too traumatised to give a statement.'

'It's been made clear that he'll be even more traumatised if he doesn't. Mary Bennet would like you to sit in.'

I must have looked worried because he said hastily, 'It's just the preliminary stuff. I suspect that getting down to the nitty-gritty will be done behind firmly closed doors. Too embarrassing for the public to know lethal drugs were being manufactured by a prominent member of the establishment. We'll just want you to sit in during the early stages and indicate any areas that might repay further investigation. And to tell us if he's lying his socks off, of course. Are you up for that?'

The Sorensen Clinic wasn't my favourite place in the world, but I'd agreed to do this. Mary Bennet was my new employer.

Michael Jones was my colleague. Officially, I was a consultant, brought in to assist with difficult interviews and such. Sorensen had spun it out for as long as he could but now the time had come, and he had questions to answer.

'Yes,' I said, with considerably more confidence than I felt. 'Of course.'

'I'll let you know when and what time I'll pick you up.'

'No need – I'll go on my moped.'

Something else that had happened at Christmas: Jones had bought me one of those little moped/scooter things. I wasn't sure what a 'cc' was, but mine had a whopping great fifty of them. I never know whether to call it a moped or a scooter but according to Jones – probably not the world's greatest expert – it's a moped if it's under fifty cc, and a scooter if you can sit on it and there's a platform on which to put your feet. Who knew?

Anyway, it was beautifully simple to operate. You sat on it, pressed the starter thing and away you went. No gears, no clutch – simple. I'd had a charging point installed in my shed, applied for a licence, taken my CBT test and was beginning to venture out and about. Around Rushford, to the supermarket – no more toiling up the hill laden with heavy groceries – and I'd explored nearby country lanes and local beauty spots. For someone whose only choice had been between walking, public transport or not going out at all, this had, literally, opened up my life. I was still a little nervous and my mind did tend to fill with visions of being laminated to the road by a giant lorry, or falling down a pothole, or being thrown off by a wonky manhole lid, but I kept telling myself loads of people had these little mopeds. They were electric and easy. Mine lived in the shed and represented freedom.

15

'OK,' said Jones amiably. 'How's that going? Ridden into a ditch yet?'

'No,' I said. 'Nor will I. I'm very careful.'

'I don't doubt it for a moment, Cage. I'll give you the details as soon as I know them and meet you at the clinic. On the steps outside. Inside if it's raining.'

'I'll be there.'

There was a pause.

'So, Chinese,' I said. 'What does everyone want?'

Well, that was a mistake. The volley of words nearly pinned me to the wall.

'Crispy fried beef.'

'Special fried rice. Three portions.'

'Prawn crackers. For Nigel. Better get two bags.'

'Those little duck things.'

'And spring rolls.'

'Are those for Nigel?'

'No. I will require six of those. And some for everyone else, as well.'

'And noodles.'

'And sweet and sour pork.'

'Hold on, hold on,' I said, and got up to find my shopping pad. I tore off a sheet and it didn't come off cleanly. I noticed that the perforations were wonky.

I started with my favourite, lemon chicken, because I'd probably end up paying for this, and then jotted down everyone else's requirements. It was actually quite a long list by the time I'd finished.

'Who's going for all this?' I said, handing the list to Jones.

'We'll both go,' he said, tucking it into his pocket and turning

16

to Iblis. 'I'll pay. You carry. Cage sets the table. Teamwork. I'll phone the order through on the way and it should just about be ready when we get there.'

'And beer,' said Iblis. 'Lots of beer.'

Jones sighed. 'Anything for you, Cage?'

'No, thanks. I made lemonade yesterday.'

'See you in about half an hour. Longer if there's a queue.'

They disappeared out of the front door.

Nigel remained. To guard me, presumably. He flung himself into this task by sighing deeply and turning over to resume his slumbers.

I put plates and bowls in the oven because my mother would have had something to say about eating straight out of the cartons. I laid the table, pulled out Nigel's dish – yes, he kept his own dish here – put the empty beer cans out for recycling, made space in the fridge for their future brethren, opened the back door to let in some cooler, fresher air, and sat down to wait, because I thought Jones's estimate of thirty minutes was a little over-optimistic.

As it turned out, I was completely wrong. They were back in less than ten. Without food.

'What happened?' I said as they came in through the front door. 'Did they refuse to serve you?'

They looked at each other. No one said anything. Something was wrong. Iblis's colour was curled tightly around him while Jones's had darkened, fringed at the edges with orange streaks of anxiety.

'What?' I said, suddenly feeling cold. 'What's happened?'

Jones walked up to the kitchen worktop, the one that divides my kitchen from the rest of the room. Iblis slipped past him

17

and opened the door to the stairs. He peered up and then disappeared. I could hear him moving around overhead.

Jones stuck his head out of the back door before shutting it and turning to look at me. 'Cage, you haven't let anyone in recently, have you?'

'No,' I said, alarmed. 'Of course not.'

'You're alone?'

'Of course I am,' I said bitterly. 'I'm always alone.'

His colour was crackling all around him. Something was very wrong.

Iblis reappeared. 'Nothing upstairs or in the cellar. Just us. And Nigel is still asleep.'

This was true. Nigel was apparently comatose – which was good because he's quite a useful barometer. I've seen him when something dodgy is about to happen and he's a fanged ball of fury. Jones says he's Rushford's answer to the Komodo dragon. His bite has only to break the skin and his victim is as good as dead – they just don't know it yet. I could easily imagine Nigel patiently tracking some poor soul as they dragged themselves around for two or three days before dying hideously of his poisonous bite.

I joined them, keeping the worktop between us. 'What's going on?'

Jones pulled a piece of paper from his pocket. 'This.'

He unfolded it and laid it out on the counter where we could all read it.

Written in my own handwriting.

> *One day soon I will send the serpent.*
> *You know I always send the serpent.*
> *It's my signature move.*

CHAPTER TWO

I picked up the note and looked at it. I turned it over, just in case, somehow, my Chinese food order was on the other side. It wasn't.

'Did one of you write this as a joke?'

They both shook their heads. For once, Iblis wasn't smiling.

Jones took the piece of paper off me and pulled over my shopping pad, carefully laying the torn sheet on the top. The jagged tear matched exactly. There was no doubt that that page had come from this pad.

I looked at it again. Black ink. I picked up the pen and made a tentative scribble. Blobby black ink. Just the same as the ink on the paper. And my handwriting.

'I don't understand,' I said. 'I wrote lemon chicken, crispy fried beef and all the rest of it.'

'Write it again,' said Jones. 'No – on another sheet.'

I tore off another page – more carefully this time – and wrote lemon chicken and crispy fried beef. When I'd finished, I laid it on the worktop for everyone to see and looked at the first note again. I think I was hoping that somehow it would have morphed back into the original list, but no. There it sat. Unchanged. Inexplicable. My paper, my pen, my handwriting.

'I didn't write this,' I said, pointing to the original. 'I didn't.

I wrote the list for the takeaway. Like that one.' I gestured to the second sheet. 'Why would I . . . ? Who wrote this? What *serpent*? Who sends a *serpent*? Why send a serpent to *me*?' I could feel panic rising. 'What's going on?' I slammed my hands down on the worktop in frustration. 'Why do I never know what's happening? Why am I always kept in the dark?'

Iblis turned to Jones. 'I will return.'

'Yes,' said Jones sardonically. 'Go and tell Melek she's entangled in her own lies again.'

Iblis stood for a moment. His colour had completely lost its sparkle. 'Nigel – stay.'

Nigel rolled over again.

The door banged behind Iblis. Jones and I were left alone.

'Well?' I said.

'No, it's not well, Cage. Come and sit down.'

I jerked my arm away. I don't lose my temper very often, but I was losing it now. 'No. *No*. I'm not going to sit down. Or have a cup of tea. Or hoover the carpet. Or do what everyone wants me to do. I'm warning you, Jones – I am *well* pissed-off and very, very tired of being the only person who never knows what's going on.'

'Of course you are,' he said, suddenly sounding very tired himself. 'I don't blame you. And, if it's any consolation at all, I was against it. But . . .' He took my hand. 'Please think very carefully about how much you want to know. Ignorance has kept you safe for a long time now and . . .'

'Safe from what? Ignorance of what? Do you honestly think you're helping?'

'No. No, I'm not. But I think it's probably best if I leave the explanations to the person whose fault all this is. If you promise not to throw it at me, can I make you another mug of tea?'

My throat and mouth were dry. I nodded. 'Yes. Thank you. And since we're discussing secrets, tell me why you're suddenly so afraid of me.'

He sat back down again. 'You've noticed.'

'Yes.'

He sighed. 'There's no hiding anything from you, is there? You are going to be so good at your new job.'

'Don't change the subject.'

'Cage, I honestly don't know what to say. Do you remember, at the beginning of this year, we had a talk?'

'About working together? Yes, I remember it well. You said because weird stuff happens to us wherever we go, the least we could do was capitalise on that. We were going to investigate other people's weird stuff. Help them. Make a little money, perhaps. I also remember you saying you would make the decisions and I would make the tea. Because it was important for me to feel I was making a contribution.'

'Yes, you would remember that, wouldn't you?'

'Nothing wrong with my memory,' I said, pointedly ignoring the fact I suspected there was something very much the matter with my memory. Not only were there the inexplicable gaps, but I was also cursed with equally inexplicable flashes – names, places, images – things of which I had no previous recollection. I sometimes felt like a badly tuned radio, picking up bits of other people's memories.

The evening had darkened. I still hadn't eaten. There was still blood on the doorstep. Nigel was still snoring. At some point he'd farted. Apparently he'd eaten a compost heap for lunch.

'That lanky witch will be here any moment,' Jones said, meaning Melek, presumably. They'd never liked each other.

21

I still wasn't absolutely sure about Melek – or Iblis, either. Most of the time I believed they were something strange and strong left over from older times, but then sometimes I would wonder if they weren't just a pair of con artists with a good act. And then I'd look at their colours – Melek's subdued gold and Iblis's swirling silver, the way they moved and the shapes that they made – and be back to strange and strong again. I had no idea what to make of either of them. I wasn't even sure if they were a force for good or bad.

Jones had no such doubts. 'Don't agree to anything she says without thinking about it very carefully.'

'What are you saying?'

'Just listen to what she says and take your time before making a decision.'

'Jones – what's going on?'

He opened his mouth, but someone tapped at the front door. He let them in. Iblis and Melek – the lanky witch, as he called her. True, she was tall. As tall as Iblis and he wasn't short.

'There you are,' said Jones, falsely amiable. 'Has Iblis explained everything to you? I can't wait to see how you lie your way out of this one. Go on – off you go.'

He settled back on the sofa and took my hand. I was unsure whether this was a gesture of defiance or solidarity.

Melek inspected me very closely. 'Elizabeth? Is everything all right?'

'Why don't *you* tell *her*?' said Jones.

'If you have nothing helpful to say, then say nothing. Or better still, leave completely.' She scowled, completely unintimidated by him. Her dark red hair was scraped back tight and hard in a bun on the nape of her neck and her boots could bring down a building.

He stood up. I'd forgotten how quickly he could move. In a second, they were eyeball to eyeball. I watched their colours clash, Melek's gold butting against Jones's crimson. Both of them tight and angry. Neither would back down. I suspected she could snap his neck in an instant if she wished. Although Iblis would probably have something to say about that. And I certainly would.

I was just so tired of everyone treating me like an idiot. Too stupid to make my own decisions. Being used for other people's purposes. Everyone wanted a piece of me. Sorensen. Mary Bennet. Melek. Jones, in his own way. And I was becoming very tired of being meek, helpless, biddable Elizabeth Cage.

'We should wait outside,' said Iblis to Jones.

'No, we really shouldn't,' said Jones, not taking his eyes from Melek's. 'Someone has to look after Cage's interests.'

'I have told you before, I mean nothing but good to Elizabeth Cage,' she said, still staring him down.

'Yeah? How's that worked out for her so far?'

I turned to him. 'Why are you so angry? What are you afraid of?'

He sighed and said more quietly, 'I'm afraid for you, Cage. And yes, a little bit afraid *of* you. Of what you could do.'

I heard myself say, 'Me? What could I do?' but I knew what he meant. I still remembered the endless, angry snow slowly covering the world. I still saw the whirlwind chaos of blood and people exploding through the roof. I still remembered lying in the blood-soaked snow staring up at the stars as I brought the Sorensen Clinic down around me. Oh yes – I've done some damage in my time.

He looked over at Melek. 'Will you tell her, or shall I?'

'Neither.'

He was becoming very angry. 'We three know who she is, but not Cage herself. Ignorance is no longer her protection. Ignorance could kill her.'

'It has always protected her in the past.'

'But the secret is out now. If everyone knows but her, then you no longer have a choice.'

She was silent for a long time. No one moved. No one spoke. The street lights came on outside. Finally, she said, 'There is still a choice.'

Jones made a movement and she continued. 'Elizabeth, the choice will be yours. I will tell you what you need to know and then you can decide. To continue with that knowledge and deal with everything that will entail – or to forget and continue as you were before.'

'But everyone else will still know?'

'Iblis and I have always known. The man Jones – well, he must find his own way to deal with it.' She didn't look at the man Jones. 'It will be his problem. My concern is for you. What do you say? I promise – whatever you decide – everyone here will abide by it.' She looked over at Jones. 'Won't they?'

He looked at me. 'Do you agree to this, Cage?'

'Actually, I can't see any other way. Yes, I agree.'

'To what do you agree?' said Melek.

I considered my words and then said formally, 'I agree to be told the truth, and then decide whether or not I want to remember it or continue as I was before.'

She turned to Jones. 'What do you say?'

'I think I've made my views known. Stay out of my head.'

'Your knowledge is not giving you peace of mind.'

'Stay out of my head.'

She stepped back from him. 'Elizabeth? Shall I continue?'

Perhaps I should have taken a little time to reflect on knowledge so terrible that it had been kept from me. I didn't.

'All right.' I turned to Melek. 'Do it.'

She came to sit beside me on the sofa and took my hands. Hers were as cold as ice. Her grey eyes bored into mine.

'Tadia, I have something very important to say to you.'

There was a bright light in my memory and then everything else was blank.

'Wake up, sleepyhead,' said Jones.

I opened my eyes. Oh, God – I'd fallen asleep. I had guests and I'd fallen asleep on the sofa.

'Right,' he said briskly, heading for the door. 'Back in half an hour, Cage. Anything else you want?'

Had I missed something? Were we still arguing about food? I scrambled for my last memories. 'Where are you going?'

'Off to get the food,' he said, opening the front door. 'Nigel hasn't eaten for hours, and I'm worried he'll start on us.'

He disappeared into the dark. Iblis followed him out.

Melek regarded me from the armchair.

'I'm so sorry,' I said, struggling to sit up and get to grips with the evening. 'My mother would have been so cross with me. Falling asleep in front of a guest.'

'You do look tired,' she said. 'The nap will have done you good. Just remember, whenever you feel uneasy or that something isn't quite right, you made your choice, and it was the right one.'

I hadn't a clue what she was talking about, but she was smiling and I should be polite, so I said, 'Can I get you anything?'

'No, thank you. As soon as they return, I must depart. How are you these days, Elizabeth Cage?'

'Um, very well, thank you.'

'There is blood on your doorstep.'

'Oh yes, I think a cat killed something there. I must wash it off tomorrow. How are you?'

'I am well.' She paused, opened her mouth as if to speak and then changed her mind.

'You won't stay to eat with us?'

'No, thank you.'

I suddenly felt very sorry for her. Iblis had no qualms at all about inviting himself for TV, free beer and food. Melek never would. How did she spend her time?

'You'd be very welcome,' I said, and meant it.

She smiled. 'Thank you, that is kind, but I have an appointment later.'

I knew better than to ask. 'If you're pressed for time, do please feel free to leave.'

'No. I will remain until they return. They should not be long.'

That turned out to be true. In less time than I expected, they were back, overloaded with foil cartons and beer.

Nigel sat up immediately. Melek regarded him without favour. He lay back down again.

She went to leave and as I stood up to see her to the door, I caught sight of my original note – the one that should have been about the food and wasn't – lying unnoticed on the worktop. I moved the kettle and tea things to make room for all the cartons and took the opportunity to slip the note into my pocket as I did so.

Jones and Melek said a polite good night to each other.

Iblis waved a spring roll at her in farewell. Nigel didn't bother looking up from his dish. I saw her into the night, looked again at the blood, a dark patch under the porch light, and went to close the door.

As I did so, a shadow moved. Across the grass and under the willow trees. I stared for a moment but saw nothing more, so I closed the door and went back inside.

Iblis, as expected, stayed the night. I made him up a bed on the sofa and brought down an old pillow for Nigel. Tactfully, Iblis took him out for a last-minute walk, leaving me and Jones alone. I'm not sure what he thought we would do with the time.

'I'll call you as soon as they're ready for you to report to the clinic,' said Jones. The food seemed to have done him some good. His colour was stronger and brighter. As it used to be. 'Any plans over the next few days?'

'Just staying at home,' I said sadly.

'Listen – that note . . .'

'Mm?' I said vaguely. I should have known better.

'The one you slipped into your pocket.'

I sighed. Dodgy eyesight or not, he never missed a thing, did he?

'Oh – *that* note.'

'When you have a minute . . .'

As if I didn't have hundreds of minutes . . . thousands, even.

'When you have a moment, sit down and make a list of anyone who might have it in for you.'

I was genuinely surprised. I could number the people I knew on the fingers of well . . . two hands, but I'd still have a few fingers left over. 'Why would anyone possibly have it in for *me*?'

'I know you tend to regard yourself as some home-loving little nonentity, but I think – in fact, I know – you're pretty badass, Cage. Sorensen thought the same and, for all his faults, he wasn't often wrong about people. Mary Bennet tends to agree as well and we're not the only ones. So, make that list. We'll have a chat when I see you next.'

'You're still working on the Ghost thing?' I said. 'That's dragging on a bit.'

'I'm only slightly involved at this stage. Uncovering the evidence and lining up the witnesses is being done by others.'

'Why?'

'Well, mostly because I'm still not completely fit, but also because my boss informs me that, for some reason, it's felt I'm not good with routine work.'

'That is astonishing.'

'Listen, I . . .'

Iblis and Nigel appeared. One of them had the appearance of one who'd performed his functions for the evening. Iblis waggled his eyebrows at us as he edged between us on the step. Jones gave it up.

'See you soon, Cage. Stay out of trouble.'

'Of course,' I said indignantly and even Nigel laughed.

Leaving Iblis with the last can of beer and the TV remote, I took myself upstairs. I climbed into bed, dimmed the light, punched my pillows to make them comfortable and lay a while, mulling things over. Then I sat up, found a pad and pen in the bedside cabinet and started to think of all the people who would have a reason to dislike me. To hate me, even. I didn't think it would take that long but I was wrong.

I started with Philip Sorensen, which would please him, since he had a very exaggerated idea of his own importance. He was the first on my list but he was in custody and had been for some time. He'd presided over the manufacture of Ghost and a lot of people had died. Cruelly and unnecessarily. And now, mostly due to me, he'd lost his job, his clinic, his reputation and his liberty. It would probably be fair to say he hated me, although how he would have the opportunity to do me any harm was a bit of a mystery. Nevertheless, he went on the list. Pride of place, in fact.

Then there was Thomas Rookwood. As far as I knew, he was still miles away in his castle up in Northumberland. He was an unpleasant man, who couldn't be far enough away as far as I was concerned. He didn't love me but he had an awful lot to lose if any of his secrets ever came tumbling out. Worth checking, I supposed.

The vengeful spirit of Clare Woods, Jones's ex-partner and girlfriend, who had been executed in a grimy basement in Droit-wich. I shivered and pulled the quilt up around my shoulders. Possible, I suppose, but again – not very likely and what if it was her? What could I do about it? Nothing. I didn't bother adding her to the list.

The Harlows – Veronica, Becky and Granny Miriam. The Mother, the Maiden and the Crone. Veronica was dead. As was Granny. Sadly, in my world, being dead never seemed to be much of a handicap when it came to bad behaviour.

And what about those malevolent standing stones who had protected them for so long – the Three Sisters? Iblis had done them irreparable harm. Dealt them what had looked to me like a fatal blow. I closed my eyes and saw the stone fall. Saw Veronica and Alice Chervil's bodies crushed beneath it. I'd wrecked their Year King ceremony. The one that went back who knew how many centuries. The ceremony that ensured the women of Greyston another year of long life and prosperity. And, most importantly, continuing power. I'd destroyed a millennia-old tradition in just under half an hour, but there might still be something nasty remaining. I remembered the moment our car had been dragged, slowly, inexorably backwards towards the standing stones. What fate would have awaited us there?

But the power of the stones had been broken – along with the stones themselves – and these days the village was surrounded by dead men. Hundreds – possibly even thousands – of them. Victims of the Year King ceremony – each and every one of them shot through with hatred and thoughts of revenge against the women who had done this to them. True, the men couldn't get in – but the women couldn't get past them. A dreadful stale-mate. I wondered how that situation had developed. Veronica and Granny might be dead, but what about Becky? She was very young but was it possible she could harness enough power to cause me harm? That also should be checked out.

Then there was the spirit of Caroline Fairbrother – I'd tied her to a wall down by the river. Doomed her to spend eternity in the cold and the dark. She definitely hated me.

Or what about Leanne Elphick – that woman who regarded the human race as her puppets and played cruel games with people's lives? I'd stood in her way as well. How difficult would it be for her to track me down?

I laid down the pad and pen, suddenly tired. There would be more. Either deliberately or unknowingly, everyone makes enemies. How many people didn't I even know about? I turned out the light, rolled over and tried to sleep.

CHAPTER THREE

I opened my bedroom door the next morning to the smell of frying bacon, which was both slightly alarming and very enticing. I put on my dressing gown and went downstairs to find Iblis had folded his bedding neatly, opened the back door to disperse the Nigel fug and was now presiding over a frying pan. The table was laid for breakfast. He really was the perfect house guest. Especially since I was almost certain there had been no bacon in the fridge. I opened my mouth and then closed it again. Sometimes it's better not to ask.

'I've had a thought,' I said, sitting at the table and pouring myself a cup of tea.

He plonked one bacon butty in front of Nigel and passed another to me. I noticed Nigel got his first.

I laid my list on the table. 'I've made a list of some of the people – and other things – who might not like me very much.'

He took an enormous mouthful of butty, picked up the list and read it through, chewing heroically all the while.

'I thought,' I said, stirring my tea and not looking at him, 'that I'd check each of them out. See what they're doing now. Discreetly, of course.'

Eventually he managed to swallow. 'You mean attempt to discover whether anyone is plotting revenge in an underground

31

cellar daubed with esoteric symbols and chanting blood-curdling spells over the body of a sacrificed virgin?'

I stared at him over my mug. 'Why would anyone do that?'

'To bring about your ruin, of course.'

'I think I had envisaged something a little less . . . vivid.'

'We could arm ourselves with protective spells, don the armour of righteousness, wield the sword of retribution, brandish the shield of valour, and brave the very jaws of Hell itself in pursuit of those who would end the world, and smite them down in our fury.'

I said carefully, 'Yes, yes, we could do that. That is certainly a possibility to bear in mind. But I think, initially, just a couple of telephone calls, don't you? You know, just to check things out. *Discreetly*.'

He seemed disappointed, so I added, 'We don't want to alert the enemy to their great peril.'

He shrugged. 'Well, no, I suppose not. We could do things your way first, I suppose.'

I wondered whether I should query 'we' or 'first', and in the end decided to do neither. Having Iblis at my side would be very reassuring. Even Jones couldn't complain about that. Although he would.

'I'll try Thomas Rookwood first,' I said. 'I've got the number somewhere. I thought I could ring the castle to enquire whether they're still taking bookings. It doesn't matter whether the answer is yes or no – I'll try to find an opportunity to speak to Thomas Rookwood in person.'

He swallowed the last of his butty. 'You are firm of purpose this bright morning, Elizabeth Cage.'

I nodded. 'Yes. Yes, I am. I'm tired of being reactive. Now I'm doing proactive.'

'Excellent. I, Iblis, can do this proactive also. Will there be music?'

He does this. Pretends not to be up to speed with modern idiom or technology. I think it amuses him.

'Not unless you want to hum a cheerful ditty.'

He frowned. 'Hm. A Spartan marching song, perhaps. Or the "Battle Hymn of the Republic". Or the "Lament of Thassa" as she stood alone before the hordes of Gorgon.'

I was determined not to ask. 'Bathroom's free if you want it and I'll clear away down here. Then we'll get started.'

'A battle plan,' he said, eyes sparkling. 'This will be a day of blood and terror for our enemies.'

Nigel belched. Loudly.

An hour later, washed and dressed, and not quite as brave as I had been an hour before, I telephoned Thomas Rookwood.

'Remember to block your caller ID,' said Iblis, confirming my belief he was nowhere near as out of touch with the modern world as he would have the modern world believe.

The phone was answered on the third ring. A man. Just a simple 'Hello'. No identification.

'Good morning,' I said briskly. 'I'm calling to ask if you still rent out holiday accommodation within the castle. A friend recommended you.'

'I'm sorry, we're not taking bookings at the moment.'

'Oh, what a shame. Will you be? Taking bookings, I mean.'

'We're not sure.'

Well, that wasn't very helpful.

'Could I speak to Thomas Rookwood, please?'

'Mr Rookwood is not available at the moment.'

'Could you tell me . . . ?'

He hung up.

'That is very suspicious,' said Iblis.

'I'm almost certain that was Thomas Rookwood himself,' I said. 'And he sounded a little drunk to me.'

We looked at the clock. Ten past ten.

'Interesting,' said Iblis. 'We could ask the man-mountain Jones to check Thomas Rookwood's financial records.'

'A couple of very small points,' I said. 'He doesn't know I'm doing this. Not that I need his permission.'

Iblis solemnly nodded, appeared to reconsider his answer, and then solemnly shook his head. 'No, you don't.'

'And I'm not sure what the position is on checking official records for private purposes. And he has one or two other things on his mind at the moment.'

'His eyesight.'

'How do you know?'

'Last night. Several times he reached for his beer and missed.'

'Could have been the beer.'

'Could have been – wasn't,' he said simply.

'I wouldn't mention it to him.'

'No. What next?'

'The village of Greyston, and that won't be so easy.'

'Courage, Elizabeth Cage. The three of us are easily equal to the women of the Three Sisters and a wood full of dead men.'

'I meant transportation. There isn't room for you on my moped so it's going to have to be the bus.'

He stared at me. 'Why?'

'It's too far to walk.'

'No, I mean – why don't we drive?'

34

'I can't drive and I don't have a car.'

'I can and I do.'

I twisted to look at him. 'You have a car?'

'Actually, I have two. Well, one is Melek's. And I have a motorbike as well. And a skateboard.'

Well, wasn't this a morning of revelations. 'Melek has a car?'

'She does indeed.'

'What sort?'

'A monstrous thing equal to any terrain, with the roar of a thousand dragons that can banish the night with their fiery eyes.'

'An SUV, then.'

'Yes.'

'What colour?'

'Mud. Overlaid with the blood of her enemies.'

Of course it was. 'What about you? What do you drive?'

He grinned wickedly. 'Something long, low, black and sinful.'

'I'm not even going to ask.'

He got to his feet. 'I will meet you at the bottom of the hill in half an hour.'

Remembering the last time I was at Greyston, I dressed for running, hiding and being terrified out of my wits. Jeans, walking boots, sweatshirt, and a small backpack with water and phone.

Iblis wore his usual black T-shirt and combats. His boots were better than mine.

Nigel wore the air of a dog rudely awakened from his mid-morning nap and not happy about it.

'Actually,' I said, 'is it wise to bring him? Given what happened to him at Greyston? Won't he be scared?'

'I have asked him. He finds the idea of revenge very attractive.'

I opened my mouth and closed it again. He might be able to speak to Nigel – he might not. The chances were fifty-fifty either way.

His own car might well have been long, low and sinful, but I wasn't going to find out that morning. We were in a battered old SUV that had certainly seen some action in its day. And never been washed since the day it left the factory.

'This is Melek's?' I asked, climbing aboard.

'Yes.'

'Does she know you've borrowed it?'

'Does Michael Jones know of your intentions today?'

It would seem we both had secrets.

He drove very well. I don't know why I'd ever supposed he wouldn't. We eased out of Rushford and set off for Greyston. Neither of us talked much. I passed the time by wondering what I would find there.

Greyston is a village of women. According to Veronica Harlow, no man had been born there for hundreds of years. They were the women of the Three Sisters.

The first time I'd visited the village, it had been chocolate-box perfect. A typical tourist trap. Neat, tidy, prosperous, a traditional English village and a joy to behold. The Three Sisters – the three standing stones – were a big draw. They stood on the village green, dominating the village which had, over the millennia, grown up around them. As Veronica Harlow had said – they looked after the stones and the stones looked after them.

The second time I'd visited, the village had been far from picture perfect because their annual human sacrifice – the Year King ceremony – hadn't taken place – all thanks to Jones and me.

The Year King ceremony has its roots deep, deep in the past.

As far back as the matriarchal societies of ancient times. There would be a ruler – a queen – and every year a man was selected to become the Year King. For twelve months, nothing was too good for him. He could have anything he wanted. Women, drink, food, a dazzling life of pleasure, waited on hand and foot.

For twelve months.

At the end of that period, he was offered up to the stones. Sacrificed. There were a variety of ways in which this could happen. In some places he was challenged and defeated by his successor. In others he was killed by the queen. Or a high priestess. In Greyston, he was upended, tied to a wooden structure and his throat was cut. His blood was collected in big bronze dishes and given to the Three Sisters to strengthen and renew them. In return, they granted the village another twelve months of prosperity. No brutal motorway would ever cut that village in half. No massive housing estate full of locally unaffordable homes would be built on their doorstep. No giant supermarket would ever darken their doors. They looked after the stones and the stones looked after them.

Not last year, however. The ceremony hadn't been completed, the power of the stones had faltered and, without their protection, the centuries had rushed back in. The last time I saw Greyston, frankly, the place had been a tip. Overgrown gardens, dilapidated houses, rusty cars parked everywhere. The stones had been damaged and now the women were vulnerable and angry. They'd planned to remedy the loss of their sacrifice by offering up Michael Jones as a belated Year King. That hadn't gone well for them. Veronica and Alice had died and Iblis had dealt the stones their death blow.

As if that wasn't bad enough, now that the power of the stones was weakened, the spirits of their victims – the Year Kings, one a year for millennia – had emerged from the surrounding woods to take their revenge.

We'd left at that point. The dead Year Kings encircled the village but lacked the power to get in. The women were trapped there and lacked the power to get out. No doubt some had tried. I wondered how far they had run before they realised that the things surrounding them were not trees.

The whole village – and the woods around it – were steeped in decay, death, blood and revenge. I wasn't at all keen to go back, but I couldn't think of any other way to find out what was happening. There might still be power there, but if so, who was wielding it? If the women had finally prevailed over the dead men, then their thoughts might well be turning to revenge. I would be top of their list. Along with Michael Jones.

And if the dead Year Kings had prevailed … well, they had no cause to love women – any woman – and I would be no exception.

I sighed and looked out of the windows at the hedgerows rushing past. Summer was getting going and everything was in full leaf. Under any other circumstances, I'd have enjoyed the drive.

We needed to be very careful. I remembered how I'd zig-zagged across the country at random, arriving at Greyston by sheer chance – or so I thought – only to have Veronica Harlow claim she'd drawn me to her. Was it possible that her daughter, Becky, the only family survivor, could be putting these thoughts into my head? Drawing me back to them. And I would have a man beside me. A new Year King, perhaps? I shook myself. If that was what she was up to, then Becky had made a big mistake.

Iblis was no one's Year King. There would be an apocalypse before that happened.

We were nearly there. Greyston was set in a bowl, surrounded by wooded hills. We were climbing now. Not far. Just over the brow of the hill . . .

'We should approach with care,' said Iblis, pulling into a lay-by. 'Stay off the road if possible.'

'Yes,' I said. 'But I'm equally reluctant to venture into the woods. You might be all right, but I don't think the inhabitants are very fond of women.'

We climbed out of the SUV. Nigel jumped down after us. I looked down, still worried for him, but he looked completely unconcerned, cocking his leg against the back wheel.

I shouldered my backpack and we set off. To any casual onlooker, we were just a couple of hikers and their dog.

We tramped along the verge at the side of the road. It was a nice day. Not too hot, not too cold. A light breeze made walking pleasant.

Up ahead, the road curved around the next bend and disappeared under the trees. Iblis slowed.

'What's the matter?' I said, alarmed in case unseen dead men were watching us from the shadows.

His next words were hardly reassuring. 'Let's let them get a good look at us, shall we?'

We slowed our pace and moved to the middle of the road – no cars had passed us in all this time. In fact, looking at the low-hanging trees and overgrown verges, I'd say nothing had been down this road for a long while. There used to be a bus service – had that been discontinued? Was Greyston completely cut off from the outside world now?

I kept going, half a pace behind Iblis, turning my head from left to right, but there was nothing to alarm anyone. Birds sang among the trees. One or two fluttered across our path. Something scuttled in the undergrowth. There was life here. Not everything in the woods was dead. I began to feel a little more cheerful.

'What do you think we'll find?' I said. 'At Greyston, I mean.'

He shook his head. 'We should wager on the outcome. I say the village is still a shithole.'

I grinned. 'Is that a technical term?'

'It is when I use it. I say the village is sinking fast. They ran out of food months ago and are eating each other.'

I shivered. 'You watch too much *Olympian Heights*.'

'It is impossible to watch too much *Olympian Heights*. Your guess?'

'I worry that somehow the power there has reinstated itself and the village will be as fresh and perfect and murderous as it was before and we're walking into a trap and the stones will eat us alive.'

He stopped, suddenly serious. 'Go back to the car. Wait for me there. I'll go on alone. It won't take me more than a few minutes. You don't have to come.'

I'd pulled myself together. 'Yes – like you and Rin Tin Tin here will even get to the treeline without falling over your own feet.'

'That is very hurtful,' he said reproachfully. 'Nigel is the Dog of Infinite Resource, and I am Iblis, International Man of Mystery. Together we are unstoppable.'

'Why have we stopped?'

'To make the point that we are unstoppable, Elizabeth Cage.'

40

I started walking again. 'So – this bet. What's the prize?'

'Our lives, probably,' he said, as we rounded the last bend.

We couldn't put the moment off any longer. Another few steps and we'd be visible from the village. If they didn't already know we were here. We stepped on to the grass verge and from there, very reluctantly, into the shelter of the trees. At least I hoped it would be shelter. Actually, I hoped they were trees.

The comfortable tramp of our footsteps disappeared, absorbed into the soft path and muffled by all the greenery. I glanced around. This was the older part of the wood. The more modern plantations were on the other side of the road. Here there were ancient oaks, a few ash trees that had survived dieback, sweet chestnut, horse chestnut, holly. And the occasional fir tree. Just a normal wood. No dark figures moved silently through the trees, thin and shifting and silent until the moment they closed in. No old shades, dead for hundreds – possibly thousands – of years. These woods had been their home for who knew how long. The trees had grown up over their graves.

The path was wide and ran parallel to the road, which was still visible to my right. We could walk side by side. Nigel trotted happily at Iblis's heels, occasionally stopping to investigate something smelly or cock his leg on a log. Normal behaviour for a dog – especially for him – and if he was relaxed, then so should I be, given that he had nearly been a part of last year's sacrifice.

The sunshine grew brighter – the trees thinner and smaller and younger.

'Stay behind me.'

I moved behind Iblis and looked back over my shoulder. No sinister figure blocked our escape, and as far as I could see, no hidden eyes watched our progress. To all intents and purposes, we were completely alone. Although I had my doubts.

Iblis stopped. 'Can you hear something?'

I listened. 'Yes, now you come to mention it. Is that machinery?'

We dropped to our knees and crawled slowly and carefully between the trees. The last few yards were accomplished on our stomachs. The ground was cool and slightly damp. A fern tickled my nose. I followed Iblis and stopped when he stopped. He motioned me to join him and I wriggled forwards.

The last of the trees straggled into nothing. The village of Greyston lay below us.

And it was not what I had been expecting.

CHAPTER FOUR

I'd made several visits to Greyston and it had managed to surprise me every time. This was no exception. I'd seen the village at its best and at its worst and now I was looking at . . . what? Refurbishment? Renovation? Repair?

Restoration – that was it. The village was being restored.

The Three Sisters had been raised again and were being permanently fixed into place. Each was encased in a cat's cradle of wooden scaffolding to support them while work proceeded. I wondered why wood. Perhaps the stones didn't like iron.

More modern scaffolding had been erected around the inn, the village hall and several of the cottages. Bricks and roof tiles were stacked in neat piles around the green, ready for use. The road between the inn and the Travellers' Rest guest house, where I had stayed before, had been coned off for resurfacing. The rusting cars and piles of scrap had all been cleared away. Hedges had been trimmed. Some of the gardens had been dug over and replanted. Others were still a work in progress. Yes, Greyston was being restored.

The stones I could understand, they were almost certainly listed; perhaps a historical society was behind the repairs. And the pub might be the responsibility of the brewery. But who was bankrolling repairs to private houses? As far as I knew, general decay was not covered by regular buildings insurance.

Most astonishingly, there were men in the village. Men who weren't dead, I mean. I could see around ten to twelve of them, all in hard hats and hi-vis vests: one driving a digger, two consulting a clipboard of some kind, one backing up a van, two crossing the green, a couple staring down into a hole in the road, one pushing a wheelbarrow and a couple rummaging in the back of a van.

There were more men here today than there had been in Greyston for the last couple of hundred years and all of them were walking about, completely unharmed and not being sacrificed in any way. Although I was willing to bet none of them would stay here after the sun went down, when the bad moon rose – that little sliver of light, low in the sky and always on its back, like a malevolent grin. Be very careful when the bad moon hangs in the sky. Don't look at it – it will look right back at you. And it will never forget you.

These men had brought a whole fleet of vehicles with them. I could see several vans parked neatly around the green. All unmarked. There were various yellow diggers, together with other vehicles whose functions were unknown to me. Cement mixers rolled lazily. There were even a couple of generators scattered around.

The last time I'd seen the village shop – the late Alice Chervil's shop – it had been boarded up, but now two more men were taking down the shutters. Obviously, someone had taken it over after its former owner had been crushed to death beneath a monolith. The bus stop was still there, as was the Travellers' Rest guest house, although today the front door was firmly closed. Was it no longer open for business or had they simply shut the doors and windows to keep the dust out?

All right, the village wasn't as broken-down as it had been. The atmosphere of decay and neglect was gone and some sort of revival was in progress. This was not what I had expected to see and now they'd certainly rocketed themselves to the top of my list of suspects. Were they now so secure they could afford to switch their attention from basic survival to thoughts of revenge? I remembered again how Veronica had drawn me to her. And how they had summoned Jones. How the women seemed able to attract their victims without them having any idea they were not operating of their own free will.

My heart chilled again.

Because I was here. The idea had come to me this morning. I'd woken up with my list of people who wished me harm. That I should check out what was happening at Greyston had felt like a high priority, but this time yesterday I hadn't given them a thought. Not for months. Now, suddenly – I was here. Suppose that hadn't been my intention but theirs? Once again, they'd called me and once again, I'd answered.

'Mrs Cage. How very pleasant to see you again.'

Very, very slowly, I pushed myself up on to my knees, then my feet. Only then did I turn around. Still very, very slowly.

She was only a little distance away on the road. I suspected wild horses couldn't drag her into these woods. I was safe as long as I didn't move out of the trees, but I wasn't confident I would retain control over my legs. I still remembered Jones getting up almost mid-sentence and setting off for Greyston on foot. Completely oblivious to his surroundings. Forging a

45

straight line across the moors. Never deviating. Like a homing pigeon but bigger and more stubborn.

I couldn't see any trace of Iblis or Nigel anywhere and I certainly wasn't going to draw attention to their absence by looking around for them. I struggled hard for a light, social tone.

'Joanna – you gave me a start. For one moment I thought it was Veronica Harlow, back from the dead to lead you all into disaster again.'

Her colour, that oh-so familiar swirl of blue, purple and turquoise – all the women here had variations of those colours – stabbed towards me. Fast and vicious. Once, twice, thrice – and then she had herself under control again. She and Veronica Harlow had always had the most self-discipline. Becky and Alice – less so. And now that Veronica was dead, I suspected Joanna was in full control of Greyston. I would have to be very careful.

She smiled now, full of confidence. 'No. Veronica will never return. *You* saw to that.'

I should keep her talking. Something would happen which would enable me to get away. I hoped. Still no sign of Iblis or Nigel. Iblis would have rolled out of sight and be circling around behind her. I hoped.

To give him time – and because I was genuinely curious – I said, 'How did you get Veronica and Alice out from under the stone?'

'To begin with, we didn't. We left them there.'

Keep it light. Unthreatening. I'm very good at unthreatening.

'Oh, yuk. Although sensible.'

'Yes. Nature did a lot of the work for us. Foxes, crows, badgers. After a few months there wasn't much left and we just dealt with what was. We chucked the remains into a pit. Granny had already been in there for some time. We covered them with lime and filled it in. Problem solved. Goodbye, Veronica and Alice. And Granny, of course. Strangely unmissed by all.'

'Yes,' I said, still striving for a friendly, casual air. 'I never understood why the women here chose Veronica over you. It was obvious to me right from the moment we met. And poor Alice was just spinning her wheels, really, wasn't she?'

She said nothing to my blatant flattery. I'd have to do better.

'So – Joanna – how are you?'

'Very well, thank you, Mrs Cage. And very happy that you cleared the way to the top for me.'

Happy – not grateful. I would have preferred grateful.

'I see you've raised the stones again. Will that actually work?'

She frowned. I had a slight advantage over her. At some point the sun had come out and she was standing in bright sunshine. I, on the other hand, was still under the trees in dappled shade.

'How do you mean – will that work?'

'Well, they're not whole stones any longer, are they? They were broken. Does the magic still work if they're cemented back together?' I paused and then said, 'Does the old malice still have them in its grasp?'

'The Old Power? Oh, yes. Very much so. Think of it as not so much restored as rejuvenated.'

I did not like the sound of that. Rejuvenation implied even greater strength than before. More power.

'Well, good for you. But a word of caution. From where does this power emanate and what price will it demand from you?'

'There will be no price. We have come to an arrangement with a new investor. Someone whose interests are aligned with ours.'

I let my shoulders slump. 'Oh, Joanna,' I said. 'I'm so disappointed in you. I honestly thought Greyston had risen again, and here you are telling me you're only under new management.'

She smiled. It would seem I'd failed to annoy her.

'To mutual benefit, believe me. We will be restored to more than our former glory. We'll catch you next time, Mrs Cage.'

'Well, if I remember rightly, you didn't even catch me the first time. The last twelve months or so have not gone well for you, have they?'

She shrugged. 'We have a powerful new protector. And attention is now turning towards you.'

I *really* didn't like the sound of that. And where was Iblis? Why hadn't he crept up behind her and slugged her with a rock?

'These are just threats, Joanna. Give me a name. Go on – give me something to lie awake at night and worry about.'

I wasn't sure I wanted to know, but this was supposed to be a fact-finding visit. Gaining information was the only thing that would save me from the wrath of Jones once he found out what we'd been up to without him.

Joanna smirked. 'Something draws close. There will be no escape for you. Not this time. The threads of your life are converging, Elizabeth Cage, and one day soon they will be pulled tight.'

She raised her hands to her throat and made a short, sharp, pulling-tight gesture.

I realised the wood had grown very silent. All movement had ceased. No birdsong. She stared me down. A breeze came out of nowhere, stirring the dust and smaller leaves into a whirlwind around her feet. She raised her arms. Her colour gathered itself and then roared towards me. Her voice throbbed with borrowed power.

48

'*He will send the serpent.*'

I felt my stomach turn over. The serpent again. I swallowed hard and forced myself to speak calmly and with a slight air of mockery. 'What serpent? And who? Who will send the serpent? Who is controlling you?'

She simply laughed. Slowly, her colour subsided and the wind dropped. I was conscious of cold sweat running down my back.

I could hear Michael Jones in my head. *Think, Cage. Get her talking again.*

He wasn't wrong – most people are very happy to tell you how clever they've been – but perhaps I needed to approach this from a different angle.

I lifted my head as if a thought had just occurred to me. 'Oh, while I think of it, how's Becky?'

'Very well indeed.'

'Tell her I asked after her.'

'Tell her yourself.'

She motioned with her head. I turned, expecting the worst. And got it. Becky had appeared while I was talking to Joanna, standing slightly behind her. Now, if I wanted to return to the car, I'd have to get past both of them.

Hatred streaked her colour. Here was the traditional blue, purple and turquoise of the women of this village, but now shot through with orange. A lot of orange. She had always been filled with massive teenage resentment but now there was almost enough to call it a fourth colour.

She'd grown. And filled out. She was a year older and more experienced than the last time I'd seen her. On the other hand, so was I, although I suspected that year lay much heavier on me than on her.

The sun disappeared behind a cloud and suddenly, now that there were two of them, these woods seemed a much darker and colder place. I was in a very bad position. I couldn't get to the car, not as things stood, and I definitely didn't want to be under the trees when dusk started to fall. This wasn't a good place for any woman to be, especially after dark. I hadn't minded when Iblis was with me, but as far as I could see, I was on my own. Suddenly, it was less about the information and more about the escape. And the subsequent survival.

A wind stirred the leaves in the trees again. A long sighing sound. Both Joanna and Becky looked around. They were as uneasy as me. I wondered how many of the women had tried to escape the village over the last twelve months. How many had made it through the encircling woods. None of them, I suspected.

Joanna looked back over her shoulder, down towards the village. For reassurance, perhaps? She was a long way from the safety of Greyston. As was Becky. We should all go our separate ways. While we still could. Because . . . under the trees . . .

I said softly, 'Joanna.'

She looked back at me.

'Be very careful. There's a man standing behind you. He's under the trees. Do not turn around.'

Her colour froze. She stood very still but her eyes flickered. 'You're bluffing.'

'No, it's true,' said Becky, her voice suddenly high with panic. I suspected she'd just realised that if we all scattered, she was probably his easiest and closest target. 'We've stayed too long. You should have killed her when you could and now one of *them* is here. I can see the wound on his neck.'

So could I. The long dark slash across his throat. The mark of the dead. That was how they had all died. Upended, tied to a diagonal cross, and their throats cut. And where there was one, there would be hundreds more. Thousands.

Joanna took off. Without a backward glance and leaving Becky stranded on the road. Good to see the old Greyston loyalties still prevailed.

I held up a hand to the man. Palm outwards. 'Halt. Stand.'

He remained still.

Mentally crossing my fingers, I said, 'Listen, Becky, I have never borne you any ill will. He will do as I say. He'll let you go if I tell him to. And I will. All I ask is for you to remember that today I saved your life. Now go. I can't hold him for ever, so go. Quickly.'

I didn't have to say it twice. She turned and raced back towards the village, running wide around the dark, motionless figure. The sounds of her footsteps faded into the distance, leaving me alone with the man with the mark of death on his throat.

I let my breath go in a long sigh and turned back towards the car. 'Nice one, Iblis. You really had me going there for a moment. Is that mud on your throat? Is Nigel with you? We really should get out of here. Joanna could be back with reinforcements any moment now.'

He didn't move. Not a muscle. We stared at each other. Slowly, the horrible truth dawned upon me. Cold panic crawled across my skin.

This wasn't Iblis and that wasn't mud and I was here alone.

Not taking my eyes off him, I took a small step to my right. Towards the road. And the car. To get myself out from under

51

the trees. And then I took another one. I didn't dare look away. I was a small mammal facing a predator, fighting the instinct to run, because that's what the predator wants you to do.

I took another step sideways. I was nearly at the road. The man hadn't moved. This was working. He was letting me go.

And then he took one long, single, silent step towards me. Out from under the trees and on to the road. Between me and the car.

All the old horror came flooding back. I'd faced them before. Rank upon rank of dead men, implacable in their desire for revenge on the women who had been doing this to them for centuries. One man every year for, say, two millennia was two thousand men. Three millennia was three thousand. I didn't want to think about four or five millennia. What would five thousand dead men look like? All gathered together in one place. Suppose they were all looking at me while I stood here like an idiot and did mental arithmetic.

And then a voice behind me said, 'No, my friend. Not this one. Not unless you want to discover that being dead is far from the worst thing that can happen to you. You know her and she has her own protection. Let her pass.'

Relief washed over me like a wave. Even though I'd known Iblis wouldn't be far away – that he wouldn't have left me – nevertheless . . .

The man didn't move.

There was the sound of someone drawing a sword. A silver light flooded the deep shadows under the trees. He spoke softly but with the authority of centuries. 'It is I, Iblis, who speaks. Let her pass.'

Things hung in the air for a long while. Certainly long enough for me to try to imagine what the fate worse than death that I was supposed to inflict upon this man would look like. And then he stepped backwards off the road and was lost under the trees.

'Even though I am Iblis,' said Iblis, his silver colour slowly dimming, 'it would be wise not to linger.'

Nigel was hiding under the car and would only come out for Iblis. I climbed into the passenger seat and put on my seat belt while Iblis tempted him out. Nigel rocketed straight into the back and gave us to understand that he would not stand in the way of our immediate departure.

'Get anything useful?' said Iblis over the noise of the engine as we pulled away.

'Yes. Someone is funding the rebuild. And attention is beginning to turn my way.'

'Any names? Details?'

'None. I did ask. Quite cleverly too.'

'I have no doubt on that score.'

'And then the man turned up and Joanna and Becky fled.'

He frowned. 'Either these women are too afraid to speak, or they are ignorant of what is happening and why, or they are lying. Any one of those.'

I sighed. 'We're not much further forwards, are we?'

'With luck we have rattled many cages,' said Iblis, who had made an entire career out of rattling people's cages. I prefer my cages unrattled.

I looked out of the window at the passing countryside. Sunset was still some way off but the day had flown by and I wanted to be home.

'Speaking of rattled cages – he's not going to be happy when he finds out, is he?'

We both knew who I meant.

'Will you tell him?'

'Oh, yes,' I said, because it would never occur to me not to. 'But he won't be happy.'

Iblis changed down to negotiate a sharp corner. His silver colour reached out towards me. 'Some advice, if you want it.'

'Yes, please.'

'Jones will be angry. Let him shout. It will be the frustration of one who has yet to come to terms with knowing his best days are done.'

'That's not true,' I said angrily. 'His days might be different from now on, but that doesn't mean they will be worse.'

He smiled at me. Not his bright beaming *I am Iblis* smile, but something rather sweet and understanding. 'Then I see you know exactly what to do.'

CHAPTER FIVE

I had the pleasure of Iblis and Nigel's company again that night. In the end, I was glad of it. The relief and euphoria of having escaped Greyston unscathed had worn off and I now found myself inclined to dwell on sentences such as *The threads of your life are converging, Elizabeth Cage, and one day soon they will be pulled tight*. None of which were contributing much to my peace of mind.

We stopped on the way home so I could buy our own body weight in eggs, bacon, sausages and potatoes, and that evening we had a massive fry-up. According to Iblis, this was the traditional celebration banquet of every triumphant champion in times gone by, when every victory – especially the rout of the murderous Assai by Keenan of Stroud – was celebrated by roasting a thousand pigs. In lieu of a thousand pigs, however, we would have two packets of bacon and sausages.

I eyed him keenly at this point, suspecting he was winding me up, but his colour showed he was telling the truth. I made a mental note to enquire more closely as to Keenan of Stroud one day. Otherwise, I enjoyed every mouthful and tried not to think too hard about cholesterol.

'Nigel and I will stay tonight,' he announced, somewhere around his fifth or sixth sausage. 'It will give Jones something harmless to shout about. Do not allow yourself to be upset by anything he says.'

I smiled and said, 'You're very wise.'

'I am Iblis, Man of Outstanding Wisdom.' He paused. His colour shimmered and reached out towards me. 'I am also the man who owes you everything. You saved me, Elizabeth. I will never forget.'

I looked down at my plate. 'You mean when I told you about Allia?'

There was a pause and his colour jumped around a little and then he smiled. 'You lifted the burden of centuries that day. I wish you would let me thank you.'

'You are my friend. It was my pleasure.'

He reached across the table and raised my hand to his lips and obviously that was the moment Jones chose to stride through the front door.

'Cage, what have I told you about leaving your door unlocked?' He paused and then demanded sarcastically, 'Am I interrupting something?'

'Yes,' said Iblis, who had obviously never heard about a soft answer turning away wrath. 'Could you wait outside for a few moments?'

I had planned to lead up to my transgressions slowly and gently, but Iblis's deliberate provocation unnerved me so much that I burst out with, 'I've been to Greyston. You won't believe—'

His gaze swung from Iblis to me and then back to Iblis again, annoying me no end, because the implication was that I was too stupid to do stupid things all by myself and had simply followed Iblis's lead.

'I made him do it,' I said, trying to salvage the situation.

'Yes,' beamed Iblis, not trying at all. 'She did.'

'By force, I suppose,' said Jones sarcastically.

Iblis forked the final sausage. 'I was completely over-whelmed . . .'

'Pull the other one.'

'. . . by the logic and strength of her arguments.'

Jones gazed at the pair of us. 'What the hell is the matter with you two? Last year I had to save the pair of you from the ramifications of your poking around the Painswicks' bungalow. Remember? When you discovered a body.'

'No, we didn't,' I objected. 'We just said there were a lot of flies. Someone else discovered the body.'

I meant to distract him from our wrongdoings at Greyston but it was the wrong thing to say. I watched his colour swirl and darken as exasperation turned to genuine anger.

'I can't believe – after everything I did to get you out of Greyston – that you would voluntarily go back and risk . . .'

'Hey,' I said, now quite angry myself. 'I got *you* out the second time – remember?'

Another wrong thing to say. I should be placating, calming, striving for a rational discussion of what we'd discovered. Not ripping up at him as he was ripping up at me. I don't know what came over me.

'You're not the slightest bit concerned about my safety. How could I be anything other than safe when Iblis was with me? You're only annoyed because we went without you. Because you can't handle not being the man of action any longer and we all have to tiptoe around you so as not to hurt your feelings.'

I couldn't believe I was saying these things. Jones had turned white while his colour was so dark as to be nearly purple.

'And don't stand there trying to threaten me. It won't be the first time you've laid hands on me.'

'No . . .' said Iblis suddenly. 'Stop. Both of you. Now.'

'You shut up,' snarled Jones. 'This is all your fault.'

'No, it's not,' I said, nearly weeping with frustration. 'For God's sake, stop ascribing all my actions to men as if I have no say in my life at all. I did a stupid thing. I persuaded Iblis to do this stupid thing with me. I. Me. Not you. Not him. Not Colonel Barton. Not the bloke in the bakery on the corner.' This list constituted nearly all the men in my life. 'Nor any other random man who happened to be passing at the time. My actions. My responsibility . . .' And before I could do anything about it, the thing in my head opened its eyes and roared, **'My life.'**

The words reverberated around my tiny house. In the kitchen, a glass bowl rang. We listened to the echoes die away.

'I think,' said Iblis carefully, 'that we should all sit down quietly before any of us make this situation any worse.'

'Cage,' said Jones. I don't know what he was going to say. Whether he would have had another shout about Greyston, or apologised, or what – I'll never know. Something inside me snapped. I felt it. Uncontrollable rage was building and any moment I would . . .

A tiny snowflake drifted down.

'Elizabeth,' said Iblis urgently. 'Look at me.'

'Get out!' I shouted. 'Both of you. Get out now.' And whether this was a command or a warning was unclear. I only knew I'd had enough. More than enough. 'Go on. What are you waiting for? Get out.'

Another snowflake settled on my arm. And then another. Invoking indoor snow – always a sign a person is normal.

'We should go,' said Iblis.

'No, we shouldn't,' shouted Jones.

'No good will come of this,' said Iblis. 'It is out of our hands now.'

'What are you talking about? Cage, what the fu—'

'Come,' said Iblis, putting a hand on his shoulder.

He shook it off. 'I'm not going anywhere until . . .'

My head was about to burst. 'Why are you still here? Get out. Now. Before . . .'

'Yeah,' said Jones. 'Before what?'

'Before we die,' said Iblis. 'I think Felda is waking up. We need to go quickly.'

He began to push Jones towards the door. Michael Jones is a big man and it takes a lot to push him from A to B, but Iblis was strong. Reluctantly, Jones moved. Iblis bent to collect Nigel from under the coffee table where he had sensibly sought refuge and then the door closed on Jones's protestations and silence was all around me.

Thoughts, pictures, emotions, memories – everything was colliding inside my head. I was in the centre of a vortex. My world was flying away from me. All control had gone. I was in the grip of something. My legs were trembling. My entire body was shaking uncontrollably. My heart was labouring. I could barely see properly. Was I going insane? Was I experiencing some kind of stroke? Was I dying?

And then the voice inside my head, soft as the settling snow, sad as the wind over the empty northern wastes, cold as ice, said, **'Elizabeth, my true friend. Sit.'**

I was gasping for breath. 'Who . . . ?'

'Sit. Regain your breath.'

I sat. I didn't particularly want to. I wanted to run away. Put some distance between this – whatever it was – and me, but it was sit down or fall down, so I sat. The table was a litter of empty plates, discarded cutlery and a single, solitary slice of bread. There was a tomato sauce bottle, salt, pepper, mugs laid out ready for the tea – an ordinary domestic scene, spoiled only by me having some kind of neural event all over it.

This wasn't the first time I'd heard this voice. All throughout my life I had been conscious of a presence. I always thought of it as the thing that lived inside my head. Mostly it slept but occasionally, in times of crisis, it would open its eyes and command me to run. Or to fight. Or to wait. Or even, occasionally, to sleep. Commands that had, in the past, kept me safe. And now it was telling me to sit down. To get my breath back. In proper words. It was talking to me.

She was talking to me. The voice was female. Was it just me talking to myself? Did I have some sort of personality disorder, perhaps? Voices in one's head are not usually good news. Whoever or whatever it was, though, I should do as I was told because this was sensible advice. So I leaned back into my seat with my eyes closed, gripping the edge of the table, waiting for my heart rate to slow and the pressure in my head to ease. I took long breaths and slowly, everything began to settle. After a few minutes I was myself again.

I tucked my hair behind my ears, drew a huge shuddering breath, opened my eyes and looked around. All right. Sickness gone. Voice gone. Room empty. I was alone. Everything back to normal. I took another breath. Never mind what had just happened, I should clear away the remains of our meal, wash the dishes and tidy up. An early night would be a good idea. A warm bath, a mug of cocoa, climb into bed with a good book and not – very definitely not – spend any time thinking about the events of today.

A good plan – practical and sensible. I did none of it.

Quite gently, the voice said, **'Are you ready for the truth?'**

I had to swallow several times before my own voice came back. 'They told me . . . Melek told me I chose not to know. She said to remember I'd made a choice and it was the right one.'

'And that still holds if that is what you want. All this is your choice, Elizabeth. This time, however, know that I am with you.'

I wasn't sure about this. No, actually, I *was* sure. I shouldn't do this.

'What is so important, so awful, that I would choose not to know?'

'You have a secret. An enormous secret. It has been hidden from you throughout all your lives, but it is becoming difficult to manage. Times change and it is taking its toll on you. Perhaps the time has come after all. Perhaps the decision is not yours but mine.'

'I don't understand.'

'Elizabeth – a mirror.'

I was too tired to argue. And too curious. I got up and groped my way up the narrow stairs into my bedroom.

'Sit down.'

I sat at the dressing table, very carefully avoiding looking at myself in the mirror.

'Look, Elizabeth. Look.'

With the feeling that I stood on the brink of something . . . tremendous . . . I slowly lifted my head, opened my eyes, and stared at myself in the mirror. Except it wasn't me. A completely different face stared back.

For some reason, I wasn't as shocked or as frightened as I might have been. I mean, really, after everything that had happened today, why wouldn't it be someone else's face? At least it seemed human. No hideous horned demon looked back at me, which had always been a worry of mine. I wasn't a monster. I wasn't hideous or terrifying. Although, as I looked more closely – this was not a human face after all. Nothing human could be that perfect. Or that cold.

Her face was a snow-white oval with sharply defined cheekbones. The word chiselled sprang into my mind. Her eyebrows were thick and white and slanted upwards. Long frost-laden eyelashes framed eyes the colour of the North Sea on a bitterly cold winter's day. Her white hair was plaited and coiled around her head. She wore something close-fitting and white. The whole effect was of a figure sculpted from ice and snow.

Her face was level with mine in the mirror, so I had no idea how tall she was but she certainly gave the impression of someone far more imposing than me. Although that wouldn't be difficult.

We regarded each other in silence. Neither of us moved. I tried not to think of huge, icy hands suddenly reaching through the mirror to seize me by my hair or my throat and drag me through to . . . wherever the other side of the mirror was. The silence dragged on. Was she waiting for me to make the first move?

I held up my hand, palm outwards. She – whoever she was – did the same. Just a fraction of a second behind me. Slowly our hands met. I could feel the icy cold striking through the mirror.

But I'd been right about her being much bigger than me. Her hand, long and white, was larger and wider than mine. My own hand looked very small, pink and fragile in comparison.

I let my hand drop away and we regarded each other, still without speaking. I couldn't think of anything to say. What words could possibly be appropriate for this sort of occasion? Were there *any* appropriate words for this sort of occasion? I stared at her. She stared at me. Waiting for me to speak first.

'I suppose I should say something,' I said eventually. 'After all, I am the host.'

For some reason, this seemed to cause her amusement. The cold mouth curled upwards. **'You are indeed, Elizabeth Cage. In every sense of the word.'**

'In that case,' I said, and my voice was all over the place. I cleared my throat and tried to speak firmly. 'Hello.'

'Greetings.'

There was more silence.

'I'm sorry,' I said at last. 'I don't know what to say. This is so . . . strange.'

'There is no need for you to say anything. I have but to say a word and you will remember everything. Explanations will then be unnecessary.'

'What word? What explanations?'

'Who you are. Who I am. What is happening. Everything.'

'You mean everything Melek has tried to conceal.'

'Do not blame her. She means you nothing but good. She is my great friend, and she has done her best for both of us, but she is slowly killing herself trying to keep us both safe. She saved me. A very long time ago. She saved you, too.'

'How?'

63

'I can open your mind and your memories, but for that I will ask your permission.'

I swallowed. 'What will that do to me? Will it hurt?'

'Physically, no.'

'And then I'll know everything.'

'You will know almost everything.'

'Almost?' I said, more sharply than I intended.

'A tiny part must remain hidden. It is not knowledge for a human. An event occurred which forced me to expose myself to something I would rather not have. I took you to a place no human should go. You met someone you should not have. I cannot say more. Trust me on this.'

'Why should I?'

'We have been together for a very long time, you and I. I have never led you astray. We have always protected each other. Let us each put our trust in the other again.'

I thought for a moment. 'This word you mentioned. The one that would make me remember. What is it?'

'Your true name.'

'My name isn't Elizabeth Cage, is it?'

Once that would have seemed impossible, but now it made perfect sense. Names from the dim past. Susannah, Eadgytha, Bianca . . .

'No, you have had many other names. Your true name will open your mind.'

'And then what?'

'Then, together, we will decide.'

'Decide what?'

'Whatever you want.'

I shifted on my stool. 'What about Melek?'

'She has done her best. She has laboured to keep us both safe. To her own cost. And she is so tired. I think, for all of us, the time has come. No more secrets.'

I thought of the question I should probably have led with. 'Who are you?'

'I am Felda, daughter of the gods.'

'You're a god?'

And then – from somewhere – a flash of memory. Jones, his face bruised and battered, shouting at me, 'You're a god, Cage? A bloody god. A living god.' And suddenly some things fell into place.

'Yes,' I said. 'Perhaps you're right. Perhaps the time has come. Should we . . . I mean . . . Should Melek be here?'

'It is, I think, better if we take the decision out of her hands. Kinder to her.'

All of a sudden I wanted to know. Whatever it was that others knew – I wanted to know it, too. This was different from the other night. That night I had sought safety in ignorance. But how wise a course of action was that? If others knew, then so should I, for my own protection. And besides, now that I could see her – now that we were actually speaking to each other – things were different. I was different.

I stared into the mirror. 'All right,' I said slowly. 'Let's do it.'

'You are sure?'

'I think the time has come, don't you? Ignorance is no longer safe for me – or for those around me.'

'I agree. Are you ready?'

'Yes.'

She smiled. Very softly, she said, **'Tadia . . .'**

I thought there would be a sudden crash of memories dumped

directly into my brain. A sort of Big Bang, something from nothing. Nothing, then everything. This wasn't like that at all.

Gently, very gently at first, like slowly falling snow, but speeding up as I became accustomed . . . my life flashed before my eyes.

Suddenly I was Tadia, the goat girl, alone in the harsh hills, day after day, month after month. Foraging for myself and slowly starving because of it. Cold, hurt, lonely, afraid of the dark. Huddled in rags between two rocks. Terrified that Div-e Sepid would carry me away to . . . somewhere. I could feel the cold, dark, gritty soil beneath my bare feet. See the glittering stars above me.

And then Melek appeared to offer me another life. Food. A warm cloak. Safety. A future. A better life. And not just one life. Many lives flashed in front of me. Susannah, Bianca, Alice, Katherine, Eadgytha . . . and all I had to do was let Melek use me to conceal a god.

I had to know. 'This thing I can do – with people's colours. Is that you?'

'**No. That gift is all your own. It is one of the reasons you were chosen.**'

'One of them? What was the other?'

'**There were many. Your compassion. Your courage. Your gentle nature.**'

'Oh, no,' I said, embarrassed. 'I didn't . . . I mean . . . I haven't done anything.'

Felda spoke softly. '**Elizabeth, you gave me rest. Peace. You agreed to become my host. You saved me. You saved the world from me. I will never be able to thank you enough.**'

'You don't have to thank me,' I whispered. 'You have saved me in return.'

66

She very nearly smiled. One side of her mouth curved upwards. I was reminded of Melek. **'I have. Would you like to see?'**

Actually, I would. Who could resist the chance to see themselves in a past life? Sometimes I was surprised at how brave I was becoming.

The mirror clouded and cleared. And there I was. Alice. That was me. Right there. I was wearing a long dark dress with what looked like a sacking apron tied around my waist and a sort of linen wimple on my head. I was standing on the steps outside a church. A big church. A cathedral, possibly. Surrounded by shouting people. A great crowd of them, hemming me in on all sides. I couldn't get out. Now I remembered the fear. I was going to die because they were angry. No – worse than angry – they were afraid. They were afraid of me and their fear would kill me.

Someone threw a stone – which missed. And then another one – which didn't, hitting me on my upper arm. And then, as always happens with a crowd, because someone else had made the first move, suddenly there were many stones. I tried to dodge. I tried to cover my head. I could feel the blood running down my face. I was going to die.

And then the thing that lived inside my head – Felda – lifted her head and I saw the world through her eyes. I let my hands fall to my side, took in a massive breath, and I roared. Something inside me opened up my chest, and a voice – her voice – roared out across the square. I saw the shock wave radiate outwards. I saw people fall, clutching at their heads. A pot shattered somewhere. The sound went on and on, spreading across the cobbled square. Dogs barked. I heard clattering hooves as a horse bolted. Above me the great bells began to sound. An alarm? A warning?

It didn't really matter. People fled in all directions, falling over each other in their panic. And then there was only me, left standing in the empty space, and I picked up my skirts and ran for my life.

A memory. Vivid. And true.

I blinked and looked at her in the mirror. 'I remember that.'

'Yes. No matter how quietly we tried to live, there was always something. But we survived. We always survived. Both of us.'

'And you,' I said. 'Will I ever know the story of your life?'

There was a slight hesitation. **'No. There is much of which I am not proud. I was not always in control. Even now . . . even these days . . .'**

I didn't know what to say.

'Yours is a gentle soul,' she went on, and her voice was laden with sadness and regret. **'Do not make me show you some of the things I have done. It would grieve me greatly to have you fear or hate me.'**

'It's all right,' I said hastily. 'Not if you don't want to.'

'I can show you a little. To help you to understand.'

I remembered Iblis's tale. The one he told me after a great deal of wine over my own dining table. About the four of them – Iblis, Melek, Felda and . . . Borin. Their achievements and their plans for a great and glorious future. And why it never happened.

I don't know what made me say it. 'Can I see him? Borin. Can you show me? But not if it's too much. I mean . . . No, I'm sorry. Forget I asked. It's just that Ted died. My husband. I loved him very much. As you probably already know. But I thought . . . we could share our grief . . . maybe . . .'

I stopped, and silence filled my bedroom.

She was silent for a long time and then said, almost to herself, **'I have held back the memories for so long. It will hurt, I warn you, but perhaps . . . just a very little?'**

I nodded and sat up straight. Afraid – no, apprehensive – but at the same time, very, very curious. What would I see? Events from long, long ago. Heart thumping, I gripped my hands together in my lap and waited.

The mirror clouded again.

This time, I saw through her eyes.

I saw a man. And not just any man. A great man – a demi-god – a man of passion and fire, striding up from the south, a land of heat and dusty plains and deserts, leading his armies as they drove the Fiori demons before them. Scattering them, killing without mercy – which is the only way with the Fiori. Giving the world a chance, at last, to wipe their evil from the face of the earth.

I was fighting my way down from the cold north to meet him. Melek and Iblis were there, too. They had moved behind the scenes – something at which Melek was particularly effective, whispering in the right ears, inspiring the right leaders, choosing the right times. There was to be a great alliance, kings, queens, champions, heroes, everyone. From great countries to tiny city states – treaties would be signed, coalitions formed. United, we would be strong enough to obliterate the Fiori for ever. Every last one of them. The future was bright and full of promise.

He and I came face to face on a rocky headland at the eastern end of the Circle Sea. The brilliant sunshine, the salt-laden wind blowing cloaks and hair, the sea birds shrieking overhead. He was wiping his sword on his cloak, frowning as someone spoke to him. He looked up as I approached. I felt the heat of him as I drew near. Saw the sudden fire in his eyes. There may have been others there – there were others there – all talking, greeting each other, doing human things. I saw only him. He saw only me.

There was wine and feasting. People talking to us all the time. We were separated. There were duties and obligations to fulfil. As soon as one group moved away, another would take its place. We were taller than everyone else there and it was easy to look over the heads of humans . . . and then someone else would speak and I would have to respond. The long day ground on. That long, long endless day.

Night fell. I slipped away from the lights and the music and the celebrations, picking my way by starlight, finding the rocky path down to the shore below. I did not look back. Not once. I knew he would follow. I found a place mostly free from rocks, close to the sea. He was there already. Waiting for me. The night was hot and full of stars. He laid down his cloak and we lost ourselves in each other.

We were ice and fire. He had the eyes of the hot southern sun – bright and golden. His skin was as black as the night sky overhead – mine as white as the snow on the mountains. He laid his hand on mine and we laughed to see the contrast between them.

That was the last time I ever laughed.

At last, he fell asleep. He lay on his back, forearm across his eyes. I rose up and walked out into the sea. I lay on my back, my hair floating around me, looking up at the stars as they wheeled across the sky above. My father spoke to me through the music of the waves. There was a choice to be made. By me.

There would be a long war against the Fiori. A long, long

war. A hard fight with no guarantee of victory, but always with the possibility of the Golden Age of which we all had dreamed. There would be glory and great deeds and heroic achievement – but at a price. And the price would be paid by me. The choice was simple – if I chose to live with the mortals then I must live as a mortal. Relinquish everything that made me Felda, daughter of the gods.

I should have hesitated, but I did not. I should have thought carefully, but I did not. I should have given consideration to all the possibilities. I did not. Some might say I deserved what came to me afterwards. I thought only of Borin. I did not think of myself.

I made my choice. There and then. Between the sea and the sky – I chose. I made my choice and called down the stars as my witness.

And then I went back to Borin.

The next day was all bustle. The treaty would be ratified by our wedding. Neither of us was willing to wait. We both wanted it to happen that day. If we had had our way – if the ceremony had taken place there and then – it is possible that the whole history of the world might have been changed. But we were overruled. There were preparations to be made, apparently. Gods to be appeased.

I informed them the gods couldn't care less – and I should know – that it was just priests trying to make themselves important as priests always do, but everyone was adamant and so the ceremony was fixed for the day after. As the sun was swallowed by the sea – we would be wed. In the sight of all. And in that moment, I would become a mortal.

We should not have waited. Not even that one day. Even now, my heart hurts to think about it . . .

71

I saw the hunting party assemble. Iblis was there, laughing and joking with all. I can still hear the jingling bits, the stamp of the horses' hooves. Then they mounted and clattered away up into the rocky hills.

I sat outside my tent with Melek. I remember they had thrown up an awning for me because the sun and the colours were too bright for my northern eyes. We drank wine and made plans.

I had no warning. No kindly premonition lessened the shock. One moment I had the whole world before me – and the next moment I had nothing. The world was ashes to me and my heart died for ever.

There had been an accident. A snake. Coiled on a rock in the sun. Startled by the sudden clatter of so many horses and riders, it struck at Borin's horse, which shied. Taken unawares, Borin fell. And died instantly.

Never mind political crises, or world-wide wars, or assassinations, or natural disasters – that was the moment that changed the world. When everything fell apart. When our plans crashed to the ground in ruins. There never was a great treaty. No Golden Age. The Fiori regrouped and are with us to this day. Without Borin to unite and lead them, mortals drifted away. Kings and queens abandoned their alliances and returned to defend their own territories. Iblis and Melek did what they could to stem the tide of desertions, but it was useless.

And I no longer cared.

There were no words to describe the pain of my grief then, and there are none now. Fierce. Searing. Savage. Brutal. Vicious. Intense. Cruel. Never-ending. None of those even come close.

To begin with, I was comforted a little by the grief of others, but that grief faded – as it does with short-lived mortals and their shorter memories. Sooner or later, everything, all of it – the deeds, the bravery, the sacrifices, everything that was great and wonderful – was lost to them. Gone for ever. But the evil against which we fought – that never dies. That evil lives on in the hearts and minds of humans, where it finds fertile soil and is never forgotten.

One by one those who had known Borin began to die, taking their memories with them. Within brief years, none were left. In time, the world forgot him. His beautiful shrine, the one I built on the headland where we met, began to fall into disrepair. Other than me, no one cared for it. I lived there for a while, easing my pain just a very little by being as close to him as I could manage, until the day I returned to find the blue-haired earth-shaker had raised his trident and the entire headland had fallen into the sea. Carrying Borin's shrine, his bones, my memories, everything, to the bottom of the sea. Now, truly, there was nothing left of him.

And I still lived. And went on living. And will go on living. Because, whether as a punishment by the gods for deserting them, or simply a cruel twist of fate, there is no kindly death for me. I had abandoned my own kind, but the marriage ceremony had never taken place, and so I am doomed to live on and on, caught between two worlds until the end of time itself. Neither god nor human, enduring the worst of both worlds. I have tried to end my life, many times – the gods alone know what I have done to myself – but always, sooner or later, I would open my eyes and find the world was still around me and I was still part of it.

I walked in deep shadows. I no longer cared what I did or to whom I did it. If I was to suffer, then mankind would suffer along with me. Before, I had been, if not loved, then at least respected. Now I was feared almost as much as the Fiori themselves. My mind grew dark and my deeds darker.

It was my friend Melek who found me a sanctuary. A refuge. A relief from the pain that never, ever, ever goes away. That never gives me a moment's respite. Never ceases to pierce my heart. She found Tadia, the little goat girl, and finally, finally, I could close my eyes and sleep away the pain . . .

I opened my eyes with a jolt. Icy tears lay on my cheeks. I was clutching the edge of my dressing table just to keep myself upright. The pain of Felda's grief was still with me and it was unbearable. And this was only a tiny echo of her never-ending agony. Grief that renewed itself over and over again down the countless years. Grief that seared its way into her very soul, day after endless day. Grief that would never end. How had she ever been able to bear it?

Well, she hadn't, had she? It had driven her mad in the end. She was probably suffering now. I should end this as soon as I could. Let her drift back into the merciful peace and forgetfulness she craved.

She was looking at me in the mirror. I forced myself not to look away. Not to judge her. Who can judge a god?

'Do not think too badly of me.'

My voice was hoarse with tears for her. 'I don't. I don't judge you at all.'

She looked at me almost shyly. **'I do not want to leave you with those images. There is still beauty in my life. Can I show you my home?'**

I nodded, wondering what I would see, prepared for the worst.

74

The mirror clouded again, and then, with a brightness that nearly blinded me, I saw snow-smothered mountains, jagged against the vivid blue sky. The brilliant sun turned them to gold, criss-crossing them with deep blue and purple shadows, reflecting the colours of the sky. Row upon row, rank upon rank of these great mountains interspersed with flat plains where nothing disturbed the white smoothness. Nothing moved anywhere. And all around was silence. Utter silence. White silence. Peace and great beauty. I could easily imagine Felda living up there among the golden peaks. Looking down on to the clouds. Solitary but never lonely. At night, the stars would shine like chipped diamonds. Shining their faint light on to the snowy slopes while the wind sang its sad song. A strange, wild landscape for a strange, wild god.

Even as I stared, the mountains faded and I heaved a great sigh at their loss. I could have gazed at their majesty for hours. 'What now?'

Her face appeared again before me. **'That is up to you. Do you wish to continue as before?'**

'You mean, not knowing who I am. Who we are?'

'Yes.'

This time, I took a moment to think. To consider the implications. 'No. No, I don't think I do.' I looked at her. 'I thought I wanted to forget, but now that I have met you . . . seen you . . . I understand . . . a little, anyway. I think I've changed my mind. Although . . .' I hesitated.

'Although what?'

'I . . . my parents. Not my real parents, who pushed me out to herd their goats until the day I died. I mean the ones that Melek . . . the memories that Melek made for me. I . . . It's hard

75

to explain, but all my life my mother and father have been a source of strength. Their memory is important to me. They are the framework of my life. I don't want to . . . to let them go. I understand now that they never existed, but they were real to me and I loved them.'

'You will always have those memories. They will never leave you. And if your parents were real to you, then they did exist. Remember them with affection.'

'I will,' I said. 'Thank you.'

There was a pause. I don't know what made me say it. 'What happened last Christmas? Something happened – I know it did. I don't know what, but things were different afterwards and I don't know why.'

She paused for a long time and then said, **'I will tell you what I can. It concerns the thing I cannot speak of.'**

I waited.

'There was an attack. On Iblis. He nearly died.'

I was horrified. 'Where? When?'

She didn't quite answer the question. **'He was stabbed.'**

'By whom?'

'With his own sword.'

Another question not quite answered. I remembered what he'd once told me. His own sword – or Melek's – was just about the only weapon in this world that could kill him.

'But . . . but he survived,' I said. 'He's still alive.'

'He is. I – we – you and I – we went in pursuit to a place I should not have taken you, to confront someone you should not have met. I cannot speak of that. Do not ask me.'

'All right,' I said. 'But he's fine now? Iblis, I mean.'

'He is. And now he is reunited with his sword. The attack

failed. He is with Melek and the two of them are strong again.'

'Did you get him? The person who tried to kill him?'

'I did not.'

She looked away. The message was clear. Stop asking questions.

'And you – us – what happens now?'

'Nothing – if that is what you want. You have always been aware of my presence.'

I blushed, because calling her 'the thing that lives in my head' was not a particularly flattering description. Especially of a god.

She sighed. **'I would very much like to sleep now.'**

'So would I,' I said with great feeling. 'It's been a tiring day.'

'No, I mean really sleep. Deeply and for a long time. The pain is . . . growing within me again.'

'Does this mean . . . Will we speak again?'

'Perhaps. One day.'

'But not soon.'

She seemed to hesitate. **'I . . . I cannot stay long. The world damages me and my presence damages the world. You know of what I speak.'**

I did. The angry snow I had once conjured, smothering everything in its path. It was no consolation to know that hadn't been me – not all me, anyway – but the cost . . . to her . . . to me . . . to Melek . . . to the world.

I nodded, suddenly desperately tired and feeling the need to sleep myself. 'I understand. I do. Now that we have spoken . . . now that I've seen . . . I . . . I am at peace. I wish you peace, as well.'

'I am not leaving you for ever, Elizabeth, but is it selfish

of me to want to sleep for a while? You have friends. Good friends, who will stand by you, come what may. You are not alone.'

'No, I'm not.' I remembered earlier events. 'If they ever come back.'

'They will. I shall sleep now. Peace to you, Elizabeth Cage.'

'Peace to you, too. Peace to us both.'

She placed her hand against the mirror again and I did the same. Again, I felt the icy cold of her touch. And then, a huge hot flash in my mind – a dark face with golden, glowing eyes. And then it was gone and all I wanted to do was sleep.

I said, 'Who was that? Was that . . . ?'

But the mirror was empty. Only I looked back at me.

For the first time in my life, I left the dishes unwashed and the table uncleared. There was no hot bath or comforting mug of cocoa. I don't think I remembered to lock the house. I didn't even undress. I just fell into bed and slept.

CHAPTER SIX

The whole world turned up on my doorstep the next morning.

Well, not the whole world, maybe, but *my* whole world, anyway. Which is not large, but more than enough for my tiny sitting room.

Melek arrived first thing. I'd showered, put on clean clothes, washed the blood off the step, and was about to clear away the remains of last night. The room stank quite badly. I wouldn't be leaving the dishes overnight again.

I wasn't in the slightest bit surprised to see her. Outwardly she looked quite calm, but her golden colour was muted and watchful.

She brought Iblis – I was expecting him, too. But not Nigel. Either he was too scared to come back here, despite all the good food or – and much more likely – Melek had refused to be seen in public with him.

Hard on their heels came Jones, who wasn't entirely unexpected either, but to have him and Melek together in a small space was always concerning. It concerned me, anyway.

'Good,' said Melek, eyeing Jones and obviously starting as she meant to go on. 'I won't have to go out and get you. That will save me a great deal of time and effort.'

'I wouldn't be too sure of that,' said Jones, standing just that little bit too close to her.

I retreated into the kitchen to finish the dishes. They could fight it out between themselves while I got on with my day.

Given I'd slept like a toppled tree, I was surprised how well I'd felt when I woke this morning. There was still a lot for me to think about and I would have appreciated some time to actually do that, but to expect the arguments of last evening to pass into peaceful oblivion was too much to hope for. I would stay out of things for as long as possible. I finished tidying the kitchen and then thought about lunch. A nice lamb stew.

I shut out the sounds of battle and concentrated hard on the task before me. Dice the lamb. Don't allow myself to be distracted. I trimmed the fat and dropped the meat into a pan to brown. Voices rose and fell as I chopped carrots, swedes and onions, humming quietly because if I didn't, then I might start shouting myself. Not that anyone would notice. Where's a light flurry of angry snow when you need one? Even if I would have to clear it out of my living room afterwards.

Still humming, still determinedly in my own world, I added the vegetables to the meat and made the gravy. This was going well and the smell was delicious. I sliced potatoes to lay across the top, salted, peppered, and dotted them generously with knobs of butter. Normally, I would make enough for several meals – one for now and freeze the rest – but I didn't want to give the impression I was catering for everyone present today, so I very defiantly made only a single portion and didn't care who saw it. This wasn't a hotel. People couldn't just turn up, have their arguments all over my lovely sitting room, decide my future, and then expect me to feed them. The way they were going at it, I could probably sit down and have my lunch and then go for a long walk afterwards and they wouldn't even notice I'd left the house. I might never come back. I might just keep on walking. Jump on a bus or train and see where it took me.

Actually, why wait until after lunch? I could walk out of the back door now, jump on to my little moped and roar away – except Jones had bought it for me and it did seem a little ungrateful to make my getaway on his Christmas present. It then occurred to me that I might need to toughen up a little. That I lacked a killer instinct.

All of this was moot. Nobody was paying me any attention at all. They were all too busy yelling at each other. I popped the casserole in the oven, straightened up and caught Iblis looking at me. He winked. I suspected he agreed with my strategy.

Still unwilling to be dragged into any of it, I looked for something else to do. I'd bake a few jacket potatoes. My mum always said never to waste a hot oven. They could go into the freezer for me to eat later. I scrubbed three potatoes, pricked them with a fork, rubbed them with oil and salt and popped them in the oven as well.

The shouting was going well. Iblis and Jones appeared to be equal recipients of Melek's displeasure. It would appear they'd both handled things badly last night and why had no one thought to summon her? Both of them were dealing with her in their separate ways. Jones looked mutinous and stubborn; Iblis was beaming at her. I decided that of the two of them, it was Iblis most likely marked for an early death.

Yes. I'd called it right. She rounded on him and was giving him an extra telling off for conveying me to Greyston, and ignoring his feeble protests that if he hadn't, then I would have got a taxi or a bus, or got Jerry to do it, or jumped on my stupid moped and . . .

'It's not stupid,' I said angrily. 'It's red and shiny and I love it.' And stopped dead because that was a statement open to a great deal of misinterpretation.

Jones snorted, which was unfortunate because Melek abandoned Iblis and turned her attention back to him. There followed a comprehensive and surprisingly accurate description of him, his appearance, his character, his attitude, his abilities in general and so on.

Wisely he didn't even try to interrupt; he simply folded his arms and waited for her to run down.

Not so Iblis. Possibly he was seeking to divert her and it worked. He'd hardly got beyond, 'I think . . .' before she switched back to him. His character – that took a long time – his appearance, his behaviour, his dog – especially his dog – his personal habits, his boots – obviously a long-standing grievance – back to his dog again – nothing escaped her . . . I would say monologue, but that in no way conveys the depth, range, and vocabulary of her diatribe. She was livid. I didn't need to look at her colour to see this anger was born of fear. She'd spent centuries covering for Iblis in his self-imposed exile, patching up the world as best she could, fighting the Fiori, watching out for me, trying to keep Felda calm, and just slowly fighting a losing battle on every front, and now the situation, like sand, was slipping through her fingers, and the tighter she clutched at it, the faster it slipped away.

I decided to stay in the kitchen and hope she'd forget I was here.

Not a chance.

'And as for you,' she raged, turning to me.

She was losing control. Her colour was all over the place. She had carried this burden for so long – and, after last night, I was beginning to have a new appreciation of how much of a burden it had been. She'd struggled to hold things together and now, no matter what she did or where she turned, it was all falling apart.

'Felda says hi,' I said brightly.

The room froze. No one moved.

Melek's shoulders dropped as her anger drained away. 'You know,' she said eventually.

'I do.'

'Everything?'

'Everything she thought I should know.'

Melek collapsed into a chair and put her head in her hands. Her thick golden colour, always so close and so rigidly controlled, now swirled aimlessly around her. She was lost.

Jones nudged Iblis and nodded towards the door.

The two big brave men edged their way out, quietly closing the door behind them, leaving me unsure what to do next. Talk to her? Give her space to pull herself together? Carry on and pretend nothing had happened? What do you do when someone as hard as nails suddenly crumbles into . . . well, someone who isn't as hard as nails? I stared at her. Was she crying? Could she cry?

I thought I'd make her a cup of tea. Even if she spurned my offer with loathing, it would give me something to do. I placed the mug in front of her and retreated back into the kitchen.

She wasn't crying, but her expression was one of complete despair. 'So,' she said, not looking at me. 'Now you know everything.'

I shook my head. 'I know what Iblis has told me, and you, and Felda herself, last night. I know about Borin and how he died and how unhappy she was afterwards and that for the sake of herself and the world, you had to find a refuge for her. I know I'm Tadia the goat girl, who should have died and didn't.

I know I had a gift – seeing people's colours – which was why you chose me. And I know that Felda and I have been together a very long time. I don't know everything she's done, because she wouldn't tell me, but I gather some of it is pretty horrible.'

'How do you feel?'

I was surprised she asked, because of the two of us, I felt I should be asking her. She looked terrible.

'Actually, I feel all right. It answers some questions and I'm . . . fine. I probably shouldn't be, but I am.'

She looked down. 'Your parents?'

'Which ones?'

'Elizabeth Cage's parents?'

'What about them?'

'Good. You still have them.'

I was puzzled. 'Why wouldn't I?'

'No reason. I'm glad. They mean a lot to you.'

I nodded.

She sighed and tried to straighten her shoulders. 'What now, Elizabeth Cage?'

'Nothing, I suppose. We came to an agreement. The world is overwhelming her and she just wants to sleep – to rest – which is fine with me. I'll get on with my own life. Why should anything change? And what everyone refers to as "my gift" is my own and nothing to do with Felda.'

'You are content for the situation to remain unchanged? You had this knowledge last Christmas and it made you deeply unhappy. And again, the other night, you chose not to know.'

'That's true, but this time Felda showed herself to me and . . . somehow, it made a difference. And I know what happened last Christmas.'

'You know that Allia attacked Iblis?'

Well, I hadn't, but I did now. I had the sense not to say anything. Melek continued. 'He lay dying. Felda chased after her and brought back his sword. Do you remember that?'

'Some of it. Did I fight her?'

'No, she surrendered the sword and . . . ran away. Iblis has his sword back.'

I picked up my own mug and came to sit opposite her. 'I suppose now no one needs to lie to anyone else, do they?'

'You are taking this remarkably well.'

'Well, I haven't really had time to take it all in yet. Perhaps this time tomorrow I'll be upset, but at the moment . . . I don't know. And what about you – you can go now, can't you? You don't have to stand guard over me any longer. You can leave Felda – for a while, at least – and me. If you want to come back occasionally, I'll be pleased to see you, but now you can concentrate on your real purpose. You can take Iblis away for a few weeks and kill some demons. You'll soon feel better.'

She regarded me. 'You are not the Elizabeth Cage you were six months ago.'

'No,' I said, 'I'm not. Now I have a better idea of who I am. I have independence. I have wheels. I have a job – if Jones can ever bring himself to speak to me again. I feel more in control of my life. It's a good feeling.' I looked into my mug. 'I could be happy.'

She finished her tea. Setting down the mug, she got up. 'Are you all right if I leave you now?'

'Yes,' I said, 'except . . .'

'What?'

'Please, if you get the opportunity, talk to Jones. He's having difficulties with all this.'

'What do you want me to say?'

'Whatever you think fit.'

She nodded. 'I promise not to kill him.' And there was very nearly a smile.

'Wow,' I said. 'Progress.'

And then she was gone, and I was alone with the smell of lamb stew.

For once, I didn't do anything stupid. I took a few days to think about everything. I sat in my window seat, looked out over the green and tried to put things into perspective. Setting aside my personal issues, there were still the women of Greyston to worry about. What was going on up there? Should I have told Melek?

No need, Iblis would do that for me. It dawned on me that for the first time ever, we were all a proper team. No one was hiding anything from anyone else. If Jones remained on board, of course. But he had to. He and I were a team working for Mary Bennet. If he left, then she'd lose me too. Surely she'd make sure there was a place for him somewhere.

So, despite all the uncertainty surrounding me, I was experiencing an unfamiliar bout of optimism. The weather was lovely and I spent the next few days doing ordinary things. I took one or two trips into the countryside on my moped, rejoicing in my freedom. I went up to Streetley, which is such a pretty little place. I explored the village and the woods, and then, greatly daring, went into the pub – by myself – and had lunch there. Nothing happened. No one attacked me. No spirits emerged from the walls to menace me. No one died. This was the sort of life normal people took for granted and now, perhaps, it could be mine, too.

I did things that kept me busy. Things that kept my mind and hands occupied. I moved the furniture around. And then moved it all back again, because my house was so small there was really very little room for furniture creativity.

I reorganised my garden shed – very necessary now it housed my moped. I banged in some nails and hung my gardening tools around the walls. I moved the clothes prop into the cellar – something I'd been meaning to do for ages, because the stupid thing kept falling on me every time I opened the shed door.

With the shed sorted, I turned my attention to my backyard. I went online and bought a ton of bedding plants. And then some pots to put them in. Everything I saw was either terracotta or stone – which was all very well but I wanted colour. Colour is important. So, I also bought some paint. Bright blue, cerise, purple and lime green. Lovely bright, vibrant colours. Full of excitement, I prised off the lids and got stuck in.

It probably wouldn't have been so bad if I'd just painted each pot a single colour, but once I had a paintbrush in my hand, I couldn't stop. As I tried to explain to Jones when he called around two days later.

I opened the door to him and could see at once that he felt better. There were still streaks of orange anxiety, which I ascribed to lingering concerns about his eyesight, but his colour was much brighter. Not completely as it had been before, but very much better.

We looked at each other.

'I'm an arsehole, Cage, but can I come in anyway?'

I suspected he and Melek had enjoyed a quiet chat together. I would have loved to be a fly on the wall for that one. However, he was here now. I had a sudden memory of him fighting for

87

me when I was snatched from his bedroom; how I'd cried over his injuries, how gentle he'd been when I told him about little Sammy's ghost and how I'd planned for us to live together. Everything we'd been through, and all the difficulties of the last months, just melted away.

'Of course you can.'

I took him through the house and into the tiny back garden, because I was still in the throes of great creativity.

He took in the scene and stopped dead. 'For the love of God, Cage – what have you done now?'

'Don't you like them?' I said, stepping back to admire the colourful pots with their multi-coloured stripes, spots and wiggly lines.

'On the contrary, I think they're very . . . striking, but won't the residents' committee have something to say?'

I frowned up at him. 'What residents' committee?'

He sighed. 'This lack of municipal organisation is a direct cause of today's urban decay. I shall take it up with the council.'

I hammered the lid back on to the cerise paint pot. It was my favourite colour and I'd used rather a lot of it. Some of it was on me, too. 'What are you talking about now?'

'Civic responsibility, Cage, and you unleashing visual pollution on an unsuspecting populace.' He paused as I began to set out the plants, ready to go in the pots now they were dry. 'No, no, you're doing it wrong. You should put those orange flowers in that blue pot, the white ones in the cerise, and the yellow and red ones in the purple and green striped pots.'

I stared at him, bewildered. 'What are you doing?'

'Joining you in bringing down civilisation.'

'How exactly are my pots bringing down civilisation?'

'You're undermining the very fabric of society, Cage. There will be letters to the *Rushford Gazette*, mark my words.'

I tipped the last marigolds from their sleeves and began to plant them up. 'Why exactly are you here?'

'I talked with Melek. Well, I sat pinned to my seat while she talked at me.'

'How did that go?'

'Some air was cleared. Interestingly, she said she has a proposition for us and she'll call in a few days.'

'What sort of proposition?'

'She didn't say. Anyway, I was told to pull myself together because apparently, for some reason, I'm not the most important person in the universe – at least in her eyes – which doesn't bother me in the slightest, as long as I'm the most important person in the universe in your eyes.'

I concentrated on the daisies. He was right. The white flowers looked stunning in the bright cerise pot.

'You want to know if you're the most important person in my world?'

'I do. Or, if not now – is there any chance I could be?'

Now what did I say?

Well, I'd made a vow to myself always to tell the truth. No more secrets. Now was obviously the time to start.

I put down my trowel. 'I've made a vow always to tell the truth, so I have to ask – are you sure you want to know?'

He took a deep breath. 'No. Personally, I'm coming round to the idea that ignorance is bliss and hope can spring eternal, but I should probably develop higher moral standards, so hit me with the truth.'

His colour was flooded with orange.

'You're the most important person in my world and have been for some time.'

He didn't move but his colour switched almost instantaneously from orange to gold. 'You mean that?'

'I do. Can you pass over my trowel, please.'

'In a minute.'

It was a good job I wasn't actually holding the trowel – he would certainly have impaled himself on it and that would have taken some explaining in A&E. And it would have been better if I'd had cleaner hands too. But there was a pleasant interlude for a few minutes, until I realised we were being watched from the upstairs windows by my neighbours, the solicitors. I had given up wondering what they thought of me. Iblis at the front and Jones around the back. It was a wonder I hadn't been run out of town.

'I'm quite badass, you know,' I told Jones.

'Come inside and prove it.'

'I can't – I've started this, so I have to finish.'

'Shall I go inside and begin without you?'

'Or you can lend a hand. Other than all that mushy romantic stuff, why are you here?'

'I thought I should see how you were. You look tired. I'm being neighbourly.'

'You live over the other side of town and honestly, I'm fine.'

He frowned. 'Not from where I'm standing.'

'Then go and stand somewhere else.'

'I love how you make me feel so welcome.' He watched me start on the petunias. 'You're doing that wrong, by the way.'

'No, I'm not. I'm doing it exactly right.'

'Seen Iblis today?' he said casually. 'Or the other one?'

'No and no. Why do you ask?'

'Just wondered.'

'I wish they *were* here. They would admire my pots and then Iblis would tell me my beauty made them pale in comparison.'

'There is something so wrong with him.'

'Well, thank you very much. Do you see that big pot there?'

'Yes,' he said, very cautiously.

'Can you carry it through and put it out on the front steps for me? I'll bring the others.'

'You're putting them at the front?'

'Some of them, yes. They'll cheer people up as they pass by.'

'Blind them, more like. You'll be sued, Cage.'

'I shan't pay.'

'They'll lock you up and throw away the key.'

'Would that mean no visitors? Ever? You, for instance?'

He smiled at me over the daisies. 'You can't get rid of me, Cage. Locks and bars mean nothing to me. I go wherever I like.'

I made a rude noise.

He sighed. 'Can you open this door for me, please?'

'Hold on.'

He carried the pot through the house and we emerged out into the sunshine again. I took a moment to stare around. I never tired of this scene. The row of crooked houses. The green opposite. Little children playing in the mud. The remains of the moat were filled with photogenic ducks that would tear you to shreds if you hadn't had the forethought to bring duck food. The accepted procedure was to throw the bag of food as far away as possible and then seize the opportunity to run for your life in the opposite direction.

Behind the willow-fringed moat stood the castle, with people strolling in and out, visiting the library or the council offices.

The castle was surprisingly undamaged. I suspect Rushford hadn't been important enough for Cromwell to do his worst during the Civil War. The council had a number of offices in there, so if they didn't like my pots then I'd soon be hearing about it.

'As you know, Cage, I'm not one to complain, but this is bloody heavy. Stop daydreaming and tell me where you want it.'

'Here. Right here. Top step. Where everyone can see it.'

'I'm warning you, Cage, I'm not going to prison for you. First sign of a riot or civil protests and I drop the pot and make a run for it. You'll have to hold them off by yourself.'

'A little more to your right. No, left. No, I meant right. Give it a bit of a turn. No, the other way. That's it. Perfect. And now your fingerprints are all over everything when the Good Taste Police turn up to take you away.'

I began to arrange the other smaller pots down the steps. I'd gone for colour and impact. I'd succeeded.

'Again,' I said, as Jones very ostentatiously donned his sunglasses. 'Why are you here?'

'Oh. Yes. Sorry, I was concentrating on saving my remaining eyesight and it went out of my head.'

'What did?'

'Sorensen Clinic. Day after tomorrow. Ten in the morning. We've begun the preliminary interviews and you are cordially invited.'

I was silent.

'Cage – you are still all right with this?'

'Oh, yes – it's just that now the time has come, I'm a little nervous.'

'Nothing to worry about. He won't be able to see you. And even if he does, he's never going to be in a position to do you any harm again. He's got a hell of a lot of explaining to do and he's going to be far too busy covering his own arse to worry about you.'

I nodded. He was right. And besides, this was the new me. No more cowering in my own home and never going out. I had a job. I had wheels. I glanced at Jones. I might even have a boyfriend.

He joined me at the bottom of my steps and we looked up. I was admiring my pots. I've no idea what Jones was doing.

He bent and peered at the third step. 'Cage, is that blood again? There. It's not like you not to compulsively clean it away and whitewash your steps while you're at it. And then everyone else's as well.'

'I did clear it away,' I said slowly. 'Yesterday morning.'

'Is there a cat bringing you something every night?'

'I shouldn't think so. Animals don't like me very much.'

Sadly, this was true. Cats hiss and run away. Horses or cows back away from me. Dogs – other than Nigel, who is easily bought with food – lay back their ears and growl quietly. They've never attacked me; they're just warning me to keep my distance. It makes me sad, sometimes. I'd love to have a pet. It would be lovely to have someone to greet me every time I came home. To share walks and curl up in front of the fire with me. But it never happens. Perhaps they can sense Felda – I don't know. All I know is that animals don't like me. Not to the extent of bringing me presents, anyway.

I was completely wrong about this, however. Something had been visiting me every night. And in a way, it had been bringing me a present.

CHAPTER SEVEN

I'd only ever had one job in my life. After I left school, I went to work for the council. I didn't like it very much and I don't think they liked me, either. No one ever said anything – not to my face, anyway – but conversations would stop when I entered a room. No one ever invited me out to lunch with them. I would bring in the traditional cake on my birthday, when it was obvious that everyone else had forgotten. Please don't misunderstand – no one ever said anything nasty – but there are a hundred ways of not being friendly. Especially in a small office.

But, fortunately for everyone, the council had needed someone to digitise a ton of records going back to the year dot. No one wanted to do it, because it was down in the dingy basement and you'd never see a single soul from one end of the day to the next.

I volunteered immediately and became popular overnight. Not only did people not have to do it themselves, but they were getting rid of me as well. People were actually quite pleasant to me. I shifted my stuff down to the basement, closed the door behind me and created my own little world.

I arranged everything the way I wanted it, smuggled in a small radio and a kettle, divided up the work the way I thought best, and made a start. I set targets and had little races with myself. Slowly, the boxes of dusty records began to dwindle, but that didn't matter because this was the council, so for every box done, two more appeared overnight. Like the Hydra.

Anyway, I'd stopped working when I married Ted – I do sometimes wonder who inherited the basement after me – and become a stay-at-home housewife. And then, after he died, I didn't need to work at all. Nor did I want to. All those people and their colours, and that not-quite nastiness, which is so difficult to deal with . . . . Not that that had kept me out of trouble, of course, but, so far, working for the council had been my one and only job.

And then, through Michael Jones, I'd been headhunted. Literally. Jones had turned up one day with an offer of a job interview. His boss wanted to meet me to talk about my abilities. So much for all my attempts to stay under the radar.

What had astonished me, however, was firstly that I'd actually gone to the interview, and secondly that I'd met Mary Bennet and quite liked her. I told myself I didn't really want the job – I certainly didn't need the job; I should stay quietly at home where I was safe – and I don't think anyone had been more surprised than me when I accepted the offer.

We'd haggled over terms and I'd won almost everything I wanted – namely that I didn't have to accept any assignment I didn't like the look of. Complete anonymity was assured – no one would know who I was – and I'd be on the books only as a consultant. They employed all sorts of consultants all the time, apparently. My job would be simply to observe interviews and give my opinion. Was the subject telling the truth? Were they afraid? How were they reacting to various questions? I'd made it perfectly clear I wasn't a mind reader and I certainly couldn't kill someone with a thought. Although when Jones was being at his most irritating, I did feel some regret over that.

Anyway, suddenly, I was one of those people who returned to work after a long absence and yes, I was very nervous. I read lots of articles online about how to handle a return to the workplace. I bought a new suit. Jones had said people mostly wore casual clothes, but I wore casual clothes all the time. I wanted an outfit that told me I was back at work, so I bought a navy blue trouser suit, some white tops and low-heeled court shoes. Definitely not the Margaret Thatcher suit with the dowdy hemline that I'd worn when Jerry and I had broken Jones out of Sorensen's clinic. Or the American Tan tights which, for some reason, had had a very interesting effect on Jones. I had a packet tucked away upstairs because – well, you never know, do you?

And best of all – because my life was full of new and different things these days – I was no longer reliant on either Jones, public transport, or my own two legs. I had my scooter.

'With the top speed of a striking snail,' said Jones, but I didn't care. Almost everything is faster than walking.

I was going back to work. I had a job for which I was uniquely qualified. I had my own transport. In fact, if I ignored the nightly mess on my steps and sinister takeaway orders harping on about serpents, then everything was good. Very, very good.

I got up early, showered and dressed in my suit. I'd laid out everything the night before. I put on a little make-up. Not a lot because it doesn't look good on me and also because a moped doesn't do a lot for eyeliner and mascara. My helmet didn't do much for my hair, either, but I could sort that out when I got there. I just wanted a little lipstick to give me confidence. Because now that the moment had arrived . . .

I let myself out through the back door, into my tiny yard and across to the shed. I unplugged my moped, wheeled it into the alleyway at the back of my house, stopped, as always, to admire its shiny redness, and checked the power levels, lights, indicators and all the other things Jones had banged on about. As if I, of all people, was likely to leap, helmetless, on to a badly maintained scooter and roar off in the wrong direction, trailing clouds of black smoke as I went.

I rode slowly down the alleyway, out into Castle Close, turned right through the archway, weaved around the bollards and down the hill.

I'd given myself plenty of time and traffic was quite light. Very carefully I drove through town, joined the bypass and chugged past the big DIY stores and supermarkets. I could call in on the way home and treat myself to something nice for supper. Just like a proper working person. I indicated off the bypass and then I was out in the countryside.

The ride was so enjoyable. The morning was beautiful – bright and sparkling because it had rained sometime during the night. There were puddles at the side of the road and the lovely smell of fresh countryside was everywhere. The sort of thing you'd never notice in a car or on a bus.

I concentrated very hard but I knew the way and there was hardly any traffic about. In fact, the only car that passed me was driven by Jones who gave me a merry toot on his horn and a rude gesture as he passed. I would have replied in kind but I wasn't yet confident enough to drive one-handed.

Finally arriving at the Sorensen Clinic, I pulled up at the

barrier. I didn't know the guard on duty. In fact, I didn't know any of the staff at all. After the Ghost incident, they'd installed an entirely new regime. New medical staff, new security, new admin, new housekeeping and gardeners. No one had been here longer than a few months. I knew no one and certainly no one knew me. I wasn't sure whether that would be a good or bad thing.

The guard logged me in, noted my registration, informed me my badge was waiting for me inside and that I was expected, and raised the barrier.

'Straight up the drive, love. Take the left-hand fork. Staff car park on your right. You'll find a little shelter for bikes and mopeds. You can leave your helmet there. It'll be quite safe.'

I thanked him and tootled off, filled with an unfamiliar sense of importance because, for just about the first time in my life – I was expected.

I looked around as I made my cautious way up the drive. There were no signs of any recent trauma that I could see. The gardens were, as ever, well designed, beautifully planted and immaculately maintained. The pots and hanging baskets were superb. Nowhere near as colourfully informal as mine, of course, but in much better taste, Jones would say.

I parked my motorbike, left my helmet as instructed, fluffed up my hair in the mirror and made my way around the building. Jones was waiting for me on the front steps.

'Morning, Cage. Everything OK?'

'Yes. Fine, thank you.'

Actually, I was quietly proud. I'd got myself here – under my own steam – and was about to begin my new job. I was more than fine – like the morning, I was sparkling.

He looked down at me. 'You look very well.'

'I am well.'

'Not worried about this at all?'

'A little, yes, but Mary Bennet said the interviewees would never see me, so Sorensen won't even know I'm here.'

'No, he won't. We've been conducting the preliminaries over the last few days. He'll have no idea you're present today. Shall we go in?'

'Is Mary Bennet here?'

'No. At the moment, Sorensen isn't saying much. We're conducting a series of fishing expeditions, which will enable us to decide the areas on which to concentrate. Then we'll sit down and map out our questions. You don't have to be present for that, if you don't want to be. Just give me your observations and I'll present them on your behalf. At some point I'll report back to Bennet with my recommendations as to whether she should attend in person or not – but until then, you've got me.'

'Is that good or bad? You being in charge, I mean. You and he have history.'

'Well, technically I'm not allowed to go at him with a telephone directory – unless he refuses to cooperate, of course. In which case . . .'

I looked at him, trying to decide if he was joking or not. His colour was a little ambiguous on the subject.

He pushed open the door and we entered the Sorensen Clinic's posh hall.

I paused to look around. Everything was different. No bad memories would linger here. They'd completely redecorated, changing the colour scheme, the layout and the furniture. The faint smells of fresh paint and new floor coverings still hung in the air.

Gone were the expensive neutrals – now the sofas and armchairs were upholstered in a plaid pattern, a soft grey, green and terracotta. The effect was striking without being in your face. There were low tables with magazines and books. The armchairs were arranged in small, friendly groups and one or two had been pushed slightly out of position. As if people actually did sit here and chat together over coffee.

Gone too were the big formal flower arrangements of Dr Sorensen's time. Small vases of slightly untidy garden flowers stood on tables and windowsills. They'd even moved the artwork around. I recognised some of the pieces from Dr Sorensen's former office.

I tugged at Jones's sleeve. 'Where's Jerry's Auerbach?'

Jones's friend Jerry was the proud possessor of some unique skills and it really wasn't a good idea to telephone him unexpectedly. Once or twice I'd disturbed him at a critical moment – just as he was entering or exiting someone's upper windows. Anyway, he'd once helped me break Jones out of here, and later come back to help himself to what he termed 'a very nice Auerbach' for his troubles.

Jones pointed silently to the fake Jerry had left in its place, fortunately concealed in a darkish corner.

'And a complete change of staff,' he said. He nodded at a tall, skinny and surprisingly young man talking to a couple of people I assumed to be patients. 'That's Dr Bridgeman. He's in charge of the medical side.'

Dr Bridgeman's colour was silvery blue and sat serenely around him. I had the impression it would take a lot to agitate Dr Bridgeman.

'Security is now in the charge of Mr Neal,' said Jones,

100

nudging me towards reception. 'He wants to meet you today as a formality, but you won't see much of him.'

'Does he know I'm Ted's wife?'

'No. No one does.'

Mr Neal's colour was a surprising soft green. I'd been expecting a strident red or purple, which was wrong of me because there are no good or bad colours. Black is not necessarily bad nor is white necessarily good. Good people don't have pretty colours. Evil people's colours are not shot through with lightning bolts of blood red, because that would be too easy, wouldn't it? As I told Mary Bennet at the interview, it's not just the colours themselves – it's their shape, their texture, their movement, their depth – I look at all those things and even then I don't always get it right. I've been deceived several times. Sorensen, by a combination of drugs and rigid self-control, had once lulled me into believing everything was fine. It all burst out in the end, but by then it was too late.

We paused at the reception desk. I was glad to see a new member of staff here as well. I hadn't much cared for the previous incumbent.

'This is Andy,' said Jones. 'Andy, this is Mrs Cage. You have a badge for her, I believe?'

Andy was nice. His colour was a strong, solid brown, rather similar to Ted's. I liked him at once. He greeted me politely and handed me a badge and a key for my locker. 'Sign here, please, Mrs Cage.'

'Report here on entrance and sign out on exit,' said Jones. 'It's Andy's job to keep track of us all. Wear your badge at all times.'

Andy grinned. 'And where is your badge today, Mr Jones?'

101

'In my pocket,' he said. 'Ready, Cage?'

My badge was on a lanyard. I put it over my head, arranged it neatly, name side uppermost, and we took the lift down to the basement.

The doors pinged open and I stepped out to a very familiar smell. Disinfectant, floor polish, and something else strange, but somehow familiar. I couldn't quite place it. I sniffed, testing the air.

'It's Ghost,' said Jones quietly. 'They were making it in a room over there. Don't worry – it's all sealed off.'

'Has it all been destroyed?'

He hesitated. 'Most of it.'

'What? Why not all of it?'

'If it ever makes a comeback, we might be able to use our stocks to manufacture an antidote.'

'And you never know when having your own supply might come in handy,' I said bitterly.

'And that.'

I tried to put all that behind me. None of it was anything to do with me. That wasn't why I was here.

'This way,' said Jones, indicating a long corridor to our left. 'Always turn left, Cage. Right will take you to the medical side – storerooms, supplies, equipment, records and so forth. Our area is down here.'

All this was new, as well. They'd completely remodelled the basements since my last disastrous visit. For one fleeting moment I remembered again the terror of something standing behind me and knowing that if I turned to see what it was then I'd be lost for ever.

We were faced with a pair of hefty doors.

'You need to use your badge,' said Jones, dispelling my memories. He swiped his through a slot. 'Both of us separately. You can't come through on mine. Forget your badge and they won't let you in, or out. Lose your badge and they'll shoot you. And me, probably.'

I ran my badge through the slot. There was a beep, the light turned green – much to my secret relief – and I joined him on the other side.

'And now everyone knows where you are,' said Jones. I wasn't sure whether he was being reassuring or not. We'd never had anything like this at the council.

We stood at the head of a corridor. There were no stores here. Nothing cluttered the long space or obscured the blank doors on either side. There was no signage, no numbers on the doors. Everything was silent and anonymous.

We started down the corridor. There was another set of double doors on the left. I used my card again. More beeping. Another green light. I wondered if someone somewhere was tracing my progress through the building.

I followed him along another corridor. More identical doors. Turn left. And another corridor. I had no idea where we were in relation to upstairs. If Jones abandoned me here, then I might never find my way back again. I pushed that thought away.

'What can I expect to happen with Sorensen?'

He held a door for me. 'We'll start with basic questions to which we know the answer. This will enable you – and us – to establish a baseline.' He pointed left. 'This way. There are no signs and no room numbers, I'm afraid – you'll just have to memorise the layout. But the chances are you'll have someone with you at all times. Me, usually, I expect. Toilets down there –

103

they're unisex so remember to leave the seat up. The canteen is at the end of the corridor. A lot of the food comes from the kitchens upstairs, so it's not too bad. You'll be charged for meals, of course. We all are – because we work for the government and they don't just give stuff away. Just tap your badge at the till and it'll automatically be deducted from your wage at the end of the month. Otherwise, there are vending machines for drinks and snacks, and since this is a government establishment, you'll never be more than six feet away from a kettle. Here we are.'

We'd reached a row of lockers against the wall. I looked down at my key. Number twenty-nine.

'You can't take anything in with you,' said Jones. 'And you can't bring anything out either, so you'll need to dump your bag, your coat if you're wearing one, and so forth. You won't even need a pen. Everything's provided.'

I opened the locker, hung up my jacket because it was warm in here, put my bag on the shelf, and turned to Jones.

'Ready?'

Full of sudden apprehension, I nodded.

We turned into a slightly narrower corridor with three doors on one side and three on another. The walls here were painted pale blue.

'This is one of our interrogation areas. Different areas for different purposes and classes of interrogation. There's a suite of rooms on each side. We're in number one on the right. Each suite consists of the actual interview room, the control room where a ton of people sit and steer the interview, and the observation room. That's where you and I will be. You'll always be in number one because the others have screens rather than a one-way window and you said you needed to see the subject in person.'

It was true. I always need to see the actual person. Colours don't transmit through cameras or screens. I don't know why. They just don't.

He opened the first door and in we went.

It was quite a small room, about twelve feet square, with a table and two chairs facing a long window on the left-hand wall. I wrinkled my nose at the slight smell of feet.

'Your window into the interviewing room,' said Jones, pulling out one of the chairs. 'It's one way. No one can see you.'

I paused in the doorway and looked around. A large notice pinned to one wall requested those using the room to leave it tidy.

On the table stood a telephone, a cellophane-wrapped headset, a small screen – currently blank – a keyboard, two writing pads, and a jar of pens.

'The headset is yours,' said Jones. 'Mine's in here.' He pulled open a drawer. 'You can leave yours in the desk when you go. This room's not often used. People prefer the other one. It's bigger and smells better.'

Other than the long table, the two not-very-comfortable-looking chairs and a waste bin in the corner, that was it. Everything was government grey. The lighting was low.

'Take as many notes as you like,' said Jones, 'but you can't take anything out of this room. Either leave them on the table or throw them in the bin afterwards. Theoretically you can talk to the interviewer through your headset, but if you're worried about someone recognising your voice, then tell me, and I'll relay your comments.'

'OK,' I said, still standing on the threshold.

105

'Coming in or are you going to do it from out in the corridor?'

His colour was quite loose and relaxed. This was just an ordinary day's work to him. I came in, closed the door behind me and sat down next to him.

He paused for a moment, turned away, and then, somewhat defiantly, took out a pair of glasses and put them on.

'Let's have a look,' I said.

He turned to face me. 'What do you think?'

I nodded.

'They're only for reading and writing,' he said.

I nodded again. 'They suit you. Do they make a difference?'

'Yeah, actually. Big difference.'

'Will you always have to wear them? I mean, will your eyesight get better one day?'

'No one seems to know. Shall we get started?'

We both turned to face the window.

'Robbie's taking the session this morning,' said Jones, donning his headset. 'It won't do Sorensen any harm to know he's not important enough for the big boys. Actually he is, but he's going to have to come across with some interesting stuff first. You and I will simply observe to begin with. You can either take notes or just tell me if anything strikes you as not quite right. Don't worry – you can speak normally in here. He can't hear you.'

Now that the moment had arrived, I was nervous. I fiddled with the pad and paper and then said, 'He doesn't know I'm working with you, does he?'

'He'll know he's under observation – he's been on this side of the window many times. Given your well-known aversion to this place, he's never going to know it's you, although he'll probably guess I'm around here somewhere.'

I took a couple of deep breaths, opened one of the notebooks and wrote the date across the top of the page.

'Do you want some water?'

'Um . . . yes, please.'

He disappeared, returning with two bottles. I made a careful note to reimburse him.

'All right? You look terrified.'

'I am.'

I was. I couldn't help thinking – suppose for some reason my 'gift' suddenly deserted me? Suppose I sat here and saw nothing. Or suppose I did but they didn't believe me. I'd been very clear about what I could and couldn't do and Mary Bennet had said she understood, but suppose I couldn't deliver anything at all? What would happen then?

'We're off,' said Jones.

I straightened up, stared through the window and clutched my pen, ready for anything.

The interview room itself was almost identical in size to the one in which we were sitting. There was a square table with a chair on either side. One of the chairs had metal rings fitted on its arms and legs.

'For restraints,' said Jones.

'Is Sorensen in handcuffs?'

'Not yet.'

The door to the interview room opened and Robbie entered.

I'd met him before. He still looked ten years younger than he actually was – a very useful talent, according to Jones. His creamy grey colour was neat and compact and completely under control.

I looked down at the small screen on the desk. The same scene in miniature but minus Robbie's colour.

He sat down and spread several files in front of him.

A voice sounded from the screen. 'This is the control room. Interview room – testing, one two three.'

Still looking down at his notes, Robbie nodded. 'Yes, fine.'

'Observation room – testing, one two three.'

'Loud and clear,' said Jones. 'Ready when you are.'

'Right,' said Robbie, pulling his chair closer to the table. 'Let's get this show on the road, shall we? You can bring him in now.'

A door at the back of the interview room opened to reveal Dr Philip Sorensen, escorted by two men in security uniforms. Even though I was expecting him, my heart still lurched in recognition.

Despite Sorensen's current circumstances, and even though he was wearing a set of very downmarket grey sweats and those slipper things that make you shuffle, he still managed to look dapper and immaculate. This was the first time I'd ever seen him out of his sharply tailored pin-striped suit.

Unlike Iblis, whose colour jumped around all over the place, reflecting whatever fleeting mood happened to be current at that moment, Sorensen's colour had always been abnormally still. A flat, off-white, pallid colour – unhealthy and thin, it always reminded me of greasy milk.

At a nod from Robbie, the two officers left the room. I suspected they wouldn't go far. They'd be on the other side of the door. Just in case things turned nasty.

That was a point. I leaned down and checked the underside of the desk. Yep – two panic buttons. And now I knew what I was looking for, another one by the door, as well. Again, I wondered how reassured I should be.

Jones grinned. 'There will be a certain amount of games-manship now. He'll make Robbie wait. Robbie will then make him wait. Who knows how long it could last? Next time, Cage, bring a book,'

He wasn't wrong. Sorensen made a great business of seating himself at the table, adjusting the position of the chair to his satisfaction, smoothing his clothing, clasping his hands on the table as if ready to begin and then doing it all again. Controlling the situation. I remembered this man was a master manipulator.

I'd never actually heard the phrase *psychological warfare* until Jones explained it to me, but that's what Sorensen did. He devised ways of misleading, deceiving and intimidating people. He was an expert on people's behaviour. He could identify a person's vulnerabilities and then go on to predict and manipu-late their responses. Which was exactly the reason he'd been engaged by the government in the first place. And he was very good. I remembered, after Ted's funeral, it had taken him about four minutes to get through my defences.

Now, though, he was technically powerless. He had no weapons other than his tongue and his mind. Which, in my opinion, still made him the most dangerous person in the building.

Robbie, bless him, sat quietly through all of this. Neither impatient nor annoyed, just sitting it out until, finally, Sorensen stopped messing around and indicated he was ready to begin.

For a moment nothing happened and then Robbie pulled out his first file, opened it, leafed slowly through the pages and began to read. Thoroughly. Every word. Every page. Taking his time. Occasionally flipping back to check a reference. Now it was Sorensen's turn to wait. His colour – off-white and shim-mering unpleasantly – remained still and serene.

I remembered I was supposed to be earning my pay. 'Sorensen seems calm,' I said. 'But he has exceptional self-control. Is he under any medication?'

'Not at present.'

Robbie closed the file and smiled. 'Good morning, Mr Sorensen.'

Sorensen's colour spiked. 'That's *Doctor* Sorensen.'

I scribbled an exclamation mark on my pad.

Jones spoke. 'He didn't like that.'

Robbie appeared to consider Sorensen's response. 'No, actually, it isn't. Not any longer. You've been struck off. After your antics last year. When all those people died. Remember?'

'No.'

Robbie was busy scribbling a note in the margin of his file. 'Good job you're not practising any longer – not with a memory that bad. Perhaps, then, given your difficulties remembering events at the end of last year, you'll allow me to recap: an illegal substance was being manufactured and distributed from your premises. Yours, Sorensen. And not only illegal but fatal, too. Not one person who took Ghost survived.

'At the end of last year, there was a serious incident here at your clinic. A number of your patients – your hugely important patients – were found naked and dead of exposure in your grounds. More bodies were found inside. There was evidence of torture.

'The body of a woman – tentatively identified as a Mrs Painswick – was found in your basement. Unlikely as it might seem, medical opinion is that she was somehow torn in half. No human being would have the strength to commit such an atrocity, so one of the purposes of our interviews will be to establish exactly

110

how this could happen, because you, Sorensen, are asking us to believe that although a number of atrocities occurred here, in your clinic, over quite a long period of time, you never noticed a single thing. You didn't even experience a mild concern as to why all your patients were standing naked in the garden when the temperature was below freezing.'

'I have done nothing.'

Still writing, Robbie said, 'That is correct, Mr Sorensen. People were dying all around you and you did absolutely nothing.'

That wasn't completely true. Sorensen had come to me and Jones for help. By that time, things at his clinic were well beyond his control and he was terrified. Unfortunately for him, both Jones and I had had other things on our mind at the time. In his desperation, he'd kidnapped me and brought me here to cover his escape. Sadly, by that time it was far too late. For him, for me, for poor Mrs Painswick, for his patients – for everyone.

Sorensen said calmly, 'I was not responsible for any of that.'

Robbie finished writing. 'What happened to Mrs Painswick?'

'I was not even on the premises when she died.'

'And her daughter's gone missing. Alyson Painswick. Not seen since that day. Anything to do with you?'

Not taking my eyes off the screen, I whispered to Jones, 'They still haven't found Alyson?'

He shook his head. 'No trace of her anywhere.'

Sorensen brushed some imaginary fluff off his sleeve. 'Of course it wasn't anything to do with me. What interest would I have in a teenage girl?'

Robbie shrugged. 'Many do.'

Sorensen's colour didn't move.

'No reaction to that,' I said to Jones.

111

Robbie bent over the file again. 'And the equipment in the basement? The drug manufactory?'

'That was nothing to do with me.'

'*Your* basement. *Your* equipment. And you knew nothing?'

Sorensen smiled disdainfully but his colour spiked again. 'All done without my knowledge. The Painswick woman misled me.'

I scribbled another exclamation mark.

Jones spoke into his mic. 'Don't let that drop.'

Robbie consulted another file. 'An illegal substance was manu-factured on your premises, Sorensen. By a woman who was later horribly murdered. Not far from this very spot. And you noticed nothing. Because you were . . . misled.'

'That is correct.'

Robbie gave a small laugh. 'By a middle-aged housewife?'

Sorensen said nothing, but his colour writhed. His vanity was his most vulnerable spot.

I scribbled a note to that effect and Jones passed it on. I suspected I wasn't telling them anything they didn't already know and that part of the purpose of being here today was to establish my credentials, as well.

'You would like us to believe a middle-aged housewife known to live a quiet family life was, in fact, a criminal mastermind.'

Sorensen said nothing.

'A middle-aged housewife whose husband was found dead at their home, whose daughter is still missing, and who was herself murdered, managed to deceive and mislead you. You, Mr Sorensen. This middle-aged housewife who manufactured and dealt drugs, was also involved in torture and murder, and you – you, Mr Sorensen – didn't notice a thing?'

'I keep telling you – I knew nothing of her activities.'

'It's not the extent of your knowledge I'm querying, Sorensen, but the extent of your gullibility. And your ignorance. And your lack of judgement. I'm afraid you're not going to come out of any of this looking good.'

'As far as I know, ignorance is not a criminal offence.'

'No, but murder, torture and drug dealing are. This is a government establishment, Sorensen. People are not happy with the way you've been running it. Sadly for you, Mrs Painswick is dead – something I'm not convinced you know nothing about – and we're looking for a scapegoat.'

Sorensen was sitting perfectly still, his head slightly tilted, his posture showing polite attention, but his colour was jumping all over the place. Normally, if a person is afraid of something specific – another person, for instance – their colour streams away from that person, but that wasn't happening here.

'He's agitated,' I said. 'No – he's afraid, but I don't think it's of Robbie. Whatever was going on here – he's still afraid. Could he be worried about repercussions? Although I don't know from whom.'

Sorensen's tone was patient. 'I keep telling you. I know nothing of any of this. I wasn't even in the clinic at the time you claim all this went down. The Painswick woman was completely responsible for everything that happened.'

'Do you often let out government facilities to random housewives, Mr Sorensen?'

'Homeopathic experiments, she said.'

'Goodness,' murmured Robbie. He wrote something in the margin again, intoning very slowly, 'Ho . . . meo . . . pathic . . . ex . . . peri . . . ments. How very interesting. And what was supposed to be the end result?'

113

'A number of revolutionary homeopathic remedies that would benefit mankind as a whole.'

Robbie smiled brightly. 'Not a whole raft of naked dead people scattered around your award-winning grounds like so many carelessly placed statues? That was just a silly miscalculation on someone's part?'

Sorensen turned his head and sighed. 'I'm not even going to grace that with a response.'

His colour spiked again and muddied.

'He's still afraid,' I said to Jones. 'I think he's scared of something that isn't present. If that makes sense.'

Jones passed this on.

Robbie continued. 'I'm curious – do you maintain that the person who tortured and murdered your patients is the same person who manufactured Ghost?'

Sorensen shrugged. 'I had left the clinic by that time, so I am unable to say.'

'What made you leave?'

'I was concerned that some of Mrs Painswick's homeopathic remedies were not as she had represented to me. Naturally I wanted to report my suspicions.'

'And did you?'

'I was not granted the opportunity.'

'In all the months between you leaving the clinic and being apprehended . . .' Robbie pretended to consult his documents again, 'no opportunity to make your misgivings known to the authorities presented itself in any way?'

Sorensen's colour had calmed and solidified.

'He's less agitated now,' I said to Jones.

'I wonder if that's because we've moved away from Mrs

114

Painswick,' he said. 'Robbie – can you go back to Painswick again?'

Robbie allowed his voice to harden. 'Not one person who took Ghost lived to tell the tale, Sorensen. Everyone died.'

I could almost see the effort it cost Sorensen to maintain his carefully open, neutral posture. 'I know nothing of this Ghost. We were developing anti-stress remedies.'

'You say *we*, so you *were* involved.'

Sorensen made a dismissive gesture. 'I was involved in only a very minor capacity. Occasionally, when requested, I offered advice. That was all. The main work was carried out by Mrs Painswick.'

'How did you first meet her? And when?'

For the first time, his colour wavered a little. 'I . . . can't remember the exact occasion.'

'He's genuinely not sure.' I turned to look at Jones. 'It's this supposed involvement of Mrs Painswick that is baffling me. I knew her and she was so quiet and shy. Surely he can't expect anyone to believe she was responsible for all the deaths, the violence . . . everything.'

'We suspect that initially he thought he was using Mrs Painswick, and that she ended up using him. Whether he genuinely doesn't remember, or his ego won't allow him to accept that – it's definitely a chink in his armour to be explored.'

'But Mrs Painswick was so ordinary. She made cakes for the Local History Society. She knitted. We even wondered if perhaps she was abused at home. Surely this can't be true.'

'It is, I'm afraid, Cage. Do you remember nothing of that day here?'

115

I shook my head. 'I remember the bodies in the grounds. And something standing behind me in the basement. Not all of it.'

'Everyone has different memories of what happened here. The survivors tell one story. Sorensen another. You another.'

'Then why am I here if I can't help you?'

He touched my arm. 'You're no longer part of the investigation, Cage. You gave your statement a long time ago. Your purpose now is to enable us to assess the validity of Sorensen's.'

Thus reminded, I turned back to what was going on.

Robbie was sitting back, idly flicking through one of the files. 'Tell me again how you met this Mrs Painswick.'

I suspected this was part of the technique. Ask the same question in a hundred different ways in the hope of eliciting a different response. It didn't work with Sorensen. His answer was exactly the same as before. Uncertainty. His colour swirled with orange anxiety. He wasn't faking it.

'I think he genuinely can't remember,' I said. 'And that seems to be causing him as much concern as the other stuff.'

Sorensen was shaking his head. 'I . . . can't quite . . .'

'Did *she* approach you?'

'I . . . Yes.'

'Where? Where were you when this happened?'

Staring down at the table, Sorensen shook his head again.

'When?'

'Last year . . . no . . . yes . . . I don't know.'

'Where is Mrs Painswick's daughter?'

'I don't know. I rarely saw her. A quiet child.'

'He's telling the truth,' I said. 'Or rather, he thinks he is.'

Jones nodded.

Robbie sipped some water and picked up another file. 'Tell me about Ghost.'

Sorensen remained silent. His colour was settling again.

'Is that a refusal to answer my questions?'

'I can't help you with Ghost.'

'He's telling the truth,' I said. 'He can't. Not won't. Could the question be rephrased?'

Robbie obliged. 'When did you first become involved with the manufacture of Ghost?'

'I was vaguely involved. I had no idea of its lethal effects.'

'What was its purpose?'

Suddenly his colour was nearly up to the ceiling. 'I don't know.'

I drew two exclamation marks.

Jones passed that on.

Robbie frowned. 'You are endeavouring to convince me that although an illegal and lethal drug was being manufactured and sold on the premises for which you are responsible, you knew nothing about it? You were unaware of its manufacture. You were unaware of its purpose. You were unaware of its lethal effects on everyone who took it.'

Sorensen's face remained calm. 'You have stated my position admirably.'

But his colour writhed.

'He's lying,' I said. 'Although we knew that because he gave me a dose of Ghost. And he was very forthcoming about what I could expect to happen to me. And I know he doesn't look it, but he's very uneasy with these questions. I wonder – with no evidence at all – whether someone or something has threatened him.'

Robbie made another note. 'And yet you administered or caused this drug to be administered.'

'I gave Ghost to no one,' he shouted.

Robbie dropped his next words into the silence. 'You gave it to Mrs Cage.'

Sorensen stopped dead. His colour stopped dead. After a few moments he swallowed and said, 'I did not.'

'He's lying,' I said to Jones. 'But we knew that anyway.'

Sorensen made an attempt to pull himself together. 'Is she dead?'

'No one survives Ghost, Mr Sorensen.' Robbie looked up and said very quietly, 'Michael Jones is looking for you. You're lucky you've got me as your interviewing officer. Very lucky indeed.' He began to stack his files. 'For the time being.'

Sorensen's colour barely moved.

'He's not frightened of Robbie,' I said to Jones. 'Or of you. There must be someone out there worse than you. Hard to believe, isn't it?'

'Yeah. Robbie, I think we'll wrap it up here. Take him back to his room. No books or magazines. No distractions. Let's leave him with your implied threat echoing in his ears, shall we? Give him something to think about. And don't schedule anything for a couple of days. He'll be expecting a follow-up this afternoon or tomorrow but let's just leave him for a while.'

He took off his glasses and rubbed his eyes.

Robbie pressed a button and the two guards entered.

I was just beginning to relax. Interview over. It hadn't been as bad as I'd thought it would be. In fact, I thought it had gone quite well. I felt I'd made a contribution. I pushed my chair back and stretched out my legs and arms.

Sorensen had got to his feet and was carefully easing himself out from behind the table when it happened. Without warning, his face changed. I stared. His features didn't move in any way but seemed overlaid by someone else's. Although I could clearly see his own face underneath, there was another over the top. For a moment I wondered if it was simply my face or Jones's somehow reflected in the glass, but it wasn't either of us. This was a man's face, quite nice, long, almost sad, and his hair fell to his shoulders. I felt a jolt of recognition, although I didn't know why.

He looked through the window, straight at me and said, 'Not long now, Mrs Cage. Not long now.'

And then the features slid away and Sorensen was back again. One of the guards took his arm and began to lead him away.

The whole thing had lasted less than five seconds and it would seem no one else had noticed a thing. Jones was quietly tearing up our notes and dropping them in the bin. Robbie was gathering his files together and putting his pen away. No one in the control room was shouting, 'Did you see that? What just happened?'

I wondered whether or not to mention it to Jones. It was perfectly possible I'd imagined the whole thing. Although how likely was that? I decided I'd speak to him about it once we were off the premises.

As it happened, I didn't get the chance.

CHAPTER EIGHT

I think I must have been more shocked by the Sorensen interview than I realised. No, that's not right. The interview itself hadn't disturbed me at all – it was what had happened at the very end that had frightened me. Although when my mind tried to focus – to remember clearly what I'd seen – the whole thing just slid away. There had been a face that I'd seen before. Somewhere. The image danced ahead of me – always just out of reach. It had happened so quickly. And no one else had noticed a thing. Had my mind played a trick on me? Even as I told myself that was a possibility, I knew it wasn't.

I stood up on wobbly legs and followed Jones out into the corridor. I was deeply unsettled. Not concentrating properly. It's my only explanation for what happened next.

'Well,' he said, and I dragged my mind back to the thing on which I should be concentrating. 'That went quite well, I think. Listen, I'm going to nip off and have a word in the control room. And I need a quick chat with Robbie as well – lay out the structure of the next few interviews and so forth. Are there any comments or observations you'd like me to make on your behalf?'

I shook my head and tried to speak firmly. 'I don't think so. Although there is something not exactly Sorensen-related I'd like to have a word about later on.'

'I'll probably be about half an hour. Why don't you go upstairs? They'll bring you a coffee and I'll join you when I've finished here. Well done, by the way. That was exactly what we wanted from you.'

I managed a smile.

'Can you remember the way out?'

'Of course,' I said, not sure at all, but privately deciding I'd find my way without asking for help even if it took me a hundred years.

'Left, right, right, then left,' he said.

'I knew that.'

He laughed and disappeared. I retrieved my things, turned left, then right, then right, then left, found the lift – to my relief – and eventually emerged into the nicely appointed hall. I could sit in one of the armchairs here, or wait in the library, or go into the restaurant itself. I paused, undecided, and then plumped for the hall. I'd see Jones when he came out of the lift.

The stairs at the Sorensen Clinic are magnificent – a real design feature – wide and shallow with a graceful curve and ornate bannisters. I glanced up at them as I crossed the hall, meaning to bag an armchair by one of the windows, find something to read, make myself comfortable, and wait for Jones to reappear.

Except . . . there was a feeling . . . and it was stronger with every step I took towards the staircase . . .

I stood at the bottom and looked up. The public rooms, the restaurant, the library, the consulting rooms, Dr Bridgeman's office and so on were all on the ground floor. The medical wards were upstairs.

I looked around. Andy was busy behind the reception desk

and I could hear voices and the chink of cutlery on crockery in the restaurant. Everything seemed perfectly normal. No raised voices. Just the normal everyday clinic noises. I craned my neck so I could see the coffee cups laid out in the library. I knew from my previous stay here that patients usually took their tea and coffee in there. Everything seemed fine. Until . . .

I laid my hand on the left-hand bannister and looked up. I knew there was a nurses' station upstairs, but in keeping with the style of the building, it was set back and out of sight. Anyone entering through the front door and looking around would see a typically gracious hall in a typically gracious country house. Which must have been exactly what the designer had wanted.

I put my foot on the bottom stair.

There it was . . . dancing just on the edge of my senses . . . If I could just get close enough to . . .

I stepped up on to the next stair.

There it was again, but stronger.

I stepped up again. And again. And then, slowly, looking up, I climbed the stairs, expecting to be challenged at any moment because, given the importance of some of their patients, un-authorised visiting was definitely not permitted.

Sounds died away behind me as I climbed. The thick grey-green carpet deadened my own footfalls. I reached the top. The landings stretched away in all directions. There was no one around. The nurses' station was empty. One or two doors were ajar but not wide enough for me to see the patients inside. I looked around again. To have no one at the station was un-usual. Had there been a crisis somewhere and they'd all gone off to deal with it? I couldn't hear anything, though. Usually a medical emergency was denoted by trollies crashing through doors, staff calling to one another, a doctor hastening down the landing, telephones ringing and so on, but this was complete and utter silence.

Which was probably why I could sense . . . something.

I turned into the women's wing.

Again, there was a new colour scheme up here. Pretty spring colours of pale green and yellow with little touches of blue. Colourful landscapes decorated the walls – most of them much nicer than Jerry's Auerbach – and there were fresh flowers on small tables pushed against the walls. I was reminded of a smart hotel. Especially as, faintly in the background, I could still catch the smell of fresh paint and new floor coverings.

I closed my eyes and turned my head. Left, then right. Yes. Yes, that way. I turned down a short corridor with only one door on the left-hand side.

The door was closed.

I hesitated. I shouldn't be here. Not without a member of staff to accompany me, but now that I was this close . . . there couldn't be any mistake . . . Behind this door was someone who desperately needed help.

Slowly, I opened the door.

The room was very dim. Thick curtains shut out the bright sunshine. I blinked a couple of times until, gradually, I was able to make out the details – bed, bedside table, small chest of drawers, a door leading into the bathroom, closed at this moment. The room was nice but very modest. This must be one of the basic rooms set aside for the clinic's pro bono work.

Lying in the bed, so small and slight as hardly to disturb the covers, lay—

Panic. Total panic. An avalanche of terror red trapped help

struggle screaming panic clawing fear emotion jagged sharp wicked spikey black fear terror confusion fear screaming trapped help crushed fear screaming screaming help terror trapped help screaming panic darkness help help help help . . .

I reeled backwards. I couldn't help it. The sheer force of it nearly bludgeoned me senseless. Something was here. A thing made solid and tangible. A thing with a will and a purpose of its own, coiled about the slender figure in thick ropes, holding her fast in a cold grip of silence. Her colour was frantic. Boiling around the room. Stretching first this way then another. Fighting to get out. To get away. Seeking . . . what? Help? An exit? A friend? I couldn't identify her colour. It was just dark. My own thoughts babbled uselessly. Panic. Terrible, terrible panic. Screaming, clawing panic. I couldn't stand it. I just couldn't . . .

I turned, bolted from the room, closed the door behind me, and leaned back against it, fighting for breath. What . . . ? What was that? What just happened? My heart was pounding its way out of my chest. I couldn't breathe. Couldn't think. I was completely overwhelmed. Being drawn down into . . .

Focus. I needed an object on which to focus my attention. I had to shut it all out. Regain some semblance of balance. Of normality. An equilibrium. Before I lost myself completely.

There was a narrow console table against the wall with a bunch of pretty summer flowers in a white vase. The flowers were real garden flowers – not a florist's bouquet. The central flower was a lovely golden rose, with white daisies, creamy delphinium spikes, yellow daffodils, yellow and orange marigolds, with silver-leaved artemisia. I focused. Delphiniums, daisies, daffs, rose, marigolds, artemisia. And again, artemisia, marigolds, rose, daffs, daisies, delphiniums. Displayed in a white vase standing on a pale blue cloth. Yellow and orange and cream flowers against a pale green wall. All standing on a light wood table.

My heart rate was slowing. And my breathing. Delphinium, daisies, daffodils, rose . . . Gradually I began to take notice of the world around me. I was standing in a short corridor with a window at the other end; there was a blue-patterned runner on the floor, pale green walls, a small table, a white vase, and flowers. And, now that my heart was no longer pounding in my ears, I could hear the silence. Thank God my unauthorised entry hadn't set off any alarms.

I straightened up and wiped my face. That had been terrifying. And yet I had the feeling it was only a tiny fraction of what the girl on the other side of the door was experiencing.

I took a breath. And then another. Was that why I'd been led here? To help this girl? I sensed that she had no voice and couldn't speak, and didn't understand what was happening to her. Could I do anything? Be a voice for someone who didn't have one? Half of me wanted to run away and never come back. I could do that. No one knew I was here. All I had to do was turn around and retrace my steps back downstairs, find an armchair and wait quietly for Jones to finish whatever it was he was doing. I looked at my watch to find hardly any time had passed at all. He'd be a while yet. Perhaps I could just . . . just try once more. And this time I would be more prepared.

The door opened smoothly and I inched my way into the room. Forewarned is forearmed and it wasn't quite such a heart-stopping shock this time. Her colour, that nasty dark thing, still beat at the walls in its efforts to escape, but she knew I was here. It flared towards me and then stopped dead. As if watching.

125

I forced myself not to step back.

I moved two paces to my right so she could see me more easily. Slowly, very gradually, her colour subsided, drawing back to nestle around her. The impression of coils was still strong. Were they comforting or restraining her?

I said quietly, 'Can you hear me?'

Nothing. Of course – she couldn't speak. I could just hear Jones telling me I was an idiot, and he wasn't wrong.

I said, 'My name is Elizabeth. You're in a hospital – well, a clinic – and you're quite safe. They're good people here.'

Her colour rushed back towards me. I should have thought of this. She would be desperate to communicate. Or for someone to communicate with her. I stepped back to keep my distance because I didn't want her colour touching me, and at the same time the feelings started up again.

Eagerness excitement desperation yes hear you hear me fear anguish don't go help terror stay despair help help help.

I held up my hand. 'Stop. Please stop. It hurts me.' I put my clenched fists to my chest. Which caused all her fear to come rushing back. Regret fear sorry guilt distress fear grief fear, all battering away at me like a stormy ocean pounding against a sea wall.

I stood my ground, and after a long while, her colour stilled and a lighter patch flickered into life and then disappeared.

I said, 'I saw that. What did you do?'

The same thing happened again. A lighter patch over her heart. Just for a moment.

'I saw that as well. Can you do that again?'

Again, the little patch of colour. And a little stronger this time. And then it broke up in a shower of fragments and disappeared.

'Please – not so fast. And not so strong. You're going too quickly for me.'

The bright patch again. Lingering longer this time before slowly fading away.

'That's much better. That's good.' I thought for a moment. 'Do you know what happened to you?'

The light patch again – a kind of creamy beige – the same colour as the delphinium spikes in the corridor – but this time tinged with a little red at the edges.

'Are you afraid?'

A very definite yes to that one. I felt her panic rise up again, and held out both hands. 'Please. Please try not to be. Please try to stay calm. I think that's better for both of us.'

Now the patch of colour didn't disappear. It faded but not completely.

'Are you feeling a little better?'

The cream turned a pale golden yellow, although still mixed with red.

'Does this help? What I'm doing?'

The flash of yellow lit up the room. Of course it was helping her. Someone had discovered a means of communicating with her. For how long had she been like this? Was she ill? Was this the result of some traumatic experience? Worst of all – had someone done this to her? And should I ask her? I suspected my first move should be to find a nurse and tell her I'd managed somehow to communicate with their patient. Now that Sorensen wasn't in charge any longer and I had Jones behind me, I felt a little more confident in publicly admitting what I could do. Of course, they might just thank me politely and tell me, even more politely, to mind my own business, but that was OK. At least I wouldn't have walked away from her. At least I would have tried.

I said, 'No one knows I'm here, so I think I'd better fetch a nurse and . . .'

Panic stay terrified panic stay frightened lost stay alone fear. It started up again. Her colour roared towards me so quickly I had no chance to step back, and the next moment I was enveloped in it.

I tried to move but my feet were pinned to the floor. Now the thing had me in its grasp as well, coiling around me, thick and black and with a terrible strength that was far too much for me, pinning my arms to my sides. I had no breath to cry out.

Now the pain was in my head. Heat. Burning. My mind was on fire. I was dying. I fought back, struggling to turn my head. Was there an alarm button I could press? Something? Anything? Blue lights flashed in front of my eyes. And then orange and red. Not colour. Flames. Real orange and red flames danced across the bed.

It was all too much for her, too much for her to contain, and now she was on fire. Her mind blazed. I felt a second's indescribable anguish – pain and failure – and then . . .

It was all gone. Everything. Colour, heat, pain, emotion, everything was gone and it was just me and her.

And she was dead.

She lay in the bed, her blank eyes staring at me in mute reproach. A trickle of blood ran from one eye, down her cheek and into her hair.

Oh my God, it had killed her.

Or had *I* killed her? I'd entered this room uninvited, unescorted, and unleashed something I hadn't been able to control and it had killed her. I'd tried to help her and I killed her.

What had I done?

CHAPTER NINE

My first thought was that I should never have come back to the Sorensen Clinic. What did I think I was doing here anyway? Why hadn't I stayed away? Why hadn't I learned from past experiences? How could I possibly have been so puffed up with my own importance . . . so flattered that someone actually wanted me . . . so . . . so . . . *stupid* as to return here. To the Sorensen Clinic, of all places. And now I wasn't just putting myself at risk – I was killing other people as well.

My instinct was to run. Run and run and run and never come back. Not back to the clinic. Not even back to Rushford. Not back to anywhere. Just keep running until I couldn't run any longer. And then find somewhere small and dark where no one would ever find me again. Ever.

What had I done?

The pain in my lungs told me to breathe. I dragged in one breath, then another. The world had not changed while I'd lost my place in it. I was still here in this dark room. And she was still dead. I realised I hadn't even known her name.

Somehow, I got myself on the other side of the door again and pulled it to behind me.

And now I had to go and tell someone what had happened.

Very slowly, because my legs were still wobbly, I set off to look for a nurse.

The corridor was silent and there was still no one in sight. The Sorensen Clinic had a very high staff-to-patient ratio. Even if it was lunchtime, there should still be people around. In fact, especially if it was lunchtime. The food here was very good. For those patients who wouldn't be lunching in the restaurant, there should be food trolleys lined up against the walls as nurses and orderlies took them their meals.

I put one hand against the wall again and struggled to pull myself together. Breathe in – breathe out. Breathe in – breathe out. My thudding heart was subsiding. I could feel cold sweat drying on my face. Slowly I regained control over myself and felt a little better.

Until I opened my eyes to find Dr Bridgeman striding down the landing towards me, his light blue colour streaming behind him. A part of my mind registered it was almost the exact colour of the carpet runners.

'Ah, Mrs Cage – I was just coming to look for you.'

I should tell him. Tell him now.

'Shall we step into my office?'

I chickened out. His office offered privacy and quiet. I could tell him there, safe from anyone else overhearing what I'd done.

I followed him down the staircase and into his office. I hadn't been in here since that dreadful day Sorensen drugged me with Ghost. In his time, it had been smart, minimalist, modern and sophisticated. Under Dr Bridgeman, it was a completely different room. His desk was comfortably cluttered with papers, files, pens and, for some reason, a stethoscope. Family photos occupied the tops of his many bookcases and the cases themselves were crammed full of books. Not all of them were textbooks – I could see colourful paperbacks standing shoulder to shoulder with professional manuals. The effect was that this wasn't just a professional space. I could easily imagine him finding himself with a spare half hour and plonking himself down in one of the armchairs with a thriller and a mug of tea.

'Do sit down, Mrs Cage.' He folded himself into his own chair.

I was glad to sit. I took a leaf out of Sorensen's book, taking a moment to settle myself, draw a breath, smooth my trousers and clasp my hands in my lap.

He smiled at me. 'Well, Mrs Cage, how do you think you're doing these days?'

'Dr Bridgeman, I . . .'

'We doctors don't pretend to have all the answers, you know,' he said cheerfully. 'Sometimes it's useful to check our own perceptions of how wonderful we think we are against those of our patients.'

I didn't know what to say. I shook my head, still seeing those thick black coils.

While I was searching for words, he pressed his intercom. 'Kevin, could we have some tea in here, please?'

The intercom squawked incomprehensibly.

'Thank you.'

He sat back and looked at me. I began to feel quite uncomfortable. What was happening here?

'Mrs Cage, I'm sorry to have to tell you this – although I don't think it will come as any great surprise to you – but we just don't seem to be making the progress I'd hoped.'

His words jolted me temporarily out of my own issues. What

was he talking about? I hadn't been on the job that long. This was my first day. What on earth had he been expecting? How bad must I have been if they were dissatisfied with my performance after only one session? Not that that was the most important thing at the moment.

I waved his words aside. 'Dr Bridgeman, there's something I have to tell you. I'm sorry – I've done wrong and I know it – but . . . the patient upstairs . . . the young girl who couldn't speak . . . who couldn't move . . . the one who didn't know what had happened to her. Her mind was screaming . . . I went in . . . to see if I could help . . . and I think it was all too much for her. She's dead and I think it might be my fault. Well, I'm certain that it's my fault.'

He stared at me, his mouth open. I rushed in with more words, making things worse with every single one of them. 'I'm sorry – I thought there might be something I could do. That I could help somehow.' I could feel tears welling up. 'I looked for a nurse but there wasn't one around and I didn't know . . .'

He leaned forwards across his desk. 'Mrs Cage, I'm sorry but I'm not sure what you're . . .'

I was desperate to make him understand. Leaping to my feet, I said, 'Let me show you. It's the patient upstairs. I think she's dead. I tried to help her but . . .'

'Which patient?'

'The one in the short corridor. In the little room on the left. I was trying to help her. We were communicating and then . . . I'm sorry, it's all my fault . . . She . . . I thought I could help. She was terrified. Her thoughts were all over the place. She was clawing at the inside of her own head trying to get out.'

'Who?'

132

Impatience was overtaking guilt. I turned to the door – as if that would help. 'The girl. The girl up there. The one who couldn't speak. Or move. She wanted me to help her but there was . . . She struggled so hard – too hard because . . . because her mind just burst into flames.'

He was shaking his head. 'What are you talking about?'

'Her,' I said, gabbling like a maniac, desperate to get him to understand what had happened. 'Your patient upstairs. I tried but she died in front of me. I'm so, so sorry and . . .'

'*Elizabeth, stop. Just . . . stop.*'

He'd raised his voice. I was so surprised I stopped talking. Exasperation clouded his colour. 'Sit down, please. Sit down. Yes, that's right. Thank you.'

I sat down with a bump and stared at him.

'Please, Mrs Cage, could you stop all this – just for one moment?'

He bowed his head and stared at his hands. 'Let's start again, shall we? I've called you in this morning because we're very concerned at your lack of progress. Please be very clear, no blame rests with you, but in view of your failure to respond to the treatment you've been receiving here, we think the time has come to review your case and possibly consider an alternative approach. At a different facility, perhaps.'

I stared at him. Words had deserted me.

'Mrs Cage, you've been here now for what – two years? We're all very fond of you – you're a model patient, and both staff and patients hold you in high regard – but the fact is – well, you haven't helped yourself much, have you?'

I found my voice. 'I . . . I'm sorry, I don't understand.'

He leaned forwards. 'Mrs Cage. Elizabeth.'

I stood up again. 'I think I'd like a word with Mr Jones, please.'

Frustration spiked his colour towards me. 'Elizabeth – for the umpteenth time, Michael Jones is not . . .'

He broke off, took a deep breath and attempted to speak calmly. 'I tell you what – let's get rid of this whole patient–doctor layout, shall we? Let's go and sit over here and be comfortable.'

He stood up and led me to the group of comfy chairs on the other side of the office. 'Oh, good. Here's our tea. Thank you, Kevin.'

Kevin – whoever he was – nodded and left.

Dr Bridgeman busied himself with the cups. 'Here you are. I think I know how you like yours. I should do by now.'

He sipped. I stared down at the tea swirling around my cup and said nothing.

'Elizabeth, I want you to listen to me very carefully. We've had this conversation many times and either you've refused to listen or become too distressed to continue, but I do urge you to listen to me today because I think this is the last time you and I will be able to talk like this. I'm sorry we haven't been able to help you here, but . . . well . . . I honestly feel you'd be better off at a different establishment. One where . . .'

I stood up. 'I definitely want to talk to Michael Jones. Why won't you let me speak to him?'

'For what purpose?'

'To discuss some things . . . Sorensen . . . his colour . . .'

He stood up and took my hand. His own was very warm. 'Elizabeth, please listen to me. Actually *listen* to what I am about to say to you. It's important and if you could just believe . . . accept what I'm going to tell you.'

'Accept what?'

'Let's sit down again, shall we? Do you know how long you've been here?'

I frowned. 'A day?'

'Elizabeth, you've been here for over two years now. Ever since your husband died. You remember Ted?'

'Of course I remember Ted,' I said angrily. 'What are you saying?'

'His death was a shock to us all. He was a lovely man and everyone here was absolutely devastated. You, of course, most of all. And that's when it started.'

I was completely bewildered. 'When what started? What are you talking about?'

'This . . . this . . . other world that you've disappeared into. With colours and swords and strange people and so forth. It's understandable, Elizabeth. You're a quiet person. You lived a quiet life and when Ted died, even that disappeared. You were left with nothing. So, your mind created a world where you had some sort of superpower. Where you had incredible adventures. Where you saved the day. You. Elizabeth Cage.'

He sighed. 'I admit now, I should have stepped in earlier but I didn't see any harm in it. It's not uncommon for people to fantasise about possessing qualities and powers they don't actually have. You fought ghosts, demons even – and won. Sadly, your own personal demons have been less easy to overcome.'

He picked up his tea and sipped. 'Elizabeth, look at me. Really, really look at me. What colour am I?'

I stared at him. His words echoed around my head. *What colour am I? What colour am I?*

I opened my mouth to tell him – the same colour as your

135

carpet, actually – and suddenly – it was gone. His colour vanished. It just faded away. Right in front of my eyes. A normal person sat opposite me. No colour. No aura. Just an ordinary person. His face showed nothing but concern and sympathy . . . Or so I thought. Because there was no colour for me to read. Nothing to tell me what he was thinking. How he was feeling.

I sat back and let my mind drift. Reaching out . . . because sometimes that works. But not this time. There was nothing. I couldn't see. I was . . . Panic boiled inside me again. I was blind. Blind and helpless and vulnerable and naked and defenceless and exposed and weak. I really was nothing. Not even a speck in all the vastness of the universe.

I swallowed hard. 'I want to talk to Michael Jones.'

He sighed and took my hand again. 'Michael Jones barely knows you exist.'

I tried to twist my hand away from his, but his grip was firm. 'He says he met you once. At some sort of function here. You were with Ted. He doesn't think he even spoke to you on that, the only occasion you ever met.'

If the earth had gaped beneath my feet, I could not have been more dumbfounded.

'No,' I said again, 'that's not right. It was Michael Jones who broke me out of this clinic when Dr Sorensen tried to . . .'

The exasperation was back. 'Elizabeth – listen to me. *There is no Dr Sorensen.* There never has been. He's a figment of your imagination. Someone you invented. A bogeyman. The anti-hero your mind constructed, in exactly the same way you turned Mr Jones into some sort of heroic champion. And these astonishing adventures in which you save the day and escape by the skin of your teeth every time . . . well, how feasible are they?'

'No. Michael Jones is . . .'

He squeezed my hand and said very gently, 'Sometimes, when we . . . when we aren't quite as happy with ourselves as we should be . . . when we're aware we're not perhaps as confident or as dynamic as other people, we . . . we create little scenarios for ourselves in which we are brave and strong and able to overcome all difficulties. There's nothing wrong with that, just as long as we remember that's all they are. Little dreams into which we can escape for a while. The problems start when we cross the line between dreaming and believing. Your life as you see it is not real, Elizabeth. None of it is. Your mind took the character of Michael Jones – who, believe me, is just an ordinary man – and turned him into someone wonderful and then slotted him into your new reality. I've spoken to him about this. Several times. He's actually quite embarrassed by the whole . . . by your scenario. He has offered to come and talk to you himself. To explain that you and he are not . . . that you couldn't be . . . He's actually in a long-term relationship with someone else.'

'Clare,' I said suddenly.

'No – where did you get Clare from? His name's Jerry. Yes, I can see that name means something to you.'

My world was spinning. They were words, I could hear them, but they were the wrong words. All wrong. I was loose. Untethered. He had no colour. Nothing for me to read. Because there *were* no colours. There never had been. It was all in my head. No one floated around in a sea of all-revealing colour. Of course they didn't. The whole idea was preposterous. Stupid. Ridiculous. Pathetic. Like me with Michael Jones. Of course he wasn't . . . I was just some inadequate little nonentity, unable

137

to cope with life, who had taken a man she had only met once for a few minutes and woven a whole fantasy life around him.

I felt myself grow hot with humiliation at the thought of it. How could I . . . ? What had I been thinking, that someone like Jones would even look at someone like me? I was a pitiful little woman, who had imagined herself to be someone exceptional – someone unique – because no one else ever would. Someone special, admired, capable, significant, worthy . . . but actually wasn't any of those things. And never would be.

My world crashed around me. Pillars toppled. Roofs caved in. Edifices fell. Everything crumbled. Turned to dust. And I was left with nothing.

Dimly I was aware of Dr Bridgeman saying my name. I blinked at him and tried to focus. He was regarding me with great kindness.

'Elizabeth, I'm so sorry but it had to be done. Your fantasy was holding you back. One day it could even have killed you. I can see you're very upset. Of course you are. This is quite a normal reaction. Please try not to be too concerned. This is the moment we can begin your recovery. I know you don't believe me right now, but this is a massive step forwards for you. From now on, you will make some real progress.'

He stood up and held out his hand to help me to my feet. 'Now, I think you need a moment alone. I'm going to walk you back to your room, settle you there and have a word with your primary nurse – it's Erin, isn't it? – and then, when you've had a little rest, we'll come in and block out a course of treatment for you. Either here or at another establishment more suited to your needs. I promise you'll be included and consulted at every stage. I suspect, Elizabeth, that you already feel very much better. That you've finally recognised the false reality in which you've been immersing yourself. Come along now. Up you get. That's it. Just take it slowly. If you like, we can take the back stairs, so you don't have to face anyone if you don't want to.'

I stood up. My legs felt as if they would hardly support me. Thoughts, words, images whirled around inside my head. I closed my eyes to block them all out.

'Take my arm,' he said gently. 'Back to your room and a nice soothing drink under a soft, warm blanket. Everything is going to be all right, Elizabeth, I promise you.'

We walked slowly towards his office door. I closed my eyes. His voice filled my head. Calm and soothing. 'That's it, Elizabeth. Just through this door here and we'll soon be there. Nearly there. Nearly there. That's it. Very good. One more step. That's it – just one more step . . . One . . . last . . . step . . .'

Something seized my wrist in a grip of iron. I'm certain I felt my bones grate together. Suddenly, there was nothing beneath my foot. I was stepping into nothing and toppling forwards . . .

And then I was jerked back. Hard. So hard it hurt. With pain came clarity.

Michael Jones stood before me. His face was . . . I can't describe it. His red and gold colour roared towards me.

'Cage? What the fu— What are you doing? Look at me. Look at me, Cage.' He shook me hard. Really hard. I could feel my hair flying around my face. '*Look at me.*'

I blinked and looked at him. The first thing I noticed was his colour, leaping about all over the place. Then I looked around. I was outside. Somehow, I was outside. Up on the roof. Not in Bridgeman's office at all. I was actually on the roof, standing on the knee-high parapet. Right at the very edge. I could still hear Dr Bridgeman's voice in my head. *'One more step. That's it – just one more step.'*

One more step and I would have gone over the edge. To my death. I had been one step from death. I would have died on the stones below. My mind couldn't move past it. I would have died. The pain in my chest told me I'd stopped breathing. And that I was still alive.

I looked up. A bright blue sky hung above me. The sun was shining. I could hear crows cawing in the trees nearby. A breeze stirred my hair. What was happening? How did I get all the way up here? Where was Dr Bridgeman? Nothing made any sense. I was four storeys up. Other people were piling out of the door behind me. There was shouting. Jones was still holding my wrist and obviously had no intention of letting go any time soon. At ground level, one or two members of staff stood staring upwards. I could see their faces. I could see the gardens. And the river beyond. And the rolling countryside beyond that.

And I could see Michael Jones. I could see his colour. Red and gold. And still roaring towards me. The word agitated didn't even begin to describe how he was feeling.

I reached out with my other hand. He took it and crushed it tightly, saying very quietly, 'I've never asked you for anything, Cage, but I'm asking now. Don't ever do that again. If anything's wrong, then talk to me. I thought we were over this. You talk to me. You don't just throw yourself . . .' He gestured to the edge of the roof, still uncomfortably close. 'You don't do that, Cage. You talk to me. Do you hear?'

I nodded. Words were completely beyond me at that point.

We took the stairs quite slowly. My mind was scrabbling for a clue. What had just happened? What had I nearly done?

Dr Bridgeman came running across the hall, his colour streaming out behind him just as it had done before. I could definitely see that. Which world was I in now? Which reality was the real reality?

This had happened to me before. My reality had split in two. There was a world in which Jones died, I died, everyone died. Then there was the other version where I simply banged my head in an accident and everyone lived. Both had happened. Both were real. Was that what had happened here?

I was ushered into his office with Dr Bridgeman asking questions all the way. Had I eaten anything recently?

I shook my head, swallowed once or twice and managed to say, 'Not since breakfast.'

'Have you drunk anything?'

'Water.'

'From the vending machine,' said Jones. 'Bought it myself.'

Dr Bridgeman examined my arms for puncture wounds. Had I been injected with something? He couldn't find anything.

He peered into my eyes. They were talking about hypnotism. Well – let them. Let them find their own rational explanation. I sat quietly and waited to see which reality would assert itself. Was I actually sitting in this office or was I dead on the flagstones four floors down with my head split open, lying in a bright red pool of my own blood?

On balance, I rather thought I'd stick with this one.

CHAPTER TEN

Two cups of tea later – and when everyone was much calmer – I was able to tell them what had happened. Or rather, what I thought had happened.

They listened with the sort of attention you only get with professional listeners. I went through it all – from leaving the basement to opening my eyes and finding myself on the roof. With a few omissions, obviously. Wild horses wouldn't have dragged the bits about Jones from me.

When I'd finished, there was a silence. Neither looked at the other. I couldn't tell if they believed me or not.

Eventually, Dr Bridgeman said, 'That was extremely ... interesting. Would you mind going through it all again so I can ask some questions?'

I nodded. 'It began with the locked-in girl upstairs.'

He stared at me. 'Who?'

'The girl upstairs. Just off the main corridor. The one who couldn't communicate. I've ... I was trying to ...'

I stopped, remembering what the other Dr Bridgeman had said about trying to make myself seem more important than I actually was and shut up.

'There is no such patient,' he said gently. 'We'd never have anyone like that here. We couldn't. We're not equipped for it.

If you are able – could you describe the set-up? Equipment, treatments and so forth?'

I saw again those dark coils twisting around her and her colour climbing the walls trying to escape.

'There was no equipment. Just a normal room. The curtains were drawn to keep out the sun and the lights were off. The room was quite dark. I could hardly make her out. The bathroom door was shut. That was it.'

I didn't want to say too much. I had a feeling I was on some very psychiatrically dodgy ground at the moment.

Dr Bridgeman was a great deal more perceptive than I gave him credit for. Well, he would be, wouldn't he? He smiled gently and said, 'Now tell me what you're not telling me, Mrs Cage. Actually, may I call you Elizabeth? I'm Stephen. We're colleagues, now, don't you think?'

I looked at Jones, who shrugged. 'Up to you, Cage. Although – and I speak from personal experience – he's very good.'

I took a deep breath and put down my cup of cold tea. 'All right.'

And I did. For only the second or third time in my life, I told someone what I could do. I talked about people's colours and seeing dead people. I didn't mention Iblis or Melek or Felda – I just told him the bits as they related to Sorensen and the clinic. Not the stuff that would get me sectioned in a heartbeat.

And definitely, definitely not the humiliating bits about Michael Jones. I do have some pride.

I ended with, 'But it was so real. It was you. I was talking to you. In here.'

'No, you weren't,' said Jones. 'I've been talking to him for the last twenty minutes. In here.'

143

Dr Bridgeman gestured around. 'You've never been in here before, have you? Not since my predecessor's time?'

I shook my head, suddenly seeing what he was getting at. 'No.' I stared around at the neat room. Gone was all the comforting clutter that had, in its own way, been so disarming. 'This is completely different.'

'Interesting,' he said. 'You couldn't replicate what you'd never seen.'

I stared at Dr Bridgeman. 'But it was *you*. You said . . .'

I stopped, unable to repeat the things he'd said. I would take my humiliation with me to the grave. 'I thought I was in here. How could I be up on the roof when I thought I was in here? And how did you know I was up there?'

'They watched you,' said Jones. 'On the security monitors. You came out of the lift, paused for a moment, then approached the stairs. You went up, stood stock-still on the landing for a minute or so, then went to the end and opened the fire door to the backstairs, which triggered a silent alarm. Given the type of patient here and some of their issues, security went into high alert and reported a non-patient going up on to the roof. I was racing up the stairs right behind you. You looked as if you were sleepwalking.'

I wondered what would happen if I said, 'Oh dear, have I started doing that again?' Would they grasp at this reasonable explanation for my bizarre actions? Somehow, I doubted it. And did I need to add sleepwalking to my already extensive list of odd behaviours?

Dr Bridgeman changed tack slightly. 'Tell me again what we were talking about? When we were in here, together?'

'You told me I'd been here for two years. Ever since Ted

died. As a patient. That I wasn't responding to treatment. That I was being transferred to another facility. He . . . You implied it wouldn't be as nice as this one. You said there was no such person as Dr Sorensen, that he only existed in my imagination.'

Dr Bridgeman frowned. 'Have you always had a fear of this place?'

I thought I should be tactful. 'Not of this place as such, but a fear of being admitted. It did happen once. I was held here against my will. I thought it was going to happen all over again but in a different, much worse establishment. And that this time it would be for good.'

My voice trembled.

Jones leaned forwards. 'Cage – I can prove to you that none of it was real. Now. This moment. That whatever it was – dream, hallucination, hypnosis, some sort of alternative reality – it didn't happen.'

I sat up. 'But it was. The details were so . . .' I ended lamely with, 'real.'

'They were, weren't they? But someone was just that little bit too clever.'

'Were they? How?'

'They hadn't banked on you focusing so hard on that vase of flowers to regain your place in the world.'

I stared at him. 'I don't understand.'

'You said you used the flowers to ground yourself again. Return to reality, if you like.'

'Yes, I did.'

'Do it again.'

'What?'

'Can you do it again for me now?'

145

'Um . . .' I stared at the floor. 'The yellow rose in the centre, delphinium spikes, daisies, daffodils, artemisia . . . um . . . marigolds . . .'

'Oh,' said Dr Bridgeman, sitting back. 'Yes.'

'Yes, what?'

Jones grinned at me. 'All summer plants except for daffodils, which only flower in the spring. It's summer. No daffodils.'

'Oh . . .' I said. 'Oh, it didn't register. Oh God, I'm so stupid.'

'Fair's fair, Cage,' said Jones. 'You had other things on your mind at the time.'

'But I *know* daffodils aren't in flower this time of the year. I know that . . .'

I tailed away. And now I came to think of it – where was Sister Cross? Why hadn't she appeared? Evelyn Cross was the ghost of a nursing sister who had served here during the war. She'd died during a bombing raid and now her self-imposed task was to be present on the admittedly rare occasions a patient died. To ease their death. To help them pass from this world to the next. She never failed. But she hadn't been here today. Not for that girl – and not for me, either.

I stared hard at the floor, trying not to cry. Because strangely, this was more upsetting than everything else.

'OK,' said Jones, standing up. 'If Dr Bridgeman permits, I'm going to take you home. Leave your scooter here. It'll be quite safe.'

Dr Bridgeman picked up his keys. 'Would you like me to give you something from my fabled box of tricks? To help you sleep, perhaps?'

'No, thank you,' I said quickly. 'I think I'd just like to go home, please. I'm sorry to have been so much trouble.'

He let me go. I suspected there would be a full-scale discussion as soon as I was out of the door. He even apologised. I don't know what he was apologising for – none of it was his fault – but I smiled, assured everyone I was absolutely fine, and finally we were allowed to leave.

I was looking forward to spending a quiet afternoon at home but, actually, this was just the beginning of quite a long day.

'*Were* you sleepwalking?' said Jones as we approached his car.

'No.'

'Have you ever sleepwalked?'

'No.'

'I got to you just in time, didn't I?'

I didn't dare look at him. 'Am I going mad?'

'Always hard to tell with you, Cage, but I don't think so. Listen, we've already paused Sorensen's interviews, so we have a couple of days off anyway. You should take things easy for a bit.'

I watched his colour. Something wasn't right with him, but I didn't think it was anything to do with me.

I sat quietly beside him as we drove down the drive. They lifted the barrier and then we were on the road home.

'So,' I said. 'Tell me what's the matter.'

'Cage, you just nearly threw yourself off the roof and . . .'

'No, not that,' I said. 'Before that. What's happened to you? What were you talking to Dr Bridgeman about?'

He started to say, 'I don't know what you mean,' and then remembered who he was talking to.

He changed down for a corner, negotiated the bend and then changed up again. 'I failed my eyesight test.'

I said quietly, 'I'm sorry to hear that.'

He shrugged.

'You thought you might.'

'Yes, but I hoped I wouldn't.'

'What does this mean for you?'

'It means I can't carry a gun any longer.'

'Officially,' I said.

He grinned at me. 'You might have some very odd habits, Cage, but you're not stupid, are you?'

I shook my head. 'After today I'm not sure I would agree.' There was silence for a while and then I said, 'Thank you for believing me.'

'I always believe you.'

'But you were with Bridgeman in his office at the time. You above everyone knew I wasn't telling the truth.'

'Cage, I always believe you.'

I felt my eyes prick with tears. 'Thank you.'

He took another bend. 'Any thoughts on how all that happened? Or why? Or who? I mean – that was a pretty sophisticated scam, Cage. That you'd been there for years . . . as a patient . . .' He paused. 'Playing on some hidden fears, perhaps.'

I sighed. 'I don't think my fears are all that well hidden.'

He let a moment go by and then said again, 'Any thoughts?'

'Well, I suppose it depends whether it was drug or hypnosis. If I was drugged, then the only thing I drank was water – and you handed me that so should I be glowering at you in a suspicious manner?'

'You do that anyway, Cage, whether there are fluids involved or not. But it seemed to begin before you even started climbing the stairs.'

I sighed. 'In that case . . .'

'What?'

'You're going to have to promise not to yell at me.'

'I refuse to commit myself. What particular folly have you perpetrated now?'

'When we were downstairs in the observation room – the interview had just ended – Sorensen was getting up to go . . .' I paused and took a breath. 'I saw something that no one else seemed to notice.'

'Was anyone else looking?'

'I'm not sure. You were tearing up our notes. Robbie was collecting his files. I don't know what was going on in the control room.'

'I can find out. What did you see?'

I gripped my hands together. 'Just at the very end – as he stood up to go – Sorensen's face changed. No, not changed – it was like another set of features was laid across his. A different face was looking at me.'

'Whose face?'

'I don't know. I have a feeling I've seen it before, but don't ask me where.'

'I'll check the tapes. We have to run through them anyway.' He paused. 'There is another possibility, of course . . .'

I nodded. 'Greyston. You're wondering if Iblis and I might have woken something up.'

He sighed. 'If I thought it would do any good, I'd forbid you to go anywhere with that blond lunatic ever again, but I know full well neither you nor he would take a blind bit of notice, so I'll spare my breath.'

'Phew,' I said, and just then my phone rang.

I fished around in my bag and pulled it out, grinned and put it on speakerphone. 'Hello, Iblis. Jones was just talking about you.'

'The man-mountain honours me. Do I bask in his high regard?'

'As much as you usually do. What can I do for you?'

'I bear a message. From Melek. You are bidden to feast with us tonight.'

I heard her voice in the background.

'She says if convenient, of course,' he added quickly.

'Well, that's lovely, but the thing is we've both of us had a very bad day and . . .'

'We have something of importance to say to you. Seven o'clock tonight.'

He disconnected.

Jones muttered under his breath and we pulled on to the ring road. 'What do you think that's all about?'

'Well, they do owe us a meal after Christmas.'

We were both silent for a while, reviewing the wreckage that had been our last Christmas. And the one before that hadn't been brilliant, either.

I shot a glimpse sideways at his profile. 'Or, of course . . .'

'What?'

'Given recent events, it could be an olive branch.'

'Yeah – I can't help feeling that any olive branch emanating from that quarter would be wired to explode as soon as I touched it.'

'Seems unnecessarily complicated when all she has to do is poison the food.' I grinned. 'Or the wine.'

He cheered up immediately. 'True.'

I glanced at him. His colour looked comparatively calm and relaxed – not like an hour ago – so I said, 'Um, they're nearer my house than yours. If you don't want to drive this evening, I can put you up. On the sofa, I mean.'

'Hasn't that flea-ridden mongrel been sleeping on it?'

I said cautiously, 'You mean Nigel?'

There was a pause. 'Of course I meant Nigel, Cage. Who did you think?'

'No idea,' I said, looking out of the window.

CHAPTER ELEVEN

'You're going to sit alone in your house, brooding over whether you've lost your mind or not, aren't you?' he said as we approached the town centre.

'No, of course I'm not,' I said defensively, although a more truthful answer would have been, 'Yes, of course I am.'

'It's a nice afternoon,' he went on, 'and we have some unexpected time off. Let's go for a walk and get a drink at the end of it. Like normal people. Then we can go on to our dinner date. Like more normal people.'

'OK,' I said. 'In fact, I was thinking the other day that perhaps I should go and check on Caroline Fairbrother. She's on my list of things that might wish me harm. We could take the opportunity to check her out and you'll be able to come with me and reassure yourself I'm not doing anything stupid.'

He frowned. 'Why does that name ring a bell?'

'She had the art gallery up by Gerald's antique shop, remember? You arrested that bloke for her murder.'

'You're going to chat with a dead woman?'

I nodded.

'She's haunting the art gallery?'

'Not exactly.'

'Cage?'

'I don't know what you're going to say to this, but actually I tied her to the wall outside.'

'Tied? Like a . . . a bondage thing?'

'The way your mind works is always interesting and frequently disturbing. No – she murdered Sammy. You remember little Sammy?'

'He fell down the steps.'

'No – he didn't.'

'She pushed him?'

'She *threw* him.'

'My God, Cage. He was practically a baby.'

'Yeah. I tied her to the scene of her crime. Well, just outside.' I waited to see what he'd say.

'Even so . . .'

'She'd tied his little ghost to the wall. He was terrified. He wanted his mum. Who was also dead, remember? I freed Sammy, he went off with his mum, and I tied Caroline in his place. She can't ever leave unless I say so.'

'Why are you telling me this?'

'I . . . I thought you ought to know I'm not as nice as you think I am.'

'I don't think you're nice at all, Cage. Nice is not the word to describe you.'

'How would you describe me?'

'Honestly?'

'Well . . . yes.'

He thought. 'I don't know. I'm not sure there are any words that even come close.'

I looked down at my hands. 'Now's a good moment for you to walk away if you want to.'

'Cage, we're in a moving car halfway around Rushford's notorious one-way system.'

'You know what I mean.'

'Neither of us is walking away. I'm pretty sure we'll be *running* away from something sooner or later, but no – I'm not walking away. And it's not as if I'm an angel myself.'

The old docks area is very pleasant since its redevelopment. All the old brick warehouses have been restored and turned into bars, cafés, boutiques and flats. They've kept their original names – Victoria, St George, Great Western, Albert, Britannia. With little Hartland Warehouse on the end. Originally it had been a fireproof repository, built to store valuable cargoes, and its robust construction and sturdy walls gave it a slightly different look to the others.

We strolled through the warehouse area, threading our way through outdoor tables and chairs, food carts and the occasional piece of carefully placed industrial equipment. A small food market was taking place alongside one of the barge arms. One of the narrow boats had been turned into an outdoor bookshop and we browsed for a while. It was all very unhurried and pleasant. The afternoon was warm and sunny and I could feel the morning's events receding further and further into the background. I don't know if it's just some sort of automatic coping mechanism, but this seems to be how things work for me. Something awful happens – there are a few moments of stomach-churning panic – and then, over the next twelve hours, the feelings slowly fade away. The memory remains but the emotional fall-out recedes. Which is probably just as well – I'd certainly be a candidate for Sorensen's clinic, otherwise.

We spent some time poking around the food fair – Jones availed himself of free samples of artisanal sausages, cheeses, bread, and wine. We wandered past the old railway yards – now also being redeveloped and eventually emerged into the open countryside. There were fields on our left, and over on the other side of the river, cows grazed placidly among the water meadows. We strolled slowly along the riverbank for a while. Occasionally, runners pounded past us, red-faced and sweating in the pursuit of fitness.

And there were fishermen, too. Jones slowed. 'Professional interest,' he explained.

I rolled my eyes. 'You mean you want to see what catching a fish actually looks like?'

'You're such a shrew, Cage. I've explained to you before – it's not about the actual catch – it's the philosophical opportunities offered by just sitting alone on a riverbank with only your thoughts and a six-pack for company. Fish are optional.'

We walked on.

'Shall we go as far as the bridge?'

He indicated the railway bridge a couple of hundred yards ahead.

I definitely didn't want to do that. I'd walked under that bridge once and encountered a troll. One of the Jötnar. True, I'd also encountered Iblis, and that had led to meeting Melek, and any number of interesting events had sprung from those encounters. I definitely wasn't in the mood to encounter old Þhurs today. There had been something in the way he had arranged the bones of his previous victims in what he regarded as pretty patterns that had made me just a little bit disinclined to further our acquaintance.

155

I shook my head. 'It's too far,' I said doubtfully. 'Let's go and find somewhere for a quiet drink.'

We turned back.

'How are you feeling now?'

'I'm fine,' I said hastily. 'No, really, I am. Whenever anything like this happens to me, it's horrible while it lasts, but only a few hours later the whole experience is . . . blunted, I think is a good word. Some sort of defence mechanism, I suppose.'

'Cage, I worry . . .'

I cut in before he could get very far with this.

'No, really. I mean, it wasn't . . . well, obviously it was a bit . . . but . . . it . . . I mean, I . . . It . . .' I tailed off because I didn't really know what I wanted to say. And I didn't want to discuss it. The thought of Jones knowing what Dr Bridgeman had said . . .

He sighed. 'There's a very useful course – *Receiving, Retaining and Transmitting Information in a Speedy and Effective Manner that Prevents Your Partner from Strangling You in Frustration* – I shall sign you up for it. Along with the one entitled *Not Doing Stupid Things as Soon as My Back's Turned*. Seriously, Cage, you frightened me out of ten years' growth today.'

'You try opening your eyes to find you're standing on the edge of a roof four floors up. I lost considerably more than that.'

'True. Let's just agree you'll cut back on doing stupid things in future.'

'I will if you will.'

He regarded me. 'It's a good job I can't shoot straight any longer, otherwise you'd be floating out to sea at this very moment.'

I sighed. 'Do you think it would be quicker and easier for both of us if I just flung myself into the river now?'

'Don't do that, Cage. I'm not facing that lanky witch alone tonight. And now, having suitably digressed . . . talk to me again about Sorensen and the face.'

'I don't know what to say, really. His face didn't change exactly . . . it was overlaid somehow. Just for a fraction of a second, there were two faces. One over the other.'

'Symbolic of what a two-faced bastard he is, don't you think? You said you thought you recognised it?'

'It was familiar. I've seen it before. It'll come back to me.'

He stopped walking. 'That's interesting, isn't it? You see a face. Ten seconds later we split up. You go one way and I go another. Five minutes later you're in your own world up on the roof holding conversations with people who aren't there.' He looked at me. 'What was Sorensen doing while his face was . . . you know?'

'Actually, I'm not sure he was even aware. He was just a . . . a vessel. It might have been nothing to do with him. Perhaps it could as easily have been Robbie's face.'

'Did it speak?'

'Yes,' I said, suddenly remembering. 'He – not Sorensen, the other one – said something like, "Not long now, Mrs Cage."'

There was a bench under a tree and he nudged me towards it.

'Any idea what he meant?'

'Well,' I said sarcastically, 'I think he meant something was about to happen in the very near future and he wanted me to know it.'

He sighed. 'It's still not too late to shoot you and toss your corpse into the river. Even I couldn't miss at this range.'

'If you shoot as well as you fish . . .'

'Tell me about the girl upstairs.'

157

'She was in a room off the main corridor.'

'I spoke to Bridgeman – there's no such room.'

Nothing was surprising me any longer.

I hesitated. 'The thing is – there was something in that room and it was terrifying. Her colour was climbing the walls trying to get away. I couldn't quite see . . .' I stopped talking. 'I don't want to have that in my mind again, but the point I'm making is that not just any person could have done something that . . . compelling. Think about it: he – I say *he* but it could be anyone – had to control me. He had to manufacture the illusion – the patient, her symptoms, her colour and so forth. It had to be interactive – it reacted to what I was saying. And then, having thoroughly terrified and undermined me, he brought in what I thought was Dr Bridgeman – who was completely convincing, by the way – to play on all my . . . my secret fears and weaknesses – and then he had to get me up on to the roof . . .' I tailed away.

'And lead you straight over the edge, without you even knowing it,' finished Jones.

I nodded.

There was a long silence as the River Rush meandered slowly past on its way to the sea. For a moment I wished I was a river, with nothing to do but flow muddily along and never have to worry about relationships or things that go bump in the night or lurked in the shadowy corners of my mind.

He sighed. 'It's a good job I love you, Cage. A lesser man would be on a plane to South America by now.'

I was still thinking *what did he just say?* when he turned to face me.

'Anything else I should know? Speak now. God knows when

we'll ever have another opportunity to talk to each other in peace and quiet.'

I took a deep breath. 'I spoke to her.'

'Your use of proper nouns needs work. Talked to whom?'

'Felda. The . . . person in my head.'

'On your own?'

'Well . . .'

'My God, Cage – don't you know how dangerous that could have been for you? On your own like that. I don't have a lot of time for that lanky witch, but if something had gone wrong, and she wasn't there to handle it . . .'

'Nothing went wrong. Felda was very careful and very gentle. I could sense it.'

'But anything could have happened. Why would you take such a risk?'

'Well, it occurred to me that no one had actually asked her – Felda – what *she* wanted.'

He sat back. 'And what did she want?'

Again, I felt the open wound of her grief. Blunted now, but still searingly painful. 'She wants peace. So much. She just wants to sleep. To forget.'

'But what does that mean for you?'

'I assume that things will be more or less as they were before. Before her public appearance at Christmas, that is. She'll be dormant. If that's the right word. And . . .' I took a breath. 'I wanted to ask you –, what do you want? Do you want to remember? Or forget?'

'What do you want me to do?'

'It's your decision. You've always made that very clear.'

'Will my decision affect yours?'

'No. I'm not putting that burden on you. Nor will I let anyone tamper with your memories without your permission. Your decision is yours alone. As was mine.'

He looked out across the river. 'I think you've made the decision for both of us. Whatever the page is – we both need to be on the same one.'

'Are you all right with that?'

'Christmas was shit, Cage. And the one before that wasn't much better. We drew a line under that one and moved on. We should do the same with this one.'

'And possibly decide to spend the next one in different hemispheres.'

He didn't laugh. He didn't even smile. In fact, he was silent for a long time. 'Cage, there's something I want to say to you. While we have this opportunity. Before the next catastrophe turns up. Remember, we have the Dinner of Death this evening and God knows how that will end.'

'Yes?'

'I'm not going to embarrass us both but . . .' He hesitated, which was unusual for him. His colour had solidified. Protecting him. I had no idea from what.

'What?'

'Is there any hope for me? For us? Sometimes I think perhaps there is, then some crisis always happens and we end up further apart than ever.'

I turned to face him properly. 'Is that what you think? I cried all over you in the hospital. I can't . . . I can't imagine . . . How could you ever think I don't . . . care for you. Quite a lot.' I swallowed. 'Although you are very irritating.'

He just stared at me.

I panicked. Lost my nerve completely. What on earth had I just done? Obviously, we'd been talking about two different things and now I'd really gone and done . . . something.

I began to gabble. 'Isn't that what you meant? Oh God, I'm so sorry. I'll go now. Sorry. Sorry.'

Still gabbling, I got to my feet, dropped my bag, bent to pick it up, dropped it again, grabbed it and began to walk off in the wrong direction, desperate, absolutely desperate to get away as quickly as possible. Coming so hard on the back of fake Dr Bridgeman's comments . . . The sooner I went back to locking myself away and never seeing a soul the better. Interpersonal relationships were obviously only for other people. I would become a hermit.

'Cage.'

'What?' I said, staring around me and wondering where Rushford had gone.

'Yes.'

'What?'

'Yes.'

'Yes, what?'

I tried to step past him. He blocked my way.

'Yes, I want to go back to the way things were as well. Let's step back from all this muddle and chaos. Let everyone else sort themselves out. We'll just concentrate on us. What do you think?'

'Yes,' I said, relief coursing through me. 'Yes, please.'

'Hey.'

I looked up. His colour, that brilliant red and gold, was surging towards me.

He kissed me. Not long. Not hard. Not demanding. Not a

bedroom kiss. Just a nice kiss, and exactly what I needed at that moment.

'You know what I miss,' he said, when we'd sat back down again. 'We never get to do things together. We only ever meet professionally, so to speak. Whenever we look as if we're about to get somewhere, something hideous turns up and engulfs us in weird stuff.'

That was true. We'd gone on a break to Scotland and all sorts of things had gone wrong with that. Or the time I'd been seconds from falling into bed with him and the next moment I'd been kidnapped. We'd even taken a seaside cottage in Rushby and been menaced by a red armchair. He was absolutely right. We never did normal things together. Long lunches, evenings at the cinema, weekends away – shopping, even. Nice, normal things. None of that ever happened to us.

'We will talk about this,' he said. 'We have a couple of days off. We'll start with what might – it is remotely possible, I suppose – turn out to be a pleasant dining experience this evening, and then we'll take some time just for ourselves and go away. It's summer so we probably won't be able to get a place in Rushby, but there'll be somewhere. Or . . .' He grinned down at me. 'You could come and stay at my place. Or I could go to yours. We have choices, Cage. We should start by making some.'

I nodded. We could be ordinary people doing ordinary things.

He got to his feet and pulled me to mine. 'Come on. As you said, we don't want to be late.'

We walked back the way we'd come in silence. Back past the cafés and warehouses.

'Listen,' he said, as we wandered through the docks. 'Are you still intending to interrogate that woman you tied in the wall?'

162

'Well, we're nearly there now. It's only just over the other side of the river. And the original problem hasn't gone away, has it? I doubt Caroline Fairbrother knows anything, and if she does, she probably won't say – especially not to me – but I suppose I should be thorough.'

'If you want my advice . . .' He stopped.

'Yes, I do,' I said. 'What's your advice?'

'It's up to you, but I would say don't do it. I don't mean don't ever do it, but don't do it today. You've had a shit day so far. Cage, you nearly died. Sorry – I can't get over that – but there's no rush to talk to this Caroline bird. Next week, maybe.'

We continued walking while I considered his words. He wasn't wrong. And now he'd mentioned it, I suddenly realised I didn't want to confront Caroline Fairbrother. Not today, anyway. I wanted to relax, enjoy the sunshine and then go to dinner with Iblis and Melek. Like an ordinary, everyday person. Although dinner with Iblis and Melek could turn out to be much more exciting than everything else that had happened today all added together.

'Yes,' I said, with some relief. 'I will take your advice. Not today.'

'Great. I need to nip off and get some cash from the machine. Coming?'

'No, I'll wait for you down by the river.'

'Cage . . .'

'What?'

'I'll be five minutes – tops. Will you be all right alone?'

I smiled at him. 'You're going to have to leave me on my own at some point. You know . . . trips to the bathroom and such.'

'Were you suggesting I accompany you or the other way around?'

'Just go and get your cash.'

We walked across the bridge. He disappeared into town and I followed the steps down to river level. In medieval times, the commercial centre of the town had been up near the castle. Then, after the bridge was built, the town spilled over the river and up the hill on the other side. The centre shifted down to the docks. Later, in Victorian times, with big, bright new shops opening up, the centre drifted across the bridge and further up the hill. A glorious, wonderfully hideous Gothic Guildhall was built. It survived repeated attempts to tear it down in the latter half of the twentieth century as 1960s architects tried to show us what hideous buildings could look like if they really put their minds to it and wouldn't everyone prefer a brutalist concrete block with no windows? – but the Guildhall won in the end and now presided, triumphant and listed, over the market square.

Down here, by the river, was where the old Tudor merchants had built their houses. Added to by the Georgians. And then the Victorians. The houses were close enough to the docks to enable them to keep an eye on their ships as they loaded and unloaded on the opposite bank, but far enough away that their wives and daughters could ignore the taint of trade.

The buildings along this side were all wonderful examples of their type – and very popular in classic TV and film dramas. It was a rare year when someone wasn't making yet another version of *A Christmas Carol* along here. Even the lampposts were olde worlde. I remember Jerry's partner, Gerald, telling me that over the years his antique shop had been Scrooge's counting house and the Old Curiosity Shop and the site of a particularly gruesome murder in the famous adaptation of a Sherlock Holmes story. At one point last year, it had been impossible for him to leave his own front door without bumping into Jack the Ripper killing his umpteenth prostitute. Or Lydia Bennet peering at bonnets in the milliner's window.

After quite a long and ragged day, however, it was very pleasant to sit on the low wall, look down at the Rush flowing silently past, admire the warehouses across the river, and just generally . . . stop. Just stop and breathe.

I stopped and breathed.

The tall houses cast a shadow on this side of the river. People wandered past, window shopping or just chatting. I could hear odd snatches of conversation. No one was having a crisis. Least of all me. I had a lot to think about but at the moment I wasn't inclined to waste my time on any of it. I was stopping and breathing. The universe could wait.

A narrow boat painted in bright green, gold and red emerged from the barge arm, close enough for me to see the ginger cat curled up on the roof in the sun. There were two tubs of bright red geraniums on the back bit and two pots of golden marigolds at the front. Slowly, it chugged off down the river. People waved as it passed.

I thought how pleasant it would be to spend a few days doing something similar. Never moving faster than a few miles an hour. Pulling over at night for a quiet meal as the sun went down. Enjoying a glass of wine. Trees hanging overhead. The sounds of nature at night.

Except it wouldn't be like that, of course. If I was there, then some river god would rise up, or a sea serpent, or some sort of vengeful water sprite. Or the ghosts of long-dead people would climb out of the river trailing weeds and ooze and try to kill us in our sleep.

165

I sighed.

'Now then, missis,' said Jerry.

I opened my eyes to see him sitting on the wall beside me.

'How are you these days?' he said. 'Jones said you weren't so well over Christmas.'

I took a breath. I didn't like lying to him but, having given the matter some thought, I'd come to the conclusion that almost anything sounded better than saying that not only was I suffering from industrial-strength hallucinations, but I also had an unstable god living inside me, who was perfectly capable of destroying the world if someone so much as looked at her wrong.

'It was a lovely Christmas,' I said. 'We ate a delicious lunch and fell over each other trying to clear it away. We played games and Iblis drank far too much and had to be put to bed. The next day Jones was called away and I returned home.'

'Oh,' he said, looking faintly astonished to be the recipient of so much information.

I tried to move things on a little. 'How are you, Jerry? And Gerald?'

'He sent me out to bring you in for a coffee and a chat.'

Jerry and Gerald had the antiques shop just behind us. A double-fronted Aladdin's cave of wonders overlooking the river. Well, Gerald owned it. As I've already mentioned, Jerry pursues a separate career. I probably shouldn't say any more, but he has some really useful skills. Including packing. He once broke into my house and packed a suitcase for me, and not only did he select exactly what I would have chosen for myself, but he folded everything perfectly and laid tissue paper between each layer.

'I'm waiting for Jones.'

'I'm behind you,' said Jones, appearing suddenly.

I was not going to give him the satisfaction of succumbing to a heart attack.

He pulled me to my feet and we followed Jerry in through the shop doorway.

I loved visiting Gerald's shop. It's like another world. Lots of other worlds, actually. As always, I was surrounded by beautiful things, enhanced by the smell of good furniture polish, potpourri and ancient wood.

It was all here. Softly glowing furniture with elegant lines, lovely faded rugs, fine china and porcelain, and quirky stuff, too – swords, music boxes, books, antique weapons, old prints, ceramics – a proper treasure trove.

The enormous Narnia wardrobe, which had played such a major role in bringing Jerry and Gerald together during the beginning stages of their relationship, now enjoyed a prominent position in their shop and was clearly marked 'Not for Sale'.

Gerald served tea in the little office at the back of the shop. 'No cake for me, thank you,' I said. 'We're going out to dinner this evening.'

'I'll have hers,' said Jones, to whom the normal rules of social intercourse do not apply.

Jerry passed me my tea. 'I was gonna come and see you anyway, missis.' He looked at Jones. 'And possibly you, as well.'

'That's me,' said Jones cheerfully, around a mouthful of Gerald's coffee and walnut cake. 'Always the afterthought.'

I was watching Jerry's colour. Usually a stable, solid brown, today it was tinged with orange and swirling at the edges. For Jerry, this was almost high anxiety.

I sat silently and waited.

He twirled his teaspoon. 'It's my sister's girl, Emily. She's a student.'

Jones finished his cake, helped himself to a home-made iced biscuit and nodded his appreciation to Gerald.

Jerry continued. 'There's three of them sharing a house in one of the streets off Hanover Square. You know. The square with them tall houses.'

I did.

'The thing is – they think the place might be haunted. Well, not the whole house – just one bedroom. Emily's.'

'What makes them think that?'

His colour was swirling. He wasn't comfortable talking about this. Not that you needed any special talent to see that. This man, who organised the Michael Jones Breakout and who was always cool and calm under pressure, was definitely disturbed.

'Well, several times now, she's woken up convinced there's something in her bedroom. Once or twice, she thought she heard breathing that wasn't hers. At first, she reckoned she'd got it wrong – you know, just woken up, drowsy, confused, mistaken. And then, the night before last, she woke up to find something licking her face.'

'Oh, yuk,' I said, putting down my cup. 'Nasty.'

'Very nasty,' said Gerald, nodding. 'Jerry and I were talking about it and I suggested you two might like to take a look. You know – both ends of the spectrum covered. If it's something weird, then Elizabeth can sort it out, and if it's something nasty, then we'll unleash Jones here.'

Jones put down his biscuit – *not* preparatory to being unleashed, I hoped. 'Where is Emily now? Has she had the sense to move out?'

'She has, yes. She's spending a couple of days back with her mother.' He turned to me. 'My sister, Sally. Who had a word with me. The word basically was, "Get it sorted, Jerry, or feel my wrath."'

I'd never met this Sally, but somehow I had no difficulty picturing her as a female version of Jerry.

'I'm assuming she was careful about the whole window-and-door-locking thing,' said Jones. 'Your niece, I mean.'

'Emily? Yes. Every night. Especially since this business started. And before you ask, she's no harum-scarum scatterbrain. Takes after her mother. Calm. Sensible. Rational.'

'Alcohol?'

'Well, they all drink – they're students and it's in the job description – but not to excess. Couple of glasses of cider and that's it. All they can afford as well.'

'They haven't got a still in the cellar?'

'No, cellar's locked. The former landlady still keeps a bit of her stuff in there.'

'Oh?'

'Nothing exciting. Crate of books. Odd bits of furniture. Treadmill. Couple of bikes.'

Jones hadn't finished. 'Drugs?'

I stiffened in case Jerry took offence but he simply shook his head. 'No, none of them. House doesn't smell of anything odd. No eccentric behaviour. No pupils the size of pinpricks or dinner plates. Sally reckons not, as well, and she's an A&E nurse.'

'Who else is in the house?'

'Monica's parents rented it for her when she started at uni. Monica has the big front bedroom. She sublets to Emily, who has the medium room, and Kyle, who's in the little one at the back. And quite happy with that, before anyone asks. Rent's reduced accordingly.'

169

'They all pay rent, then?'

'Yes. Monica's parents took the house only so they knew she'd have somewhere safe, but they all pay rent.'

Jones finished his biscuit and started on another. 'Tell me about them.'

Jerry sighed. 'Well, Monica's studying economics, Emily design, and Kyle sociology. All good kids. Quiet. Well, they're students, of course, but they're quiet for students, let's put it that way. They're all in their first year. Kyle's a bit late with the rent sometimes but he always pays in the end. Emily reckons his parents help him out.'

'Who was the last to move in?'

'Kyle. The girls tried it with just the two of them, but they couldn't make ends meet so they took him in.'

I sat back, thinking.

Jerry mistook my silence. 'You don't have to do it, missis. Just thought I'd ask because, you know, you talked about maybe doing this sort of thing as a business, so I thought there was a chance we could help each other out.'

'And because you're shit-scared of your sister,' said Jones.

'You've met her,' he said.

'Yeah, I have.'

They both looked at me.

'What about it, Cage?' said Jones. 'I'm game if you are. If you're not, then neither am I.' He looked at Jerry. 'We've had a very dodgy day.'

I appreciated the 'we'.

'It wouldn't hurt to take a look,' I said. 'See if we can help. We might not be able to.'

'That's understood.'

170

'We can't do anything today,' said Jones. 'We've received a royal summons for this evening, but how about tomorrow or the day after? We could go round there, meet them, have a bit of a poke about. See if anything jumps out. Although in a student house that's almost certain to happen.'

'Thanks. Appreciated. I'll give Sal a ring and tell her to expect you.'

After we'd finished our tea, Gerald gave us a guided tour around the shop, telling us the histories of various objects. Some were interesting – some were even funny. Nothing strange occurred. No long-dead spirit haunted a particular piece of furniture. There were no sinister creaks or groans emanating from obscure corners. No items flew across the room all by themselves. It was lovely to potter about and chat with friends. We spent a very pleasant half hour and Jones bought himself a letter opener shaped like an Italian stiletto which, he thought, would lend a touch of class to his new desk.

'What new desk?' I said, laughing.

'My new desk in our new office.'

'What new office?'

'We need an office.'

'Whatever for?'

'For protection.'

I blinked at him. 'Protection from what?'

He sighed. 'Because of what we do, Cage. You take the weird stuff and I take the shitheads. Between us, we have everything covered. But – and this is the important bit – shithead or spook, we don't want anything banging on our front doors in the small hours. Basic precaution.'

'But an office?' I said. 'Isn't that a little high profile for us?'

'We need a separate space to operate out of. Somewhere we can lock up at night and walk away from. Therefore – office.'

'Well . . .' I said, still unconvinced.

'And a smart new letter opener for my new desk in our new office.'

I frowned. 'Don't I get a desk?'

'What would you need a desk for? By the time you've made the tea, switched on my laptop, opened the post, nipped out for my mid-morning bacon butty, done some filing, made the tea again, sorted out my dry cleaning, swept and dusted the office and made the tea again, it'll be time to go home.'

Gerald, who was just finishing wrapping the stiletto, stared at him open-mouthed.

Jerry was quite blunt. 'Mate – how are you even still alive?'

'Not for much longer,' I said darkly.

'What?' said Jones, apparently bewildered by our reaction.

I held out my hand to Gerald. '*I'll* carry the knife.'

Gerald grinned. 'I'm afraid to give it to you, lest we're all featured on the evening news tonight. *Bloodbath in sleepy rural town.*'

Jerry came straight back. '*Oppressed office assistant runs amok.*'

And Gerald again. '*Man found face down in river. No one is surprised.*'

I was laughing. Which, if you'd asked me three or four hours ago, was not a thing I thought I'd ever do again. Not this year, anyway.

Jones put his hand on my shoulder. 'Better now?'

'Yes, much.'

'Good. In that case, I shall send you in first this evening.'

172

'Where on earth are you going?' enquired Gerald. 'You make it sound like some sort of trial by ordeal.'

'Dinner with some friends of Cage's.'

I looked up at him. 'Don't you count them as your friends too?'

There was a pause. 'They tolerate me because of you.'

I shook my head. 'Not true. Not in Iblis's case.'

'What about the other one?'

'Hers is not an outgoing, friendly nature, but let's face it, if she didn't have at least some small liking for you, then you'd be dead by now. And she wouldn't need a stiletto knife.'

'True. But I'm still sending you in first.'

I was reluctant to leave Jerry and Gerald, but time was ticking on.

'We just have time for a drink before this evening,' said Jones as we walked across the bridge. 'If you still want to go, that is. Just say the word if you don't feel up to it. You had quite a morning, even by your standards.'

'I'm fine,' I said. 'Jerry and Gerald are the perfect answer to anything sinister. Don't you want to go? Aren't you curious to find out what she wants?'

'I have to say I am quite keen to see what their gaff looks like. Aren't you?'

'Well, when I first met Iblis, he was living in the woods and dining off squirrel, so I'm not sure what we'll get.'

'No wonder he gets so excited over fish and chips. And television must seem like a miracle to him.'

I thought of Iblis's expert handling of Melek's SUV and bit back a smile. This evening promised to be quite interesting.

CHAPTER TWELVE

After all our speculations, their gaff – as Jones insisted on calling it – was lovely. I don't know what I'd been expecting, but given our hosts, I suppose I should have expected the unexpected.

There wasn't time to go home and change so Jones and I stopped at one of the trendy bars in the docks for what Jones referred to as a pre-ordeal drink and I grabbed the opportunity to tidy myself up a little in their very posh toilet. I applied some lipstick and emerged a few minutes later reeking of free hand lotion. Because it had been a work day, I was still wearing my new suit, so I looked reasonably smart, but that didn't stop me feeling somewhat underdressed as we set off for what Jones persisted in calling our last night on this earth.

I knew Melek and Iblis lived in Hartland Warehouse. Just around the corner, Hartland was the last and smallest of the two rows of warehouses bordering the barge arm. While the others all looked very smart now they'd been converted into cafés and pubs at ground level and flats above, Hartland alone retained its pre-renovation shabbiness with many of its windows boarded up and steel shutters across its doors. Almost as if it had been forgotten in the regeneration of ten years ago. All the others had been tarted up, but not, for some reason, this one. And

174

while all the others were six or seven storeys high, Hartland had only three floors.

I'd always thought it was empty. It certainly looked it with its heavy doors and blind windows. You never saw any interior lights.

There was a keypad by the door, however. We pressed the bell and waited. And waited.

'Is anything happening?' said Jones, stepping back to look up. 'Are we even in the right place?'

The door swung silently open – shutter and all – and there stood Iblis, looking just as he always did. Black T-shirt, black combats, big smile, and mischief written all over his face.

'Welcome,' he cried, flinging out his arms in his usual dramatic style. His silver colour reached out towards us. 'It is I, Iblis, who welcomes you to our home. Cast aside your cares and enter.'

I, for one, was very happy to do so. I cast my cares in all directions. Jones, I suspect, clutched his even closer. His was not a care-casting nature.

Iblis closed the door behind us. Now that we were on the inside, I could see there were some pretty hefty locks and bolts on this side of it. I stood looking around while Iblis secured them all. That done, he made a small gesture and muttered a word under his breath. I felt the hairs on the back of my neck lift gently. He had always told me I was safe in my own house because it was warded – nothing could ever get in – and I suspected this one was, as well. Heavily warded.

We were standing in an unprepossessing, narrow, dusty hall with a very inconvenient dog-leg. Anyone breaking in would have an immediate awkward left turn. I wondered if that was deliberate.

The walls were bare brick – and not the modern trendy bricks so beloved of today's interior designers, but ugly, cheap engineering bricks. The floor consisted of bare concrete. Again, not the fashionable, industrial polished stuff but the *slap it down any old how because no one will ever see it* type.

Jones was gazing about him. I had a horrible feeling he was expecting squirrel on the menu after all.

Iblis gestured. 'This way.'

We negotiated the dog-leg and turned right through an arch into a wide space that was obviously their garage. There was the familiar SUV – encased in even more mud than the last time I had seen it – with a shiny black car parked alongside, and a powerful-looking motorbike alongside that. And Iblis hadn't been joking about the skateboard. It was over there, propped against the wall.

I know nothing of motorbikes but Jones paused, impressed. 'Nice.'

Iblis nodded and led us to a big goods lift in the corner. He pulled back the grille, and we stepped inside and clanked our way noisily upwards. I wondered if the lift rattled deliberately. To give notice of approaching visitors. Or people whose intentions might not be entirely friendly.

'We're on the top floor,' said Iblis.

Jones looked around. 'Who's in the middle?'

'No one. It's empty.'

He was surprised. 'You have the whole warehouse to yourself?'

'Yes. Well, not me – Melek.'

'How did she manage that?'

He shrugged. 'No idea. But if she wants a thing, she usually gets it.'

176

Jones was scowling. I hoped very much this wasn't going to be a difficult evening. Not on top of my already difficult day.

The lift opened on to a landing. Another dusty concrete floor and the same brick walls. Three grubby windows let in just enough light to make dim patterns on the floor. The smell was of dust and concrete and disuse. It was very hard to believe anyone could possibly be living here.

Directly opposite the lift stood a pair of heavy metal doors with a completely smooth surface. There were no hinges or handles visible. These were the doors of someone who did not expect all her visitors to be particularly friendly.

Again, I hoped we weren't in for a difficult evening.

The right-hand door swung open and there stood Melek. I'm sure it was only a coincidence that, with the light behind her, she looked even taller and more menacing than usual. Unlike Iblis, her colour, a soft gold, remained firmly in place, rigid and unmoving.

'Welcome to our home,' she said, somewhat stiffly. I don't think she meant to sound ungracious or unfriendly – it was more that the phrase was unfamiliar to her. 'Please come in and be at peace.'

'After you,' said Jones, stepping aside for me to enter.

Nigel bustled up to say hello, stopped halfway and began to scratch. Melek looked down at him. He stopped immediately.

I suppose I should call it a flat – because it was – even though that word really doesn't do it justice because it was . . . amazing. Just amazing. And beautiful. And huge.

As I said, I don't know what I'd been expecting. Something temporary, I think, given the outside of the building and their unsettled lifestyle. A couple of camping beds plus a few basic cooking facilities. They might not even have water laid on.

I was completely wrong. Melek stepped aside. My first impression was of dazzling light and infinite space. The whole top floor lay before me. And while Hartland might have been the least large of all the warehouses, it still wasn't small. This huge space was flooded with light from windows on three sides. The fourth wall, behind me, contained two doors which I guessed led to bathrooms and bedrooms.

A handsome, well-equipped kitchen occupied at least a quarter of the space. Gleaming white tiles and units, dark granite worktops and chrome appliances winked in the low evening sunlight. You could have dropped the entire downstairs of my house in the kitchen area alone.

The rest of the room was their living space and it was even bigger. My downstairs would have fitted three times into this part. And probably still have room to spare.

I say 'they' and 'their', but this was Melek's flat. She'd been here a while now, keeping a discreet eye on me, so of course she'd had time to make a proper home. Until very recently, Iblis had pursued more of a *small tent in the woods with something unknown bubbling over a campfire* lifestyle.

She'd used the space cleverly. There was a seating area with three large sofas around a low table. There was a worktable under the windows, cluttered with what looked like balsa wood models of things my eyes couldn't quite grasp, plans, blueprints, charts, pieces of wood and leather, what looked like a welder's mask and tons of other stuff. I'd love to have had a really good look, but sadly my mother had brought me up to be polite and not rummage through other people's belongings.

On the other side of the room, bookshelves had been placed between the windows with seemingly random ornaments operating as bookends. A reading couch with a side table stood nearby. Here was another person who read more than one book at a time. Two or three lay open on the table; another couple were riddled with bookmarks. One ancient, leather-bound tome seemed to be handwritten in a language I'd never seen before. The symbols were strange. Some were arranged in vertical columns – others in rectangular blocks. Some symbols were larger than others. Ominously, one or two of them were written in red.

'Bound in human skin and written with the blood of virgins,' whispered Jones.

I never knew whether he'd meant to be heard or not. I heard Iblis snort.

Melek turned to face us. 'Cookery book,' she said briefly.

On reflection, that sentence wasn't particularly reassuring.

'An ancient recipe for cooking cattle in red wine,' said Iblis helpfully. He grinned. 'A favourite of Eveth, seventh king of Fradd, famous for his wife, Frith, who could not only sit on her own hair but frequently sat on other people's as well. That's what we're having this evening. The beef in red wine, I mean – not Queen Frith and the hair-sitting thing.'

Jones met his innocent gaze. 'I've been looking forward to it all day,' he said, and the side of Melek's mouth twitched.

I breathed out in relief.

Melek seemed unsure what to do next. I think we all did. This was a very different situation to the casual sessions at my house – me with my feet up on the coffee table, Iblis drinking Jones's beer and Nigel snoring in front of the fire while we avidly digested the latest episode of *Olympian Heights*.

A rather awkward silence fell. I couldn't think of anything to say.

'I like what you've done with the place,' said Jones, saving, if not the whole evening, at least the next few minutes of it.

'Drink?' suggested Iblis. 'It is I, Iblis, who will be your host for the evening, while Melek has many tasks in the kitchen she must attend to.'

She took the hint and disappeared. The atmosphere lightened a little.

We seated ourselves on the very comfortable sofas around the table.

Iblis flourished a bottle of wine and four glasses.

'We should have brought wine,' said Jones to me.

'No need,' said Iblis, catching my eye. His expression of blinding innocence was the most suspicious thing I'd ever seen. I stared at the bottle, which looked strangely familiar. It couldn't be, surely. On the other hand . . . this was Iblis. And that, unless I was very much mistaken, was the unemptyable Bottle of Utgard-Loki. It used to be the Horn of Utgard-Loki but, as Iblis had said, we all need to move with the times.

I opened my mouth, had second thoughts and closed it again. An unemptyable bottle of wine could be just what this evening needed. And I looked forward to seeing Jones rise to the challenge.

Iblis poured four glasses of rich, ruby-red wine, took one to Melek in the kitchen and passed the rest around.

'A toast,' he declared. 'To us.'

'To us,' I said, and sipped. The wine was lovely. I'm not usually a big fan of red wine but this was good stuff. Even Jones nodded his appreciation. Perhaps this wasn't going to be such a bad evening after all.

I settled back and tried to look around without being too

obvious about it. Over to my left, the space between two windows was covered in what looked like framed sketches of faces, torsos and hands, done in charcoal, Conté and ink.

Iblis noticed me looking. 'I, Iblis, invite you to view our treasures. Come.'

He led us to the sketches.

I blinked.

So did Jones. 'These look like . . . Are these genuine?'

'Oh yes,' said Iblis. He pointed at three or four. 'Titian, Botticelli, Leonardo, Michelangelo . . . Some were studies for actual portraits – this one, for instance, was a preliminary sketch for his *David*.' He took up the pose. 'Recognise anyone?'

Jones pulled out his spectacles. 'You're kidding.' He squinted. '*You're David?* I don't believe it.'

'Behave yourself,' said Melek, appearing suddenly behind Iblis. Whether he was being reprimanded for telling the truth or telling porkies was not entirely clear.

Iblis stepped back and pointed. 'Do you recognise this one?'

Jones stared. 'Is that . . . ? Mona Lisa herself?'

I peered more closely. 'She looks . . . different somehow.'

'Pissed as a newt,' said Iblis. 'The only way we could get her to sit still and shut up was to ply her with wine. Unfortunately, she had the capacity of Lake Avernus. There was a very small window between calming her down and oblivion. Obviously, he painted her eyes open in the portrait – and her mouth shut – but believe me, most of the time she was out for the count. We had to prop her up with an old easel and a couple of cushions. Hopeless, of course, and her husband certainly wasn't pleased with the result and tried to get out of paying so we had to send some of the boys round to have a word.'

181

The way he said it left me in no doubt as to who one of the boys would have been.

'We?'

'I am Iblis, man of many skills. I was apprenticed.'

'You were apprenticed to Leonardo da Vinci?'

'Only for a short while. I was chasing something unpleasant that lived on the banks of the Arno, emerging at night to . . .'

'To make off with beautiful young women,' interrupted Jones who, I could see, wasn't buying any of this.

'Old men, actually.'

'Why?'

'We never found out.' He shook his head sadly. 'And then there was that embarrassing business with one of his Virgin paintings.'

Jones blinked. 'Which Virgin?'

'Can't remember – he painted so many of them.' He frowned, apparently in an effort to recall. 'The Annunciation, perhaps . . . ?'

'What exactly was the business with the Virgin?' I enquired.

'I was never quite sure. He said it was to do with his experiments with optics, but I always thought the problem was him starting from the left-hand side of the canvas on Monday, getting pissed that night, and then starting from the right-hand side on Tuesday. Just asking for trouble – as I told him at the time. When he met himself in the middle of the picture, he found he couldn't join the two sides together unless he made the Virgin's arm about nine feet long. Can't remember who commissioned it now and I certainly never thought he'd manage to sell it – not with the Virgin's Muppet arm – but sell it he did. I suspect he plied the client with so much vino they couldn't even see the picture, let alone the arm.' He sighed and gazed into his wine. 'Happy days.'

Jones grinned at me.

'And here,' said Iblis, moving on to one of the bookcases, 'is a piece of the altar from the Temple of Athena at Troy.'

He pointed to a piece of stone propping up half a dozen leather-bound books. I peered at the carved inscription, trying to make it out.

'Luwian,' said Iblis.

'I'm sorry?'

'They spoke Luwian – not Greek.' He said a few strange words.

'What was that?' said Jones suspiciously.

'I welcomed you into our house in the Luwian tongue,' said Iblis, his face an open book of simple innocence. 'What else would I say?'

I gestured around the room, taking in the exquisite rugs – their jewel colours glowing in the light of three or four lovely bronze lamps that looked even older than the rugs themselves – the astrolabe, the artwork, and the small tapestry hanging between the bedroom doors. 'How did you acquire all these lovely things?'

'Souvenirs,' he said briefly.

I saw Jones open his mouth to argue, but at that moment Melek called us over to eat.

'This all smells wonderful,' I said, as we sat down at a small square table. Jones was opposite me, Iblis to my left and Melek to my right. 'What are we having?'

'Coquilles St Jacques,' said Melek. 'Followed by boeuf bourguignon with dauphinoise potatoes. And Iblis has made chocolate pots.'

'My world-famous Chocolate Pots of Great Renown,' said Iblis, obviously feeling he'd been undersold. 'Guaranteed no squirrel.'

I waited a moment, just in case they wanted to say a form of grace, but Iblis picked up his knife and fork and tucked in. 'Mm,' he said to Melek. 'Excellent.'

She smiled slightly and their colours reached out. Nothing dramatic. Just gently touching. I remembered, when I first met him, when he was weighed down with guilt and regret and shame, how his colour would surge towards her. Melek's would recoil and his would creep back to him, rejected and forlorn. Every single time. It had been so sad because he loved her. Loved her with everything he had. How she felt about him, I had no idea. She was always difficult to read.

Now, however, both their colours moved naturally around each other, gently intermingling. Just two friends who had known each other for a very long time, whose relationship had healed after a lengthy rift, and who were now enjoying each other's company again. I was so pleased for them.

The food was delicious and nicely presented. Everything was lovely – the crisp white cloth, the elegant crockery, the small bowl of flowers carefully placed in the centre of the table. They had obviously gone to a great deal of trouble to make the evening pleasant. The least we could do, as guests, was to respond appropriately.

By unspoken consent, we kept the conversation strictly non-controversial. No gods were mentioned. Felda obviously wasn't the reason for this evening. What the actual reason was I still had no idea, but I was certain there had to be some purpose behind the invitation. I wasn't going to ask, though. I'd leave it to them to introduce whatever it was in their own time and in their own way.

We admired the flat and the food. The unemptyable Bottle of Utgard-Loki went around several times and more than lived up to its name. Even I had a second glass and I don't drink a lot as a rule. There are things that live on the very edge of consciousness, and alcohol can sometimes open a door to something best not invited in. And I definitely don't like that feeling of not being quite in control of myself. Because if I'm not in control, then something else might be. There are always things – unpleasant things – looking for an opportunity to force their way through into this world.

This evening, however, I recklessly embarked on a second glass and waited to see which of them would introduce the burning topic of the evening.

'Have you lived here long?' enquired Jones, holding out his glass for another refill. His colour was close and still but I could see he was beginning to relax. He might even start to enjoy the evening if he wasn't careful.

'Yes, I've been here – in this place – for some years now. Iblis only moved in fairly recently. After . . . Christmas. To . . . recover.'

We all veered away from last Christmas.

'Iblis tells us you have the whole building?' enquired Jones. She nodded.

'Wow,' I said, feeling somewhat . . . flushed. 'This place is huge. You must pay a fortune in council tax.' And stopped, embarrassed, because my mother always said it was rude to talk about money.

There was a baffled silence. I saw Jones grin to himself.

Melek turned to me. For enlightenment, presumably. 'Council . . . tax?'

'Yes,' I said. 'You know. The money you pay to the council for your property and the services they provide.'

She looked at Iblis and there was more baffled silence as they both grappled with this novel concept.

Jones was openly grinning at them. 'I shouldn't ask this but I'm going to anyway,' he said. 'Does the council even know you're here?'

Iblis waved his fork in a manner that managed to be both vague and discouraging of any further questioning in that area.

No one spoke for a while.

'So, tell us,' said Iblis, carefully casual, and I could tell by his colour – this was it. This was why we were here tonight. 'Tell us about your plans for the future. I understand you are to seek out situations where your expertise might prove . . . useful.'

'I doubt we'll have to seek them out,' said Jones, sipping his wine. 'In our experience, situations like that seem to happen to us wherever we go. In fact, we might have one job already.'

'Really?'

'Though our current problem is where we'll operate from. We were discussing it this afternoon.' He turned to Iblis. 'We don't want people knowing where we live. We don't want them knowing our private email addresses or telephone numbers. And we certainly don't want something that might, or might not, be human following us home one night.'

I nodded. 'I suppose we could move in together and operate out of the other property, but then that property's compromised. And Jones likes his flat and I love my house.'

Melek picked up the dish of potatoes and offered it to Jones. 'Yes, I can see that would be a problem.'

He took the dish and helped himself. 'Thank you. Sadly, we don't all have your advantages when it comes to flying under the official radar.'

Iblis and Melek looked at each other across the table. What was going on?

'Well,' she said. 'We might be in a position to assist you.'

'How?' said Jones, at exactly the same time I asked, 'In what way?'

'And why?' he went on. 'Why would you do that?'

'Because,' said Iblis, 'both of us – Melek and I – in our separate ways, owe Elizabeth Cage a great debt. This is a small – a very small – gesture towards repaying that debt.'

'Really,' said Jones, carefully neutral. 'And how exactly are you to set about repaying this debt?'

'Well,' said Iblis, 'we would like to offer you a part of this building to use as your business premises. A room on the ground floor. There is a separate entrance – your comings and goings would be nothing to do with us. There is water and power. And you would be able to piggyback off our WiFi.'

I looked at Jones to see how he was coping with Iblis's use of the term *piggybacking off our WiFi*. However, he remained silent and I was too astonished to speak at all.

'There is a security camera at the front door,' continued Iblis. 'You would be able to monitor all your callers. The door is industrial-strength security. You'd need a tank or a dragon to break through it. Won't keep out the demons, of course, but it would deter any human thugs who might be after you. What do you think?'

Jones laid down his spoon and wiped his mouth on his napkin.

'We've had a lovely meal, and you've obviously gone to a great deal of time and trouble, for which I thank you, and I hate to be the one to break up the evening, but this is clearly just another scheme of yours to ensure Cage is still under surveillance.'

This was going well, wasn't it?

Melek sighed. 'To some extent – yes. But before you raise objections, consider this. You will both be ... not exactly placing yourself in harm's way, but you will certainly attract attention. From both worldly and otherworldly sources. Surely these are basic precautions you should be considering. And if the worst does come to the worst – we would not be that far away. I urge you to consider the advantages rather than the disadvantages.'

I think if she'd denied their motives or tried to downplay Jones's concerns, then that would have been the end of the matter, but her reasonable response gave him pause. He picked up his spoon again and frowned at his chocolate pot.

Iblis turned to me. 'Your thoughts, Elizabeth Cage?'

I was halfway down my second glass of wine and now people wanted intelligent comment from me. And coherency.

'I can see the advantages,' I said to Jones. 'But I think security matters come under your remit, so I'm content to leave this decision to you.' I gulped down a little more wine and returned to my own dessert.

I could see he wasn't happy – his colour was more red than gold. I could see Melek wasn't either. She'd made a genuine offer – an olive branch – and it was being rejected. I looked up. Iblis was watching me. He's by no means the airhead he'd like you to think he is. I flashed a quick, meaningful glance at Melek and Iblis flung himself into the breach.

'Has Nigel peed in the corner again?'

Her head whipped round. 'What?'

We all regarded Nigel, flat out in his bed, legs in the air, and not something you'd want people of a nervous disposition to encounter.

'No, he hasn't,' she said.

But the difficult moment had passed.

'Why don't we go down and have a look?' suggested Iblis. 'After we've finished dessert, of course. Let me top up everyone's glasses.'

'You're going to need another bottle,' said Jones.

'No need,' said Iblis. 'Tonight we enjoy the bounteous gifts of the unemptyable Bottle of Utgard-Loki.'

'The what?'

'Just drink,' I said to him, smiling somewhat muzzily.

We finished with coffee, made with the latest top-of-the-range gleaming chrome coffee maker sitting on the worktop. The conversation ran fairly smoothly – all things considered – and when our cups were empty, there was a slight pause and then Iblis got to his feet, gestured towards the door, and we all went down to inspect our possible new premises.

We had to go outside and then in again. Physically, this part of the building was separate from the other. Iblis unlocked the door and pushed it open, Melek flicked on the light, and in we went.

I was actually quite excited – although that might have been the wine. This could represent yet another new chapter in my life. I had a job, I had my own transport, and now I might have a business partnership with Jones, as well. My life was changing

189

beyond all recognition. And it was a little scary, too. I pulled myself together, frowned with intelligence and concentrated.

The room was just the right size. Not too big, but not poky, either. Brick walls and grimy concrete floor, but that could be dealt with. There was a dusty window. I looked up – yes, office strip lighting with the covers full of traditional dead flies. 'It was an office once,' announced Iblis. 'Toilet and sink through there.' He nodded towards a door in the corner.

I stood and thought. This could work. This end of the barge arm was quieter but there would still be a reasonable footfall. And it had a good feel about it. I waited to see what Jones would say.

He was prowling around, peering at the walls, scuffing the floor with his foot. I had no idea why. Perhaps it was something prospective new owners did. He opened the other door and stared at the toilet in a critical manner. Again, I had no idea why. I was beginning to suspect that two and a half glasses of wine might not be contributing anything useful to my ability to . . . contribute anything useful. I shook my head. That was not a sentence on which I should have embarked without giving consideration to the ending. Surreptitiously, I leaned against a wall.

Eventually, Jones finished his perambulation and stood in front of me. Aha. He was going to ask my opinion.

'What do you think, Cage?'

I decided to play it cool. I would be Mrs Enigmatic. Not giving anything away. Maintaining a tough bargaining position.

'It's fabulous,' I said, the words tumbling over themselves in my enthusiasm. 'Just what we were looking for. Or would be if we had been. Looking, I mean.'

He sighed and looked at Iblis. 'Well, the brains of the outfit quite likes it.'

Hey, how about that? I was the brains of the outfit. Who knew? I leaned back against the wall, again. Just for a moment.

'We could get a couple of second-hand desks,' he said. 'Easy enough to pick up. But good chairs are important because back problems are a bitch. No landline, Cage, we'll get a couple of extra mobiles for business use only. No one will know where we live or any of our personal contact details.' He frowned. 'We'll probably need a WiFi extender. Or our own hot spot. And the tea things over there by the socket.'

'Filing cabinet?' I said.

'I don't think we want to write anything down, Cage, do you?'

'But,' I said, 'surely there will be official paperwork. Invoices? Bills? Electric and so forth?'

'And rent,' said Jones. He looked at Iblis and Melek. 'Who pays the utilities?'

It might have been the wine, but I thought they looked mildly baffled.

'And did we resolve the question of council tax?'

They exchanged glances. Melek shrugged.

'All right,' said Iblis. '*We'll* cover this . . . this . . . ?' He stopped.

'Council tax,' I said.

'Council tax. And electricity and water.'

Jones frowned. 'Do you actually pay for electricity and water?'

Iblis waved this aside as irrelevant.

'Rent?' persevered Jones.

Iblis scratched his head. 'How about – we take a percentage of your takings? Ten per cent of whatever you make. Payable on the first of each month,' he said, presumably in an effort to look businesslike. 'We only take cash,' he added, completely ruining the effect.

Jones turned to me. 'What do you think?'

'Seems like a good deal to me,' I said, because it did.

'You'll provide your own furniture and equipment,' said Iblis.

I nodded. Jones was still looking for a flaw.

'Starting officially on the first of next month,' I said.

Everyone nodded.

'OK then,' said Jones. 'If my partner is happy . . . ?'

'I am,' I said, wondering if more coffee might be beneficial.

'In that case – done.'

'Great,' said Iblis with relief. 'We shall return to the feast and drink to our success.' He wheeled about, shouting, 'More wine!'

Oh my God. I couldn't believe it. This was actually happening. We'd talked about it – on and off – but it hadn't seemed real to me. Now, suddenly, it was.

'We'll start with Jerry's niece,' said Jones as we slowly made our way home. The pavement was very uneven. 'Our first job, Cage. I'll give Jerry a ring and we'll go and see her . . .' He threw me an appraising look as I weaved my way around a lamppost. 'The day *after* tomorrow.'

'We're really doing this,' I said, still in a state of shock.

'We are, Cage. Looking forward to it?'

'Yes. Yes, I am.' I think perhaps the wine was beginning to wear off. 'But . . . I mean . . . what about tax and paperwork and . . .'

'Well, your friend Melek doesn't seem too bothered, so why should we be?'

'But when the authorities find out . . . ?'

He sighed. 'I thought it wouldn't be long before your touching but misplaced faith in the authorities surfaced again. Think about it, Cage. How long has she been living there without them knowing anything about it? I don't think we need worry. It'll be one of the few advantages of being under their umbrella. In fact, look at it this way – they've used you for their purposes and now it's time they gave something back. It's a good deal for us. I propose we give it six months and see how it goes. If we don't get any clients, then we'll just thank them politely and hand it all back. There's no risk to us at all. And virtually no financial outlay. And, looking on the bright side, the chances are that some tentacled monstrosity will get us long before the council does, so we don't have anything to worry about, do we?'

'Yes – you're absolutely right.'

He grinned. 'You should drink that second glass of wine more often. It's doing wonders for your appreciation of your business partner.'

I would never drink that second glass of wine again. I had real trouble getting up the hill. In the end I tucked my arm into Jones's and let him tow me along. Halfway up my mobile rang.

I couldn't think who could possibly be ringing me at this time of night.

'Do you recognise the number, Cage?'

I shook my head.

'Don't answer it if you don't want to.'

I couldn't not answer it. I didn't get many calls.

'Hello?'

A female voice, young and breathless, said, 'Can I speak to Mrs Cage?'

'Speaking.'

'Mrs Cage, you told me to remember . . .'

'Remember what? Who is that?'

'It's—'

The voice broke off. I heard another voice, speaking sharply, but before I could make out the words, the line went dead.

I stared at the blank screen.

'What was that all about?' said Jones.

'I don't know.' I sighed. 'This really has not been the best day I've ever had.'

'No,' he said quietly. 'I'm taking you up on your offer to stay the night, so don't argue, Cage.'

'I wasn't going to,' I said wearily.

I do remember there was more blood on my step again that night.

194

CHAPTER THIRTEEN

The next day was very quiet. I used my indoor voice.

I was awoken mid-morning by Jones bringing me a mug of tea. Being the size he was, he'd had to sleep on the floor because he didn't fit on to the sofa. No matter how we arranged him there had been considerable overhang. The wine and I had had a fit of the giggles. Now, I was blinking at the tea and wondering who had glued my mouth together.

Around about lunchtime we enjoyed a gentle breakfast. Jones logged on to my laptop and scoured the web for second-hand office furniture. There was plenty about – we wouldn't have any problems getting just what we wanted.

I did as little as possible, as quietly as possible.

The day after that we went to see Jerry's sister, Sally. By some strange coincidence, she lived on the same estate as the Painswicks. Only a few streets away, but in a modern semi-detached rather than a bungalow.

Everything was as neat as a new pin. The tiny front garden was well maintained. The conventional square lawn was surrounded by flower borders bright with bedding plants. The drive was clear, the windows shone and the brass door knocker gleamed in the mid-morning sunshine.

Sally looked so much like Jerry I couldn't believe it. Same colour, too. Brown, steady, sensible.

'I didn't really want Emily to live out,' she said, as we sat around the kitchen table with a pot of tea between us. 'There was no need for it. She could easily have stayed here.'

'I think you've both got the best of the deal,' said Jones, stirring his tea. 'She's living out, being a student, enjoying her freedom and so on, but you have the reassurance of knowing she's only just over the other side of town, rather than the other end of the country.'

She nodded. 'That's what Jerry says and I suppose he's right, but I don't like what's been happening in that house.'

'What's Emily like?' Jones asked.

She laughed. 'You're asking her mother?'

He laughed too. 'Who better?'

'Well, she looks a lot like me. She's very quiet. She's never really given me any trouble at all. No massive teenage meltdowns. No drugs – and I'd know, before you say anything.'

I remembered Sally was a nurse in A&E.

'She tries to drink but doesn't really like it. There's only ever been the two of us since her dad walked out. He didn't quite do the traditional *just popped out for some cigarettes and never came back* routine, but he moved away – for his job, he said – and we never saw him again. No way to contact him. No financial support for me or Emily. To be fair – he wasn't much of a loss.'

'A bit of a shock, though,' said Jones.

'Initially, yes. And it wasn't easy to begin with. I'd probably have taken him back if he'd asked. Which would have been a huge mistake. Six months later, I'd realised how much better I could do without him. The only reason I'd welcome him back now is to give him the good kicking he so deserves.'

'And Emily?'

'Same, I think. Obviously, in the beginning, she kept asking where he was and when he was coming back, but as time went on, the questions became less and less frequent. Now she never asks at all.'

'OK,' said Jones. 'Please don't bludgeon me senseless with the teapot – could she be in contact with her father and not told you? For any reason – not necessarily sinister. I just want to get an idea of Emily and her world.'

'It's possible,' said Sally, 'but not likely, I think. Why would he? Money is the only reason he'd ever come back and neither of us has any. I mean, I have my job, and we have just enough. But Emily's a student – they're not noted for their spending power.'

'Any thoughts about this business?'

She shook her head. 'None. I mean, initially I thought it was Kyle playing some sort of silly trick. But this latest thing . . . the face-licking . . . that's a bit more serious, don't you think?'

'I do, yes,' said Jones. He drained his mug just as the front door banged.

Sally looked up. 'Here she is now.'

Emily was a younger Sally. And I could see Jerry in her, as well. And her colour was also brown, just like Jerry's. Except while his was still and serene, hers was jumpy and nervous. Orange anxiety hovered around the edges. She was considerably more upset than she was letting on.

'We have one of those houses behind Hanover Square,' she said, dropping her backpack on the floor as Sally poured her tea. 'Thanks, Mum. There's three of us – me, Monica and Kyle.'

197

'And you all get on?'

'We do. We don't actually see a lot of each other. Monica has a boyfriend – Elliott. I'm busy with my studies.' She looked up, laughing. 'And I'm not just saying that because Mum's here. She and Uncle Jerry made sacrifices to give me this opportunity. I'm not going to waste it.' She smiled warmly at her mother.

She was telling the truth. Emily was exactly what she seemed. A nice girl. Family-oriented. Conscientious. Polite.

Jones smiled at her. 'And Kyle?'

'Kyle? Well, we – Monica and I – always describe him as aimless but harmless. He doesn't always pull his weight around the house, but if you throw his smelly socks at him, then he usually takes the hint and clears his stuff away.'

'When did these events start?'

She frowned. 'I think . . . just after Christmas.'

'Tell me about them.'

She sighed and put down her tea. 'I remember three definite instances. I think there were a few other times when I thought something was in my bedroom, but I was sleepy and convinced myself I'd imagined it. The first one that I remember clearly was last month. I woke up thinking I could hear breathing, but it was too cold and I was too sleepy to get out of bed and investigate. I just pulled the covers over my head and went back to sleep.

'The second time I could definitely hear breathing. I sat up and said, "Who's there?" No one answered – obviously – and everything stopped for a while after that. There was no more night-time breathing. The third time – I woke up to see someone standing at the bottom of my bed. I hadn't drawn the curtains and I could see a shape against the window.'

198

'Could you hear breathing that time?' asked Jones.

'I don't think so. I don't remember. Yes. No. I don't know. Sorry.'

'It's OK,' said Jones. 'Not a problem. So that was three times at least. Probably more. Then what happened?'

She pushed her mug away from her. 'The other night, I woke up. For a moment I didn't know why. And then there was breath on my face – and then . . .' Her voice wobbled. 'And then something warm and wet licked my face. All up one side. From my chin all the way to my hairline.'

'What did you do?'

Her face creased. 'Nothing. It was . . . it was horrible. I couldn't . . . I just froze . . . I couldn't move. I couldn't believe . . . It was so awful. And then it did it again. Drool ran down my face. And it smelled. Stale and horrible. And that was even worse. I didn't dare move in case . . . in case it did it again and . . .'

Her colour was jumping around all over the place and deepening with every second.

I tried to smile at her. 'It's all right. You described it very well. We don't need to talk about it any longer. Drink your tea.'

She nodded and picked up her mug with shaking hands.

Sally looked at us. 'It's that Kyle, isn't it?'

'It can't be,' said Emily, somewhat wildly. 'My door was locked. And the window. I was very, very careful. There was no way to get in. And no way to get out either. Unless they unlocked the door or windows. Which they didn't.'

'And I'm guessing when you turned on the light, there was nothing there. Do you have a bedside light?'

She shook her head. 'Money's a bit tight . . . you know how

199

it is. There's an overhead light. I keep looking at the student notice boards for a cheap bedside lamp but nothing so far.'

Jones nodded as if this was perfectly normal. 'Do you have a cord over the bed, to turn the light on?'

She shook her head again. 'No, I have to get out of bed and find the switch over by the door.'

'How long did it take you to get the light on?'

'Well, I was in such a panic that I tried to get out of bed without throwing off the quilt first and I got a bit tangled up. When I eventually sorted myself out, I had to get across the room. Then I ran into the wardrobe door which had swung open, and hurt myself. I found the wall, groped about a bit because I was panicking and finally found the light switch. Probably about fifteen to twenty seconds. Possibly more.'

'And when the light came on, obviously the room was empty.'

'Yes.'

'And the door?'

'Locked. Definitely locked. I remember scrabbling at the key because my hands were shaking so much.'

'Then what?'

'I went straight into the bathroom and washed my face. Several times. Then I went downstairs and made myself a mug of tea. I slept on the sofa. Well, I wrapped myself in a throw and huddled on the sofa until the sun came up. Then I told Monica what had happened. She stood in my room with me while I grabbed a few things and came home. She was nearly as upset as I was.'

'Who was in the house that night?'

'All of us. And on the other nights as well.'

'No one staying over with any of you?'

'Well, Elliott, probably. He's there with Monica most nights.'

'OK. Well, you've been really helpful. Do you mind if we go over there and look at your room? We won't disturb anything, I promise. We just want to look.'

'Do I have to . . . ?'

He smiled at her. 'Come if you want to, by all means, but we don't need you.'

'Then I won't. If you don't mind.'

'Do both Monica and Kyle know why you left?'

'Yes, they were really upset.'

'They believed you?'

'Yes. Well, they said they did. Actually, I think Monica's a bit scared now as well.'

'Can you give her a ring and tell her we're coming over?'

'OK.'

'And can we have your keys? Just in case. Mrs Cage and I will take a look. You carry on as normal, if you can.'

She stood up. 'Yes, I have a lecture at three.'

'OK. We'll come and see you again.' He stood up. 'Mrs Blundell – Sally, thank you for the tea. We'll talk soon.'

'Did we mention money?' said Jones as we walked back down the road.

I stopped. 'No – I forgot.'

'Me too. Have we even discussed what we'll charge?'

'No.'

He sighed. 'We're never going to be rich, are we?'

Kyle let us in. Obviously he had no lectures that day. No lectures that he was attending, anyway.

The house was typical student accommodation. Sparsely

furnished and in need of modernising. They'd had a curry fairly recently. The kitchen was at the rear, overlooking a tiny yard. The sitting room's bay window looked out over the street. Two saggy sofas faced the TV and there was a bookcase stuffed with a mixture of textbooks and paperbacks. Every electrical socket I could see had some sort of charger dangling from it.

The stairs were narrow and dark and quite steep. Upstairs there was a tiny bathroom at the back and a very small bedroom – more of a box room, really. That would be Kyle's room. Monica's was the one at the front, quite large and with two windows, and Emily's was in the middle.

I didn't like the look of Kyle. Not one bit. But that didn't make him the guilty party. I smiled politely. Fortunately, he didn't offer to shake hands.

He was a typical immature adolescent. Tall, skinny, but with a curiously flat face. I wondered if he realised he was everyone's prime suspect. Including mine. His colour swirled between a kind of khaki green and browny-yellow. I would have expected more orange anxiety to show but its movements were slow and sluggish. I didn't like that, either, but as I said, I shouldn't let that prejudice me.

'Um . . . would you like some tea? Or coffee?'

He opened the fridge, took out a carton of milk, sniffed it and recoiled slightly. Rummaging, he pulled out another, clearly marked *Monica's milk – hands off you thieving toerag Kyle.*

I noticed now that two of the cupboards were padlocked. I suspected these belonged to Monica and Emily. They weren't great big massive padlocks but they were definitely sending a message. I'd never been to university but obviously it wasn't all sex, drugs and missed lectures. There were Milk Wars as well.

'Not for me,' I said quickly, remembering his recoil. 'But thank you.'

'Nor me,' said Jones.

Before Kyle could offer anything even more dubious in the hospitality area, we heard a key in the lock. It was Monica. She was very petite, dark, and extremely pretty, sparkling with life and the joy of it. This sparkle was reflected in her colour – a deep, rich, glowing indigo – and its restless movement reminded me very much of Iblis.

Kyle greeted her with relief. 'Can I use your milk? I'm desperate for a coffee.' He paused. 'Can I borrow some coffee as well. Please.'

She smiled sunnily. 'Of course you can.'

'Aw – thanks, Mon.'

She whipped open a cupboard door and flourished a beer mug in front of him. It was full of fifty-pence pieces.

Kyle's face fell. 'Actually, I'm a bit skint at the moment.'

'Then no.'

'Aw . . .'

She replaced the mug and closed the door.

Kyle groaned and began to rummage in his pockets. 'I think I've got . . .'

Penny by penny, he assembled fifty pence on the worktop. And a fair amount of fluff and what might have been biscuit crumbs as well.

Monica looked at it with distaste, reminding me very much of Melek. 'I am not touching any of that.'

For one moment she sounded exactly like her as well.

Kyle sighed and swept the pile of loose change into the beer mug. 'All right now?'

She nodded.

We all watched Kyle depart with his coffee and then she turned to us. 'You're Emily's friends?'

'We are,' said Jones. 'We don't want to get in your way – just to take a quick look around.' He paused. 'I think I've got fifty pence somewhere.'

She laughed prettily. 'No, you're all right. Emily told me.'

'We've got the layout of the house,' said Jones, 'and now we'd like to look in her room.'

'OK. This way.'

She led the way up the stairs and paused at the door.

'We do have Emily's permission to look around,' said Jones.

Monica took the hint and left us to it.

'I used to live in a place like this,' said Jones as she disappeared downstairs. 'When I was a kid. I wonder . . .' He stepped back and looked up at the tiny loft hatch.

I sighed, because I could see whose job it would be to check that out. He'd barely be able to get his head through the hole.

'Right,' he said briskly. 'A bit of on-the-job training. The first thing to do is look. Not just at what we've come to see but all around. Look for ways out before you look for ways in. You never know when you might have to run for it, and obviously we want to run to safety, not hurl ourselves into even greater peril. So – if we open the door and there's a socking great dragon in there, then you head straight down the stairs and out through the front door.'

'And where will you be?'

'Belgium,' he said briefly.

He opened the door using Emily's key and, as per instructions, I stood on the threshold and looked.

'Tell me what you see.'

I drew a breath. 'A narrow room, not large. Doesn't get a lot of light. One tall window at the far end. One bed, one wardrobe, one old dressing table cum desk. A painted wooden chair. Ghastly wallpaper, mostly obscured by various posters. Scruffy carpet. Half-drawn curtains. One's been wrenched back. Wardrobe door open and a blue sweatshirt on the floor which she might have dropped on the way out since the rest of the room is quite tidy. The bed's unmade. Drawers half open. Signs someone departed in a hurry, perhaps. No smell of cigarettes or . . . anything. Just a bit stuffy.'

'Doesn't look as if anyone's been in here since she left,' said Jones. 'Or any*thing*, of course, suggesting . . . ?'

'It's Emily that's the target, rather than the room or the house,' I said. 'Although whatever it was didn't follow her back to her mother's house.'

'Possibly too scared of the redoubtable Sally,' he said absently. 'Right, I'm going to have a look around – I'll give you a running commentary. You stay back.'

'Why?'

'Different perspective.'

'Oh. Not just staying out of your way, then?'

'Not at all. Although yes, a little bit.'

I noticed the light switch was just inside the door and the bed was as far away from the door as possible. Jones inspected the lock, which was good quality, he said. Reputable firm. Pickable but not easily.

'Duplicate key?' I said, keen to contribute.

'Her key was in the lock so no one would be able to get in from the outside whether they had a duplicate or not.'

205

The dressing table under the window held a neat pile of books, a mug of pens and two notepads. In her hurry to get out, she'd taken her laptop with her but left the charger.

Jones unplugged it and put it in his pocket. 'We'll take it round to her.' He knelt to check under the bed.

An old-fashioned dark wood wardrobe stood against the short wall, the door still open. Remembering what Emily'd said about the door, I touched it. It moved slightly. I closed it and waited. It stayed closed. I bounced gently.

'What are you doing?' said Jones, withdrawing his head from under the bed.

'Emily said the door had swung open – I'm trying to get it to . . . yes.'

The door swung open. The catch was broken and I suspected the floor wasn't level, which tilted the wardrobe forwards very slightly. That would be why the door had swung open in the night when she ran into it. Easily fixed, though. All she needed to do was wedge it with a piece of card and it would be fine.

I looked down. Yes, there was the piece of card, half under the wardrobe itself. I picked it up and wedged the door closed.

A second later, the card fell out and the door swung open again.

Jones had his head out of the window, looking up and down the building. 'No nearby downspouts to climb up or roofs to climb down,' he said, pulling his head back in and closing the window. 'Just unbroken vertical walls.'

I walked slowly around the room, checking out the posters, all of current bands whose names meant nothing to me. Their average age appeared to be about twelve years old.

I sighed. To me, everything looked quite normal. A bit shabby perhaps, but definitely normal.

Jones had his head in the wardrobe. I could hear the sounds of hangers being shoved aside.

I should justify my existence, so I sat at the desk and tried to let my mind drift because sometimes that works. I closed my eyes. No – there wasn't anything. When I opened them again, Jones was next door, talking to Kyle, who said something and they both laughed.

I walked slowly around again, but it was just a bedroom. Our first job looked like being a bit of a failure.

For something to do, I stood in the doorway and looked up again at the loft hatch.

'Anything?' said Jones, closing Kyle's door behind him.

'No, I've got nothing.'

He frowned. 'How would you fancy spending the night in Emily's room?'

'Would you still be in Belgium?'

'I could be if that's what you want, but actually, I thought you'd prefer me to be on the premises somewhere.'

'Why can't you spend the night in this room and I'll be on the premises somewhere?'

'Because I'm not young and female. OK – plan of action. We'll go back downstairs and tell them we haven't found anything out of the ordinary. Which is perfectly true, Cage. Always tell the truth where possible. And if you're going to lie – make it a big one. Politicians do it all the time and it works for them.'

'Tonight . . .' I said, dragging him back to the business in hand.

'Yes. We'll tell them that on the strength of our inspection and report, Emily has reluctantly agreed to return tonight. We'll

207

escort her here – see her settled and then depart. In reality, you'll swap with her and I'll take her home.'

'Leaving me alone with the face-licker.'

'But not for very long. Ten minutes – tops.'

'How will you get back in?'

'Emily's key. I'll let myself in when everyone's in bed. You won't see or hear me, Cage, but I'll be around, I promise.'

I sighed. 'All right.'

'You're a trouper, Cage.'

Monica was waiting for us in the kitchen, her indigo colour streaked with anxiety. She was more than a little bit suspicious of us.

She barely gave us time to sit down. 'What do you think it is?'

'No idea at this stage,' said Jones cheerfully. 'You?'

She shook her head. 'I don't know what to think. Initially I thought something just startled her awake – like a noise in the street – and she was sleepy and imagined it. And then it happened again. And then again. I told her to lock her door – my dad had locks put on all the bedroom doors before I moved in – and to make sure her window was shut as well, although I don't know what – I mean *who* – could climb up the outside wall and get in.'

'Or down, either,' said Jones.

She looked puzzled. 'How . . . ?'

'From the roof,' he said.

'But how would they get down off the roof?'

He pointed upwards. 'Through your loft hatch.'

She went a little pale.

'Don't worry,' he said. 'Your hatch is very small.'

'I'll ask my dad to put a padlock on it.'

'Good idea. And only one key. Keep it yourself. Anyone wanting to be up there will have to ask you for it.'

I had a sudden picture of something lizard-like running up the back wall. Not a nice picture. I tried very hard to put it from my mind.

'All right. How is Emily – is she OK?'

'She's fine. Talking about coming back tonight. We'll stay with her for a while. See her safely settled and so on. Provide a reassuring presence.'

'You will?' Monica looked at me.

I smiled and nodded. Because I'm a trouper.

CHAPTER FOURTEEN

I went home and packed an overnight bag.

'You took your time,' said Jones, meeting me at the bottom of the hill.

'Well, obviously it's not easy selecting the appropriate gear for having my face licked in the dark by something unpleasant.'

'I can imagine,' he said thoughtfully. 'What did you go for in the end?'

'Kimono, beekeeper's hat and wellingtons.'

'You're supposed to be attracting weirdos, Cage, not frightening the living daylights out of them.'

I gave it up and we set off for the students' house. Monica let us in. 'Emily's on her way back. Come into the kitchen.'

I could see at once Monica wasn't happy. She'd had time to think things over while we'd been gone. Was she regretting having Emily as a housemate? I didn't blame her, but I couldn't see this problem going away by itself. Even if this was just an unpleasant hoax – or what Jones would consider 'typical Elizabeth Cage weird stuff' – it needed to be addressed. Before it escalated into something more serious. I caught his glance and flicked my eyes to Monica.

'Smells good,' he said casually. 'Spag bol?'

'Yes.'

'You should have said – I'd have brought along a nice Chianti.'

She grinned. 'And some fava beans? What are fava beans, anyway?'

'Broad beans,' he said. 'Very tasty in their place . . .'

'But not in spag bol.'

'Definitely not.'

Her colour relaxed a little.

'I lived off pasta for three years when I was at Exeter,' Jones said chattily. 'Made me what I am today.'

I sighed. 'I suspect the Italian Tourist Board would be upset to hear you say so.'

Monica smiled reluctantly.

'Do you always cook supper?' said Jones.

'Usually,' she said. 'I enjoy cooking.' She scowled. 'Although my efforts aren't always appreciated.'

'Tell me about it,' said Jones and a moment later, the two of them were knee-deep in recipes. I could see her thawing. Her colour was brightening by the moment as she grew more reconciled to us – well, to Jones, anyway. I cast my mind back to the day I'd met him and wondered if I'd been so easily and quickly charmed. I'd like to think I wasn't, but I have my doubts.

Emily came in, gave us an uncertain smile, and went up to her room. Kyle turned up about five minutes later. I don't know where he'd been but he wasn't heaving around the traditional student backpack stuffed full of books, notebooks and tablets, so he probably hadn't been attending lectures.

We all sat around the kitchen table. There was just about room for all of us. The spag bol was delicious and both Jones and I said so. Every scrap disappeared.

'Well,' said Kyle, dropping his fork and spoon back into his bowl and pushing himself back up from the table, 'I'm off out. See you later.'

'Dishes,' said Monica and Emily in unison. They didn't even look up, so Kyle skipping out without doing the dishes was obviously a regular thing.

He sighed and began to fill the sink. There was a great deal of dish-clattering – which both girls ignored. I watched his colour. That greeny-brown thing . . .

'All done,' he said, wiping his hands. 'I'm off to the students' union. What about you, Em? Fancy a pint?'

Following instructions, Emily shook her head. 'Not tonight, thanks, Kyle. Tomorrow, perhaps.'

To his credit, he hesitated. 'Monica's going out tonight as well. You all right here on your own?'

Emily nodded. 'Have to be, won't I?'

'And we'll be staying for a while,' said Jones. 'We'll make sure everything's OK before we leave.'

'OK then. I'm off.' He made himself scarce, slamming the front door behind him.

'I'm off too,' said Monica, getting up. 'I'm meeting Elliott at the Cider Tree. You'll be OK, Emily?'

Emily smiled faintly. 'Early night for me.'

Monica hovered uncertainly. 'Well, OK then. You'll, um . . .'

'I'll be fine,' said Emily, obviously not believing a word she herself was saying.

'Well, Elliott's coming back with me. We won't be late. If you think everything will be . . . um . . .'

'Everything will be fine,' said Jones easily. 'We might even still be here when you get back. Enjoy yourselves.'

212

I think Monica was glad to get away. This situation was such a shame. Three young people who should be enjoying their time at university and instead had to cope with . . . whatever was happening here.

She closed the door behind her – much more quietly than Kyle.

Jones turned to Emily. 'I'll drive you home.'

She protested. 'It's only around the corner.'

'Go out the back way; I'll pick you up at the end of the street. Don't leave your mother's house tonight.'

'Are you . . . ? Do you think something will happen?'

'No. But I want to be able to concentrate on here and not have to worry about you.'

I noticed he had no qualms about leaving me on my own and said so.

He grinned. 'Cage, my heart goes out to anyone trying anything with you. Ready when you are, Emily.'

They disappeared. I stayed sitting at the table for a moment, just letting my mind drift . . . There wasn't anything. Just an elderly house, shabby but with good bones, smelling of spaghetti bolognese rather than curry. There was the occasional creak as it settled for the night.

I checked the back door was locked, went into the living room, switched on the light and left the door open. I did the same with the hall and landing. I went upstairs and checked over the bathroom.

Monica's bedroom was locked. Kyle's wasn't. There was a single bed, heaped with clothes, and another wardrobe similar to Emily's, although this one had a working door. That was it – there wasn't really room for anything else. It had a certain atmosphere but the smell was locker-room lilac, rather than decomposing bodies. I switched off the light and closed the door. The house seemed very silent.

Back out on the landing, I paused for a moment, looking up at the loft hatch again. Jones had been right – it was on the small side. Not much could get through there. I probably could, but not him.

I paused, to let my mind drift once again ... further and deeper than before ... and perhaps ...

The front door opened, making me jump. I managed not to emit a very unprofessional squeak.

'All right?' said Jones. He'd brought my small overnight case from the car.

'Yes. Emily?'

'Safely disposed of.'

'Do you think either Monica or Kyle fell for it?'

'Probably not.'

'I'm not expecting anything to happen tonight – are you?'

He shook his head. 'I'm still not sure what we're dealing with here. Someone with a face-licking fetish or something else.'

I wasn't either.

'Well, don't just stand there,' he said. 'Go to bed.'

'Where will you be?'

'Around. Take this.' He handed me a lipstick.

I stared at it. 'Why ... ?'

'Mace.'

'Oh. Isn't that illegal?'

'A professional tip, Cage – don't let yourself get caught up in irrelevant details.'

'So, yes.'

214

'You've used this before, Cage, so you know what to do. Just point and press. Do that first. Panic second.'

'Oh God . . .'

'You'll be fine. Come on.'

I let myself into Emily's room and Jones locked me in. I wasn't happy about that but there was only one key and, as he said, he might need to get in fast if I was injured. I tried to feel reassured by this. I checked the windows were shut tight, pulled the curtains and looked around.

Emily had picked up the sweatshirt and straightened the quilt. I turned out the light and groped my way back to the bed. Three or four seconds – no more. If there had been something in Emily's room that night, it must have moved really quickly. And where could it have gone?

I slipped the mace under the pillow where I could get to it easily, kicked off my shoes, pulled the duvet over me and lay back.

I was quite surprised at how dark the room was. The curtains were very thick, and with the room being at the back of the house, there was no street light outside.

Time passed. I lay quietly, letting my mind wander as it pleased. The house was silent. So silent I actually wondered whether Jones had pushed off to the Cider Tree as well and I was here all on my own.

I heard Monica and Elliott come in. They shut the front door quietly, which was considerate of them, and came straight upstairs. I could hear them whispering together. I heard Elliott go into the bathroom and then the door into Monica's room shut behind him. I distinctly heard him lock the door.

They chatted quietly for a little while, Monica giggled, and then there was silence. I tried hard not to think about what they could be doing.

Kyle didn't actually slam the door behind him, but he didn't appear to be making any effort to be quiet. I heard him clatter around in the kitchen for a few minutes and then he too came upstairs. I kept expecting him to stumble over Jones somewhere and when he didn't, I went back to worrying whether Jones was still here. Or asleep. Or dead.

I lay in the darkness as Kyle put himself to bed in the next room, and once again the house settled back into silence.

I thought I'd be too scared to sleep – I would have put money on it – so I was quite surprised when I suddenly opened my eyes. Had I actually dropped off? For how long? I turned my head on the pillow and stared into the darkness. What had woken me?

There was someone in the room. I could hear breathing. Not mine. And not close. Other side of the room. I heard a slight movement. A rustle of clothing. This was a real person making real person noises. I slipped my hand under the pillow and touched the spray.

And then – suddenly – it was here. With me. Next to me. In the dark. Now. Afterwards, when things had returned to nearly normal, Jones congratulated me on not panicking and giving the game away, but the truth was that I was too terrified to move. They say there are two responses – fight or flight. I'd like to add a third – freeze.

I froze.

And then – as if all that wasn't bad enough – something warm and wet and alive touched my face. Starting at my chin, lingering around my mouth and then slowly meandering its way up

216

to my hairline. Drool ran down my cheek and hot breath gusted into my face. And Emily had been right. There was a smell.

The spell broke. I dragged out the pepper spray, screamed and squirted. Just the way Jones had told me to. Well, no, actually I was supposed to spray first and scream second, but I hit the target and that was the main thing.

Someone yelped and a second later Jones burst in, switching on the light as he entered, with Monica hot on his heels, then Elliott behind her. Monica was wrapped in her duvet and Elliott was – actually Elliott appeared to have come as he was. I averted my eyes. Anyway, everyone was clustered in the doorway, except Kyle who was lying on the floor clutching his face and making bubbling noises.

For long moments, everyone stared and then Monica said, 'It's Kyle. It was him all along.'

'Thought it was,' said Jones with satisfaction. 'Always gratifying to be right.'

'I was right too,' said Elliott.

'And me,' said Monica.

'Are you all right, Cage?'

I nodded and sat up. 'I need the bathroom. And a good wash.'

'Hands first. In case you got mace on them. Don't put them anywhere near your face until you're absolutely sure they're clean. Swill with soapy water. Don't rub. Don't spread it over your skin.'

'What's that smell?' said Elliott who, I now saw, was a tall, dark boy, as handsome as Monica was pretty. They made a very good-looking pair. His colour, a silvery lilac, complemented hers.

'Mace,' said Monica with deep satisfaction.

'Well,' said Jones. 'Mostly mace. I have a friend who has a lab and a twisted mind.'

Kyle was moaning and snorting. I scrambled past him on my way to the bathroom. What I could see of his face was a deep red. And swollen. And running with tears and mucus. He was a very unattractive sight.

My instinct was to wash my face first – to rid myself of that horrible warm, wet tongue – but remembering Jones's words, I washed my hands very, very carefully. I didn't think I'd got any of Jones's magic substance on them but I wasn't prepared to take any chances. And then I refilled the basin with hot water, borrowed some of Monica's luxury handwash and washed my face twice. And then a third time, until I felt clean again and smelled of orange and bergamot.

When I returned to the landing, Monica and Elliott had disappeared – to put some clothes on, I hoped – and Jones was just hauling Kyle out of his room and on to the landing.

'Look out,' he said, shaking Kyle by the scruff of his neck. 'You don't want to fall down the . . . oh, dearie, dearie me.'

There was the sound of Kyle bouncing from stair to stair on his way down, eventually ending as a pool of self-pity and snot at the bottom.

Jones followed him down, picked him up one-handed and dragged him back up again. 'Get your stuff together – you're leaving. Now.'

Kyle snorted a ton of mucus. 'My rent . . . I'm paid up until the end of . . .'

'Thank you for reminding me. Cough up.'

'What?'

'Empty your pockets.'

For someone who'd had to scrabble for fifty pence, Kyle had a surprising amount of money in his wallet. Jones took all of it. Then he made Kyle stuff his few possessions into a bin bag which he, Jones, knotted and threw down the stairs. Possibly terrified the same thing might happen to him again, Kyle made his own way down. Jones dragged him into the kitchen where Monica, Elliott and I were in the midst of calming our nerves with tea and bacon sandwiches.

'Kyle has come to say goodbye,' said Jones. 'He's had to leave. Suddenly.' He turned to Kyle. 'I have ears and eyes all over this town. You try anything like this again and I'll tie something heavy to your feet and chuck you in the river. No one will miss you. No one will care. Get it?'

Shaking with reaction and mace, Kyle nodded, apparently still too scared to speak.

I got up and slipped past the pair of them, into the hall and then out through the front door.

The night air seemed very cold after the warmth of the kitchen. The nearest street light was some way away and the hedge cast a long shadow. I stood quietly and waited.

I heard voices and then Monica shouted, 'Just get out, will you!'

Kyle shot out of the front door – possibly Jones-assisted – clutching his bin bag of possessions, and ran out of the gate.

Now he was away from the house – and especially away from Jones – he was smirking. Because he thought he'd fooled us.

I stepped out from behind the hedge. 'I know you.'

That brought him up short. I could see him staring at me in the dark. He looked back at the house, possibly wondering why I wasn't there.

'What?'

'I know you. I know what you are. They all think you're just some sleazy kid who licks girls' faces in the night. Did you enjoy the taste of her? I hope so, because that's all you're getting. Don't ever come back to this town.'

Away from Jones, he was suddenly cocky. 'Yeah? Says who?'

I stepped up close, emboldened by justifiable anger and the knowledge I had an unstable god living inside me. To say nothing of Michael Jones in the kitchen.

I said very quietly, 'Never mind what Jones said. This is me talking and if I ever see you again, I'll send a Fiori to suck out your soul and leave you naked and exposed to the Eternal Void. Until the end of time.'

He stared at me. Heart hammering, I forced myself to meet his gaze. And – yes – there it was – just for a split second – a flickering purple tongue tasting the air. And then it was gone and just Kyle stood in front of me, smiling that insolent smile.

Because none of this had been about Emily, she had only been the bait. This had all been about me.

He leaned forwards, whispering, 'But we have the taste of you now, Mrs Cage. You can run. You can hide. But he will always find you.'

I refused to step back. 'What are you?'

He smirked again.

'Not long now, Mrs Cage. Not long now.'

I felt my blood run cold. 'Not long until what?'

That was the moment when whatever had given him false courage now abandoned him. I saw it go. His colour collapsed around him.

I said, 'Run. Run far and run fast and don't ever come back.'

220

Grabbing his bin bag, he ran.

I took two or three very deep breaths and returned to the house.

Monica and Elliott had moved on from tea and were now having a much-needed glass of wine in the kitchen. Jones poured himself a small glass and joined them. I stuck with tea.

Monica sighed. 'I dread to think what sort of state his room is in.'

Jones sipped his wine and shook his head. 'He was induced to clean it before he left.'

Monica sat back in shock. 'He what?'

Jones pushed Kyle's wad of cash across the table. 'And pay his rent until the end of next month in lieu of notice. And then add in a bit extra because he was very sorry for all the trouble he'd caused.'

They gaped. 'Kyle?'

'It's all ready for the new tenant that you'll have no difficulty finding. Just be a little more rigorous in your vetting next time.'

They nodded, awestruck.

'I must know,' said Monica. 'How did he do it? Emily locked her door at night. I swear she locked it. I heard her.'

'She did lock the door,' said Jones. 'As did I this evening.'

'Then how did he get in?'

'He came through the wardrobe.'

'What?'

'Like Narnia,' he said, as if that made things any clearer.

They stared at him. I think I stared at him as well.

'If you look closely, there is a door in the wall.'

Monica stared at him in complete bewilderment. 'Is there? No, there isn't. Is there? Where? I never noticed.'

'No, because at some point, someone locked it, put a wardrobe across it on each side of the wall, and forgot about it. Kyle removed the door and took the back off Emily's wardrobe. Should Emily ever check – and why should she? – the back of his wardrobe is still in place and one piece of wood looks very like another. He probably did it one afternoon when you were all out. And then, whenever it suited him, he would gently slide the back of his wardrobe to one side and cross through into Emily's room. He probably deliberately broke her wardrobe catch as well.'

'But why?'

Jones shrugged. 'Perhaps just a bit of pilfering initially, and then he began to get other ideas.'

'And you knew what to look for?' said Monica, in disbelief.

He shook his head. 'I grew up in a house like this. That small back bedroom was often a nursery. A connecting door between nursery and bedroom made life easier. Most have been plastered over long ago. This house was converted on the cheap. Student accommodation.'

'So the place isn't haunted at all?'

'Well, we can't guarantee that, but the face-licker has definitely gone. I'll tell Jerry and he'll sort someone to come and plaster over the door and see to the wardrobes. Problem solved.'

'You're certain?' said Monica.

'Although . . .' He looked at me. 'Cage, I need you.'

This did not bring the joy to my heart that you might expect. 'Why?'

'To check out the loft.'

'Again – why?'

'This is a long terrace. A lot of them had interconnecting

doors in the attics. You could move from one house to the next quite easily. Most of them have been bricked up now, of course – security and fire regs – but it's one last thing I want to check out.'

I remembered the tiny loft hatch. '*You'll* check it out?'

He just grinned at me then turned to Monica. 'Do you have a stepladder?'

Five minutes later – and very much against my better judgement – I was clutching a torch and peering up through the hatch.

Jones had been right – he'd never have got through this tiny hole. I shone the torch around. The attic was surprisingly cool and draughty. It was also large and empty. I could see almost all of it, apart from the corner behind the cold-water tank. I was tempted to leave it, but no – I was a trouper – I should be thorough.

Grumbling, I clambered up into the attic and picked up the torch, intending to make my way from rafter to rafter. Just a little further and I would be able to . . .

Eyes.

There were eyes in the corner.

I very nearly overbalanced. I did drop the torch. Now the attic was almost completely dark. But I could still see the eyes. And now they were coming towards me. Fast. Faster than anything could possibly . . .

I screamed and, forgetting where I was, I stepped backwards and fell through the hatch. I hit the stepladder, knocking it flying, and we both hit Jones, standing at the bottom.

I lay on my back, dazed and winded, staring up through the hatch into the darkness of the attic. I heard footsteps pounding on the stairs as Monica and Elliott came running.

223

Everyone made a huge fuss over me. They pulled off the stepladder, picked me up, dusted me down and asked what had happened.

'I thought I saw something,' I said, which was absolutely true. 'And I forgot where I was.' Also completely true. 'And I stepped back and fell out of the loft.' All of it absolutely true. Just not *all* the truth. I made a judgement call. This was not the time to start burbling on about eyes. Not if Monica and Emily ever wanted to sleep soundly in this house again.

Jones straightened the stepladder, climbed up and spent some time shining the torch around. 'Oh. Yes.' He deepened his voice. 'Eyes.'

'What?' shrieked Monica.

He grinned. 'There's a broken bottle in the corner and I think it reflected the torchlight. Looks exactly like eyes glowing in the dark.'

Monica heaved a sigh of relief.

'Well,' said Jones, 'it's been exciting, but Mrs Cage needs her rest. As do I. Job done and done, I think, but let Jerry know if there are any further problems. And don't forget the padlock for the loft hatch.'

Monica and Elliott nodded, hero worship shining from their eyes.

'You are now worshipped as a god,' I said as we drove home through the dark streets.

He laughed. 'Yeah – that really doesn't happen often enough.' He smiled down at me. 'I think that went well, don't you?'

'Well, it would have gone even better if I hadn't fallen out of the attic.'

I rubbed my elbow. And my shoulder. And then my other elbow.

'We put a stop to Kyle's little game, though, didn't we? Good to see it's not always something dark and sinister from another world. Sometimes, it's just ordinary human shit.'

'Actually . . .' I stopped.

He pulled up for a traffic light and turned to me. 'You're not going to tell me it wasn't him after all?'

'Oh, it was him, all right. It was the human wickedness you were wrong about. Kyle was a rather nasty something. Before you ask – I don't know what.'

'How do you know this?'

'He told me. Outside. I had a quick word with him after you threw him through the front door.'

The light turned green and was ignored. Good job there was no traffic around at this hour.

'What else did he say?'

'Not a lot.'

'Why didn't you tell me? I'd have put the fear of God into the little shit.'

'Well, that's very kind but I managed that for myself.'

'You? How?'

'Successfully.'

The light turned amber and then red.

'I mean – what did you do?'

'I threatened him with a Fiori demon to suck out his soul and condemn him, naked and helpless, to the Eternal Void. It's quite enjoyable, isn't it – frightening the wits out of people, I mean. I felt quite empowered afterwards.'

He groaned and rested his head against the steering wheel. 'Did he say why he did it?'

225

'I think . . . it was for me.'

'For you?'

'Possibly.'

'Not Emily?'

'No.'

The light turned red and amber.

'Shit, Cage. Did he say any more?'

'No – I think I frightened him.'

'Very likely. You terrify me.'

'You're such a wuss.'

'You just told me I was a god.'

'I told you Monica and Elliott thought you were a god. Pay attention.'

'What do *you* think, Cage?'

'I think, astonishingly, I'm hungry.'

The light turned green again and he pulled out towards the ring road.

'Where are we going?'

'All-night services. Twenty-four-hour breakfast. My treat.'

'Oh,' I said. 'Thank you.'

CHAPTER FIFTEEN

The following Saturday we picked up the keys for our new office, gave it a good sweep and mop, and waited for our bits and pieces to be delivered. Jones brought in two new mobiles and a laptop.

'Business only on these,' he said. 'No personal stuff of any kind.'

I nodded. Excited, scared, apprehensive, eager all at the same time. If I had a colour, I'd probably look like a rainbow.

We stripped off all the packaging and started to arrange the furniture. We set up the two desks at right angles to each other and placed two extra easy chairs between us so visitors could face whichever desk they liked.

'Which desk do you want, Cage?'

'Is there any sort of tactical advantage to having you nearer the door or the window?'

He was assembling my chair. 'Sorry – not with you.'

'Well, if one of our clients turns out to be an axe-wielding lunatic, then obviously it makes sense to have you between him and me.'

'True, but if some tentacle-waving entity from the nether-world materialises, then it makes sense to have *you* between it and me, don't you think?'

'OK,' I said. 'I'll sit at the desk nearest the door and you can take the other one.'

'Thus putting me next to the kettle, which means I'm assigned permanent tea-making duties. Nice try, Cage. I'll sit nearest the door.'

Having thus painlessly acquired my favoured desk by the window, away from the possible draughts from the door and next to the tea and biscuits, I said nothing and let him get on with it.

Jones finished assembling my chair and I began to arrange my desk. Stuff I would need every day went in the top drawer – pens, stationery, spare notebooks and such. Regularly needed items – stapler, staples, spare printer cartridges and suchlike went into the second drawer down. Stuff I hadn't a clue about – headphones, lunchbox, cardboard file covers, hand cream and so on – went in the bottom.

I arranged my pens in my pen mug – one black, one blue and one red. And a sharpened pencil. I'd brought a coaster for my mug because I didn't want nasty rings all over my nice desk. My desk diary – empty so far except for my birthday noted in red – was on the right-hand side of my desk, together with a mouse mat, should I ever be granted permission to use the office laptop. My new mobile phone sat on my left. A handy office notebook – entitled Handy Office Notebook – sat in front of me, open at page one and all ready to start making important notes as soon as the first client turned up.

I adjusted my seat to the correct ergonomic height, sat down, clasped my hands in front of me and waited for our first customer.

I have no idea what Jones did. None of the above, anyway.

We discussed what I called office procedures and he called rules.

'I have another job, Cage, and they expect me to show up for it every now and then. How would you feel about being here alone?'

'I'd be fine,' I said, carefully not mentioning that help would only be upstairs.

'OK. Don't accept any jobs without consulting me first.'

I closed my top drawer slowly and with menace. 'Because . . . ?'

'Because if the situation were reversed, I wouldn't do it to you. We decide together what jobs we accept. If anyone wants us, thank them politely, take the details, and tell them you'll discuss it with your partner and we'll get back to them.'

I nodded because that made sense.

'And promise me faithfully you won't go racing off on your own.'

I said quietly, 'I've been alone nearly all my life. I've almost always faced everything by myself.'

'I know – and I didn't mean what you think I meant. We're a team. I handle the rough stuff and you do the weird bits. That's the way we work, Cage. I want your promise on this. No matter how seemingly unimportant or harmless the circumstances, you don't go anywhere on your own. Promise me.'

'OK,' I said. 'And you tell me everything. You don't keep me in the dark for my own good. You don't shelter me or protect me. We're both full members of this team.'

'Agreed.'

*   *   *

229

For a long time, nothing happened. Nothing at all. Having acquired one client – non-paying – before we had even set up, it would appear we had shot our commercial bolt. Days passed. We weren't there for every one of them, of course. Jones had his other job. We manned the office two or three times a week. We would roll up around nine a.m. and make the first tea of the day. Jones would bring in newspapers. After two days I brought my Kindle.

Nothing happened.

I took to monitoring the news bulletins in case there was an item that obviously required the attention of Cage and Jones.

Nothing happened.

Jones took up sudoku. None too successfully by the sound of it. I contemplated learning a foreign language.

Nothing continued to happen on an hourly basis.

And then, one day – a Saturday morning – I was deep into my thriller when Jones heaved a massive sigh. 'Ten per cent of nothing is nothing. Our landlords aren't going to make much money out of us.'

This was true. I hadn't thought people would be beating a path to our door but given the frequency with which we were overcome by the bizarre – usually when we least wanted or expected it – I'd thought we would be busier than this.

We discussed taking out some advertising, but both of us were against it. For me, years of a reluctance even to discuss what I could do were not easily overcome.

Jones was even more blunt. 'We'd be knee-deep in nutters.'

'We would.'

He looked down. 'Bugger, I've got two fives in this row. How did that happen?'

'I've heard those sudoku puzzles can be fiendishly difficult. What level are you on now?'

There was a long pause during which the word 'easy' was not spoken.

And then, having said all that, that very afternoon, someone tapped on the door and pushed it open.

'Hello – there's no sign outside. Have I come to the right place?'

The first thing I noticed about her was her colour. Green, shading through to hazel, which was quite unusual in itself – but mostly I noticed the shape. Sharp. Almost pointed. Angular. Not stabbing in and out; there wasn't actually a great deal of movement. Not until she saw Jones, anyway.

She was extremely good-looking. Tall, willowy, with hazel eyes and a wonderful complexion. Her skin actually glowed. If she was wearing foundation, then the manufacturer was missing a golden advertising opportunity. Her long dark glossy hair showed exciting red glints if she stood in the sun. Of which it seemed she was well aware. I watched her select the seat by my desk, presumably because it was in sunlight, but turned it to face Jones, effectively cutting me out of the conversation.

She sat herself down and regarded Jones with her head tilted to one side. He regarded her back. I passed the time by assessing her clothes – which were lovely. Fashionable but comfortable. Black ankle-grazer trousers and a pale yellow top with a really nice short black and gold quilted jacket. I would have worn that outfit in a heartbeat.

She smiled at him and I was completely unsurprised to see her teeth were flawless as well. The green in her colour deepened, seemed to gather itself and flowed towards him.

I put her down as ambitious, clever, charming and sharp. And very attracted to Michael Jones.

I sat back to see what would happen next.

Jones put down his pen. 'Good afternoon, Mrs . . .'

'Miss,' she said, seemingly very keen that he should know this. 'King. Lorelei King.'

From the way she said it, she obviously expected some sort of recognition. I looked over at Jones and shook my head.

'I'm sorry,' he said. 'You seem to feel that name should mean something.'

She laughed charmingly. 'Well, sometimes it does, although obviously not today. I write for the local paper – and the national ones as well – and I have a slot on local radio on Saturday mornings.'

Jones nodded.

I made a note in my notebook. That was what it was there for, after all.

She turned to me. Obviously, I was only the assistant. 'Do you think I could have a cup of tea? I'm sorry to ask, but I've galloped here straight from the studio and I'm absolutely parched.'

Normally I'd have been happy to oblige, especially for a client, but for some reason . . . not today.

I continued to write busily in my notebook, a shining example of workplace efficiency, and far too busy to make the tea.

Jones got up and switched on the kettle. He didn't return to his seat, either, coming to perch on the corner of my desk, forcing her to turn and face both of us. I decided he could have as many bacon butties as he liked next week.

'So, what can we do for you, Miss King?'

232

'Lorelei, please.'

He didn't introduce either of us. I didn't need to look at his colour to see he didn't like her. This should be interesting.

The silence lengthened.

Eventually, with a deprecating laugh, she said, 'Well, it's what I can do for you, actually.'

'And what would that be?'

'I'd like to write a short piece about you, Mr Jones.'

So, she knew our names. His name, anyway. And she was telling the truth – but not all the truth.

Jones was ploughing on. 'Why would you want to do that?'

'Well, firstly because there are all sorts of rumours flying around town about you and your assistant. There was that supposedly haunted house off Hanover Square. And before you deny it, I've talked to Sally Blundell.'

'I doubt that,' said Jones.

'Well, admittedly it was more what she didn't say than what she did, but there was that business last year with James Monroe – I know you were involved in that. And rumour has it something happened out at the Sorensen Clinic recently, with which you were not unconnected. So, I thought I'd do a little piece about you.'

'Why?'

'To find out who you really are. What you do. And, most importantly, to keep the public informed.' She smiled charmingly, her colour reaching out towards him. 'That's kind of my job.'

I saw his colour harden. 'Really? That's not what I heard.'

Her smile faded and her own colour slithered away from him like a receding wave. 'I'm sorry?'

'So you should be after that debacle last year. You remember – that piece you did about people abusing disabled parking schemes.' He turned to me. 'I thought her name sounded familiar.' He turned back again. 'You really should have realised that not all disabled people limp. You were so desperate to get out of small-town reporting that you didn't bother to check your facts properly, did you? Or even at all.'

He was speaking to me now. 'A woman – a blue badge holder – came to pick up her mother who'd had a funny turn in Boots. Naturally, concerned about her mother, she shot out of the car as fast as she could go and didn't limp even a little bit, causing Miss King, who witnessed the speed and agility with which she moved, to write a somewhat scathing piece on what she called the sort of people who "abuse" the blue badge system and identifying someone she deemed to be a culprit. The lady in question was actually severely disabled in both arms and a perfectly legitimate blue badge holder and not very happy at being so publicly stigmatised. Miss King's paper – the *Rushford Gazette* – was forced to issue a grovelling apology and make a substantial donation to charity. You're not really very popular in this town, are you, Miss King? And now you're desperate to reinstate your reputation and thought you'd use us to do so.'

Her smile was completely gone by now. And her colour was shying away from him as if the touch would poison her.

Sitting up straight, she said, 'I've heard rumours about you and Mrs Cage and I simply wanted to give you the opportunity to tell your side of the story.'

'What story? There is no story.'

'Well, why don't you give your side of the story there isn't.'

'Why don't you go away instead?'

234

She shifted in her chair to face me. 'How much do you charge, Mrs Cage? For your services, I mean.'

There was no correct answer to that and saying nothing would simply morph into 'Mrs Cage refused to reveal details of her charges'.

I couldn't see any way of getting rid of her. In fact, I couldn't see any way out of this at all. I suspected she already had her narrative. Anything we said, anything at all, would be twisted to suit her already written story.

I sat back and let my mind drift a little . . .

The kettle switched itself off. No one made any move to make the tea.

I put down my pen and said, 'Tell me about being a reporter.'

That threw her. 'What?'

'Tell me about being a reporter.'

She half laughed. 'Why would I do that?'

This was where I made my big mistake. All throughout my childhood, my father had told me never to speak about what I could do. Never to tell anyone. To keep quiet and keep my head down. Not only did I forget all that, but I forgot it in front of the very worst person possible.

I blundered on. 'I'm trying to keep you here long enough for you to avoid the accident.'

She stared at me. I took the opportunity to stare right back. 'What accident?'

I shrugged. 'I don't know yet.'

She stared at Jones, who remained silent and still.

I was taking a chance here. An accident could be anything from a major traffic pile-up to dropping her favourite mug to losing her keys to twisting her ankle stepping off the kerb. The odds are that nearly everyone will experience something in their daily lives that could be classed as *an accident*. Although a small thing had come to me . . . when I'd let my mind go . . . just enough to put the idea into my head and the fatal words into my mouth.

I smiled at her. The silence went on and on.

When it became apparent that neither Jones nor I were going to say another word, she grabbed her bag and stood up.

Unhurriedly, Jones reached out and took it from her.

'What are you doing? Give me back my bag.'

He passed it to me. 'Probably best if you do it, Cage.'

I shook out the contents, picked up the tiny recording device, and passed it to him.

'Oh dear,' he said. 'I hope there wasn't anything important on this – besides us, of course,' and did something I couldn't see.

Her colour hardened. 'You can't do that. I'll report you.'

'Recording a person without their consent is illegal. You really are desperate, aren't you?'

He popped her stuff back into her bag, zipped it up and returned it to her.

She snatched it from him.

He looked at me. 'Have we kept her long enough?'

'I think so.'

'Good day, Miss King.'

She slammed the door on the way out.

'Nice strategy, Cage. I can see you're going to be a real asset.'

I grinned at him. 'If only I could return the compliment.'

'You're such a shrew.'

'So you often remark.'

'And the beauty of it is that when nothing happens to her

today, she'll decide you're a complete fraud and, with luck, never darken our doors again.'

He was completely wrong.

Forty-five minutes later she was back, and this time she didn't even bother to knock. And strangely, I was included in the conversation. She faced me, her face sheet-white. I could see a tiny spot where she hadn't blended her foundation into her hairline.

'There was a big pile-up on the Whittington road.'

I really, really wanted to say, 'I know.' Just to show off a little. And to see the look on her face. And then I stopped myself. Just because I didn't like her ... A year ago – six months, even – I would never even have dreamed of doing such a thing. I was already regretting my earlier comments. Boasting about what I could do wasn't my style at all. And I certainly shouldn't use my dislike of people as an excuse for what my mother would have described as showing off, and my dad would have called very unwise. A scene from my childhood flashed into my mind. His garden shed, rich with the smell of the wood he loved to work with. Me holding his screwdriver and some sandpaper as he worked away while telling me always to be careful. Always to think before I spoke. It was a little late in the day now, but I resisted the temptation anyway.

'Oh dear,' said Jones, breaking the long silence that followed. 'Anyone hurt?'

She looked at me. 'Not now.'

I had a horrible feeling I'd made a big mistake.

'You look a trifle shaken,' said Jones. 'You'd better come in properly and sit down. Interesting you didn't stay to cover the accident.'

237

She didn't speak until he handed her a mug. Although she did say thank you.

She sipped away, her hand shaking. For her, this had hit a little too close to home. I suspected she was making a few mental readjustments.

Eventually she looked up at Jones. 'I'm not an idiot, you know.'

'Then stop writing like one,' he said, lifting her wrist to take her pulse.

She stiffened.

'Relax. Workplace first aider.'

She snatched her wrist away. 'And where exactly is your workplace?'

He gestured vaguely.

'Mr Jones, I'm not the sort of woman who just goes away quietly, you know.'

'Great,' he said gloomily. 'Just what every man needs in his life. Another difficult woman.'

I leaned forwards over my desk. 'Mr Jones has fond memories of the days when women knew their place.'

'Good God,' she said to him. 'How old *are* you?' And I suddenly liked her better. I caught a sudden impression. Trapped. Frustrated. Time passing. Early promise not being fulfilled . . .

Jones fiddled with his pen. 'Why did you come back?'

'I told you. I want to do a piece on you and Mrs Cage.'

'No, you don't. You came to expose what you'd decided is another fraud. Cage did her best to help you because she has a kind heart. In return, you're about to write some poisonous muck accusing her of deception, fraud and preying on the vulnerable – something you'd know all about, of course – and

238

any good you might have done in bringing Mrs Cage's unique talents to a wider audience – some of whom might have been in desperate need – will be submerged in the sea of bile and spite about to spew from your pen.'

My mouth was hanging open.

He didn't stop. 'She could have let you go. She could have kept quiet. She didn't have to keep you here for those vital extra minutes. But she did. Remember that when you write your piece.'

The room quivered with silence. And then, very slowly and carefully, she placed her mug on my desk, picked up her bag and walked out.

This time she didn't slam the door.

CHAPTER SIXTEEN

After that brief flurry of excitement, even more time passed. Nothing happened. Neither in the office nor out of it. There was still the occasional smudge of blood on my step in the morning, and I still had no idea to whom it belonged. I never heard a thing. Whatever was going on occurred in complete silence. I tried hard not to find that unsettling.

On the other hand, I wrote myself several shopping lists and none of them morphed into anything sinister about serpents, and I was rather hoping that whatever that had been about was over with.

Jones went back to his sudoku and I continued to think about learning a foreign language. I'd done French and German at school – of the two, I preferred German – and I was scouring online language sites.

Jones admitted to speaking German. I told him I looked forward to the day we could enjoy intelligent conversations *auf Deutsch* because we certainly weren't enjoying them in English.

A fortnight passed before we had another customer, although that sounds worse than it actually was because Jones was busy on another job at the time. We were only going in two days a week and one of those was Saturday.

The call came through late Friday afternoon. For a moment

neither of us could think what the noise was and then we both scrabbled for our phones. I lost because I'd forgotten mine was in my top drawer where it had been for . . . well, ages. It didn't matter anyway, because it was his phone doing the ringing.

He sat silently for the most part, taking copious notes. He said 'Yes' and 'No' and 'All right' a couple of times and then ended the call with, 'We'll get back to you very soon.'

'Well?' I said, in high excitement.

He pushed up his glasses and read through his notes. 'That was a call from one Oliver Shotton. Or, as he was very keen to be known, Oliver Shotton of Shotton Hall.'

He paused and frowned.

'What did he want?'

'Us. Or, more strictly speaking – you.'

'Me?' I said, not very intelligently. 'What for?'

'Oliver Shotton has recently inherited a property . . .'

'Shotton Hall,' I said, just to show I'd been paying attention.

He frowned. 'We're not going to get far if you continually interrupt the briefing, Cage. Anyway, he's inspecting the property and could we – by which he meant you – join him on the 22nd?'

'Tomorrow?'

'Well done, Cage. Yes.'

'Why?'

'It would seem he has a big building project in mind but it's a property with history.' He frowned at his notes again. 'And he wants to be absolutely certain it's what he calls . . . "clean". He's tied up a lot of money in the project and can't afford to have dodgy rumours frightening away potential investors.' He looked up. 'Does the name Shotton Hall ring any bells with you, Cage?'

I shook my head.

'I'll have a poke around online while you make the tea.'

'No,' I said, picking up my Kindle. 'You can do both.'

'We're supposed to be equal partners, Cage.'

'We absolutely are equal partners. One sugar, please.'

There was a lot of muttering over the kettle, but eventually he dumped a mug in front of me and retreated to study his laptop.

After only a few minutes, he looked up. 'I was right. I thought I'd heard of Shotton Hall.'

I closed my Kindle and picked up my tea. 'Look at us acting like professionals and ascertaining all the facts, instead of barging in blindly as we usually do. What did you find?'

'The Shotton Massacre.'

I sat up. 'The what?'

'I knew I'd heard the name Shotton before. There's tons of stuff about it online.' He read a little further. 'It's not a pretty story. If you're a lover of romantic nineteenth-century love stories, Cage, you should look away now.'

'Have you ever noticed how few spirits haunt a place because they've had a long and happy life there?'

He sighed. 'Shall I carry on or do you want to change the subject and maunder on about something completely different?'

'Sorry. What have you found?'

He passed over the laptop while he drank his own tea. He was right. It wasn't a pretty story at all.

The Shottons had lived at Shotton Hall. They were prosperous and well-to-do but George Shotton made his money in trade which was a bit of a no-no in those days. Earning your own money and making your own way in the world was definitely not the thing to do. Old money was good – new money

242

was bad – and despite their substantial moneybags, and to the frustration of Mrs Shotton, the family only ever managed to hover on the very fringes of genteel society.

That was the state of play until near the end of the 19th century, when things began to look up. George Shotton had two daughters – Elizabeth and Georgiana. I know lots of people are named Elizabeth, but it always gives me a slight shock to see my own name written down. I often wondered afterwards whether I'd have done things differently if she'd had another name.

Georgiana was staggeringly beautiful – quite exceptional, apparently, and widely admired. There was never any mention of the other sister. I wondered if perhaps she'd have been considered pretty enough in any other company but stood no chance in comparison with her stunning younger sister who, in the way of her world, was being groomed for an exceptional marriage. Entrée into the upper-classes was at last within the reach of her ambitious parents.

Shotton Hall was – still is – situated at the northern end of the county, about seventeen miles from Rushford, sitting in its own grounds and, in those days, the epicentre of a prosperous estate. The Shottons were well-off and, had they been content to remain within their own social sphere, they'd probably have been happy enough – but the widely admired Georgiana was definitely their hope for the future. All family resources were diverted towards grooming her for and providing her with a season in London, where it was confidently expected she would take the fashionable world by storm. A suitable townhouse was hired. An elderly peeress – poor but with excellent connections – professed herself willing to guide Miss Georgiana through the intricacies of the social scene. For a price, of course. A vast wardrobe of ball gowns, morning dresses, walking dresses, riding habits, shoes, dancing slippers, hats and bonnets, cloaks, reticules, muffs, gloves and so forth were commissioned. Music, deportment and drawing lessons were provided. Her careful mama schooled her in manners and social behaviour. Georgiana Shotton was to be presented as the perfect young lady, who would make the perfect match. Certainly a viscount, possibly an earl, perhaps even a duke. Mrs Shotton's imagination probably knew no bounds.

And then, almost on the eve of their departure for London – utter disaster of the very worst kind. The other sister caught the smallpox. The red plague.

This was a huge blow. No one knew how or where or from whom she'd contracted the disease. Family plans were thrown into turmoil. What of Georgiana's carefully planned season? The family had gambled everything on this. Mr Shotton was up to his ears in debt and there would be no second chance. It was now or never.

Mr Shotton dealt with this disaster in the traditional masculine fashion and retired to his library with the brandy. Mrs Shotton took a more practical approach.

Under no circumstances must her elder sister be allowed to infect the daughter on whom all their hopes rested. That night, two heavily bribed local men carried the presumably too-sick-to-protest Elizabeth into an outhouse. They left the district immediately afterwards. No one knew what happened to them, but it was rumoured they went abroad.

Elizabeth was left to fend for herself. None of the servants would go anywhere near her. I assumed some food and drink must have been left nearby, although whether she'd have the strength to eat it – or even fetch it – I didn't know. But, with their problem satisfactorily resolved, Mr and Mrs Shotton and the lovely Georgiana climbed into the first of four baggage-laden coaches and departed, all ready to take London by storm.

The family arrived in London, Georgiana was unveiled, and her season was easily the triumphant success her parents had gambled everything upon. Things could not have gone better. Noblemen queued up to buy her hand in marriage, and less than two months later, she became the Marchioness of Somewhere or Other. She was married in London at St James's, Piccadilly. I could just imagine the huge society wedding that probably bankrupted George Shotton all over again.

I looked up. 'I wonder how Georgiana felt about her sister being abandoned so she could reign, triumphant over fashionable London for a season.'

'We'll never know, will we.'

I frowned. Something made me say, 'I think we should use her name. Stop referring to her as the other sister.'

'Yes. Even in her own time, she appears to have been pretty well forgotten. Women were worthless unless they were beautiful or well dowered. Character counted for nothing, as long as they had a pretty smile.'

I couldn't help remembering Lorelei King and thinking that things weren't that different even today.

He picked up his mug. 'I didn't get that far into the story. Did the parents return to Shotton Hall or did they remain in London reaping the benefits of their daughter's wonderful marriage?'

I was scrolling down. 'They stayed for the remainder of the season and then returned home, probably hoping the problem of Elizabeth had been solved – one way or another – in their absence.'

'And had it?'

I scanned the page. 'In a way. They returned to Shotton Hall to find that, against all the odds, their daughter had survived the red plague. However, the disease had wreaked its usual destructive havoc and she was horribly disfigured, so once again Elizabeth was about to bring disaster down upon them.'

Jones looked over at me. 'How so?'

'The happy couple's first wedding anniversary was to be celebrated with a visit to the bride's family home. Mrs Shotton was planning a massive ball to celebrate their daughter's brilliant marriage. All the new husband's relations were expected, along with the leading local families, and it was to be a glittering occasion – a once in a lifetime event. Unfortunately for these grand plans, however, the problem still hadn't gone away. Elizabeth hadn't done the decent thing and died, which would not only have solved the problem but resulted in lots of sympathy for the family. But she hadn't, and the story says her loving mother didn't want a face like that around, not when the house was to be full of important people and her beautiful daughter.'

I gave Jones the laptop while I finished my tea.

He frowned. 'It says here that Mrs Shotton issued instructions whereby Elizabeth was never again to be admitted to the house.'

I put down my mug in shock. 'They kicked her out?'

'Not completely. It seems she was allowed to live in a tiny cottage in the grounds somewhere. Alone, obviously. I'm assuming they fed her. Probably a few supplies were sent over – I'd bet barely enough to keep her alive.'

I was surprised at the anger inside me. How much pity I felt for another unhappy Elizabeth – whose only crime was not being as pretty as her sister and then not dying to make things easier for her family.

Jones was reading on. 'The family were strongly religious. In fact, George Shotton was a sidesman. I suppose Christian compassion prevented them actually killing her, so they created conditions which more or less ensured she wouldn't survive.'

'But she did?' I said.

He nodded.

'Good for her.'

'Well . . . no. They *thought* she'd survived. Every day she appeared outside the front door. Waiting to be let back in, the story says. Her loving parents sent the servants to drive her away but she always came back. She would appear at the front door with the dawn and disappear with the sunset. Every day.'

'And at night?'

'Legend has it that she spent the nights walking around the house. Those inside could hear her rattling the doors, trying the windows, looking for a way to get in. The servants were having hysterics and leaving in their droves.'

'Poor Elizabeth. When did she actually die?'

For the first time he hesitated, scrolling down the page. And then another. 'Oh.'

'What?'

'Cage, she didn't live – she died.'

I sat up in a hurry. 'What?'

'She never survived the smallpox. She died while her parents were still in London. Which sounds much more likely than somehow surviving, un-nursed and abandoned, don't you think? What greeted them on their return was not their daughter – although no one knew it at the time. Not until someone thought to visit the original outhouse – presumably while ghost Elizabeth was patiently waiting outside the front door to be let in – which was when they discovered she'd been dead for some time. Her body had melted into the thin blankets which were all she'd had to keep out the cold. What they'd been seeing – what they'd all been seeing – was not their daughter.'

I tried not to shiver. 'And she's haunted Shotton Hall ever since?'

He shook his head. 'The worst was yet to come.'

I was still angry on behalf of Elizabeth. 'Did they even bury her?'

'It doesn't say.'

'Was her . . . her ghost still patrolling the house, trying to get in?'

'I think we can assume yes. They probably had to pay the servants an absolute fortune to stay on. If the legend is true, of course. Anyway, there's no further mention of the very inconvenient Elizabeth, who had almost ruined everything . . .' He looked over at me. 'Until . . .'

I felt the hairs on the back of my neck rise up. 'Until what?'

'Until the long-planned anniversary celebrations. The lovely Georgiana – probably even more widely regarded than ever, now she had fulfilled her duty and given birth to a son and heir – was to return in triumph to her family home, along with her husband and various members of his family, and a month of marvellous festivities was planned, culminating in a magnificent Christmas ball. And that, apparently, was when the ghost struck.'

He paused.

'How?' I said impatiently. 'What did she do?'

'Well, the Shottons had instructed all their guests to arrive

248

during daylight – although in those days not many travelled at night, anyway. Over the previous twelve months they'd planted trees, hedges and bushes all around the house – not so much to keep Elizabeth out but to conceal her from their guests. According to reports, George was nearly insane by then, incessantly checking the house was all locked up. He had shutters installed and went round and round, testing the windows, turning keys and so on. Like a man possessed. The servants were forbidden ever to open a window on pain of death. Everything needed for the ball was to be brought into the house and stored there. It took all the guests the best part of a week to assemble, but once they'd all arrived, no door or window was to be opened until they departed.'

I frowned. 'Elizabeth let other people go in?'

'So it would seem.'

About to enquire further, I remembered he'd called it the Shotton Massacre. 'What happened? What went wrong?'

'An outside manservant belonging to one of the guests, not realising the significance of all the bolted doors and windows – and obviously the Shottons weren't going to tell anyone – left one of the servants' doors open while he brought something inside. The door was only unattended long enough for him to come in from the kitchen garden, deposit his load on the table, and then go back to shut and lock the door behind him, but the damage was done.'

'She was inside?'

He scanned down another page. 'She was. Worse – now she was *locked* inside. Stands to reason, I suppose – if the locks were strong enough to keep her out, then they'd be strong enough to keep her in as well.'

249

'What happened?'

'One of the biggest unexplained mass-dyings in British history. Estimates put the number of people in the house that night at around forty. Including servants. Less than half of them – mostly servants – walked out three days later. Well – ran out three days later. They ran and ran – the records don't say who they were or where or to whom they ran – but they certainly never came back. Inconveniently for us, but conveniently for the tellers of internet tall tales, there are no names or details of any of them. Rumour had it they were all dead within a year, anyway, but that's certainly unfounded.

'At some point, two maids and a young girl from a local family who had somehow managed to barricade themselves in somewhere made their way down to the village. Every one of them was drenched in blood. Two were injured. One was insane.'

I'd gone very cold. 'What about the baby? What happened to the baby?'

'Hang on.'

He scrolled some more. 'Fortunately, Georgiana Shotton was the last word in modern motherhood and they hadn't brought the baby with them. Because you didn't, in those days.'

I nodded. 'Georgiana probably didn't even see him until he was about nine years old.'

'Anyway, it . . . he . . . stayed safely in London.'

'Did Georgiana survive?'

'No. Nor her husband. Nor her mother. Nor her father.'

'Elizabeth killed them all?'

He shook his head. 'No. That's just it. According to the three girls, they all killed each other. There were no forensics in those days, of course, so no one was ever quite sure what had happened and to whom and in what order, but two of the three survivors – when they were recovered enough to speak – told terrible tales of possession, murder, torture, blood, dismemberment – even cannibalism.'

I stared at him. 'You're kidding.'

'I'm not – no. Upon hearing this tale, a group of local men – strongly fortified by drink, I suspect – got together, entered the Hall and . . .'

'Don't tell me. A terrible sight met their eyes.'

'It certainly did. But not for very long.'

'They fled too?'

'They did, gabbling their tales of terror to anyone who would listen. Which was everyone, obviously. When a group of county officials – two magistrates, the local constable, a couple of retired army officers and the local vicar – eventually plucked up enough courage to return to Shotton Hall – they described the place as a scene from hell. The lower rooms were full of corpses and parts of corpses. The highlight, apparently, was a splendidly dressed but somewhat dishevelled young lady wandering the rooms covered in blood, singing folk songs and gnawing on a body part that the writer of this lurid piece is too shy to mention – but we can both guess, I think.'

I swallowed. 'This is just a legend though, surely. It's far too sensational to be true. I mean – it has to be – doesn't it?'

Jones remained silent.

'What happened to Shotton Hall?'

'Abandoned. Not surprisingly.'

I don't know why I said it. 'I think we should give this one a miss.'

He looked up. 'Why?'

'Hello?' I said. 'Blood-crazed ghost. Torture. Murder. Insanity. Cannibalism. Are you out of your mind?'

'We could charge the earth for this one, Cage.'

'And I could end my days covered in blood. Singing nursery rhymes and gnawing on . . .'

I stopped in time. Fortunately, he was too engrossed in internet sensationalism to notice. I took a deep breath. 'Is that the end of the legend?'

'Apart from the usual nonsense, of course.'

'The usual nonsense being . . . ?'

'Oh, some tosh about the curse of the Shottons. A minor branch of the family moved in, but after what are described as *some incidents*, they took themselves off to the other side of Rushford and kept their heads down for a long time. Every now and then, a young Shotton would return to the scene of the massacre – out of curiosity, I expect. Or a dare. Or pissed. Whatever. None survived. According to this, anyway. And now, no one's been near the place for years.'

I frowned. 'Did they actually die in the house?'

He read some more. 'I don't think so. All the bodies seem to have been found within the grounds.'

'Any recent accounts of supernatural activity at Shotton Hall?'

'No – nothing at all. Mind you, the place has been empty for ages.'

'What do they need us for? If I was a Shotton, I wouldn't go within fifty miles of it. Why don't they just bulldoze it and have done?'

'Well, that's what they want us for. Not the bulldozing. The

252

current Shotton – Oliver – wants us to investigate, Cage. He has plans for the place. What do you say? We shoot up there – it's less than an hour away – we wander around, you do your thing, we tell them the place is as clean as a whistle, pocket our enormous fee and come home again. We wouldn't even have to stay the night. Money for old rope. Think about it.'

I did think about it. As he said – the story was far too lurid to be credible. A legend, built on and embellished over the years and with very little foundation. There might once have been a sister who contracted smallpox and somehow, in her fever, escaped the sickroom and roamed the grounds until discovered and returned. The rest was pure fantasy. An exaggerated tale fuelled by internet fantasists. And Jones was right – this could be easy. And yes, we certainly would be charging them a fortune for it.

We talked about it for the rest of the day.

'This is up to you,' said Jones. 'It's your area of expertise. What do you want to do?'

'I think it can't possibly be true. I think it's likely something did happen there, once upon a time, and the story's grown over the years into something quite preposterous.'

'But . . .'

I looked at him. 'What do you mean – but?'

'There's something bothering you, Cage. I can tell.'

'No, you can't.'

'Hey – master interrogator here, remember? Your body language, the tone of your voice, your expression – there's a *but* coming.'

'My doubt is not that tangible,' I said.

'But . . .'

'Yes. But . . .' I shook my head. 'It's nothing I can put my finger on. Should we let that affect our decision?'

'Not necessarily,' said Jones. 'Let's be sensible about this. Basic precautions. We tell someone where we're going and why.'

'Iblis.'

'I was thinking Jerry.'

'Iblis *and* Jerry.'

'We tell them we expect to return the same day.'

'And we call them on our return.'

'We take our work phones and keep them fully charged at all times.'

I nodded. 'And we don't split up. That never ends well in films. Especially for the heroine. We stick together. So, one phone on us – mine – and yours in the car. A spare, in case we have to make a quick getaway and need to summon assistance.'

'Yes. Good thinking, Cage.'

We stopped and looked at each other.

'So, we're doing it?' he said.

'Looks like it.'

He sat back in his seat. 'Well, this is it, then, Cage. Our first proper paying job. You sure you're all right with this?'

'Just a little nervous. We stumble over so much by accident, I'm rather worried about what we'll discover if we actually go out looking for trouble.'

'Not with this one, Cage. Just think of it as a glorified building inspection. And we'll be home in time for tea.'

Oliver Shotton rang back just as we were switching off the lights prior to going home.

'I'll put it on speaker,' said Jones.

'Well,' said a voice, before Jones even had a chance to speak. 'Are you going to do it?'

I looked at Jones. He grinned. I grinned back.

'I don't think so,' he said. 'We talked it over and we don't think we're quite the right people to help you. But thank you very much for thinking of us.' And ended the call.

We switched the lights back on and waited. Four minutes later, the phone rang again. They'd increase the fee by thirty per cent. All expenses paid.

I looked at Jones. He raised his eyebrows. I nodded.

'We accept the job,' he said.

CHAPTER SEVENTEEN

Jones picked me up on the other side of the medieval bridge the next morning and we set out. The day was lovely and while I was somewhat apprehensive over the job, it would be nice to work on something that didn't involve the Sorensen Clinic.

'By the way,' said Jones, apparently reading my mind, 'they're going to rename it. The Sorensen Clinic. Get rid of his name completely.'

'He really won't like that,' I said, trying not to smile.

'Yeah. We're just waiting for the right moment to tell him. It'll be interesting to see how he reacts to this massive blow to his vanity.'

'Can they do that? After all, it is his clinic.'

'Initially, yes, it was. Then we moved in. He was allowed to keep the private patients' side as a cover while we took over the rest of it for our people. Now it all belongs to us. Bridgeman's already been installed so there's not a lot Sorensen can do. Especially with this cloud hanging over him. The legal eagles will thrash out all the details, but the bottom line is that he's finished. And rightly so after everything he's done.'

I watched the scenery flash past while I thought about this. 'Is it my fault, do you think?'

He didn't pretend to misunderstand me. Nor did he tell me that of course it wasn't my fault.

Eventually, he said, 'I think things started to go wrong for him the minute he met you. He wanted you and his efforts to acquire you caused him to cross the line.'

'He'll blame me.'

'He'll blame everyone except himself, Cage. Don't worry about it.'

'He must hate me.'

'I think he fears you. Which is much better, trust me.'

The countryside sped past. I'd never been to this part of Rushfordshire before. The area was heavily farmed. Neat fields were surrounded by neat hedges. Gradually the roads grew narrower and the trees hung low over the lanes.

'Nearly there,' said Jones. 'I can't believe you're not fast asleep and snoring your head off. You're not usually the world's most stimulating travelling companion, you know.'

'It's the company I keep,' I said. 'I always find it hard to stay awake when you're nearby.'

'Hurtful,' he said, changing down and turning left, up what had once been a narrow lane and had now degenerated into an overgrown track. We'd arrived at Shotton Hall.

I caught fleeting glimpses of a building until we swept out from under the trees into a wide area thick with weeds. I suspected it had once been a very imposing carriage sweep. There was some kind of stone basin in the centre, almost invisible in the undergrowth. The remains of a fountain, perhaps. I tried not to remember that most of these bushy shrubs and trees would be the descendants of those planted by George Shotton to save him from having to look at his dead daughter.

Shotton Hall itself loomed over us, encased in overgrown trees. I could see oak and cedar in the distance, and closer to the house, alder, birch and sycamore. Even on the brightest day it would be dark inside.

The house was much bigger than I'd thought it would be.

'Grade II,' said Jones briefly. 'With a Palladian front.'

'Impressive,' I said, still squinting up at the blind windows. 'Your architectural expertise, I mean. Did you study architecture?'

'No, I googled Shotton Hall. Built in the mid-nineteenth century by some nobleman whose name I forget because he immediately went bankrupt and the property was bought by Josiah Shotton, George's father. Eighteen-sixty, I think. Or thereabouts.'

The whole front of the building – whether Palladian or not – was thickly covered in ivy, which in some cases was growing right across the windows, which could only add to the dark and sinister atmosphere. I found it hard to imagine this as a family home with children running around the gardens, horses being led to and fro, servants moving around, cheerful fires within and all the hustle and bustle of late-nineteenth-century life.

I squinted upwards. Shotton Hall was wider than it was tall, being only three storeys high, excluding the attics. The square central block was flanked by two smaller one-storey wings with arched windows currently all boarded up. The front door, however, was clearly visible in a small porch between pillars supporting a portico. Tall brick chimneys sprouted from the roof and small trees sprouted from the chimneys.

We pulled up alongside a vast, over-egged SUV that had almost certainly never been off-road in its entire life. All that was missing was the cowcatcher.

'Set in about ten acres,' said Jones chattily, climbing out of the car. 'All equally decrepit, I expect.'

I was looking around. There had been no reported sightings of the ghost for decades. On the other hand, no one had lived here for a very long time, so perhaps the other Elizabeth couldn't be bothered to get out of bed if there was no one to be terrorised.

I climbed slowly out of the car. The afternoon was hot and still; there was no wind. No leaves fluttered in the breeze. No birds sang. No fluffy clouds scudded across the sky. Time not only ran slowly here – it had practically stopped. The only sound was the faint tick-tick from the car as the engine cooled.

It was, as they say in all the best films, too quiet.

'Cage?'

I closed the car door very quietly, unwilling to draw attention to our arrival.

'Cage?' said Jones, again.

'Mm? Yes?'

'All right?'

'So far, so good,' I said with fake cheeriness and followed him through the knee-high weeds and brambles to the front door.

'Yes – two and a half minutes into the job and we're unharmed. Must be a bit of a record for us.'

He scanned the front door for a knocker or bell or anything to announce our arrival, and finding nothing, thumped on the door.

I stood behind him, scanning the wilderness around us. It was so quiet I could hear my own breathing.

'Poor sight lines from the house,' said Jones. 'An entire army could be concealed out there and we'd never know anything about it until it was too late and our bodies were stretched, lifeless, across the porch.'

'I always think it's your light-hearted insouciance that puts the sparkle in our working day.'

'Believe it or not, Cage, I was a cheery chappie until I met you. All my girlfriends remarked on it. Sometimes in a complimentary manner but, it has to be said, sometimes not. These last two years have worn me to a shadow of my former self, however, and I have no hesitation in blaming you for that. Have they forgotten we're coming, do you think?'

At that moment, the front door creaked open in the traditionally sinister manner. Both Jones and I refrained from comment.

I disliked both the Shotton brothers as soon as I saw them. And then, as if things weren't bad enough, Lorelei King appeared from a downstairs doorway, and I knew that whatever was going to happen, none of it would be good.

'Hello, there,' said the taller of the two men. He made ushering gestures. 'Come in. Come in.'

He seemed in a great hurry to get us inside and shut the door behind us. I didn't much care for the emphatic way he shot the recently oiled bolts, either.

Turning to face us, he held out a hand. 'I'm Oliver Shotton. Of Shotton Hall. Thank you for coming today.'

Jones – who has his own instincts – ignored the outstretched hand. 'Michael Jones. And this is Mrs Cage.'

'Mrs Cage, what a pleasure to meet you. Lorelei – you remember her, I'm sure – has told me so much about you.'

There was something wrong, but I couldn't quite put my finger on it. Given the number of people who'd died here, I'd half expected the house to be full of sinister shades, all shrieking curses and demanding blood and retribution, but this house was as silent inside as out.

I closed my eyes and tried to let my mind drift a little, but Oliver just wouldn't stop talking and I couldn't concentrate.

'And this is Adam, my younger brother and the junior partner in my little venture.'

I think I disliked Adam even more than Oliver. I made a mental note for the future – meet the clients face to face before we actually committed ourselves. Although, given Jones's reluctance to give out personal details before we agreed to a job, it was hard to see how that could be managed. A neutral meeting place, perhaps? I wasn't sure how helpful that would be. If we were going to meet at say, a café, what was the point of having a room in Hartland Warehouse? Some sort of preliminary meeting, maybe, *before* taking them back to our office. I sighed. This was all becoming very complicated.

I surfaced to find everyone looking at me.

'I'm sorry – I was miles away.'

'Jolly good, jolly good,' said Oliver, rubbing his hands together. 'On the job already, I see.'

I wondered what would happen if I instructed Jones to inflict a little very gentle violence on this prat, prior to us returning to Rushford with all speed. However, we were supposed to be professionals and we were charging them the earth, so we needed to do this properly.

The two brothers were standing close together. There was a strong family resemblance between them both, except that Adam was a weaker, paler copy of his brother. Oliver was tall, with light-coloured hair brushed back from a high forehead. He wore carefully casual country clothes that looked as if they were having their first outing. His boots were very shiny and stiff-looking.

Adam, on the other hand, hadn't bothered with trying to fit in at all. He wore city clothes. As a concession to country living, however, he'd taken off his jacket and loosened his tie. His hair was darker and thinner than his brother's. The distance between his eyebrows and hairline was already greater than Oliver's. There was a faint smell of whisky about him. His colour flopped helplessly around him, indecisive and vague.

Oliver's deep purple colour was unusual – alternately bright and glowing with excitement – or possibly greed – and then withdrawn and tight. A man with something to hide was hardly a wild guess on my part.

Adam's colour was a much weaker blue-lavender and didn't glow at all. Didn't do much of anything, actually. I wondered if he was on drugs. Some sort of sedative, perhaps? He definitely seemed a little out of things.

Unusually for brothers, their colours were entirely separate. There was no mixing or mingling of any kind. These two didn't like each other very much.

Lorelei King stood off to one side. Her green colour had darkened and was close and still. Orange curdled around the edges. She wasn't very happy about something.

Oliver was still talking.

'. . . like to make a start,' he was saying. 'It might be a good idea if I came with you – some of the floors are a little spongy, you know. Or I could give you a potted history of the family, although I'm certain if you hadn't heard of us before, you certainly had after you'd googled us.' He crinkled his eyes in what he probably thought was a charmingly deprecating manner. 'Not a particularly nice bunch, are we?'

Receiving no polite denial, he pushed on. 'Anyway, this place has been empty since for ever. I'm . . .'

Adam stirred.

'Sorry Adam – *we're* – actually the first Shottons to set foot in Shotton Hall for more than a decade.'

'Why are you here now?' enquired Jones, looking around. 'Personally, I mean. You could have engaged an agent to meet us here.'

'To satisfy my own curiosity, I suppose. My father never came near the place. Not after my brother died here. More than ten years ago. I was the second son. Never thought Shotton Hall would be mine.' He looked around. 'But my father died and now it is.'

His colour said that wasn't quite right. He wasn't lying – but he wasn't telling the truth, either. Not the whole truth, anyway. He was holding something back.

'I – *we* – have great plans for this place.' Oliver gestured around. 'Convert this main building into flats. We're looking at six luxury apartments in the main body of the house, plus another two super luxury affairs. One in each wing.'

Adam's colour was flooding through with . . . what? Resentment? Greed? No – fear.

Oliver was *still* talking. 'There'll be a spa, of course, a well-equipped gym and heated indoor swimming pool, plus another twenty or so houses built in the grounds, each set in its own half-acre garden. Yes, I'm – *we're* – really going to clean up here.'

'Doesn't your planning application include some affordable housing?' enquired Jones, who had done our homework.

Oliver shrugged. 'Well, yes, but we'll fling up half a dozen hovels around the back where no one can see them. Separate entrance, big hedge and everything. Just one of the ways to keep the council off our backs. Apart from the traditional methods, of course.'

He jingled the coins in his pocket and laughed a *look at how clever I am* laugh. No one else even smiled.

'So,' said Jones, 'just so we're all on the same page: this house's reputation is standing in the way of what is obviously going to be a sizeable profit and you want Mrs Cage to confirm . . .'

'No,' I said slowly. 'That's not quite right – is it?'

The atmosphere changed. Oliver's colour contracted sharply and deepened to an almost-black. 'Well, actually – no. I must admit to a slight – a very slight – withholding of . . . one fact.'

The atmosphere changed again. From the corner of my eye, I saw Adam and Lorelei move closer together as if for mutual support. From the way their colours mingled, I guessed they were a couple. I'd think about that later because something was definitely going on here.

Jones also moved slightly. I recognised the stance. Weight on both feet, hands loose at his sides. Ready for anything. I moved behind him because that was what he always said: *Stay behind me so I know where you are, Cage, and don't get in my way.*

I half turned to check behind us.

We were still in the generously proportioned entrance hall, no more than ten paces from the front door. Neither Oliver nor Adam would give Jones any trouble at all and, I'm ashamed to say, if I was very lucky, an opportunity might arise to give Lorelei King the slapping she so deserved.

'Let's get this straight,' said Jones. 'You want us to establish whether or not you have a ghost?'

'Oh, no. No, no, no. We know the answer to that question. We do have a ghost. Elizabeth Shotton.'

'So, what exactly is the problem? Has she started to walk again?'

'She never stopped. She's here right now.'

He was right. Something was coming . . .

Oliver's colour was brightening again. He was almost gleeful. I wondered if perhaps he enjoyed frightening people.

I turned my head to look at Lorelei. Her colour was almost vibrating. Thick ropes of orange colour ran through it.

I moved to face Oliver Shotton. 'Why exactly have you brought me here?'

'I want you to send the ghost away.'

'Mrs Cage is not a performing seal,' said Jones angrily.

'Why now?' I asked, turning my head, trying to focus . . . My heart rate was increasing. I could hear the beat inside my head. 'Have people started to die?'

'Not yet.'

'I don't understand.'

'And we don't want to,' said Jones. 'I don't like the look of any of these dodgy buggers, Cage. Let's go.'

He began to head for the door.

'I'm afraid,' said Oliver, stepping into his path, 'that opening the door is out of the question. You see, unfortunately for all of us, there's one rather important piece of information that isn't generally known. I wasn't completely sure of it myself until it was too late.'

'And what's that?' I asked, although I was horribly sure I'd guessed the answer.

Oliver's colour surged around him.

'Elizabeth Shotton. She lets people in – but she never lets them back out again. You say Mrs Cage is not a performing seal, but if she ever wants to see the outside world again, then, I'm afraid, perform she must.'

CHAPTER EIGHTEEN

For a while – quite a long while, actually – no one moved. Or spoke. Or, in my case, breathed. What was Oliver saying? That now we were inside Shotton Hall, we might never get out again?

I looked over at Jones who was staring at the floor, frowning heavily. I suspected his thoughts were running along the same lines as mine. We could be trapped. Trapped in an old house with no power, no food – probably no water, either. And no way out. Because Shotton Hall was like flypaper. Once it touched you, it never let go.

Jones stirred. 'Exactly how long have you been here?'

'This is our second day.'

There must be a mobile phone signal. Oliver Shotton had called us yesterday. From here, presumably. We could do the same. Call on Iblis or Jerry for help.

No – no, we couldn't do that. We'd be no better than the Shottons themselves if we dragged someone else into this. Later, perhaps – as a last resort.

I looked across to Jones and once again I saw his thoughts had followed mine.

I took a deep breath. It wasn't all bad. At least Oliver had stopped talking.

Jones drew me aside, saying quietly, 'Stay here.'

'What are you going to do?'

'Open the front door. See what happens.'

'What do you expect to happen?'

'I don't know.'

'Don't you believe them?'

He gestured to the two brothers, now standing, heads together at the foot of the stairs, watching us. 'This place has been deserted for years. Decades. There's no food here. No water. No electricity.'

'Unless they've brought supplies with them. But if that's so, then did they know what would happen?'

'I think they at least had a very good idea of what *might* happen. Remember Oliver's brother died here. Suppose he'd had similar development plans, popped over for a quick survey and . . .'

'And she wouldn't let him out.' I swallowed. 'And he died. But of what?'

'Starvation? Or possibly dehydration. Perhaps she actually . . . got him.'

'Surely not. These are modern times. He could have called for help at any time. On his mobile. There's obviously a signal.'

Jones looked down at me, moving to shield me from the others. 'Keep your face still, Cage.'

'All right.'

'Perhaps he did call someone. Suppose he called Oliver to get him out. After all – who else would he contact?' He drew a deep breath. 'And Oliver didn't come.'

'But all his brother would have had to do was call someone else. And then Oliver would be in real trouble.'

He dropped his voice even lower. 'Not necessarily. Picture

the conversation, Cage.' He held his hand to his ear in the traditional telephone shape. '"Oh my God, brother, you're trapped? How terrible. Don't panic. Sit tight. I'll get something organised and we'll have you out of there in no time. Don't call anyone else – you need to save your battery. And don't ring me – I'll ring you. You'll need your phone to talk to us when we arrive. Hang on, brother mine, help is on the way."' He sighed. 'Only it wasn't. Oliver did nothing. Nothing at all. He probably sat by his phone counting down the hours. Maybe every now and then he called his brother: "Yes, yes, we've assembled a team. Helicopters, security and so forth. Sit tight. We're on our way. Hang up and save your power."'

I stared, hardly able to believe my ears.

'How long does your phone last, Cage?'

'I don't know – I charge it every night.'

'Most people do. But no matter how much charge he had when he arrived here, sooner or later it would have run out.'

I shivered. 'I wonder at what point he realised Oliver wasn't coming.'

'I think we can assume after his phone was dead, otherwise he would have called someone else.'

I remembered what he'd said about keeping my face still. Forcing myself not to look around, I whispered, 'And that was ten years ago?'

'Which makes Oliver a very dangerous man.'

'Ruthless, certainly, but why dangerous?'

'Because having killed his brother – indirectly – he had the patience to sit back and wait to inherit normally. He knew Shotton Hall would come to him eventually. All he had to do was wait. He probably passed the time with dreaming and scheming over how best to use this unexpected windfall. I think he's been planning this for years.'

'But, sadly, the ghost who cleared his way is now standing in it.'

'Yes. Hence – us. That was what Lorelei King was doing when she came to see us. Sounding us out.'

I looked around. 'If Oliver's brother died here – where's the body?'

'I think we can assume he died outside somewhere. That at some point he made a run for it. I wonder how far he got. He might still be out there, somewhere. In that great tangle of undergrowth. We might even have walked straight past his bones. Or perhaps he made it as far as the road before he died, and was found. We don't know and I'm not going to raise their suspicions by asking.'

I swallowed. 'But that makes Oliver a particularly cold-blooded murderer.'

'Well, not technically. His defence was probably that his brother rang him with some ridiculous ghost story which he didn't believe until it was too late. Who would? Obviously the balance of his mind was disturbed. "How sad. If only I'd acted more quickly. Such a tragedy."'

'Still a murderer, though.'

'A very cold, calculating bastard of a murderer,' Jones agreed.

'And if he'd do that to his brother – what wouldn't he do to us?'

'There's a lot of money at stake here and I think he'll do anything to get it. So, for the time being, we need to play along. Some sort of opportunity will present itself, Cage, and then, trust me, we're out of here. And I might as well tell you now that taking any Shotton or King with us will be very optional.'

I was rather shocked to find I had no problems with that.

269

What an unpleasant person I seemed to be turning into. Was it increased exposure to unpleasant things? Or – a nasty thought – was the bad side of Felda bleeding through? Or had I always been this way and never noticed? Whichever it was – now was not the time to worry about it.

'All right,' I said, again. 'And we should take a look around, get the lie of the land, identify possible escape routes, and so forth.'

'Agreed,' he said. 'OK – meek and mild, Cage. We need them to believe we've been outwitted. Full cooperation with these little turds, because it might be the only way out of here. Smile and do as you're told.'

'I always do.'

'Oh Cage, you and I have such diametrically opposed points of view.'

I glanced back at the brothers, who were still watching us. 'Are you still going to . . . you know . . . open the door?'

'I think we have to, don't you? First rule, Cage – always establish the facts for yourself. For all we know, these people are lying through their teeth, and imagine how embarrassing it will be to starve to death when we could have walked out at any time. I'll do it. You stand well back. And remember – if anything happens to me . . .'

He stopped.

'What?' I said, alarmed.

'Avenge my passing.'

'Oh . . . um . . . well . . .'

'Cage!'

I pulled myself together. 'Yes, of course. May a blood curse fall upon me should I fail to avenge your terrible fate.'

He patted my shoulder. 'Don't get carried away.'

270

He was right, of course – not about the getting-carried-away thing – but we should establish the facts before deciding on a course of action and the first thing to establish, obviously – was there an actual ghost?

The short answer was – yes, there was. And she was a monster.

I'd read up on smallpox, of course – one of the most disfiguring diseases ever. It's been eradicated these days, but for centuries – millennia, even – it was a scourge. A hugely contagious, bloody, agonising, and almost always fatal scourge.

Until you've seen a victim face to face, you can have no idea.

Jones had reached the door. Carefully, he shot the top and bottom bolts. They moved soundlessly. I suspected liberal applications of WD40. I wouldn't mind betting the key turned equally easily. Oliver – because it wouldn't have been Adam – had thought of everything. I should be careful of underestimating Oliver. Just because he looked like everyone's idea of an upper-class twit didn't necessarily mean he was.

Obviously anticipating what Jones would do, Oliver retreated back through an open doorway into the room beyond, closing the door behind him. I noticed he left his brother and Lorelei King to fend for themselves.

I ran to a front window, knelt on the sill and tried to squint out and sideways for a view of the front door. 'There's no one there. The porch is empty.'

'Wait,' shouted Adam, slightly behind events. 'What are you doing? Stop.'

Too late. Jones wrenched open the door.

The porch was *not* empty. She was there. I don't know where she came from. Or how. One moment the porch was unoccupied, and the next – she was there, surging towards us.

271

Tall. She was very tall. It was only later I realised her feet didn't touch the ground. She was just hanging in the air. Perhaps towards the end, in her last days, her legs hadn't worked properly.

I had a vague impression of a ragged, dark dress hanging off her scrawny body, but it was her face that would always stay in my memory. And later her hands, but right now, looking down on Jones – it was her face.

I tried to look away but horror held me rigid. There were hundreds and hundreds of pus-filled spots on every visible area of her body. She must be riddled with them. Some were old and scabby, some fresh and raw. Many were weeping. She herself was filthy dirty and many of her open sores were badly infected.

Only one eye was visible. The other was buried under a mound of suppurating blisters. Her thin hair hung stringily around her face. I could see huge lesions all over her scalp.

And she was so close to Jones. I knew the disease was horribly contagious. That it could be passed through coughing or sneezing, or by touching the pus from a blister. Even just by handling an infected person's bedding or belongings.

And there was no cure. Not in her time, anyway.

She was far too close to Jones. Towering over his head. Only a few feet away. All it would take was one cough, one sneeze, one touch. She might even hawk and spit.

The next bit was very confused. She seemed to surge forwards, filling the doorway. If she should cross the threshold . . . I shouted a warning. At the same time, Lorelei King screamed. Adam yelped or screamed – it was hard to tell – but Jones was already slamming the door in her face. The boom echoed around the hall, and plaster and dust dropped from the ceiling. He'd had the door open for less than five seconds.

272

For a moment, I couldn't move. Even though she'd gone, my eyes could still see her, hanging in the air above him. My heart was pounding. I could feel cold sweat on my forehead.

Forcing my shaky legs to work, I went to join him, looking him up and down for signs of . . . something. 'Are you all right? Did she touch you? At all?'

He was bolting the door. 'Yes and no, Cage. I'm fine.'

His colour was dark and swirling – not surprisingly – but his face was calm.

Now that it was safe, Oliver emerged from wherever he'd been hiding and crossed the hall.

'Now will you believe me?' he said.

'Yes,' said Jones, and fetched Oliver a punch that sent him reeling backwards to sit down hard on his bottom. The flagstones wouldn't have cushioned his fall even a little bit.

I tried to remember that violence never solves anyone's problems and failed. Quite spectacularly.

'Nice hit,' I said, in admiration.

Jones was shaking out his hand. 'Thank you, Cage.'

He turned to Adam and Lorelei. 'I'm going to ask questions, which you will answer fully and truthfully. Cage and I will find a way out of this. Cooperate with our efforts and we'll consider letting you two tag along with us. Fail to cooperate and we'll leave you to rot with Obnoxious Oliver here. Please indicate if you're too stupid to understand a word I'm saying.'

They shook their heads. I was reminded of two naughty schoolchildren called to account in the head teacher's study.

'Right. Cards on the table,' said Jones. 'You've brought us here to get rid of her. Elizabeth Shotton.'

Oliver climbed slowly to his feet and touched his nose. To see if it was still there, presumably.

'Yes. I can't bring in architects, surveyors, engineers, only to have them trapped in this house. Or die trying to get out. Word would soon get around and then the project would never get off the ground.'

This was obviously his main concern. Not the architects, surveyors, etc., who would slowly starve to death.

'So, obviously,' he said, pulling out his handkerchief and dabbing at his non-bleeding nose. 'I want her gone. She's vicious, she's mindless and she's in my way. Get rid of her.'

The words seemed to echo around the cavernous hall with a strange kind of resonance. It was fanciful, I know, but I had a horrible feeling Oliver might just have signed his own death warrant. Adam and Lorelei looked at each other and then away again.

'Moving on from that,' said Jones. 'Resources. Is there any food?'

Adam nodded.

'For how long?'

'A week.'

'For all of us, or just for Oliver?'

'All of us. He planned for this. He heard there was a woman in Rushford who could . . . well . . . deal with this sort of thing. He sent Lorelei to check you out and . . .'

And if I hadn't shown off about the accident on the Whittington road . . . If I'd just shut up and made the tea . . . been the timid little assistant the universe obviously wanted me to be, then we might not be here at this moment. I could only hope I lived long enough to learn my lesson.

Jones was forging on. 'And water?'

They nodded again.

'Phones?'

'We had to leave them behind,' said Adam resentfully. 'Oliver thought we might tip you off.'

Thus reminded, I looked around for my bag on the window seat. Just in time to catch Oliver emptying its contents all over the floor. My diary, comb, purse, notebook, pen and keys skidded in all directions. And there were other things, too. Private things. I felt my face burn hot with embarrassment.

Before I could move, however, Oliver brought his foot down hard. My phone shattered. And Jones's phone – according to our very own safety protocol, as suggested by me – was outside in the car.

Jones turned to me. 'We definitely need to rethink that part of the plan.'

I was on my knees, picking up my belongings and ramming them back into my handbag. 'Agreed.'

My phone was in pieces. I extracted the sim card out of the wreckage and tucked it away.

Jones turned back to Lorelei and Adam. 'Are any of these rooms habitable?'

'Yes,' Lorelei said. She certainly wasn't attracted to Jones now. Her colour was shrinking away from him. About time she realised she'd got a tiger by the tail.

'Have any of you been able to go outside? At all? Even for a moment?'

She and Adam both shook their heads.

'What happens if one of you opens the front door and the other the back? Don't tell me she can be in two places at the same time.'

'That was our thought,' said Lorelei. 'But she moves so

275

fast. The second person wouldn't get more than ten feet.' She scowled at Oliver. 'And then Oliver locked the back door and took the key.'

'Is she here all the time?'

'Sometimes she goes round and round the house,' volunteered Adam. His voice was thin and reedy. 'You can hear her at night. Her nails scratch against the windowpanes.' He shivered.

'Are there any broken windows she could get through?' said Jones sharply.

'No. Everything broken is boarded up. First thing we checked.' Lorelei was looking resentfully at her broken fingernails and ruined manicure.

'So, as things stand at the moment, she can't get in?'

'Not unless someone lets her in.'

Jones looked around. 'Anyone likely to do that?'

Silence was the only answer to that question.

'No,' said Adam eventually. 'We're safe. As long as we stay inside.'

Lorelei caught at his arm. 'But the food will run out and . . .'

'Oh, Cage and I will be gone long before then,' said Jones cheerfully. 'Not sure about you lot, of course. Let's have the promised guided tour, shall we? No, not you, Oliver. After you, Miss King.'

'Um . . . OK. Well, we're standing in the hall.' She gestured, and obediently I looked around. She continued, 'This is one of the oldest parts of the house.'

'What about the wings?' asked Jones, staring up at the high ceiling.

'Both boarded up. There's no access to and from the main part of the house.'

'Other doors?'

'Only the kitchen door at the back. Locked.'

'So just this front door,' he said, still looking around.

'Yes.'

The hall was a big square space, one and a half storeys high. A massive fireplace occupied part of the left-hand wall. I stared at it thoughtfully.

Adam shook his head. 'No – that's one good thing. The flues are all closed and have been for years. They can't be forced open.'

Well, at least nothing unpleasant would be coming down the chimney.

I looked down. The floor was part flagstones and part dirty cracked terracotta tiles, all of which looked solid enough, so it seemed safe to assume nothing would be coming up through the floor, either.

There was no furniture anywhere – the hall was completely bare and the walls were covered in crumbling wooden panelling to above head height. Several doors opened off.

'Drawing room,' said Lorelei, pointing right. 'Library. Study.' She pointed left. 'Dining Room. Morning room. One other room, purpose unknown. Most of the furniture's piled up in there.' She swallowed. 'We think, at some point, someone tried to build a barricade.'

'Anything of value in the house?' said Jones, setting off. 'Portraits, and so forth.'

She trotted along behind him. 'No one knows. There's no inventory. The house was more or less abandoned overnight. There probably were portraits, books, old masters, china, tapestries, Turkish carpets – all the usual stuff – but with no one to look after it, it seems a lot of it has just mouldered away.'

All the rooms were similar, with high ceilings and tall windows, but the trees and bushes growing only feet away kept them dark.

Jones headed for the stairs. 'Let's try up there.'

Lorelei followed him. 'Be careful. The steps are a bit wormy. Keep to the edges, and it's probably best not to put any weight on the bannisters.'

She was being unusually helpful. I wondered if she'd worked out that she stood a better chance of escape with Jones than with Oliver.

'Are we looking for anything in particular?' I said to him, as we walked slowly up the stairs in single file, only one of us standing on each stair at any given time.

'A way out for us – a way in for her.' He turned to Lorelei, several stairs below us. 'Were there any signs of her when you first arrived?'

'No. Because . . .'

'Because she lets you in, but doesn't let you out again.'

'Yes.'

He lowered his voice. 'Did you know about this? Did you know the story before you came here?'

'No,' she said quietly. 'He just said it was an old house, nearly derelict, but he had big plans for it and would I like to come along with him and take a look? Get in on the ground floor of what could be an important story locally.'

Her colour had wrapped itself around her. She was lying. No – she was hiding something. The bit about Oliver was true but there was more to it than that. I glanced at Jones, who was obviously thinking along the same lines. He turned back to her.

'Why you?'

'Adam and I . . .' she said, and just for a moment her colour flickered.

I had no idea what that meant. She was obviously in a relationship with Adam, who, frankly, didn't have a lot going for him. Not for someone like Lorelei King, anyway. I would have thought Oliver, unpleasant specimen though he was, was more her cup of tea. On the other hand, if this property deal came off, even if Adam only came in for a minor share, that would still be a lot of money. Was that the attraction? I could easily believe that.

'Where are you sleeping?'

'Um . . .'

'I don't mean who are you sleeping with; I want a room which is habitable enough for Cage and me to sleep in and that doesn't have any of you in it.'

'Oh. Yours is at the end of the landing on the right.'

There were four windows in the room. Two on each side of the grubby marble fireplace. The windows were very tall – from knee height nearly up to the ceiling, with small panes of glass. The outlook was to the front and a little more open here. The trees stood further away.

'It's a miracle none of these are broken,' I said.

'Protected by trees and tall bushes, I suspect,' said Jones. 'But not for much longer. The putty's gone. Some of these panes must be hanging in there out of sheer habit.'

'And there's been no vandalism,' I said. 'Other than local wildlife, no one's been here for ages.'

'Too scared, probably,' said Jones.

As everywhere else in this house, this room smelled of dust and mushrooms because, of course, no one could ever open a window.

279

Jones looked up. 'What about the top floor?'

'Most of the ceilings have come down up there. It's very unsafe.'

'Do you know that for a fact?'

'Um . . . no. Oliver told me.'

I'd been standing with my back to the window, looking around as I listened to them talk. Now I turned to have another look outside.

She was there. On the other side of the window. About twelve inches away from me. We were on the first floor so she must be at least fifteen to twenty feet off the ground. She was so close. I could see the dirt in her pores. See the grease in her hair. I could see where her gums had receded, showing her long teeth as she drew back her lips in a vicious snarl. Her face was flat up against the glass. She raised her hand. Was she strong enough to punch her way through?

I don't know what made me do it. It wasn't bravery. I was terrified. Too terrified to run. Too terrified even to step away from the window. For a long, long moment – an endless moment – we looked at each other. I lifted my hand and placed it flat against the glass. Because, suddenly, I wondered – was she reaching out *for* me? Or *to* me.

The moment stretched on and on. Behind me, all movement had ceased. There wasn't a sound from Jones or Lorelei King.

And then, for no reason that I could discern, almost faster than the eye could see, she whirled about. There was a brief impression of swirling brown fabric, flying hair, and in the blink of an eye, she had disappeared.

CHAPTER NINETEEN

I think all of us were happy to discontinue the tour after that. We went back downstairs – slowly and in single file again.

Oliver was in the kitchen staring helplessly into one of several rather upmarket food hampers. He turned as we approached. 'Oh good. Perhaps the girls could rustle us all up some sandwiches.'

'I can't think of anything more unlikely,' said Jones, folding his arms and grinning at him.

There was an embarrassed silence. Jones continued to radiate unhelpfulness. Adam had drifted off to Planet Adam. I certainly wasn't going to budge. Which left Lorelei. She shifted her weight to step forwards and I gently caught hold of her gilet and pulled her back. She looked round and I fractionally shook my head.

The embarrassment factor was off the charts. I was interested to see who would buckle first.

It was Oliver. Turning to Lorelei, he said, 'I don't know why I brought you here, if you're not going to make yourself useful.'

'You didn't,' said Adam, suddenly waking up. 'I did.'

Oliver made an exasperated noise and strode from the kitchen.

'Good,' said Jones, unfolding his arms. 'Because I'm starving. Cage, you slice the rolls in half, because you're the only one here I trust with a sharp implement. Adam, you butter. Lorelei, you stuff the rolls.'

She looked at him.

'With ham,' he said, as if to an infant.

'And what exactly will you be doing?'

'Lighting the camping stove and heating the soup. Chop-chop, everyone. We should get this done before dark.'

'Water?' I said.

'There's a pump in the scullery,' said Adam, peering at the butter. Possibly he expected it to spread itself on the rolls under its own steam.

Jones set off. 'I'll pump some up now, while we can still see. Then we can have tea afterwards.'

'Boil it well,' I said, because I couldn't help myself.

No one was surprised when Oliver reappeared just as we were sitting down to eat. On the floor, obviously, backs against the wall. He grunted and helped himself.

I curled my hands around my picnic mug. The hot soup was very welcome. This house was damp and the floor cold and hard.

'Well?' said Oliver, apparently not noticing no one was speaking to him. 'I'm keen to hear what progress you've made.'

Jones swallowed down the last of his roll. 'I don't anticipate any difficulties getting myself and Mrs Cage out of here. Not so sure about the rest of you.'

'Why – what is the problem?'

'No problem. I just don't particularly feel like bringing you along. For two pins, I'd leave you here to rot for ever.'

'Mr Jones, you will find I can be very, very generous and I'm certainly not prepared to pinch the pennies in this case.'

Jones shook his head. 'Not entirely sure I trust you to pay up when all this is over.'

'No need to be so suspicious, Mr Jones. I can pop the money into your bank account any—'

He stopped and at that moment Lorelei screamed and pointed with a shaking hand. 'She's there. Looking at us through the window.'

We all looked up. If she had been there, she was gone now. Although night was falling and with our two camping lanterns going, it was impossible to see outside.

Oliver had jumped a mile. He was by no means as blasé as he would have us believe. 'You stupid cow. Keep your screaming and squeaking to yourself.'

She tossed her hair. 'Don't speak to me like that. Adam, are you going to let him speak to me like that?'

Adam had been enjoying a more liquid meal from his hip flask and wasn't really capable of preventing anyone doing anything.

Oliver sighed. 'Whatever does he see in you?'

She glared hatred at him. Her whole colour was flooded with red and orange. Colours that don't mix well with green. Dark grey patches appeared, spreading outwards. I'd never seen such a strong reaction from anyone. I cast a glance at Jones, placidly sipping his soup and missing nothing.

He dipped his head at me. Very fractionally. For some reason that made no sense at all, I felt comforted. We'd been together so long we didn't always need words.

By the time we'd finished eating and cleared away, it was nearly dark and I'd had my fill of Shottons. And Lorelei King as well. She wasn't blameless in this mess.

Jones looked at Oliver. 'We need to sort out our sleeping

283

arrangements. Do we just stretch out on the floor somewhere and freeze to death?'

'Of course not,' he said, quite offended. As if, up until this moment, he'd been the perfect host. 'Mrs Cage, please do not imagine I haven't prepared for this. There are sleeping bags and a pack of toiletries for each of you. They're in the library. I believe Lorelei will already have shown you the room I've allocated to you. There are shutters at the window but I don't recommend touching them. I suspect it wouldn't take much for them to slip their moorings and we don't want to run any risk of breaking a window, do we? Lorelei, go and get their sleeping bags.'

'Don't bother,' I said, getting up. 'We can manage.'

There were indeed sleeping bags. And more camping lanterns. And toiletries.

'Interesting,' said Jones as we made our way upstairs by the light of a solitary lantern.

'What is?'

'That he came so well prepared. He obviously didn't expect this to be a ten-minute job.'

I waited until we'd shunted all our stuff into our room and more or less got the door closed before finally voicing my fears. Standing in the small pool of light cast by our lantern, I took a deep breath and said, 'You should know – I'm not sure what I can do to fix this. Or even how to make a start. I'm afraid, when the time comes, I won't be able to do anything to get us out and if I can't then we're stuck here. For ever. We'll die here. And it'll be my fault because I did that thing with Lorelei and the road traffic accident and I'm not as clever as people think I am. As you think I am.'

284

I wasn't sure he was listening to me. 'Actually, I'm rather wondering if Oliver didn't make his first mistake just now.'

'But . . .'

'We'll work the problem together,' he said. 'Like we always do. Now, sleeping bags over there, I think.'

By mutual consent we laid our sleeping bags against the wall furthest from the windows and investigated our packs. Oliver was right – there was everything we needed, even including a cheap white T-shirt to sleep in.

Jones indicated one of the dark windows. 'Would you like me to stare outside while you . . . ?'

'Thank you, but no,' I said. 'There's no way I'm taking any clothes off. If anything kicks off, I'm not being the token totty rushing around in her nightie.'

'Shame,' he said. 'I'd give a lot to see that. It's dark and we shouldn't waste the lantern, Cage. Let's get everything laid out. We'll talk once we're in bed.'

I laid out my sleeping bag and unzipped it. My toilet bag contained wet wipes, a toothbrush, toothpaste and deodorant. As did Jones's. But no razor.

He sighed. 'Well, I've been considering a beard.'

I took off my jacket and shoes and zipped up my sleeping bag around me. 'Good heavens. Why?'

'I thought it might enhance my manliness.'

'Well, it's your decision, of course, but I really think it might take more than one.'

'You won't be saying that when the full impact of my masculinity bursts forth tomorrow. Watch what I'm doing, now. If anything kicks off in the night then it will be dark. The door is along the wall and to our left. There's nothing between it and us to fall over or walk into. Once out of the door, turn left and head for the stairs. Take this torch and tuck it in your sleeping bag with you.'

'Why?'

'So you can find it easily. And so no one can sneak in and pinch it.'

'Why would they do that?'

'Because then we'd be in the dark, wouldn't we, and all sorts of things can happen in the dark.'

I waited until he was zipped in his own sleeping bag and then said, 'Well, go on. I know you're dying to tell me. What was the mistake that Oliver made?'

'You heard it as well as me.'

'Yes, but I'm tired, frightened and lying on this incredibly cold, hard floor alongside a man so deluded he thinks beards can perform miracles, so let's assume I missed it.'

'No assumption needed, Cage. You did miss it. He stopped himself just in time. And then, fortunately for him, Lorelei started screaming.'

'All right – what did he nearly say?'

'He was about to say he could pop the money into my bank account.'

'Really? What money?'

'Wrong question, Cage.'

I sighed in the dark. 'All right – what was the right question?'

'How?'

'How what?'

'How would he do that? He's stuck here with the rest of us.'

'Well, obviously he'd . . .' I tailed away. 'That's a very good question.'

'It is, isn't it?' He lowered his voice although who he thought might overhear us was a bit of a mystery. 'I think it's pretty obvious Oliver Shotton has a second phone stashed somewhere. He called us on his own phone – quite openly – and now I suspect it's run out of charge and there's no power here. He'd be an idiot if he didn't have a spare tucked away somewhere. So – first thing tomorrow – we find it.'

The noises started almost at once. I lay still, listening to the silence of the night all around us and then—

A gentle scratching sound. For a moment, I couldn't think what it was and then I could. She was outside the window, running her fingernails over the glass. Looking for a way inside.

The noise stopped. Had she moved on to another window? Another room?

No, she had not. A tapping sound. Gentle at first and then getting louder and louder. Now she was banging. Banging on the glass with both hands. Oh God, suppose one of the panes broke. She be inside in a flash and we'd be dead. Or would she play with us first? Drive us mad? Cause us to kill each other? Would we be reduced to eating each other when the food ran out?

Tap tap tap. Bang bang bang. I curled up small and tried very hard not to imagine that terrible face pressed against the glass, looking in at me as I lay helpless on the floor. Willing me to get up and open the window and let her in.

We weren't going to get out of this one. My stupidity – my hubris – had killed us both. We were going to die. At her hands or our own.

'I'll tell you something,' said Jones, beside me in the dark, startling me out of my terrors.

I swallowed. 'What's that?'

'If I go, I'm taking that prick Shotton with me.'

'Which one?'

There was a pause while he considered this.

'Both of them.'

I barely slept that night. Every sound jerked me awake. Everything outside was silent. The countryside is usually quite noisy at night but not here. No foxes barked. No owls hooted. We were surrounded by silent, velvety blackness. And then there would be that sound again. At the window. A soft brushing noise as if someone was dragging their hand across the window. The knowledge that she was always there, testing for weaknesses, looking in at us as we lay in the dark, was not conducive to sleep. Not in any way.

'She can't get in,' said Jones beside me. 'If she could, she would have. And as long as she's scratching at the window, we know where she is and it's not in here with us.'

'No, I know.'

'We'll get out of this, Cage.'

'How?'

'You'll think of something.'

'Thank you. That's very comforting.'

'Hey – it's what I do.'

I lay in the dark and listened to the ghost of Elizabeth Shotton endlessly searching for a way inside.

Oliver and Adam met us as we came downstairs the next morning.

'Well, Mrs Cage,' said Oliver, attempting joviality. 'Your

288

turn to make the breakfast. And someone's going to need to pump up some water.'

It was obvious that whoever that someone was, it wasn't going to be him.

'You don't want Cage anywhere near food,' said Jones. 'Worst cook in the world.'

Justifiably indignant at this slur, I opened my mouth and then closed it again, saying meekly, 'That's true.'

Oliver tutted and disappeared, presumably to bully Lorelei into making his breakfast.

'Come on,' said Jones to Adam. 'We'll get the water.'

They wandered off, leaving me standing alone which, no doubt, was exactly what Jones had intended.

I'd spent half the night thinking about where I would hide a phone. Small. Flat. Rectangular. Somewhere it could be accessed quickly in the event of an emergency. Would he have it on him? I rather thought he would and, if so, then Jones would have to handle that. My job was to eliminate the possibility he might have hidden it somewhere around the building. Somewhere no one else would go. His room, obviously. I made my way up the creaking stairs and along the landing. I decided that should anyone come after me, my excuse would be that I wanted a quiet word alone with Oliver, since he was best placed to give me the information I needed to rid Shotton Hall of its troublesome spirit. Or that I was walking around to get the feel of the place. Something like that, anyway.

No one did. Jones would be keeping them all breakfast-oriented. The Shottons' rooms were at the other end of the landing. I tapped gently at Oliver's door just in case, received no answer and slipped inside.

It wasn't in his sleeping bag. Or among his toiletries. Or his small sports bag. I slipped next door and started on Lorelei's gear. It would be typical of Oliver to have hidden it there, because then if it was accidentally discovered, he'd be able to blame her.

It wasn't. Lorelei's gear was as phone-free as Oliver's. As was Adam's.

I returned to Oliver's room and stood in the doorway, looking around the room. Time was passing. I needed to get a move on.

There was no furniture in here. I walked the floor, looking for possible loose boards. I crossed to the fireplace. The grate was full of soot and there were no signs anyone had even been near it, so not up the chimney.

I straightened up and tried to think. Where would I hide a phone? Most of me was still convinced he'd have it on him.

Adam and Lorelei's stuff had spilled halfway across their room but Oliver was neat. His toiletries were packed away and his sleeping bag unzipped to air. Even his boots were neatly parked against the wall. He wasn't wearing them today. They still looked stiff and shiny; I suspected they'd hurt his feet.

Actually . . .

And there it was. Stuffed in the toe of his right boot. I pulled it out. Switched off.

We should have guessed sooner. There was no way Oliver Shotton would have left himself out of contact with the outside world. My guess was that he would have a helicopter on standby. Would a 19th-century ghost be equal to modern technology? I would think about that later.

I removed the phone from its cover. The cover went back into his boot in case he wanted to check it was still there. The

290

phone itself went in my bra strap. Probably the safest and least visited place in the entire world.

I let myself carefully out of his room, down the creaking stairs and into the kitchen. Someone was making toast. Lorelei, I think. Adam was boiling water. Jones was assembling mugs. I caught his eye and nodded, casually placing my hand over the phone.

He grinned and said, 'Adam, how's that water coming on?'

'Just coming to the boil,' said Adam, who looked even worse in the mornings than he did in the evenings.

'Cage, can you give me a hand with this bucket, please?'

I followed him into the scullery, glanced over my shoulder and handed over the phone.

He switched it on. 'Locked. Obviously.'

'Do you think you can force him to open it?'

'Probably, but I have something more subtle in mind. Time to start frightening the living shit out of Oliver Shotton. Stay out of the way, Cage. He's not going to be a happy bunny.'

I followed him back into the kitchen and went to stand with my back against the far wall.

I never saw him do it. I swear I never took my eyes off him, and I've no idea when or how he did it. He carried on pottering cheerfully around the kitchen, laying out the mugs for tea, passing the toast around until, finally, casually, he came to rest next to Oliver.

'Where's that tea?' said Oliver, quite jovially for him.

Lorelei bent over the saucepan. 'It's nearly . . .'

She jumped back with a scream.

Oliver was irritated all over again. 'For God's sake – what now?'

She was peering through the steam, holding her hair out of her eyes. 'It's . . . There's a phone. In the water. There's a phone in there.'

Oliver scrambled to his feet. 'What?'

Shoving her aside, he too bent over the saucepan, and stared for a few seconds. Grabbing at the handle, he yelped.

'Be careful,' said Jones innocently. 'Those handles can get very hot.'

Cursing, Oliver grabbed at it, yanking the saucepan so violently that water splashed everywhere. Including down his own leg. He yelped again.

'Do be careful,' said Jones, grinning.

Oliver kicked over the saucepan. Boiling water ran across the floor. People jumped back and a mobile phone clattered on to the flags.

'A phone,' cried Lorelei. She peered more closely. 'That's not . . .' She straightened up. 'You had another phone.' She turned to him, furious. 'All this time you had another phone?'

Interesting that she was instantly able to identify the culprit.

'Not any longer,' said Jones. 'I know they make sim cards tough these days, but I doubt they're designed to survive boiling water . . .' He tailed away and sighed sadly. 'If only Mrs Cage's phone hadn't met with a tragic accident.'

Oliver wheeled around. 'You. You did this.'

Jones loomed over him. Half a head taller and a couple of shoulders wider. 'Yep. Guilty as charged.'

I saw the exact moment Oliver abandoned thoughts of vengeance on Jones and opted instead for the weak link. He rounded on me. 'You went through our things. You're not only useless at getting us out of here, but you're a common little thief as well. I've a good mind to throw you to the bitch outside.'

For a moment I thought he was going to hit me, but Jones was suddenly there and Oliver hastily moved on to Lorelei.

'This is all your fault. You told me this woman could do it. I believed you and now we're all trapped. We're all going to die here, thanks to you, you stupid, stupid little trollop.'

He backhanded her across the room.

Adam rose to his feet. 'Hey.'

I ran to Lorelei, who was sprawled on the floor, and tugged at her arm. 'Get up. There's going to be a fight and you don't want to be trampled.'

There was a fight. Well, a bit of a fight. It was actually quite funny. Brought up as I'd been on TV and film violence, I think subconsciously I was expecting carefully choreographed punching and kicking and so forth. This wasn't quite that. Oliver and Adam each brought their own style to the proceedings. There was a lot of wild arm swinging. No punches connected. Or even came close. Abandoning that, they grappled with each other, staggering around the kitchen, bouncing off the walls. Lorelei and I just kept out of the way, but Jones helped himself to a piece of toast and settled down to watch. It was very obvious that, having got hold of each other, neither Oliver nor Adam knew what to do next.

Eventually they fell back, panting, each eyeing the other balefully. And yes, it was a funny moment, but I couldn't help remembering that according to the original story, it hadn't been the ghost who killed the inhabitants – they'd killed each other. Elizabeth Shotton hadn't lifted a finger. Was this the beginning

293

of the end for us? The first step in a dance that would end in an orgy of violence, insanity, and ultimately – death?

I mustn't think like that. I should concentrate on now, rather than the events of the past. Jones was eating – I should do the same. I snagged myself a piece of toast.

Jones stirred the broken phone with his foot. 'Well, now we're all in the same boat. We're out of contact with the outside world.'

Oliver wiped his face with his sleeve. 'Are you insane? Do you know what you've done?'

'Yeah – like you were ever going to let us out of here, knowing what we know.' He looked across at Lorelei, not without some compassion. 'You weren't going to let her out either, were you?'

'What?' she screamed and flew at Oliver.

I looked across at Jones. There was something about this situation that wasn't quite right. Almost – but not quite.

Jones gave her a few moments to enjoy herself and then, as Oliver bunched his fist, he stepped in and pulled her off.

'Understandable reaction,' he said to her, swinging her aside and dumping her on her feet, 'but he's not worth going to prison for. Adam, make the tea.'

'Who are you to . . . ?'

'Now.'

Jones and I ate more toast, drank our tea and then left them to it. I think we both hankered after some Shotton-free space.

'Well, Cage,' he said, as we strolled aimlessly from room to room, getting the layout into our heads. 'Any thoughts?'

'I've had an idea,' I said. 'It's stupid and dangerous, but it's all I can think of.'

'Go on.'

'Well, we're not going to get out. No one ever has and there's nothing special about us . . .'

'Hey,' he said, wounded.

'So, we turn it around.'

'How exactly . . . ?'

I turned to face him. 'We invite her in.'

CHAPTER TWENTY

I thought he'd argue. Or shout. Or stamp about and wave his arms. Or simply refuse to do anything that stupid. I thought there would be demands to know what the hell I thought I was playing at. I thought he'd go on and on and on – and he didn't. He didn't do any of that.

He stood very still for perhaps a whole minute – which is quite a long time – not looking at anything in particular, and then he said, 'Yeah – actually that might work.'

We must have been on the sunny side of the house. Dappled sunlight shafted through the dusty windows. We stood together in a patch of warm sunshine and made a plan.

We spent the next hour in the kitchen. Adam was nowhere to be seen – I suspected he'd taken himself off somewhere quiet for a spot of recreational-substance reinforcement. Oliver wasn't around either, but Lorelei was still with us. Jones took her aside for a quiet word, after which she nodded and then set to, buttering bread as if her life depended on it, which, now I came to think of it, it did.

We were all busily working away when Oliver reappeared and stopped dead. There were plates of food everywhere. Because it was important to do this properly. We had to put on the best show we could. Anything else would be an insult and that wouldn't end well.

He surveyed the plates of finger sandwiches, the tiny slices of Battenburg – a favourite of Adam's, apparently – and me, polishing our picnic crockery in an effort to make it look special. 'What the hell are you doing?'

'We're having a tea party,' said Jones, busy gathering plates and stuff.

'What do you think you're . . . ? You've used up nearly all the food – there's barely anything left.'

'That's right.'

'Why? What the fuck do you think you're playing at?'

He really wasn't a happy camper. We'd taken away his phone and now we were using up all his supplies. As Jones had said, when things are going to be bad, always make sure they deteriorate at the time and place of your choosing.

'We're inviting her to tea. Elizabeth Shotton. We thought it would be nice if you could meet socially. Get to know each other. That sort of thing.'

Oliver literally staggered backwards. 'You're letting her into the house? Are you mad?'

Lorelei began to open a tin of tuna.

'Stop that,' he shouted, and tried to pull her away. I noted he didn't dare try that with me, and if he had wanted to shift Jones, then he would have needed heavy-lifting gear.

Lorelei shrugged him off and continued with what she was doing.

On the other hand, Oliver did have a point. We'd pillaged his stores. In addition to the sandwiches and the Battenburg, we'd found some biscuits. The nice ones with the thick chocolate.

And some cheese – which I'd cut into attractive shapes and arranged with some cherry tomatoes. Now, far from having another three or four days' supplies, we barely had enough for tomorrow's breakfast. This really was make-or-break time.

We had no tablecloths with us, but Lorelei had found some sad remains in a worm-eaten dresser. Something had given them a good chew, but by laying two or three on top of each other, we would be able to cover most of the holes.

Jones and Lorelei went off in search of the most suitable room. Small, not too dusty, not too smelly, that would respond to a quick tarting-up. They came back to say they'd discovered a small room at the top of the stairs that would do nicely, plus there were the remains of a table and some chairs that could be used. Jones was to wrestle with the flue and, if possible, light a small fire. They disappeared full of enthusiasm while I carried on cutting the crusts off the sandwiches and arranging the biscuits in a pattern I thought would appeal to an angry ghost with a vicious streak and a not-unjustified hatred of everything Shotton.

'Ready?' enquired Jones, reappearing in the kitchen. He looked hot, dishevelled, dusty and sooty. His arms were black to the elbows.

'Yes. Lorelei and I will get this lot upstairs. You glam yourself up a bit. Even one-day-old stubble isn't making you look particularly attractive.'

'Actually . . .' said Lorelei thoughtfully, watching him disappear into the scullery.

I held up my hand. 'Don't tell him that.'

She grinned. 'What?'

'That it suits him. Trust me, you'll regret it for ever.'

We carried the plates carefully upstairs. She and Jones had done a great job in here. The room wasn't wonderful, of course, but compared with the rest of the house, it looked warm and welcoming. A small fire burned in the hearth. A couple of the more dilapidated chairs had been broken up and used as firewood. They'd placed the small table near the fire and set three mostly intact chairs around it.

'Will I have to be here?' said Lorelei nervously, trying to smooth the creases from the tablecloths.

I shook my head and said quietly, 'Find somewhere safe near the front door. Stay away from Oliver and Adam in case they try to stop you leaving. Be ready to move. Don't waste time trying to bring anything with you.'

'All right.'

We laid things out as best we could. The tablecloths helped. Two plates of tiny finger sandwiches, the chocolate biscuits in their attractive pattern, the colourful Battenburg cake and the plate of cheese and tiny tomatoes. Three picnic plates and three travel cups ready for the tea. Being Oliver, of course, it was all high-quality picnicware in a smart blue and green geometric pattern. We didn't put out any cutlery other than teaspoons. Certainly nothing sharp.

'Boiling water,' said Jones, appearing at the door with the saucepan. He set it close to the fire to keep it hot. 'Have you got your scarf?'

'Yes.' I laid my carefully folded scarf alongside one of the plates.

'What's that?' said Lorelei, instantly suspicious.

'Greasing the wheels,' said Jones.

'A present for her,' I said. 'Because every little helps.'

'Oh. Yes. Good idea.' She stood for a moment. 'Wait.' She began to fumble around the back of her neck. 'Bugger . . . I can't . . .'

'What?' I said.

'Locket. If you think it will help.'

'Good thought,' said Jones.

She laid a little golden heart across the scarf. I wondered if Adam had bought it for her.

And then – suddenly – there was nothing more to do. I wiped my hands down my jeans. We'd been so busy that I'd almost forgotten the point of all our preparations. Now it all came crashing back. We were about to do something amazingly stupid. These could be the last moments of our lives.

'Does everyone know what to do?' said Jones quietly.

Lorelei and I nodded.

'Off you go, then,' he said to her. 'Good luck. Stay safe.'

She slipped out of the room.

'OK,' said Jones. 'Well, let's hope this works.'

No sooner had the words left his mouth than the door opened. Oliver and Adam stood across the threshold. Oliver was wearing his *you shall not pass* expression. Adam contented himself with swaying in a threatening manner.

I wasn't that concerned – I had might on my side. Or Michael Jones, as many others called him.

'I won't let you do this,' said Oliver furiously. 'You're endangering us all. You know what will happen if you let her in.'

'Yes,' said Jones. 'You'll die.'

'We'll *all* die.'

Jones considered this. 'Not necessarily.'

'But . . .'

300

'We're negotiating our escape,' said Jones patiently. 'And yours as well, so shut up and let us get on with it. Stay out of sight. Don't let her see you. She doesn't like Shottons. When you see us coming down the stairs – and not before – get ready to leave. Don't run. You don't want to upset her. Wait for us because this will only work if we all leave together.'

By now, Oliver was very nearly frothing at the mouth. 'You're insane. You've heard the stories. You've even seen her. You know what will happen once she gets inside this house. It will be another massacre.'

'That's a point,' said Jones. 'Thank you for reminding me.' He raised his voice slightly. 'I'd like to make it perfectly clear that anyone attempting to gnaw on my penis will get a thump round the side of the head that will solve all their problems for ever.' He looked down at me. 'Present company excepted, of course.'

I put my hands over my eyes. 'Why are you saying these things?'

'I'm trying to cheer you up. Has it worked?'

'I've certainly just realised that death is not the worst thing that can happen to me this afternoon.' I smoothed down my hair and endeavoured to look, if not respectable, at least as if I hadn't slept in these clothes.

Oliver wasn't giving up. 'I'm warning you, Jones . . .'

'We're opening the front door in ten seconds,' said Jones. 'This is your last chance to find a room in which to barricade yourself while Mrs Cage and I take all the risks. Nine . . . eight . . .'

'I won't let you do this. You'll die. We'll all die. I forbid it. This is my house. You work for me and I'm telling you . . .'

'Oh, do shut up,' said Jones wearily. 'I honestly think I prefer facing Elizabeth Shotton to listening to you whingeing on and on all day long.' I had to admit I was in complete agreement with him.

'Adam, for God's sake, do something useful and help me out here.'

But Adam had gone.

'What . . . ?' Oliver spun around as if Adam might be hiding behind the door.

'He's been sensible and found himself a little hidey-hole,' said Jones. 'Come on, Cage – you're up.'

Shouldering Oliver aside, he made his way to the door. I gave Oliver a wide berth and followed him out. I'm not sure what Oliver did but I heard running footsteps along the landing and a door banged somewhere. More dust fell from the ceiling.

'Bugger it,' said Jones, trying to shake it out of his hair. 'This has to work, Cage – I've used all the water to wash in and I have a feeling that in ten minutes' time I'll lack the strength to pump up any more.'

'Look on the bright side,' I said. 'In ten minutes' time, we'll probably both be dead.'

He looked down at me. 'There's always a silver lining with you.'

'Remember – formal, late-nineteenth-century manners. Polite at all times. Do not enrage her.'

'As if,' he said.

I looked at him. 'I honestly don't know if this is going to work. This could be the most stupid thing we've ever done.'

'And the last,' he said cheerfully.

By now we'd reached the top of the stairs.

302

'I can't remember,' he said. 'Is the correct form of address Miss Shotton or Miss Elizabeth Shotton?'

'She's the elder, so she's Miss Shotton,' I said. 'The younger sister would have been Miss Georgiana Shotton.'

'Got it.'

The house was very silent as he followed me downstairs.

'You wait here,' he said. 'I'll get the door.'

'Good luck.'

'You too, Cage.' He hesitated for a moment as if about to say something else, and then thought better of it.

I watched him tread across the hall to the front door and twisted around to look upstairs. Yes, everything was ready. We'd done everything we could.

Jones had reached the front door. He looked across the hall to me.

I tucked my hair behind my ears, lifted my chin and nodded.

Slowly and noisily, he pulled back the bolts, waited a few seconds, and then unlocked the door. He gave it another few seconds, then swung it wide. Not a few cautious inches, but a full, wide-open, *welcome to our house* gesture.

She was there. Right on the threshold. Looking down on him. Just as she had before.

He said nothing. I had a moment's panic. Had he forgotten? Was he too frightened to speak? Was he already dead?

No. None of those. He was giving her a minute. Then he stepped aside and made a gesture of welcome.

'Miss Shotton? Good afternoon, we've been expecting you. Would you like to come inside?'

303

CHAPTER TWENTY-ONE

I stood at the foot of the stairs in the traditional pose of the mistress of the house waiting to greet her guests. Jones's thinking had been that if anything went wrong, then she'd start on him first and I'd have a few seconds' head start. Which was rubbish. At the speed she moved, I probably wouldn't even have time to get one leg off the ground. I clenched my fists at my sides, decided that wasn't a good look for a hostess waiting to welcome her guests, and tried to remain calm. Staying calm was key.

Suddenly she was in front of me. I don't know how she moved. I certainly didn't know how she contrived to move so quickly. There was a faint blur about her that left me feeling slightly disoriented and unsteady. As if the world had suddenly slammed to a halt but I'd carried on, just for a moment. It was the strangest feeling. I took half a step to the left to regain my balance. And my composure.

What I hadn't noticed before – because Jones had got the front door shut so quickly – had been the smell. The smell of rotting meat. Of sickness. Of dirt and decay. Neglect. Of something foul that went straight to my stomach. My mouth filled with bile. I was going to throw up. Worse – I was going to hurl. My stomach heaved.

No. Everything depended on this. I had to control myself. Throwing up would ruin everything. Swallow it down. Breathe through my mouth. *Do not throw up.* Under the guise of a welcoming gesture, I took another small step to the side. The smell was slightly less intense. That helped a little.

She was considerably taller than me. And she was very close. I had to tilt my head back to look at her.

My voice was too high. Much too high. 'Miss Shotton, you are very welcome.' I made an effort to pitch it lower. 'I do hope you will take some tea with us this afternoon. And there are sandwiches and biscuits which I hope you will enjoy. Would you like to come this way?'

I crossed my fingers, stepped to one side and gestured up the stairs. Jones and I had talked about this and we were banking on two things. Curiosity – hers, of course – and the fact she hadn't been inside her home for a very long time. How would she react? We had no idea, but Jones reckoned the longer she didn't attack, the less chance there was of her attacking. Unless one of us said or did something stupid, of course.

She didn't move, so I turned, expecting to feel her weight on my back at any moment as she bore me to the ground and enveloped me in her stench. Not daring to turn around, I made my way slowly up the stairs. Back straight. Head up. One hand resting lightly on the bannister. I told myself no sudden movements. And definitely don't show fear. Just put one foot in front of the other. I knew she was with me because the smell followed me up the stairs.

Reaching the top, I half turned. She was there. Right behind me. Far too close. Invading my space. I would not step back. Mustering a polite smile from somewhere, I gestured to the

305

open door. 'We thought you'd like to have tea in here. It's very pleasant when the sun shines.'

She'd know that. She used to live here. I should stop gabbling.

I have to say, compared with the way it had looked a couple of hours ago, this was a definite improvement. Jones and Lorelei had worked hard to make it look slightly more presentable than this time yesterday. The colourful picnicware made the table look cheerful. The sandwiches were beautifully cut, even if I say so myself, and the teapot stood ready. It wouldn't be what she was accustomed to, but on the other hand, surely she must be aware of the house's continuing dilapidation.

I pushed that away. Such thoughts weren't wise. Confidence and good manners would see me through.

'Shall we make ourselves comfortable?'

I pulled out a chair and carefully seated myself. The chair creaked but held.

Jones had followed us into the room and now pulled out the chair opposite me. The one nearest the door. The decision not to place ourselves between her and the door had been unanimous. 'Miss Shotton?'

I held my breath. If she sat – if she actually sat down – then I reckoned we'd have a chance. She might listen. She might let us go. I waited, determined not to speak until she actually sat. Jones, too, remained motionless. The only sound was the crackling fire and the gently bubbling water in the saucepan.

She sat. She seemed to fold herself horizontally and the next minute she had taken her place. Another wave of rot and decay blasted across the table but this time it was easier to withstand. I wondered if my brain had overridden my stomach. With me, it's usually the other way around.

Her hands lay on the table. Long grey talons ending in thick, jagged purple fingernails. Claws might be a better description.

She looked down at the table. My pretty pale blue and gold scarf lay beside her plate, neatly folded. Lorelei's locket lay across the top.

She still hadn't said a word.

I leaned forwards, as if about to share a secret. The smell didn't seem so bad in here. Or I was getting used to it.

'A few small gifts for you, Miss Shotton.'

She was still staring down at the table.

'Where I come from,' I said, wondering why my voice sounded so strange to me, 'it's customary for the hostess to present her guest with some small gifts. We do hope you will accept them.'

She stared at them for a long time.

I tried very hard not to imagine her springing across the table, enveloping me in bones and dust and open sores, and eating me alive. That was not a pleasant thought and now, not only must I not throw up – I must eat, as well.

I forged on. I mustn't lose my nerve. Not now. This was just an ordinary social occasion. I had a guest to entertain to tea. I took a deep breath, tried not to let my voice wobble, and channelled my mother.

'My name is Elizabeth, too. It's not as fashionable as it once was, but I like it. Do you like your name?'

There was no answer. *Could* she speak? Or had no one spoken to her for so long she had forgotten how? I pretended not to notice her silence.

'May I pour you some tea? Do you take milk? Sugar?'

She watched me. She watched my every move. I wondered

how much she could actually see. Weeping sores had gummed up one eye and the other was hidden behind her hair.

The teapot wobbled all over the place but somehow I was able to pour some tea into her cup. Jones picked it up and placed it beside her plate. He hadn't sat down. Presumably he was holding himself ready in case she attacked. As if there would be anything either of us could do.

I poured myself half a cup of tea and splashed in a little milk. I didn't want it but my mouth was so dry I doubted I'd be able to speak otherwise.

'Now, we're a little short on supplies, but these . . .' I gestured, 'are tuna sandwiches. Have you ever tried tuna? It's very popular these days and I think you will like it. If not, however, these are best Wiltshire ham. May I serve you one of each, perhaps, Miss Shotton?'

I placed two sandwiches on a plate with a hand that hardly trembled at all and Jones put it in front of her.

She still faced me across the table. Her face was difficult to look at. I tried to glance at her every now and then, just as one would do in the normal course of conversation, but it really wasn't easy. Pity, revulsion, sheer terror – I could only hope none of it showed in my face. I wondered what she was thinking. I suspected, at that moment, she was a little bewildered by our antics. I'd been right about her curiosity.

Now we needed to keep her here long enough to listen to what we had to say. Because we'd given her what she wanted. To be inside. I hoped and prayed she'd give us what *we* wanted. To be outside.

Jones now seated himself at the table. His chair creaked even more alarmingly under his weight, but by now I was in

308

full Victorian-hostess mode. 'Mr Jones? I know you too well to ask whether you would like a sandwich.'

I placed a tuna sandwich carefully on his plate. If I concentrated hard on these tiny actions, I might not give way to the fear bubbling inside me.

Jones's party manners were exemplary. 'Thank you, Mrs Cage. Might I trouble you for a cup of tea, please?'

'Of course.'

I poured him a cup and passed it over. The mug trembled in my hand. I had to do better than this. Showing fear could prove fatal. Outwardly, Jones was calm, but his colour was spiking all over the place. I was too strung up to eat, but one of us had to.

He never hesitated. Biting into his sandwich, he smiled at us both. 'Delicious.'

I sipped at my tea, hoping it would settle my stomach. And it was something to do while I wracked my brains for suitable topics of conversation that didn't include smallpox, family life, mass murder and the fact that she was between me and the door.

As if she read my mind, she turned her head – slowly and creakily – to look at the fire, which was beginning to get going now. In fact, with the weak sun shining through the windows and the cheerful flames, the room looked moderately pleasant, and if we really, really used our imagination, we could pretend we were just three people enjoying a normal afternoon tea.

My mug rattled against my plate as I set it down. She was still silent and hadn't touched either her sandwiches or her tea – not that I expected her to. There were no clues at all as to how she was feeling or what her next move would be. Would she hurl herself across the tea table, teeth bared, to rip out my throat? Would she move so quickly I'd never know anything about it?

309

Or would she reach slowly across the table to claw out my eyes with those long grey and purple claws of hers?

She was looking around. This house had been her home. How often had she been here in this room? How many times had she taken tea here? This was the first time in more than a hundred years that she'd actually been invited inside her own home. That she'd been made welcome. That she hadn't been driven away. That people had actually spoken to her, as if she was a normal human being. Would she respond in kind? Or would she turn on us all? Had I made a terrible mistake by admitting the woman responsible for the Shotton Massacre? The woman who inspired such frenzied insanity that people actually killed each other?

Now she was looking at Jones. Would she turn on him first? He was still calmly eating his sandwich. As if he caught an echo of my thoughts, he looked up. 'These sandwiches are delicious, Miss Shotton. I do urge you to try one.'

She stared at him.

I moistened my lips. 'I am so pleased to hear there might be rain on the way. This has been a very hot, dry summer and the farmers will be grateful.'

'I quite agree,' said Jones, and with that, our little conversation dwindled and died.

She still hadn't moved. Her tea sat cooling in front of her and her sandwiches remained untouched. She never took her eyes off us. What was she thinking at this moment? And more importantly – what would she do when the tea, sandwiches and small talk ran out?

I looked at Jones and he nodded slightly. We couldn't put it off any longer.

I cleared my throat and went for it. 'I'm so glad to have had this opportunity to meet you today, Miss Shotton. Mr Jones and I will be leaving this afternoon and we very much wanted to make your acquaintance before we left. We are so pleased you could join us. I hope you are enjoying your tea.'

I picked up my tea and sipped. It tasted awful, so I put it back on the table. I shifted my position so both feet were on the floor and my hands were free. This was it. I'd stated our intentions. What would she do now? Would she eat us where we sat? Would we be here for ever? Would we be driven mad like the Shottons' guests all those years ago? Would she kill us or would we kill each other?

Or would she let us go? We weren't actually Shottons – but then, the majority of the massacre victims hadn't been Shottons either, and look what had happened to them. Don't think about that.

Still, she sat motionless, her sore-ridden, withered grey hands resting on the table in front of her.

Well, she hadn't said no. I was unwilling to break eye contact, but I had no choice. Slowly, I bent and picked up my handbag. Jones rose politely and held my chair for me. We both turned to face her.

He bowed. 'Good afternoon, Miss Shotton. A pleasure to have met you today.'

He held out his hand.

She looked at it. We all looked at it. The moment dragged on and on. I could see dust dancing in the shafts of sunlight.

She moved. Very slowly. Almost as if she didn't want to frighten us. That was what I told myself, anyway. She lifted her right hand and placed it over the scarf and locket.

That was good enough for me.

I stepped around the table and Jones took my arm. She turned her head to watch us, but she still hadn't moved from the table. We already knew she could move faster than thought, but what was she thinking now?

We began to head for the door. Slowly. Don't run. Don't give way to panic.

Jones held my arm very tightly. As if he feared we'd be torn apart for some reason. 'Are you ready to leave, Mrs Cage?'

'I am,' I said and couldn't think of anything else to say. I didn't want to give the impression we couldn't wait to get out of here, but I didn't want her getting the idea we'd be happy to stay, either.

Five slow paces to the door. There was no logical reason for it, but I couldn't help thinking if we could just get through the door then the rest would be easy. Which was nonsense. We could race along the landing, hurl ourselves down the stairs, sprint across the hall and still find her standing at the front door, teeth bared, barring our way. That might yet happen.

Jones was just reaching out for the door handle – and that was when we heard it.

The front door slammed. In fact, it slammed so hard we felt the reverberations all the way up here.

For a moment I thought part of the building had come down. I think I'd been half expecting that ever since I walked through the door. Then I realised what it meant. They'd gone. Oliver and Adam had gone. They'd taken advantage of our diversion and pushed off, leaving us here, alone, with Elizabeth Shotton. We could all have left together, peacefully, normally. We could have just walked out of the front door, climbed into our cars and driven away. All they'd had to do was hold their nerve.

And then I had second thoughts. Had they done this on purpose? Because not only had they ensured their own get-away – they'd prevented ours. They'd sabotaged any possibility of our escape. Of course – now no one would be left alive to tell the story of their treachery. They'd be free and we'd be dead. How long would we take to die?

Another part of my mind wondered whether Lorelei King had gone with them.

'Shit,' said Jones very softly. 'Go, Cage. I've got your back.'

I looked back over my shoulder.

Elizabeth Shotton was rising up like the wrath of God, her face twisted with a terrible ferocity. Because she thought we'd tricked her. That we'd deliberately lured her here to enable the Shottons – and Lorelei – to escape her clutches. And while the Shottons might be gone, we were still here.

This was very, very bad.

Jones pulled me behind him, which wouldn't benefit either of us in any way. Elizabeth Shotton surged across the room, long discoloured teeth bared.

Once again there was that odd action. As if she was gliding. As if she had no feet. My head swam again. She flew across the room, rage written in every movement.

The stench was overwhelming. So sudden and unexpected that I wasn't prepared for it. I couldn't hold it in this time. I leaned forwards and gagged.

Which might have saved us because it meant she got to the door first. It shattered into a million pieces as she blew straight through it. Large parts just disintegrated. Shards of wood blasted out into the landing beyond. Sawdust hung in the air.

She was furious. Livid. She paused in the doorway, threw

313

us one look – possibly promising retribution later – and then she was gone.

'She thinks we deliberately distracted her,' I said, wiping my mouth.

'Yes,' said Jones, pulling me through the remains of the door, 'you're right, but I don't think we have time to discuss it now. We have to get out of here. Come on.'

We ran. In my case, on very wobbly legs. We ran down the stairs, ignoring their creaks and groans. The front door stood wide open. I could see the outside world. Bright sunshine and brown, dry weeds. And Lorelei King standing in the doorway, staring out down the drive. There was a small bag at her feet. She'd planned to go with them.

'Where did she go?' demanded Jones.

Hand shaking, she pointed out of the door. 'They left me behind,' she said in disbelief. 'They told me to watch the other windows and they went off and left me. They did it deliberately. They left me.'

In the distance, I could hear a car's engine roar and squealing tyres. The Shotton brothers were making their getaway and leaving us to the mercy of Elizabeth Shotton.

'They left us all,' said Jones, pushing past her. 'But we're out of here now and we're not waiting. Come with us or take your chances on your own. Your choice.'

Not much of a choice, really. The three of us flew out of the front door. Jones's car was still where he'd left it. I had a sudden fear the Shotton brothers might have let down the tyres or sabotaged the car in some way, but they hadn't. Fortunately for us they'd been in too much of a hurry to save themselves.

We piled in.

'We've left the front door wide open,' said Lorelei, glancing back.

'Good,' said Jones. 'Are you going back to close it?'

She stared around fearfully. 'No.'

Jones started the engine and we headed to the gates.

'Not that way,' she said suddenly, leaning over the back seat. 'There's a quicker way. Go around the back and take the right-hand road past the old stables.'

We skidded past all sorts of outbuildings – I couldn't help but wonder if one of those had been Elizabeth Shotton's final home – past the wreckage of a once magnificent kitchen garden and down an overgrown track. We were travelling much faster than was wise, but I think the desire to get as far away as possible as fast as possible was unspoken but unanimous. We roared through a dark and tangled wood. The trees met over-head, shutting out the bright sunshine.

'Keep your eyes peeled for her,' said Jones and we did. I stared out of the passenger window and Lorelei was on her knees, peering out through the back.

'I can't see anything,' she said, craning her neck. 'Faster. Drive faster.'

Jones ignored her. The track was rough, there were obs-tacles – hidden rocks and fallen branches. The last thing we needed was a puncture or a damaged wheel.

We emerged from the wood with no warning. The track ended abruptly at a public road. There were old wrought-iron gates here – this must have been the tradesmen's entrance – but one gate had fallen long ago and lay half buried in the long grass, and the other hung askew from one hinge.

We roared between the crumbling stone pillars and out on to the lane.

'Left,' said Lorelei. 'You'll pick up the Rushford road eventually.'

We turned left. The road was narrow and twisty, forcing Jones to moderate his speed somewhat.

'We're not out of the woods yet. We've no idea of her range and she's not happy. She might well hold us responsible for the Shottons getting away and come after us. Keep watching out for her.'

'Seat belts,' I said, fastening mine.

I heard Lorelei snort in the back. She was laughing at silly, timid, fuddy-duddy Elizabeth Cage but, unfortunately, silly, timid, fuddy-duddy Elizabeth Cage was to have the last laugh.

We turned on to the main Rushford road and only half a mile further on, came upon an accident. A car had gone off the road.

'Don't look, Cage,' said Jones, slowing as we approached.

'That's Oliver's car,' said Lorelei from the back, her voice rising in hysteria. 'That's them. Oh my God. Oh my God. That looks bad.'

It was bad.

We slowed even more.

Their vehicle had skidded for some reason – I could see black tyre tracks burned across the road – and had come to a halt, nose down, half in and half out of a shallow ditch.

Adam must have been in the passenger seat, but not any longer. He'd gone straight through the windscreen. No seat belt. And the airbag hadn't deployed.

He lay, face down, spreadeagled across the bonnet. There was a lot of blood.

Oliver had been driving. His airbag hadn't deployed either. He was slumped back in his seat. I could see a terrible wound to his forehead. Had he hit his face on the steering wheel? His right arm hung limply out of the window.

Crouched on the bonnet, her mouth, chin and cheeks stained red with blood, sat the woman with whom we'd tried to make polite conversation over the tea table. Elizabeth Shotton. As I watched in horror, she grasped a handful of Adam's hair, wrenched his head back, and buried her face in his throat.

Lorelei screamed.

'Shut up,' said Jones, but it was too late.

The bloody thing looked up and saw us inching our way slowly past.

Just as we drew level, she threw herself on Oliver, worrying at his face, ripping and tearing with her teeth. His arm was still dangling from the window. I saw his fingers spasm.

My lips were stiff with horror. 'Oh my God, he's still alive.'

Jones cursed and slowed even more. 'Cage, you can't drive, can you?'

'I can,' said Lorelei King.

'No one trusts you not to drive off and leave us here,' said Jones.

'Switch off the engine and take the key with you,' I said.

'Are you insane?' screamed Lorelei. 'You can't stop here. Drive on. Drive on.'

Jones stopped the car and slowly opened the door.

Lorelei King was having hysterics in the back seat. I think I would have been doing the same thing if I'd been able to get any part of my body to function.

He walked slowly towards the SUV. Elizabeth Shotton watched his every move. Blood ran down her face.

Standing as far away as possible, and without taking his eyes off her, he picked up Oliver's wrist and felt for his pulse.

Still she watched him. Motionless.

Moving very slowly and carefully, he began to edge his way around the bonnet. Towards Adam.

She made a movement. Protecting her prey.

He stopped.

She stopped.

He began to move again. 'Let me see him, please.'

She began to inch towards him. Sliding slowly across the bonnet already slick with blood.

I opened the car door and got out.

She looked around him to me.

I called on every ounce of authority I possessed. 'Leave him alone, please, Miss Shotton. Let him do his duty.'

Jones edged around the car until he had a clear view of Adam. He didn't bother taking his pulse. It was very clear that Adam was dead.

I whispered, 'Don't turn your back on her.'

Jones couldn't possibly have heard me but he began to back away. Slowly.

She changed her position, gathering her legs beneath her. Was she ready to spring?

No. She turned her attention back to Oliver. The last Shotton to die.

I too walked backwards until I felt the car behind me. I opened the door and slithered in, pulling it to. And then I locked it. Not that that would do me any good if she suddenly pounced.

Jones climbed back into the car, quietly shut his own door and started up the engine. We pulled slowly away.

I watched in the wing mirror as the scene of the accident grew smaller and smaller. Then the road curved to the left and it was lost to view.

No one spoke but at least Lorelei King had shut up.

I turned to Michael Jones. 'I am so very proud of you.'

Just for a moment, his colour lit up the car. Then he reached across and briefly put his hand on mine. His own hand was icy cold and mine was vibrating like a tuning fork. I know the rest of me was, as well. He kissed my hand and then gave it back to me.

There was complete silence from the back seat.

Jones said, 'Cage . . .' and I pulled our other phone from the dash, dialled 999 and put it on speakerphone.

He gave his service number and reported a bad accident five miles north of Rushford on the Whittington road. 'One of them has gone through the windscreen. I checked but they're both dead.'

He switched off the phone and I shoved it back in the glove compartment.

We continued to Rushford in silence.

CHAPTER TWENTY-TWO

We dropped Lorelei King at her house on the new estate being built along the ring road. Four- and five-bedroomed executive-style houses. The sort of houses Oliver Shotton probably dreamed about at night.

Not any longer, of course.

She grabbed her bag, staggered out of the car and stood for a moment, leaning on the door. I remembered she'd been in a relationship with Adam, who was now dead. What would she do now?

'Will you be all right?' I said. One of my more stupid questions, but I felt bad about just leaving her at the side of the road. How implicated she'd been, what part she'd played – how far she'd been prepared to sacrifice us – I had no idea. Nor did I care.

'Got your keys?' enquired Jones, always practical.

She nodded and patted her pocket.

'I recommend a long bath and an even longer drink,' he said, putting the car in gear and preparing to drive away.

'You're going?' she said in disbelief.

'Can't get away quickly enough,' he said cheerfully.

'But . . .' She looked around helplessly. 'What do I do now?'

'No idea.'

'But you can't just . . . leave me.'

'We can and we are,' he said grimly. 'You and your little friends led us into a trap. You personally set us up and your charming colleagues did the rest. That you're safe at this moment is thanks entirely to Mrs Cage here – frankly, I'd have left you there. May I recommend that you resist the temptation to publish any articles denigrating the person generous enough to have saved you today. We've delivered you safely to your doorstep, which was a bloody sight more than you were prepared to do for us. A friendly warning, Miss King – stay out of my way in future.'

She was pulling herself together now she was safe. 'Actually, I could make things very difficult for you.'

'Not half as difficult as I can make them for you. You are one seriously stupid woman. You and Adam planned all this, didn't you? Yes, I'll grant you Oliver's was the original idea, but you and Adam took that one stage further because you were plotting to kill Oliver and blame it on the ghost. Or possibly on me and Mrs Cage. Depending on the circumstances, I suppose. Well, that didn't work, did it?'

Suddenly, everything fell into place. All along I'd had the feeling something wasn't quite right. Especially when I looked at Lorelei and Adam together. Jones had worked it out.

He continued. 'Listen carefully, because I'll tell you how this is going to work. You stay well away from both of us and keep your mouth shut. I'll write up my report this evening – that will be my *full* report, chock-full of fascinating but potentially embarrassing details – and the file will sit harmlessly in the cloud until the end of time. Or until you try to make trouble for us – whichever comes first. Good luck convincing the police

321

about all the supernatural stuff. At best, they'll remand you for psychiatric reports – at worst, you'll find yourself looking down the wrong end of an investigation as the fraud squad move in to look at the Shotton company's books. You might even find yourself implicated in their deaths.'

As usual, he'd hit the nail squarely on the head. Her colour darkened and recoiled from him. She stepped back from the car and we drove off and left her standing there.

'Was that wise?' I said.

He shrugged. 'She picked the wrong side, Cage, and when the going got tough, they abandoned her to save themselves. We got her out, which makes us better than them.'

'Plus, they're dead.'

'And that. Do you want to come back to my place for a shower and a decent meal or do you feel the need to go home, turn out all your kitchen cupboards and shampoo the carpet?'

There was no malice in his words.

'Hot shower and something to eat, please,' I said, suddenly very unwilling to be alone. 'I just want to sit for half an hour and pull myself together.'

'Yes,' he said. 'Quite a lively weekend even by our standards.'

I looked across at him. 'You knew the Shottons would make a break for it, didn't you?'

He hesitated then said, 'Yes, I thought they might.'

'It was Oliver and Adam who were the real decoy, weren't they? Not us.'

Again, he hesitated and then said, 'Yes.'

'You sacrificed them for us.'

'I didn't make them sneak out of the front door and leave us behind to deal with the consequences. If they'd stuck with our plan, they might have made it. Elizabeth Shotton might have come around to letting us all go.'

'You don't really believe that would have happened.'

'No. No, I don't. I think once she was over her confusion at what we were doing, she would have gone for all of us.'

'So, you gave Oliver and Adam the opportunity to make a run for it. Knowing they would and she'd go after them. That's just a . . . a little ruthless.'

He was silent for so long I thought he wasn't going to respond, and then he said, very quietly, 'I had you to save, Cage.'

That was one of the best showers of my life. I scrubbed myself from top to bottom, seeking to rid myself of the filth encountered at Shotton Hall. And not just the physical dirt.

What would Elizabeth Shotton do now? Oliver and Adam were dead, so presumably the plans to convert the house into luxury flats and create a spa centre and so forth wouldn't go ahead. Would she finally let go and make her way to wherever she should have gone after her death all those years ago? Or would she return to brood and wait? I had no idea whether there were any other Shottons still alive, so Shotton Hall might simply sink back into its habitual silence, as the trees slowly closed in and the brickwork crumbled to dust. And we'd left the front door open, which could only hasten its end. What would she do then? And did I actually care?

I emerged from the shower wearing one of Jones's T-shirts, which came down nearly to my knees, and enveloped in his dressing gown. I had to turn back the cuffs and it trailed on the ground behind me. I actually felt quite regal.

He made giant burgers in giant buns. He had two and I had one. He filled a glass with a substantial amount of whisky for himself – I had a hot chocolate.

'Mm,' I said, taking a giant bite out of my giant burger.

'Mm,' he said, doing the same, and we chomped in silence for a while.

'Your clothes are in the wash,' he said eventually. 'I didn't think you'd want to carry any part of Shotton Hall back to your own house.'

I nodded. 'I'm never going near that place again.' I swallowed the last of my burger and picked up my hot chocolate. 'What do you think she'll do?'

'Who?'

'Elizabeth, of course.'

'I think she'll go back to Shotton Hall. I think she'll wander the empty rooms for ever. Or until the house falls down and the rooms don't exist any longer.'

'Poor Elizabeth. Her death is as tragic as her life.'

He nodded too. 'Actually, despite Elizabeth's predilection for bloody and violent revenge, I'm not half as bothered by her as I am about the other one.'

'Lorelei?'

'Yes. She is a journalist, after all, and I'm wondering how much of our adventure she'll make public.'

'She's in a difficult position, surely. She set us up. She can't say anything without us telling the world what she did.'

He finished his second burger. 'I think I might have a word with someone though, just in case.'

'You can do that?'

324

He sighed. 'You're an asset, Cage. You have to be protected.'

'Oh,' I said. 'Oh.'

We watched a little TV. I snuggled up to him on the sofa and he put his arm around me. There was nothing in it. His colour lay quiet and placid.

'All right?' he said, looking down at me.

'Better by the minute. You?'

'Same. Hush now. The football's starting.'

I watched it, because after a weekend like ours, anything looked good. As I told Jones, the mind-numbing tedium of ninety minutes of football – plus extra time for those whose brains hadn't already melted out of their ears – was just what I needed. What the final score was and even who was playing was of little importance. He tutted loudly and shook his head, but I noticed he didn't let go of either me or his whisky.

I spent a quiet couple of days catching up on things that needed doing around my house – changing the sheets, doing the laundry, checking my cupboards to see what needed replacing – even reorganising my backyard. I rearranged the pots, did a bit of deadheading, swept the steps, and carried some stuff down into the cellar. Which was next on my list of things to be sorted out.

I was enjoying a cup of coffee, prior to getting stuck in, when my phone rang. The same number as the other night.

The caller got straight down to it. 'Can I speak to Mrs Cage, please?'

The voice sounded familiar, but I couldn't place it.

'Who's calling?'

'It's me. Is that you, Mrs Cage? It's Becky – Becky Harlow.'

My stomach turned over. Something had happened. Something bad. I just knew it.

'Becky, what's happened?'

There was a long silence and then, as if the words were being dragged out of her, she said, 'You saved me. That time in the wood.'

'Yes.'

'You said not to forget it.'

'Yes.'

'I . . .'

'Becky, what's happened?' I repeated.

'I'm trying to help you.'

'How?'

There was a long silence.

'Did you call me the other night?'

'Yes. But they nearly caught me. I had to hang up. Listen – there's a man. He's using us. For a sending. They've been trying for ages and it's just not working quickly enough. Something keeps turning it back, but now . . .'

I tried to think. 'What do you mean – but now?'

'Now he's here. Actually here.'

'Where?'

'In Greyston.'

'A man? Living in Greyston?'

Her voice sank to a whisper. 'He's not a man.'

'What's he doing?'

Her voice was quickening with panic. 'He told us he wanted to help us. Rebuilding. Restoring the stones. But he's not. He's using us. Using us up. Every time he tries a sending, some of us burn away. We're dying here. Every day.'

'Why are you telling me this?'

She was gabbling now. I had to concentrate hard to make sense of what she was saying. 'Because it's you he wants. Joanna did a deal with him because she hates you. It's every night but he can't get through. Something's turning him back and we're dying. If you run away, he'll stop. You have to get away.'

'And so must you by the sound of it.'

Her voice was rising. 'I can't. None of us can. The dead men are in the woods. We're trapped here.' Her voice dropped to a sudden whisper. 'With him.'

'Becky – it's broad daylight. Can you get out of the village somehow? Is there a way?'

'I . . . don't know.'

'I'll call you back. Wait where you are.'

I thought for a moment and then rang Iblis.

'Can you pick me up? I have to get to Greyston. Becky Harlow just rang for help.'

He didn't waste time arguing.

'Where are you?'

'At home.'

'Bottom of the hill. Ten minutes.'

'Thank you.'

I rang Becky again.

'Hello?'

'Be at the place I saw you last. Hide and wait.'

I grabbed my keys and ran out of the house.

Iblis was at the bottom of the hill, waiting in Melek's big muddy SUV. He started the engine as I climbed in.

I looked around. 'Where's Nigel?'

'Under the blanket in the back. Tell me what she said.'

I did so, finishing with, 'Is this a trap, do you think?'

'Yes.'

'She sounded terrified.'

'She might well be if they forced her to do it.'

'Who is *he*?'

'I'm sure we'll soon find out.'

'It's just that as soon as she said *send*, I remembered. I nearly remembered it that night with the Chinese food but then everyone was talking . . . and it went out of my head.'

'What do you remember?'

'A voice. I remember a voice. *I always send the serpent.* And then it says something like, *It's . . . it's my signature move.* Do you know anything about that?'

'I couldn't say before – when we had that business with the note – because you'd chosen not to know, but now . . .' He stared at the road ahead. 'It's not about you. He's someone you – Felda – met last Christmas. This is not aimed at you. Please try not to . . . .' He stopped.

'Worry,' I finished for him. 'Except Felda and I are one and the same so something tells me I should be doing more than worry.'

Iblis drove fast but the journey still took long enough for me to regret every moment of it. Of course it was a trap. We'd get there and the Greyston women would be waiting for us. Yes, Becky had sounded terrified, but I can't see a colour down a phone so she might simply have been acting a part while Joanna and all the others stood around grinning and sharpening their sickles. And even if Becky was genuine, how would we get her out? The women wouldn't let her go and neither would the dead men. The more I thought about it, the more recklessly stupid our actions seemed.

I suspect Iblis had followed my every thought.

'She might be genuine,' he said. 'I imagine living conditions in the village – even under their supposed new management – are not that salubrious. It's a long time to have been confined to one place, their power gone. Resources would have become scarce. There would be arguments, recriminations, factions springing up. Fights, even. And none of them are strangers to murder, are they? They might even have tried to reinstate a form of sacrifice using one of their own instead of a Year King. You know – putting your bins out on the wrong day is punishable by being sacrificed to the stones.'

I looked at him.

'It's very possible,' he said. 'They had great power and people don't give up that sort of thing lightly.'

I shivered. He wasn't wrong.

He went on. 'From what you told me, it's possible Joanna has struck a deal with someone she shouldn't have. No one ever comes out on top with him. He offered them everything they wanted . . .'

'In return for what . . .' I said, already knowing the answer. 'You.'

'How would he know? About me, I mean.'

He smiled sadly. 'Well, that would probably be my fault. Last Christmas, when Allia tried to kill me with my own sword and you went after her . . . Well – not you – your co-pilot.' He stared ahead for a moment and then said quietly, 'There really is no limit to the damage one mistake can do, is there? The people I care for . . . Melek . . . you . . .'

I put my hand on his arm. 'Iblis, stop. Turn around. I'm not risking you for Becky.'

He shook his head. 'I will, if that is your command.' He paused. 'Is it your command?'

I sighed. 'Yes. No. I don't know. I don't know anything any more.'

He pulled over and switched off the engine and turned to face me. 'What is wrong?'

Now the time had come, I wasn't sure I could say it.

'Last time I was at the clinic – something happened to me. And I have to tell you because you're doing this out of gratitude and I'm not sure I deserve that gratitude and you should know why.'

He waited.

'A patient died. Well, she wasn't a patient. Actually, she didn't exist, but I thought she did. I was trying to help her but she died. Dr Bridgeman came to talk to me. He said . . .' I swallowed. 'He said . . . there was something wrong with me. He said I was a patient there and I'd been suffering from delusions ever since Ted died. That I imagined I had some kind of superpower. That I was always *saving the day*, as he put it. That Michael Jones barely knew who I was and that I'd created a fantasy world with you and Melek and swords and demons simply to compensate for being a sad, inadequate little woman whose life was . . . well . . . insignificant and worthless. Jones and Dr Bridgeman – the real Dr Bridgeman – said it wasn't true, but while it was happening, I believed every word of it, and how do I know that's not what I'm doing now? How do I know this is the right reality? How do I know I haven't somehow slipped into the other one? You're special to me and I don't want to get you killed.'

My voice was very wobbly at the end. I couldn't look at him. He took my hand. His was very warm. Mine was very cold.

'Then what happened?'

I took a deep breath and, not very coherently, told him the whole story, ending with, 'Jones caught me about to jump off the roof. For a moment, there were two different realities side by side, and then I was me again – the me that is here now. But suppose the other me is the right one? Suppose this is all just some stupid dream I'm having.'

I stopped before I started on about my supposed relationship with Jones, telling myself that wasn't relevant at this moment.

'If you are not the Elizabeth Cage of legend, and all this is a dream, then no great evil awaits us at Greyston, does it?'

'No . . .' I said uncertainly. 'I suppose not. But how do I know you're real? What if you're not?'

'It is true that many women dream of me, but I assure you I am Iblis – Man of Great Reality. Together with Nigel the Ninja, Dog of Overwhelming Pungency.'

'That's not very reassuring,' I said, trying to smile. 'Only the worst sort of diseased brain could conjure up Nigel.'

'Clever, though,' he said, staring through the windscreen. 'Very, very clever. It sounds as if he very nearly succeeded.'

'Who's "he" and how?'

He blinked while he disentangled my question.

'He is the person behind Allia, and the how is that you were within half a step of destroying yourself, Elizabeth Cage. Success was very nearly within his grasp. From what Becky said, I suspect he has been using the women at Greyston as his power source. That was a very powerful illusion he unleashed at the clinic. He must have burned through many lives to achieve it.

331

And that might be the reason for Becky's sudden panic and desire to escape.'

I thought about this for a while.

'It wasn't true, was it? What Dr Bridgeman said. About me.'

'Of course not. It was a delusion. Did your Dr Bridgeman – the real one – say how it was achieved?'

'He suspected hypnosis or drugs.'

He shrugged. 'It always boils down to spells and potions, doesn't it?'

'What do you want to do?'

'I shall proceed alone.'

I sat up in a hurry. 'No, you won't.' Which wasn't at all what I'd meant to say. 'Except – I don't have any sort of weapon.'

He started the engine. 'Elizabeth Cage – *you* are the weapon.'

Ten minutes later we were at Greyston. I was pleased to see an almost cloudless sky. Sunshine was good. Things hide in the dark. Things with their throats ripped out, their blood given to the stones, and with a big grudge against women.

To my surprise, Iblis stopped a hundred yards ahead of the rendezvous and turned the car around. Having done that, he reversed us to the meeting point.

'Quick getaway. We want to be facing in the right direction,' he said. 'Don't get out of the car until you see her.'

I nodded and looked around. The sun continued to shine. Trees overhung each side of the road, casting their welcome shade. They were in full leaf and swaying softly in the breeze. Nigel snored gustily in the back. Just a peaceful, sunny summer day.

I looked towards the village. The dusty road dipped over the crest of the hill. There was no movement anywhere. No solitary figure plodded up the hill towards us. 'She might be in the trees somewhere.'

'Unlikely. Would you be?'

I shivered again. 'No.'

We waited and waited but Becky didn't come. We waited some more. Becky still didn't come.

I began to fret. Clouds were gathering overhead. At some point the wind had picked up. The sky was darkening. This was no longer the lovely summer day we had left behind in Rushford. Perhaps there was a big storm on the way. I tried not to feel this might be a very bad thing, and it would seem I wasn't alone with that thought.

Iblis was peering out of the window. 'This is not right.'

'No,' I said, peering up at the darkly roiling clouds overhead.

'Have we been tricked after all, I wonder? We're exactly where Becky wanted us to be, but we've been here for some time. If it is a trap, then they're taking their time about it. No, I'm actually more suspicious of this weather.'

'If Becky made the arrangements in good faith, surely we can't abandon her?'

'No, but we can give ourselves a better chance. In case things turn nasty.'

'How?' I demanded.

'Reinforcements.'

'Who?'

'Your partner and mine. The man-mountain and the stroppy one. Perhaps even Jerry.'

I frowned. 'They won't be happy. We'll be hearing about it for the rest of our lives.'

'Which, happily for us, could be very short.'

333

'Even with reinforcements, what can we do?'

'Split up. You and Jones could create a diversion, while Melek and I go down into the village.'

'Why?'

'To locate and extract Becky. And possibly discover what is happening there.'

I drew a breath. 'Jones will go ballistic.'

'But he will do it?'

'Yes, if he can. But he won't be happy.'

'Neither will Melek.'

'There will be a heavy price to be paid.'

He looked sideways at me and grinned. 'There will.'

'Let's hope we live long enough to pay it.'

He said nothing.

I sighed. 'How many times have I had to escape these women?'

He tutted. 'Nigel and I have discussed this and we agree that under-confidence is frequently an issue with you.'

'I notice Nigel is not making his views known at this moment.'

'Well, no, he is asleep.'

'What are you doing?'

He'd pulled out his phone. 'Summoning assistance.'

'I don't know,' I said feebly.

But it was too late. 'Watch the road,' he said.

I watched the road for dear life, unsure whether it was safer to be in the car or out of it. Melek was not going to be happy.

Sensibly, Iblis confined himself to a simple request for assistance, gave our location and disconnected.

'That seemed to go quite well,' I said cautiously.

'Retribution will come later. I will now attempt to contact the man-mountain.'

I continued to watch the road as instructed.

'He wants to speak to you,' said Iblis, passing over the phone.

I took it. 'Don't start.'

I might as well have spared my breath.

'Cage, what did I say to you?'

'You are not in charge of me.'

'We're supposed to be partners.'

'That still doesn't mean I need your permission.'

'We're supposed to discuss . . .'

'Why? You never discuss anything with me. You get a phone call and it's all "Got to go, Cage. Probably back on Thursday," then the door slams behind you and you're gone.'

'That's my other job,' he said. 'Nothing to do with you.'

'This is *my* other job. Nothing to do with you.'

'If it's nothing to do with me, then why are you ringing for my assistance?'

'I'm not – Iblis is.'

There was a pause long enough for him to grind his teeth. 'Put the idiot back on.'

'I've put you on speaker,' I said to Iblis. 'You talk to him. He's being very unreasonable.'

Iblis sighed. 'Have the two of you ever considered just ripping off each other's clothes and going at it like rabid rabbits until your hearts give out?'

'Of course not,' I said. 'No one has – ever,' and at exactly the same moment, Jones said, 'Yes, all the time.'

'What?' I glared at the innocent phone.

'Oh, come on, Cage. You'd be furious if I'd said I hadn't.'

'Hadn't what?'

'Considered ripping off your clothes and all the rest of it.'

I gritted my own teeth. 'Look – forget it. By the time you get here, it'll be dark. We'll manage without you.'

'No, you won't.'

I was annoyed. 'You don't think we can pull this off?'

'No, I don't, but as it happens, you don't have to. I'm behind you.'

I twisted round in my seat. 'Oh no, you're not.'

'Well, no, but it was such a good line. I was already on my way home but now I'm driving like stink while engaging in one of the most unnerving conversations of my life. Give me ten minutes.'

He ended the call.

'Well,' I said, 'I hope your partner is in a better mood than mine.'

Iblis sighed. 'I think we both know that's highly unlikely.'

Melek arrived first, in Iblis's car. She too must have driven like stink to get here in such a short time. Actually, going by the state of Iblis's car, she must, at some point, have left the roads and cut across country. The shiny blackness had vanished. The bodywork was plastered with mud that had sprayed across the windscreen, as well. There was enough greenery hanging off the front to start a florist's shop.

Iblis gave a faint whimper. 'My car.'

I patted his arm. 'Courage, Camille.'

We watched her turn and park behind us. We watched her walk towards us. She wrenched open the door and climbed into the back. Nigel immediately scrambled into the front, with me. She folded her arms and we waited in silence. Occasionally, she fanned the air in front of her.

Jones turned up about ten minutes later. By unspoken consent, we got out and met him in the road.

The wind was getting up. Dust stung my eyes and leaves skittered along the road. But there was blue sky over on the horizon – was this just a local storm? Or something much more sinister?

Our plan was simple: Jones and I would stay with the getaway car until required. Iblis and Melek – for whom the woods held no terrors – would make their way down to the village, locate and retrieve Becky. In the event of any trouble, Jones and I were to cause some sort of diversion.

None of us was particularly happy with this plan, but it made sense to keep Jones away from the women, and if things went wrong for Iblis and Melek – not that that was likely – then we were the rescue team.

'Don't like the look of this,' said Jones, looking up at the murky sky.

I didn't like the look of things down here, either. 'Are you armed?'

He looked down at me. 'Of course not. I failed my eyesight test. My permit has been rescinded and carrying a gun would be illegal.'

'Give it to me, then. I can see.'

'Yes, but you can't shoot.'

'Then teach me.'

He paused. 'OK – but not right at this moment.'

'Do you want me to shoot you if you're captured?'

'What? No. Why would I want you to shoot me?'

'Isn't that what they always say? *Don't let them take me alive?*'

He sighed. 'In the unlikely event of us getting out of this unscathed, Cage, you and I are going to sit down and have such a long talk.'

Iblis and Melek made their preparations in silence. She shrugged off her coat and threw it in the car. She smoothed back her hair. Iblis swung his arms. Without looking at each other, they lined up, side by side. Iblis on the left – he was left-handed – and Melek on the right. They were quiet and professional. Doing their job. They didn't speak. They didn't even look at each other. They didn't have to. They'd been doing this for a very long time. Some of my fear ebbed away. Whatever the women of Greyston might be up to, my money was on these two.

Iblis was looking around, sniffing the air. 'Ready?'

'Whenever you are.' She turned to us. 'Stay in the car.'

With one perfectly synchronised movement, they drew their swords. One gleamed gold – the other silver. They nodded to each other and vanished silently into the growing gloom.

'Well,' said Jones, watching them go. 'I think I'd much rather be behind those two than in front of them.'

I could only agree.

338

CHAPTER TWENTY-THREE

We stood by Melek's SUV and then Jones said, 'Cage, get in the back seat.'

'Why?' I said, instantly suspicious.

He sighed. 'If they do come back with Becky then they'll be in a tearing hurry and won't have time to mess about with car doors. If you sit in the back, in the middle, then they'll have three doors for three people. Quick getaway.'

'Oh. OK. Is this what they call on-the-job training?'

'No, this is what they call rank stupidity ending in unnecessary and painful death. Mine, mostly.'

I slipped into the back.

He opened all the doors and stood by the car. Then we waited.

The sky grew darker. Somewhere in the far distance, thunder growled. I could feel electricity in the air.

'I wonder what's going on down there,' I said, trying to see out of the back window.

'Whatever it is, they'll handle it. And if Becky's still alive, they'll get her out.'

'You think she might be dead?'

'I'm sorry, Cage, but I wouldn't be at all surprised.'

Actually, neither would I. Could I have handled this any

better? Had I, by trying to help, only made things considerably worse? Was this going to be the Sorensen Clinic all over again?

It was difficult to make out any details. The tossing trees were simply dark shapes among darker shadows, but the road was still clear. Which was both good and bad. No dead men, but no Iblis or Melek either. Nor Becky.

'Given the lack of screaming, flames, earthquakes, riot, and Armageddon, I think we can assume they haven't yet made their presence known,' said Jones, obviously reading my mind.

'I wonder what's going on down there,' I repeated.

'Not our responsibility, Cage. Concentrate on the job in hand. And that *is* on-the-job training. In any job, everyone is given a specific task. Everyone concentrates on their own task and trusts everyone else to do the same.'

'That's really good advice.'

'Could you manage not to sound quite so surprised, please.'

The thunder growled again. Closer this time. Dark clouds swirled overhead.

'I don't like this,' I said, shunting across the seat to peer out of the left-hand door. 'This doesn't feel right. Is it worth putting on your headlights, do you think?'

'We're facing away from the village and it'll give away our position. What's the problem?'

'I don't know,' I said, now peering out of the right-hand door. 'This storm feels – wrong.'

'I feel really stupid asking this,' said Jones, 'but could this be something those women have raised?'

'It's a good question,' I said. 'And possibly.'

Lightning flickered in the distance.

'I can never remember if you're safe in a car during a storm or not. Surely it's made of metal.'

'The tyres are rubber, Cage.'

'Oh. Good.'

'But they'll melt if we're struck by lightning, so not a lot of use if we need to get away. And we're in the woods. You know – tall trees attract lightning. And the woods are full of dead men who don't like women. Really, it's not an ideal situation, is it? We'd probably be safer in the village with all those madwomen.'

'Remind me never to make you morale officer.'

The wind grew stronger. The car rocked occasionally.

Jones climbed back inside the car and I slid across the seat to peer out of the back window again. The road was still clear in all directions.

'What's that?' said Jones suddenly.

'Where?'

He pointed. 'There.'

Behind us, back in the village, a faint golden glow lit the sky, growing stronger all the time. I stared. Fire? Beacon? Lightning strike?

'It's bonfires,' I said. 'Oh God, they must be making a sacrifice. *Becky.*' I went to climb out of the car.

'No,' he said. 'Stay where you are, Cage. And now I really am telling you what to do. You don't know what's going on down there. Iblis or Melek might have started the fire as a diversion. There's every possibility our team could come flying up the road with Becky any moment now and they'll be relying on us to be ready. This is how missions get screwed, Cage. People do what they *think* is right rather than what is *actually* right.'

'Sorry,' I said.

'No, it's OK. It's instinctive to want to do something, but that's not our function today.'

I nodded, feeling rather stupid.

'Hey.'

'What?'

He reached between the seats and took my hand. 'This will end well, I promise you. I'd back those two against anyone. And you and I have already taken on these women twice and won both times. Just have a little faith.'

I smiled. 'Thank you.'

'Just doing my job. Morale officer, remember?'

I had opened my mouth to make some sort of reply – I can't remember what it was now – when, without warning, an almighty clap of thunder exploded directly overhead. Even Jones jumped, and I nearly banged my head on the roof of the car. Followed by lightning. Both types. The sky flickered pink and yellow, pink and yellow, while great forks of blue-white lightning jagged overhead.

'Bloody hell,' said Jones. 'Close the car doors, Cage.'

I kept ducking. I couldn't help it. I'd never been in such a violent storm. Even with the doors closed every clap of thunder hurt my ears. This was not natural. More than ever, I was coming to believe this was something to do with Greyston. What the hell were they up to down there? Had something gone very badly wrong?

'No rain though,' said Jones thoughtfully.

'No,' I said. 'That would put out the bonfire.'

We looked at each other.

'Get ready, Cage. My instinct tells me it – whatever it is – won't be long now.'

The lightning flashed again. And again. Violent thunderstorms were all very well when I was safely tucked up at home, but not now. Not right this moment with madwomen and dead men and sacrifices and ancient stones demanding blood and goodness knows what else.

I pressed my face against the glass.

'Shit,' shouted Jones, and the next moment his gun – well, *a* gun – appeared between the seats.

I jumped a mile. 'What?'

'Something moved. Right next to you. Get in the front, Cage. Quick as you can.'

'Oh, no, no. It's fine. It's Nigel.'

The gun disappeared. 'In what universe is that fine? And what's he doing?'

'Trying to get out from under Melek's coat. She must have tossed it on top of him.'

'Understandable, but why?'

'She was preparing to . . .'

'I mean, why is Nigel here?'

'He's Iblis's inseparable . . .'

I paused, looking for the right word, finally going with 'companion'. A word which completely failed to describe Nigel's pungency, insatiable appetite, unspeakable personal hygiene, and fierce fighting spirit.

I turned back to the window just as the next flash of lightning lit up the inside of the car.

A face looked in at me.

And then it was dark again.

I stared at the window, frozen with fear. Perhaps it had been my own face reflected in the glass. Although I knew it wasn't.

343

Another fork jagged across the sky. And another. And then another.

For an instant – just for an instant – there were men everywhere. Rank upon rank of them. Each flash revealed hundreds and hundreds of dead men. A whole army of them. We were completely surrounded by an army of dead men.

Every single one of them was naked. With dark, dead eyes. And great, gaping wounds slashed across their throats. And they were all around us. So thickly clustered that I couldn't see the wood for the dead men. Most were staring down the road towards the village, but those nearest the car were looking in at us.

We were trapped.

'Shit,' said Jones again, very softly.

I whispered, 'Keep very still.'

'No problem. I'm paralysed with fear anyway.'

The lightning flashed again. They hadn't gone away. They were still here. Motionless and waiting.

But for what?

They couldn't possibly be waiting for me to get out. That was never going to happen. Not in a million years. I'd expire of hunger and thirst before stepping outside this vehicle.

Not that I'd have to wait that long. There were so many of them clustered around the car that they could probably overturn it at the drop of a hat. Or rip off the doors and drag us out and do something unpleasant. In fact, I was surprised we were still intact and safe inside it.

Yes, we were, weren't we. Time was passing and still the dark figures were crowded around us. This didn't make sense. Was it the presence of Jones that was confusing them? After all, he was nominally the current Year King – even if the ceremony had never been completed. Surely they harboured no hostility towards him.

Or Nigel – who had very nearly suffered the same fate.

And, now I came to think of it, they'd never really threatened me directly, and I'd been the person who ended the women's millennia-old reign of terror.

We couldn't sit here for ever. Iblis and Melek were down there somewhere. I had a thought. Mentally crossing every finger I had, I shunted over to the door.

Jones reached through the seats and caught my wrist. 'Cage, what are you doing?'

'I'm wondering . . . Perhaps they don't mean us any harm.'

'Are you sure of that?'

'No – not at all. Wait here.'

'Cage – no.'

I opened the door. Very slowly. Quite prepared to slam it shut at the first signs of danger.

There were none. In fact, the two or three nearest the car stepped back to give me room.

Nigel hopped down beside me. His tail was between his legs and he wasn't happy, but he wasn't half as afraid of these men as he was of the women down in Greyston.

I heard a sound on the other side of the car. Jones was climbing out. He wasn't leaving me to face this alone. A warm glow spread through my heart.

'Well,' he said, edging his way around the car to stand by me. 'Now what?'

A very good question, because the men were no longer looking at me. They were looking at Jones. Their eyes flickered in the dark. That was when I realised.

'It's you. It's you they want.'

He laid his hand on the door handle again. 'Shit. Really?'

'No – no, that's not what I meant. You were last year's Year King. You got away but you were never replaced. They still regard you as their king. Lead them.'

He stared down at me.

I persisted. I was right. I knew I was right. 'They're not attacking. They're not even threatening us. They're just standing here. I think they're waiting for instructions. From you.'

Still he said nothing.

The sky flashed again. I could see Jones looking at me and I could see the dead men looking at him.

As if he'd come to a sudden decision, he stepped away from me. 'All right.'

In the long silence that followed, I realised that night had fallen and the temperature had plummeted. Still no rain, though.

I kept my back against the car because I thought that would prevent anyone creeping up behind me. An action that would have been of no use whatsoever if the hundreds and hundreds of women-hating men suddenly turned on me. I might have time for one small squeak and that would be it.

Amazingly, I felt laughter bubbling up inside. Hysteria, obviously. Or my mind had buckled under the strain and I'd gone mad. One of the two, anyway.

Jones took my hand. 'Stick with me, Cage.'

'Like glue,' I said, and my voice hardly trembled at all.

Jones raised his voice. 'These women must be stopped.'

There was silence all around us. The lightning and the wind continued but the thunder had paused.

'We have friends in the village below. They were attempting a rescue and haven't come back. I am going to their aid. If you wish, some of you may accompany me, but the greater number must remain in the woods. It's likely the women will scatter, and none must be allowed to get away and start up somewhere else.'

Their eyes glinted under the flickering sky.

'You will know our friends when you see them. You may have seen one of them before. You know who I mean.' He looked down. 'And the dog is on our side. He too was a victim of the women.'

He turned to me. 'Anything I've forgotten?'

I cleared my throat. 'I can't think of anything. Actually, I can't really think at all.'

'Right – off we go, then.' He raised his voice again. 'Stay in the woods until we need you. Cage, you're with me until the first bend. And you're responsible for the scruffy fleabag.'

I assumed he meant Nigel.

We set off down the road. A hundred paces later and we'd left the cover of the trees. The wind was stronger now. I zipped up my jacket.

The village lay below us, brilliantly lit. Every light in every house was on. There were street lights with strings of outdoor fairy lights strung between them. Four blazing bonfires had been built, one at each corner of the village green. The Three Sisters themselves stood in darkness. At their base, where the shadows were deepest – something moved.

I stopped. Jones stopped. Nigel edged between us. We were in no danger of being spotted – anything outside the ring of bright lights must be in complete darkness.

It would seem that Jones thought the same. 'Rather careless

347

of them,' he muttered. 'They can't have any night vision at all.'
He halted. 'OK, Cage, this is as far as you go.'

'No,' I said.

'Think about it. We don't know whether they've got Becky
or not. She might be making her way to the car at this very
moment. She'll arrive and you won't be there.' He paused and
then nodded at the dark shadows under the trees. 'But *they* will.'

I didn't like it, but he was right. Poor Becky – to fight her
way out of the village only to be torn apart because I wasn't
there to protect her.

He pointed back the way we'd come. 'From here you can
see the car.' He turned and pointed the other way. 'And you
can see the village. You'll be well positioned to do whatever it
is you do so well. Nigel will stay here with you.'

He looked down and said commandingly, 'Sit.'

Nigel sat. Even I nearly sat.

I grabbed his arm. 'Take care.'

'Yeah, well, I'm actually spoiling for a fight, so don't worry
about me, Cage. And don't you do anything stupid.'

'Pot. Kettle. Black.'

He handed me the car key. 'Never leave the key in the car,
Cage.'

'Why are you . . . ?'

'If things get really bad – save yourself.'

'I can't drive.'

'You'd be surprised what you can do if you have to. Good
luck.'

The sky flickered again. And again. He turned to the shadows.
'Those of you coming with me . . .'

Keeping to the grass verge, he set off. It seemed to me that a large part of the wood went with him. Within seconds, Nigel and I were alone. The car was still in the centre of the road. Jones had switched on the interior light and the dim glow marked its position. It too stood alone. The wind blew and the lightning flashed. There was electricity in the air. Even under my jacket, I could feel the fine hairs on my arms stand on end. On such a night as this, anything could happen.

I looked up. Torn storm clouds scudded across the sky and the bad moon looked down at me. Almost directly over my head. Watching and waiting. People say the full moon is the one to watch. When ghosties and ghoulies walk abroad and A&E is full of people who have done stupid things. That's not actually true. A full, golden moon is just pretty. Romantic, even. A bad moon means you harm. Never venture outside when the giant horns hang in the sky.

Too late for me, of course. I stood exposed in the wavering moonlight. It was not a romantic moment.

I stared down at the village. I could clearly see the women of Greyston milling about. The combination of brilliant lights and the deep shadows made it hard for me to estimate their numbers, but I reckoned about twenty to thirty. Certainly a lot less than the last time I had encountered them, when there had been several hundred, at least. Were these all that were left? Had their numbers been reduced so drastically? What had been going on here?

Their colours – that pretty combination of blue, turquoise and purple – were a lot less vibrant than I remembered. Subdued might be a good word. With all this light and fire and the obvious build-up to some sort of ceremony, I would have expected them to be flaring with excitement, but they were very restrained. In fact, all of them seemed to be huddling close to the Three Sisters. For protection, perhaps? Yes, of course – there was to be a ceremony, but clearly not the one they'd been used to. I remembered what Becky had said about 'a sending'. I wondered – was it possible that tonight *they* were to be the sacrifices?

I cupped my hands around my eyes, squinting, trying to shut out the glare of bonfires, spotlights, street lights, and torches, because something lay concealed at the foot of the Three Sisters. Where the shadows were very thick and very dark. Darker than the night.

I began to grow cold. Beside me, Nigel whimpered.

'It's all right,' I said, more to myself than to him. 'We don't have to go down there.'

There was no sign of Iblis. Or Melek. Or even Jones. They must surely be in the village by now. Or had they all been taken? Quickly and quietly. Had the women learned from previous experience? Never mind the ceremony, the trappings or the rituals – just kill. Kill whenever you have the opportunity and throw the blood at the stones. No messing. Just get it done.

Was that what I was looking at now? The post-sacrifice party? Iblis and Melek already dead, Jones about to die, and only I was left? Standing alone and exposed and far from home while women crept through the woods towards me? I remembered them from before – their faces caked white with huge dark eyes and mouths, smeared with the blood of their victim. Maenads come to life. Were they actually watching me now? At this very moment?

No – that was ridiculous. The dead men would never let them through. The hatred in their hearts was far too great for that to happen.

I shivered – so much cold evil crammed into such a tiny area.

Something was happening. I could hear a man's voice in the distance – not Jones and definitely not Iblis – raised in a kind of chant. There was a brief pause and then the women responded. Then fell silent. Then the man again. The women chanted a response, reminding me of a religious service. Each time he raised his voice, the bonfires blazed brighter and the shadows grew darker. And all the time that shadow lurked under the stones. Waiting . . .

A huge explosion split the sky. I jumped so high my feet literally left the ground. The sudden flare of bright light left me blinking green and purple shadows. I felt the earth shake beneath my feet and the inn just . . . blew apart. The roof was blown high into the air atop a pillar of fire. The windows exploded outwards. I saw lumps of masonry fly through the air, trailing flames and smoke behind them like comets.

Women screamed and ran for cover. Not that it did them any good because the Travellers' Rest – the boarding house where Veronica Harlow had once held me prisoner – also disappeared in a mushroom of fire. Nearby trees erupted too, the flames rushing from one branch to another, until they reached the next house. Its thatch went up with a roar. Within seconds that house was burning as well. And then, all around the green – in less time than it takes to tell – one by one, more explosions, more fires.

There was pandemonium. Women scattered into the shadows. Whether to escape or to try to save their burning homes was not clear. Neither did I care. I had no idea how, but those explosions – all that destruction – had to be Iblis-and-Melek-related. And probably Jones too.

I should get back to the car. There was the very faintest

possibility that Becky – if she was still free – could use the screaming chaos to escape. Or perhaps Jones had found her and they were on their way back. Whether they were or not, standing here was not a good idea. I shifted my weight, all ready to go, and in that instant – something happened. The world changed.

The moon dimmed. The wind changed direction, blowing strongly from behind me now, whipping my hair past my face. So strong was it that I was actually blown a step or two towards the village. Was Greyston attempting to drag me back? Not for the first time.

I dropped to a crouch, clutching at the cool grass with both hands. For all the good that would do. These women had once possessed enough power to drag a whole car backwards, with the engine screaming to move forwards and Jerry gunning the accelerator for all he was worth.

Beside me, Nigel had spread his legs, lowered his head and was bracing himself against the wind.

I pulled my hair back off my face and tried to see what was happening around us. It wasn't smoke or the dust, I was certain of that, but I simply couldn't focus. Imagine covering one eye and looking at an object. Then covering the other eye. The object appears to have shifted. It hasn't actually moved but that's how it seems. This was what I was seeing now. The world was shifting back and forth. My eyes couldn't focus. Nothing was right. My brain, unable to cope, took refuge in blind terror. My stomach – slightly more sensibly – jettisoned its contents. All of them. I fell sideways and vomited. I screamed at myself to get up. If anything turned up now, I'd be easy meat. I was completely unable to move. All I could do was wait until the nausea passed.

I closed my eyes. That helped. I'm not sure what happened next or how long it happened for, but Nigel whimpered and nudged me. I opened first one eye and then the other. He was butting me with his head. An unpleasant pool of my own making lay nearby but at least I'd kept my hair out of it.

Somewhat groggily, I climbed to my feet. There was a nasty moment when I thought my stomach was about to misbehave again. I took two or three deep breaths, pushed my hair out of my eyes and stared down into Greyston.

A dark figure stood, black against the flames, his back to the stones. The clouds curdled. The moon was dying.

Nigel whimpered again, trembling with terror but determined not to desert his post.

I said, 'Good boy,' and reached out for him. Time to go. Definitely time to go.

Around me, dust, leaves and twigs were still being sucked back into Greyston. As if the village had inhaled. I had no idea what was happening. Was this something Melek or Iblis had done? I doubted it. This didn't feel right at all.

This was . . .

This was definitely a trap.

With or without Becky's assistance – this was a trap.

I clutched Nigel tight to my chest and risked another glance down into Greyston.

I wished I hadn't. For one merciful moment, I thought they were young trees burning. Saplings planted on the village green as part of the renovations that had gone up in flames after the explosions.

I was horribly, horribly wrong.

People – women – burned like torches. Flames leaped from

one to another. They didn't scream. They didn't run. They just stood silently and burned.

I couldn't look away.

Not all the women were dying in flames. I could see dark figures fleeing everywhere. Running mindlessly, just as I wanted to do. Without thought, without direction – they just ran. Straight into the surrounding trees. One by one they vanished from view. And then the shadows moved. Swift and silent. Someone screamed but there was no escape for them. The dead would hunt them down.

Still clutching Nigel, I took a shaky step backwards. And then another. Desperate to get back to the car. Away from the flames, the shadows, the bad moon – everything.

Whether the ceremony had ended in success or chaos – it would appear the women of Greyston had served their purpose. The dark figure walked past human torches, smoking craters, burning buildings. Unseeing and uncaring, it vanished into the stones.

CHAPTER TWENTY-FOUR

Jones appeared first. He was pulling Becky along with him but she appeared to be coming willingly enough. Iblis and Melek were twenty paces or so behind them, covering their escape. No one seemed to be following them.

There was no sign of the dead men but I knew they'd be around.

I already had the engine running and the doors open. Melek scrambled into the driver's seat.

'Get in the back,' she said, and Becky scrambled to obey.

Iblis headed for his own car. As did Jones.

'Get out of here,' he shouted. 'Go.'

We went.

I could feel Nigel pressed against my legs, shaking, but I was busy with Becky, who was nearly hysterical with terror.

'You're safe,' I kept saying to her. 'You're safe. You're safe.'

She put her hands over her face and sobbed. I didn't blame her. For two pins I'd have done the same.

I knelt on the back seat, staring out of the rear window. Alongside the car, keeping pace with us, the trees were bursting into flames.

'Faster. Drive faster.'

Melek put her foot down. I felt the big car surge forwards.

Slowly, the burning trees fell away behind us. Then we were round the bend and skidding away into the cool night.

Half a mile down the road, we pulled over. Engines running, we held a hurried conference.

I looked at the time. Only ten past eight. So much had happened I felt it should be midnight. At least. I had to remind myself it was still a summer evening everywhere else.

'Tesco will be open,' said Jones. 'We'll meet in the car park. Let's move.'

He pulled away. Melek was behind him, with me and a slightly calmer Becky. And Nigel. Iblis brought up the rear.

None of us spoke. Becky hiccupped the occasional sob. Her colour was riddled with orange and flying around all over the place. Watching her run up the road towards us, it had crossed my mind that she'd been allowed to escape – or even that she was deliberately deceiving us – but there was no doubt at all that she was utterly terrified.

Nigel sat as far away from her as possible. Which was actually on my lap. Unbelievably a combination of exertion and terror had made him even more whiffy than usual. I remembered this was Melek's car. She was not going to be happy.

Never were the lights of Rushford more welcome. Real lights. Proper lights. With traffic. And pedestrians. And no one was on fire. It had been raining here. Quite heavily, judging by the puddles. A light drizzle was still falling.

Our convoy turned into Tesco's car park, hissing through the puddles. Jones found a quiet corner next to the recycling pods. We pulled in together. Melek switched off the engine and we sat in silence for a moment.

356

Jones appeared at my window – Iblis at Melek's. We lowered the windows and cool, fresh evening air flooded in.

Becky was weeping fresh tears. 'I can't stay here. You can't keep me here, I haven't done anything. I tried to warn you. I have to get away. They'll find me.'

And on and on.

I rummaged in my pockets and found some mostly clean tissues. 'Here.'

There was the sound of long and bubbly nose-blowing. I felt sorry for her. She was terrified, she'd betrayed her own people, and now had nowhere to go. On the other hand, she was sobbing her heart out in a public place. People were hurrying to get out of the rain, but sooner or later someone would notice.

'Be quiet,' said Melek, but not unkindly. 'You'll attract attention.'

'I'd do as she says,' I said. 'You won't like her methods of dealing with hysterics.'

Becky mopped at her face.

'Well,' said Jones. 'What was that all about?'

Everyone looked at Becky, who gave her nose one final blow and made an effort to pull herself together.

'They made me do it. Call you. Get you to come. And then . . . when I'd done it . . .' Wrapping her arms around herself she whispered, 'They were going to kill me. Give me to the stones.'

These were the same stones she'd served all her life, sacrificing men year on year without a second thought. It would seem she viewed them differently now.

I found her another tissue. This was a power move by Joanna, of course. An opportunity to rid herself of the last Harlow in the village. 'It was a trap, wasn't it?'

357

She nodded. 'They waited for you to turn up. Only you didn't.' She stared resentfully at Iblis and Melek. 'They did.'

'Why did they want me at Greyston?'

'I don't know. They never talked about anything in front of me.' Her colour said she was telling the truth.

'So they could finish us off,' said Jones. I saw Iblis frown at that and I wasn't sure I agreed either, but Jones was still speaking. 'We need a plan. We can't keep her here in Rushford. First place they'll look.'

'But they can't get out.'

'Physically, no. But there's still the telephone. Or emails. Suppose they call the police and say we kidnapped Becky. In a way, that could be more difficult to deal with than . . .'

Iblis peered in at Becky. 'What was tonight all about? The ceremony? The sacrifices? Was it another attempt at a sending?'

'I don't know. As I said, they never told me anything.'

'How do you feel, Cage?'

'Fine,' I said. 'Well, cold, exhausted, and terrified, of course, but otherwise fine.'

'Whatever that was, it wasn't aimed at you, then,' said Iblis.

We fell silent. Because if not me, then Becky. Either to kill her or get her back.

Melek twisted around to see Becky. 'Who was that man?'

She shook her head. 'I don't know his name. I wasn't important enough for him to speak to me. He only ever dealt with Joanna or one or two of the others, but I'm sure he paid for all the repairs.'

'Why?' I said. 'Why go to all that trouble?'

'For the resources of Greyston,' said Iblis. 'For the power of the stones.'

Melek nodded. 'They were old and malevolent. And very powerful. Until they were damaged. He wanted that power, so he paid for the restoration. I suspect the women thought they were using him, but actually the boot was on the other foot. Their weakness meant they were easily controlled.' She paused, and then said, 'And, ultimately, expendable.'

Becky sniffed again.

'Just to be clear,' said Melek. 'He was not their new Year King?'

Becky sniffed but I'd run out of tissues. 'He was – sort of. But he was much different to all the others. He raised the stones. He promised us power.' She stopped and the tears began to fall again.

'But . . .'

'He used us,' she said, obviously completely forgetting she was one of a bunch of women who had been murdering men in their thousands down the centuries. 'To get to Mrs Cage. He was doing something . . . I don't know what. Calling on the stones. But with every attempt . . . well, he said he was being turned back.' Her eyes closed and she whispered, 'The stones betrayed us. They belong to him now. And every time it happened . . . some of us burned.'

Iblis looked at Melek. 'He was using the women as a source of power. Human batteries.'

'For what purpose?' said Jones.

'There was something there,' I said slowly. 'In the shadows. Moving around the stones.'

'What?' said Melek sharply. 'What did you see?'

'Just shifting shadows.'

'But what about me?' cried Becky, tears falling down her face again. 'They'll want me back. To kill me. Where can I go?'

There was a long silence. Where indeed?

'Leave this with me,' said Jones suddenly.

Melek looked at him. 'You?'

'Yeah – me. I know a safe place. Well, I know several. I'll take her. She's in too much of a state to go anywhere alone. I'll talk to her on the way when she's calmed down a little. It's a fair distance so I'll be gone a day. Possibly two.' He looked at me. 'Will you be all right?'

All right was relative, but any moment I wasn't actually surrounded by dead men or burning women was good, so yes, I was all right.

'I will go with you,' said Melek to Jones. 'In case.'

In case of what, she didn't say, and he didn't ask. It wasn't such a bad idea. Jones would easily be able to deal with any conventional threats that might arise and Melek could take on the more imaginative stuff. Between them, they should have everything covered. It might even give them a chance to bond. Perhaps.

Melek turned to him. 'Same car?'

'No. I'll take Becky in mine. You follow on.'

'I shall stay with Elizabeth Cage,' announced Iblis.

There was a moment's silence and then Jones said, 'Yes, good idea.' He took my hand, and for a moment we were the only people there. 'Please – stay safe.'

'I will.'

He looked at Iblis. 'Keep her safe.'

'I will.'

'All right, then.' Jones paused and then said, 'See you when I see you, Cage.'

'And you. You stay safe too.' I paused as well. 'You have to.'

He squeezed my hand. 'See you soon. Come on, Becky.'

Somewhat reluctantly, she climbed out of the SUV.

'Get in the back,' he said. 'Stretch out on the seat and get some sleep. It's a long way.'

Silently, she did as she was told. No backward glance. No thanks.

I was doubtful. 'Are you sure you'll be OK with her?'

'I'll be fine. At the first sign of trouble, I'll pull over and set the lanky witch on her.'

About to climb into Iblis's car, the lanky witch paused for a moment, wisely decided she hadn't heard anything and closed the door.

Jones smiled down at me. 'I won't call. Not until I'm on my way home. Calls can be traced.'

'All right.'

'And for God's sake, try not to get into any more trouble. Not until I'm back, anyway.'

'When you come back,' I said, 'we really need to sit down and talk.'

'Yes, we do. Properly. Over good food and wine and without something climbing out of the woodwork or manifesting itself all over your kitchen. See you in a day or so.'

He jumped into his car, started the engine and drove out of the car park. I watched his rear lights disappear into the thin drizzle, followed by Melek in Iblis's car. Then it was just us. And Nigel.

'Home?' I said to Iblis.

I should have known better. He pointed to the brightly lit supermarket. 'Provisions first.'

361

CHAPTER TWENTY-FIVE

We left the car at the bottom of the hill and walked up to my house. We were very quiet and very careful. It wasn't that late – only just coming up to half past nine. There were still people on the streets. There had been a real downpour here but the rain had dwindled to a soft and gentle sprinkling. Drains and gutters were still gurgling, trying to cope with all the water, and wide puddles lay everywhere.

In Castle Close itself, the moat had overflowed its banks and was sending out fingers of water across the green. Surprised ducks would wake up tomorrow to find they could holiday in formerly inaccessible areas.

I had my house keys ready. Jones was always very clear about not wasting time fumbling for them in the dark, when I might need to get inside quickly. *Given your lifestyle, Cage* . . . he'd said, and left the rest unspoken.

I opened my mouth to wonder whether I'd find the usual splash of blood on my doorstep but never got to ask the question. Because while the rain might have washed away this evening's blood, it appeared to have left a body in its place. Something black lay across my top step and it wasn't moving.

I reached out to put my hand on Iblis's arm but he'd already

362

seen. My porch light came on as he climbed the steps. I stood behind him, trying to see what was going on.

At first, I thought it was a dog. It was certainly big enough.

'It's a cat,' I said in surprise.

Iblis said nothing.

'Is it dead?'

'Not quite. Can you find something to carry him on?'

I stepped carefully over the pair of them, opened my front door and found an old wooden tray in the kitchen.

'Careful,' he said and I was. The cat had a floppy feel about it that spoke of many broken bones. It moaned slightly as we lifted it on to the tray.

'I'm sorry,' I said, as if it could hear and understand me. 'I'm sorry. We're just trying to help.'

Iblis carried it inside. I went on ahead, turning on the lights for him, and then went back to bring in the shopping and close the front door.

'Lock it,' he said over his shoulder and I did. And bolted it for good measure and drew the curtain across.

When I turned back, he had switched on the fire and laid the cat, still on his tray, in front of it.

Seen now in the light for the first time, I could see why I'd mistaken it for a dog. It was huge. Easily the biggest cat I'd ever seen.

I always think there are two types of cats – the wide-bodied, short-legged kind, often with longish fur – and the leggy short-haired sort. This was the second type. Long legs, lean but not skinny, with big ears and a long, strong nose. And black, I thought. At the moment he was a sodden heap of hurt, but his nose and paw pads were black, so it seemed likely the rest of him was as well.

But, most astonishing of all – he had a colour. Animals do, but mostly it's just a very pale outline of grey or brown that fades away into nothing. But this was blue. Faint and frail at the moment, but I could imagine that normally it would be a bright, pure blue. Lapis lazuli blue. He lay unmoving. I wasn't convinced he was still alive. Iblis knelt over him.

'Well now, old soldier – I haven't seen one like you for a long, long time. What have you been up to, eh?'

Not unsurprisingly the cat made no response.

'I'll get a blanket to wrap him in,' I said.

I ran upstairs and found an old pashmina I'd never worn because I'd thought the colour was lime green until I saw it in daylight and realised it was a particularly virulent shade of mustard. And yes, I am aware of the irony of me getting a colour wrong, but, finally, it could do something useful.

We lifted the cat off the tray and very carefully wrapped him in the shawl's soft folds. He was in a dreadful state. One ear was crusted with blood and looked as if it had been almost ripped from his head. His left eye was hugely swollen – in fact, the whole left side of his skull had a crushed look about it. His right front leg was broken and I think one of his back ones was as well. His hips didn't look right, anyway. And his ribs were the wrong shape, so I suspected massive internal injuries as well.

'Has he been hit by a car?' I said, although he surely hadn't dragged himself all the way up here from the road. 'Or has he fallen? Or, no . . . crushed. Perhaps something fell on him. What about a vet?'

'Oh no, I don't think a vet would do that.'

364

'I meant – should we take him to one?'

'Actually, no.'

'Why not?'

'I don't think it would do him any good.'

'Why ever not? Look at the state of the poor thing.'

'He's been fighting,' said Iblis.

I was astonished. 'Fighting what? A tank?'

Iblis shook his head. 'Fighting is the wrong word. I think he's been battling.' He disappeared into the kitchen to do things with mugs, tea and the kettle. Nigel heaved himself out from under the table in anticipation of food and I stayed on the hearthrug where I could see all three of them.

Iblis plonked two mugs of tea on the table. Nigel hung around hopefully, in case biscuits turned up.

I wasn't going to let Iblis off the hook. 'This is no ordinary cat, is it? Why did you call him "old soldier"? What's happened to him? Who is he?'

'He is a soldier in the army of Bastet and I think it has been his blood on the doorstep every night.'

I think I was more astonished that I accepted this statement without question than at the statement itself.

'That rings a faint bell. Wasn't Bastet an Egyptian god? And weren't cats sacred in Egypt?'

He nodded, drained his mug and stood up. 'Will you be all right if I leave you? Just for a little while.'

'Yes, of course,' I said, meaning the exact opposite. 'Where are you going?'

'I shall return with medical supplies.'

'I already have a first aid kit.'

He looked at the horribly injured cat. 'It won't be enough. I know a woman – she does potions, salves and the like. I shall return.'

After he'd gone, I watched the cat for a while, tried to pull my scattered thoughts together, gave that up and fed Nigel instead. He gulped down his food and came straight back to the cat, sniffing around. Fearing he'd hurt it somehow, I gently fended him off. 'No, Nigel.'

He ignored me, pushing past my arm. Carefully – delicately, almost – he lowered himself alongside the unconscious cat. Of course – body warmth.

I left him to it and took refuge in normality. I unpacked the shopping and put it all away. Iblis would be hungry when he got back. I switched on the oven and shoved in a vast number of sausages and pulled out two giant frozen Yorkshire puddings. I chopped onions and made stock for the gravy, all the while keeping an eye on the cat who, sadly, hadn't moved an inch.

That done, I re-boiled the kettle, because people always call for boiling water in a crisis, and returned yet again to hover anxiously over the cat. I'd never seen such a stricken animal. I suspected the best we could do for it was just leave it alone to die in warmth and peace.

Iblis was back much quicker than I expected. 'I have brought assistance,' he announced.

I think I still thought he would at least have brought an animal medic of some kind – a white-coated professional who would deal swiftly and efficiently with the problem. Or, possibly, given that this was Iblis, an elderly shaman crushed by the weight of time, full of lore and wisdom, festooned with garlands of herbs and reeking of slightly sinister ointments.

He was actually followed inside by a young woman wearing a smart grey business suit, trendy glasses and sporting a sharp hairstyle with a crimson streak. Her colour varied between pale green and primrose yellow. Spring colours.

'This is Ursula. She's a witch.'

'How do you do,' I murmured, determined to take all this in my stride.

She was already kneeling on the rug. 'Let's have a look at you, shall we?'

She had a strong Liverpool accent.

Smiling at Nigel, she said, 'Yes, my friend, you can move away now.'

Nigel shifted himself up on to the sofa.

Ursula looked up, saying sharply, 'This cat has been bitten. There are puncture marks as well as all the other damage. Do either of you know what's happened here?'

We shook our heads. 'He was stretched across my doorstep when we arrived,' I said.

I thought she'd X-ray the cat – don't ask me how she would have managed that; I'd had a long day and my thought processes weren't at their best – or possibly that she would manipulate his limbs – gently, of course. I thought she'd peer at his eyes, clean his wounds, or at the very least shave off various bits of fur and stitch him back together again.

She did none of that.

She sang a song over him. I didn't recognise the language, and the rhythm was strange. Nothing I'd ever heard before, anyway. The words and music resonated around my little room. I could hear my crystal wine glasses singing their own song in response. Her colour swirled over the cat, glowing slightly, and

367

when she finished, the cat's colour – that very faint outline in blue – had strengthened and thickened a little.

'There,' she said, sitting back on her heels and looking exhausted. 'I've done what I can. Either he lives or dies. It's out of my hands, now.'

'Thank you,' said Iblis, helping her up.

She looked down at the cat. 'I didn't know there were any of them still left in the world.' She raised her glance to Iblis. 'Must be something serious.'

'I rather think it is,' he said quietly.

I reached for my bag. 'How much do we owe you?'

'I work for free,' she said. 'Especially for such a one as this.' She looked down at the cat again. 'May the great Ubaste have you in her care, soldier. I will mention you to the Mother in my prayers tonight.'

'But surely I must give you something,' I said.

'One day, perhaps,' she said, smiling. 'Let's see how this turns out first.'

'Do I need to do anything? Dress his wounds or . . . feed him . . . or . . .' I ran out of ideas.

'He looks after himself, this one, but a drink, maybe. If he asks for it.'

'Well, thank you,' I said. 'And thank you for coming so quickly.'

'My pleasure. Good luck, old soldier.'

Iblis saw her out and bolted the door behind her.

I checked the cat one more time, shunted Nigel off the sofa and began to lay the table. Time for some answers.

'OK, Iblis, what's going on? What's this all about?'

He pulled a beer out of the fridge. 'I told you. He's a soldier in the army of Bastet.'

'The Egyptian goddess.'

He nodded and chugged back some beer.

'Hasn't she been dead for thousands of years?'

'Gods don't die, Elizabeth Cage. You of all people should know that.'

I couldn't help glancing around. 'She's not here, is she?'

'Oh no – long gone.'

'To where?'

'Wherever it is the gods go.' He looked at me. 'They all leave sooner or later. Some are replaced. Some simply fade away. Some move on. One day there will be none left in this world. Whether that will turn out to be a good or a bad thing remains to be seen.'

This was too much for me to think about. I'd made a quiet resolution to put all god-related stuff from my mind. I couldn't help what I was, but I could ignore it. Work around it. For the time being, anyway. Felda and I had made our arrangement and I would stick to it as best I could. I certainly didn't want to talk about it, so I reverted to the original subject.

'So, why exactly is he here? And what has done this to him?'

'Those are very good questions. Did anything strike you about this evening?'

I banged the cutlery down on the table in a sudden fit of temper. 'You mean other than exploding villages, evil stones, burning women, bad moons, dead men and mysterious cats? No, not really. Just a normal evening so far, don't you think?'

I rested my hands on the table and let my head hang down.

He looked at me. 'This is not like you, Elizabeth Cage.'

I sighed. 'I've had a couple of bad weeks.'

He waited.

I lifted my head. 'All right – other than the obvious, what should have struck me about this evening?'

He waited some more.

I stopped having a strop and tried to think properly. 'It's stupid, I know, but when Jones said we'd walked into a trap . . . well, I wondered.'

He said nothing.

I looked across at him. 'We *were* lured to the village, weren't we?'

He finished his beer and crushed his can. 'Yes, but take that one stage further.'

I stared at him. 'No, sorry . . .'

'We weren't lured *to* – we were lured *from*.'

'From here? For what purpose?'

'So we wouldn't be here when it happened.'

I looked round wildly. 'What? What happened?'

'I think – nothing. Thanks to this old soldier here.'

I looked down at the cat. 'The one who's a soldier in the army of . . .'

'Bastet. Yes. Tonight was a special effort – you saw how those women burned – but the cat turned it back. Think what you might have come back to if he had failed.'

The cat made a faint sound.

I abandoned the table-laying. 'I'll get him some water.'

I filled a bowl with water and found a teaspoon. I knelt and very gently trickled a little water into the cat's mouth. A pink tongue appeared and lapped at the spoon.

'That's good,' I said. 'He can drink.'

'Oh yes,' said Iblis. 'He'll be fine in a couple of days. He just needs to rest.'

I replenished the spoon and held it for the cat to lap again. 'Is there anything else you're not telling me? Because if there is, I warn you, there are saucepans over there and I'm not afraid to use them.'

'Well, yes, I am very hungry, but I sense that preparing a meal for me and Nigel is not your meaning.'

I ground my teeth – my dentist says I shouldn't do that – and continued to give the cat water. Just a little at a time. After two or three spoonfuls, the cat ceased to lap, laid its head back down and closed its eyes.

I regarded it anxiously. 'Is it dead?'

'No – only resting.'

'But what has happened to him? What could do this awful damage?'

'You've had blood on your doorstep for how long now?'

I couldn't think for a moment. 'I can't remember. Yes, I can. It started – no, I first noticed it that day you came round to watch *Olympian Heights*. The night I got that note.' I stared at him. '*I will send the serpent.*'

I had the impression he was choosing his words very carefully. 'I think . . . every night . . . something has been trying to get in, and every night our soldier here has been keeping it out.'

I stood up on creaking legs and took the bowl back into the kitchen.

'That's what Becky said. That those women were sending something and it kept being turned back.'

'And every time that happened, some of them died. Because

if you raise something and it misses its target, it can't return empty-handed. Failure rebounds on the summoner, so, to protect themself, the summoner always works through others. They're the ones who pay the price of failure.'

I looked across at him. 'It's a snake, isn't it? The note said they were sending a snake.'

Oddly enough, I wasn't as terrified as I thought I should be. I'm not afraid of snakes. I know some people are – there's a name for it that I couldn't remember at that moment – but I'm not. Nor rats or spiders. I sometimes wonder if, because I can see things from the other world, threats from this one don't seem that scary. Snakes can be dealt with. Throw a blanket over them, then ring the council's pest control department and let someone else deal with it.

'Did tonight's summoning fail?'

He put the empty beer can out for recycling and said slowly, 'I think it must have. I wonder if our intervention disrupted their ceremony before they'd finished? If that is so, then we almost certainly saved this soldier's life. He would not have given up while there was breath in his body, but he couldn't have lasted much longer. Thanks to us, the summoning failed before our soldier died doing his duty.'

'And this has been going on for how long?'

'Most nights, I think.'

I took a moment to think about this silent battle that had been raging on my doorstep. Every night. Presumably the cat had won every time – except for tonight. That was how his bones had been broken. The snake had curled itself around him and tried to crush him to death.

I blinked away a tear. 'Poor little fellow.'

'I think you're missing the point.'

'I wouldn't be at all surprised,' I said bitterly. 'What is the point I'm missing?'

'Are you familiar with the story of Bastet?'

I shook my head. 'The cat goddess?'

'She is the daughter of Ra and Isis, and consort of Ptah. Her titles include Goddess of the Sun, Protector of Lower Egypt, Protector against Evil Spirits, Slayer of Apep, and Defender of the Sun God Ra, whom she saved by slaying the serpent.'

'Apep.'

'Yes, a giant snake.'

'Or serpent.'

'Yes.'

'How giant?'

'Well, big enough to swallow the sun.'

Oddly, this was reassuring. It seemed safe to assume that had something big enough to swallow the sun turned up on my doorstep, then someone would have noticed and rung the council to complain.

'This Apep – is he a god too?'

'No. Apep has always existed. When time began, he was already here, lurking in the waters of primeval chaos.'

I took a moment to concentrate very hard on the place settings. Knife on the right. Fork on the left. Other way around for Iblis. Salt. Pepper. Glass. Table mats. It was very important that I did this properly.

Iblis was continuing. 'Every day, Apep lurks below the horizon and as the barque of the sun god drops below the world, he attacks.'

Present tense.

I took out the water carafe and filled it up, saying, 'And do we know why he does that?'

'To return the world to the dark chaos from which it was born.'

'How interesting,' I said politely.

'Every night hundreds of thousands of Egyptians would pray for Ra's survival. Every day the king would perform the rituals necessary to ensure the sun would always rise that morning. It was one of the most important parts of his job.'

'Yes,' I said. 'I can see it would be. Just one teeny tiny query. Why would this sun-swallowing monster be interested in me?'

'You're looking at this the wrong way around.'

I sighed. 'Of course I am.'

'Every society has legends of a giant snake – Nidhögg, Ouroboros, Hedammu, Leviathan, Quetzalcoatl . . .'

'Are they all after me, too?'

'No,' he said patiently. 'I'm saying it's not the serpent that's after you – it's the person behind it. The serpent is the weapon. The sender is the person wielding that weapon.'

'All right – who is this sender?'

But even as the words left my mouth – I knew. The memory I hadn't quite been able to grasp was suddenly as clear and sharp as if it had happened yesterday. Or, to be more accurate, last Christmas. Just a flash. Just for one very quick moment. A snowy landscape, a pale man sitting under a cedar tree, his bare feet buried in the snow. A long, sad face. And a voice. *I sent the serpent. I always send the serpent. It's kind of my signature move.*

I felt the blood run from my face. My skin felt tight and cold. '*I will send the serpent.*'

He nodded.

'But he wasn't talking to me,' I said slowly. 'That was Felda. What does he want with me?'

'He wants Felda and . . .' He stopped suddenly, leaving the words unspoken. *He would tear me apart to get to her*.

I couldn't speak.

'He was happy to leave her to her grief – it drove her mad and she was no longer a danger to him. And then Melek hid her in you and he couldn't find her. He must have thought she had passed on to the next world, and forgotten about her, but then, suddenly, you crossed his path and now, Elizabeth, he knows exactly where and who she is. And now he knows all about you, too.'

CHAPTER TWENTY-SIX

I felt my heart stop. My blood really did run cold – in fact, it felt as if ice water was running through my veins. At that moment I was more afraid than I'd ever been in my entire life. More than when Clare Woods came back to haunt me. More than when facing down Elizabeth Shotton. Even more than the time a thing waited behind me in the Sorensen Clinic. I stood in my own kitchen – the one place in all the world where I should have been safe – held fast in the grip of a bone-deep, inescapable terror that numbed my senses. I couldn't move, couldn't think. I couldn't even panic – not just at that moment. I had a horrible feeling panic would come later. Hysteria, even.

Iblis had come to stand beside me. He gripped both my hands. 'Breathe,' he said, much in the way Jones would have done.

I did as I was told. I breathed.

'Drink your tea.'

I drank my tea. It was a shame Jones himself wasn't here to witness my docility.

'Iblis, I . . .' I couldn't say any more. Words wouldn't come.

'You are safe. The serpent was turned back today.'

'But it will come again tomorrow and the cat . . . he's in no state to . . .' I gestured at the unconscious cat.

'No,' he agreed. 'We need help. Leave that to me. But take

heart. Given the state of things at Greyston, they almost certainly are in no condition to mount another attack tomorrow. We have time, I think.'

I got up and knelt over the cat again, too scared to show Iblis my face, which must have terror written all over it. 'Iblis, should I run? I could catch a train. Or you could drive me . . . There must be somewhere . . . I . . . Oh God.'

I put my face in my hands.

He came over to put his hand on my shoulder. 'Be calm. I promised the man-mountain I would keep you safe and I will.'

I let my hands fall. 'Iblis, I don't think I can do this for much longer. Ever since Ted died, my life has just tumbled from one crisis to another. It's getting worse, isn't it? I thought, once I'd made my peace with Felda and we came to our arrangement, that things would get better, but it's everywhere I go. Everyone I meet. Every situation I encounter.'

He held my face between his warm hands. 'No, it's not. And you have friends, Elizabeth. More than you know. Think of the people you have helped. Remember them – not those you think hate you.'

I nodded and closed my eyes. Tears ran down my cheeks. Angrily, I brushed them away and lifted my chin and struggled for some courage. This was no time for crying. This was a time for . . . not crying.

All right. Stop. Think. What would Jones do? He would seek to gain more information. Knowledge is strength. Ask questions. Focus.

I turned to Iblis. 'You keep saying "he". Who is he?'

He shrugged. 'He rules the Fiori. If he has a name, then none have ever heard it.'

I'd heard of this before. To know a person's true name gives you a power over that person. I knew that Iblis and Melek weren't their real names. I knew that Elizabeth Cage wasn't mine. And now I came to think of it, Michael Jones wasn't Michael Jones, either. None of us were who we seemed.

The timer pinged. Which was probably the best thing that could have happened to me just at that moment. Automatically, I went to check the oven. Doing what I did best. A 1950s house-wife – that was me.

Iblis was on my heels. 'Something smells good.'

I stopped dead. 'You're still hungry?'

'Of course I am. Aren't you?'

I didn't think I was – not after the day I'd had – but as soon as I whipped the sausages out of the oven, I realised that yes, I was. Very hungry, actually. I topped each golden Yorkshire pudding with crispy sausages and fried onions and anointed the whole thing with thick, rich gravy.

Nigel awoke – obviously – and I set aside some for him.

'When it's cooled down a bit,' I said severely, ignoring the growing pool of dribble around his feet.

We ate in silence until there was nothing left.

'Better now?' enquired Iblis.

Reluctantly, I nodded. 'I'm so shallow – my life is full of trauma and crisis and unknown threats, but three sausages later and I'm feeling fine.'

His eyes sparkled. 'Never underestimate the restorative powers of a good sausage.'

'For that,' I said, getting up, '*you* will be doing the dishes.'

He laughed. 'Other than that, Mrs Lincoln, how has the evening been so far?'

I had to smile. 'Actually? Given what happened last weekend, about par for the course.'

He began to fill the washing-up bowl. 'Yes? Tell me what happened.'

'Well,' I said, passing him the dirty dishes. 'Jones and I were lured to a sinister mansion. Once inside, we discovered a malevolent ghost who wasn't going to let us back out again. Not until we'd descended into lunacy and cannibalism, anyway. Jones got stroppy and refused to let anyone gnaw on his . . . arm . . . other than me, but I didn't fancy it, so we devised a successful getaway plan and escaped. On the way back, we came across our ghost feasting on a couple of family members, which, I believe, might have been the last of their line. Whether the curse is ended or not, I'm afraid I have no idea. How was your weekend?'

He shook his head. 'My exploits are as nothing compared with those of the magnificent Elizabeth Cage.' He headed towards the door. 'Please do not panic but I must leave you again for a while.'

I did panic, but invisibly, I hoped. 'Is it safe for you to go?'

'Yes. There will be nothing more tonight. I will leave Nigel but I don't think you'll need him.'

We both looked across at Nigel, overwhelmed by two enormous meals and oblivious to his equally enormous respon-sibilities and snoring gently.

'Where are you going?'

'For assistance,' he said.

'Oh.' I had no problems with that. Although . . . I narrowed my eyes – this was Iblis, after all. Assistance could range from a spell knocked up from a couple of eyes of newt and two spoonfuls of gravy browning, to an entire tank regiment. Or a dragon. The Kraken, even. I said doubtfully, 'What sort of assistance?'

'The very best.'

'But . . .'

He drew himself up and declaimed, 'I, Iblis, shall return,' took my key and let himself out.

In the sudden silence, I realised he'd stuck me with the dishes again.

Once again, he returned more quickly than I'd expected. I'd barely had time to clear the supper things away and contemplate making up his bed on the sofa when my phone rang.

'It is I, Iblis,' he announced, even though he knew the screen would have his name emblazoned across it.

'Hello. I've just finished the dishes. It's safe to return.'

'In his epic poem, *GogMagog*, Karnak of Thame, Chief Bard of Queen Dorice the Fair, says occupying the hands and mind is always beneficial in times of great crisis. And he should know. I need you to go upstairs and look out of your bedroom window. Tell me what you see.'

'Why?'

'I am setting up the defence of your house.'

'Oh. OK.'

I ran up the stairs into my bedroom and peered out through the window. I couldn't see a thing. Well, yes, I could see the dark outline of the castle, the green, the trees, the street lights and so forth, but nothing out of the ordinary.

'Um, no, nothing. I can't see anything. Should I?'

'No. Now try the bathroom.'

I shot across the landing, stood in the bath, opened the window and leaned out into the cold night air. There were still lights speckled all across Rushford. Windows, street lights, headlights. Someone had had a BBQ – I could smell woodsmoke. The rain had stopped, the sky had cleared and the stars looked down.

I heard the front door open.

'There is no cause for alarm,' he called. 'It is I, Iblis, Champion and Hero. Protector of the beauteous Elizabeth Cage. Are all your windows secure?'

I closed the bathroom window, calling over my shoulder, 'They are now.'

'OK,' he said. 'Well, that's upstairs checked. I'm doing the downstairs now. Wait up there until I give the word.'

I switched off my phone, climbed out of the bath, and reflected briefly on my life choices.

His voice came from the bottom of the stairs. 'You're all secure. You can come down now.'

He was just closing the cellar door as I trotted down the stairs.

'I think,' I said carefully, unwilling to admit even to myself that I didn't fancy sleeping upstairs on my own, 'I think I'll sleep down here tonight. You know – keep an eye on the cat. In case he needs anything. You know.'

'A very wise decision,' he said solemnly.

Nigel shot out into the back garden for one last whatever it is dogs do before going to bed, while I checked the cat. I dragged my quilt and pillows down the stairs. Iblis called Nigel in and locked up. I checked the cat again and then we all went to bed. There was a lot of shunting around but we finally settled down at around one a.m. I was exhausted. Too exhausted to sleep.

That was what I told myself anyway, because it sounded better than being too scared to close my eyes. I think I might have dozed once or twice, but mostly I lay and waited for the sun to come up. I got up once to offer the cat some more water – he didn't want it, which was worrying – and Iblis got up twice to walk around and check the doors and windows. He even went down into the cellar.

At around six a.m. I gave it up, switched on the kettle and checked on the cat again.

He was still alive. I could hardly believe he'd made it through the night. And not only was he still alive, but his eyes were open. They were the most beautiful, vivid blue. Just like his colour. He'd dried out – his fur was as jet black as I'd suspected – and he seemed warmer. I settled the pashmina around him again and very, very gently stroked his head. Just one finger. The very lightest touch—

And suddenly there was light. Brilliant, dazzling light, bouncing off white marble and gold. And heat. Lovely, bone-warming, healing, sleep-filled heat.

I walked the Sacred Path. Date palms and pomegranate trees cast welcome shade. The air smelled of dust and spices and incense. Twin canals bordered the path, one on each side, with white and pink lotus flowers standing proudly above the sur-face, and before me, blindingly white under the golden rays of Ra – Per-Bast, the House of Bast.

There were small groups of people here, waiting patiently in the shade as, gently and with great respect, the priests accepted the bodies of beloved household cats, brought here to sleep the long sleep under the protection of Bastet herself, while their kas frolicked in the afterlife.

I passed through the propylaea – the guards saluted me and the golden collar of my office – and approached the temple. My presence was required by the goddess.

The temple itself was cool and silent. I walked the halls. My feet welcomed the cold marble after the heat of the sand. Here, the smell of incense was even stronger and not unwelcome.

I walked slowly but without hesitation, weaving my way between the tall pillars, each topped with the head of the goddess in her early incarnation as the lioness warrior and facing in four directions. I knew the way. I had been here many times before. Past the painted walls. Past depictions of the goddess, sistrum in one hand, aegis in the other, standing with Hathor, Sekhmet and Isis, presiding over pregnancy and childbirth. The bronze lamps flickered, giving the images depth, movement and life.

There were other soldiers everywhere. Tails high, trotting through the halls on silent feet. Or sitting, statue-still, watching the world through unblinking eyes. Some, like me, wore the golden collars of high rank. Some wore jewels. I greeted my friend Pakapu, with whom I had shared many a kill. He butted me with his head and passed on his way. And here, tawny as a lion and with glowing topaz eyes, the lady of my heart, Miu. She paused and we touched noses. She rubbed her head briefly against mine and then she was gone. Those of us in the service of the goddess have very little time for anything else.

And finally, as I turned the last corner before the inner sanctum, there it was, spread from one side of the wall to the other: the depiction of the Great Battle itself, when Bastet defeated the Lord of Chaos, the Eater of Souls, He who Encircles the World, Dweller in the Tenth Region of the Night – the serpent himself – Apep, the Great Enemy of Ra.

Even after all this time, I paused. Out of respect.

There was the golden barque of the Sun God, resplendent in fire and light. There, erupting from the darkness of the void, was the Great Enemy, its coils already wrapped around the Ship of the Sun, its huge mouth agape to swallow it whole. Before him stood the goddess, mighty in her wrath, her lance raised to smite the World-Encircler and cast him down to the depths from whence he came. That Ra rises every day is due to Bastet, Lady of Ankhtawy. All thanks to her. Glory to her name.

Two white-clad priests bowed and pulled aside the curtain and I passed into the darkness of the inner sanctum. The home of the goddess.

I entered, paid my respects and waited. The statue rose high above me. Made of alabaster – which takes its name from hers – the lion-headed goddess regarded me with her golden eyes and made her wishes known.

The lamps blazed in a sudden intensity – her eyes flashed fire – the temple faded and suddenly I was lying on a rug in a world that had no colour, no light, no fire. There was pain, and I was a long way from home.

I drew a long shuddering sigh.

'Well,' said Iblis quietly. 'Now you know.'

'Yes, I do. And he has done his duty. And now he's hurt and in pain.' I bent over the cat, whispering, 'Thank you.'

There was a short silence.

'That's all settled, then,' said Iblis cheerfully. 'Now everyone knows who everyone is. How would you like to do this next bit?'

I blinked. 'How would I like to do what next bit?'

'Well, would you like to get the next shock out of the way

384

now, while you're still reeling from the last one? Or would you like to pause, have a cup of tea, get over things a little, and brace yourself for the next impact?'

I stared at him. 'What? What impact? Did something happen while I was . . . ?'

I stopped. *While I was communing with a goddess in Ancient Egypt* isn't really something you want to say out loud. 'Just tell me.'

He rubbed his forehead. 'All right, but you have to promise me you won't be cross.'

I stared at him with deep foreboding. 'What have you done?'

'Well – and I want you to bear in mind that I've done it with the very best of intentions . . .'

'What have you done with the very best of intentions?'

'And I'm certain, after you've sat down and thought about it for a while – carefully and calmly – you will agree that . . .'

'*Iblis!*'

He sighed and braced himself. 'There's a troll in your cellar.'

CHAPTER TWENTY-SEVEN

'I ... Wh ... ? I ... You ... Wh ... ? Tro ... ? Wh ... ?'

It was no good. I couldn't get anything out. Five million words struggled to get through the Door of Coherence. Simultaneously. All of them failed. Lacking any useful direction from my brain, they gave up and went home.

I stared at him. What can you say to someone who has put a troll in your cellar? And thinks they've done you a favour? What words could possibly convey ... ?

The cat, wisely, had closed his eyes again.

Nigel, even more wisely, was behind the sofa.

I continued my struggle with words.

Iblis watched with interest. 'You need to work through your emotions,' he advised. 'That's what Melek always does. Start with the need to inflict a violent and painful fate upon me. Dwell on that for a few enjoyable moments, then move on to something slightly more constructive, such as the reasons for my actions. And then we can move forwards – together – towards the sunlit uplands of comprehension and appreciation.'

A single solitary word fought its way through my overwhelming urge to lay him out cold with a handy piece of Le Creuset.

'Why?'

He settled back. 'Ah. The right question. And congratulations on achieving your state of tolerance and forbearance so quickly. Melek usually pushes me out of the door with instructions not to return for a month.'

I reached for the poker. But in a very tolerant and forbearing manner. Zen-like, almost. 'Again. Why?'

'To keep you safe.'

'Trolls *eat* people. One nearly ate me, once.'

'Ah. Yes. About that . . .'

I closed my eyes. 'He's downstairs, isn't he? It's Þhurs. He's in my cellar at this very moment.'

'Well, yes, that is *one* interpretation of the facts . . .'

'You intend to keep me from the serpent by sacrificing me to a troll.'

He waved this aside. 'He's not hungry at the moment, you're perfectly safe.'

I knew better than to let this statement go. '*Why* is he not hungry at the moment?'

'Well, you know those purple and green things down there . . . ?'

My grasp on reality slackened even further. 'What?'

'Like sweets.'

'What?'

'The pretty ones.'

Inspiration punched me between the eyes. 'You mean laundry pods?'

'That's them.'

'What about them?'

'He might have eaten a few. Or a whole tubful.'

'*Might* have eaten . . . ?'

'All right – he has eaten them. Yes, the downside is that you won't be able to wash my socks, but the upside is that he's not hungry any longer.'

'He's probably not alive any longer. They're deadly poisonous.'

'You wash your clothes in deadly poison? Very wise. Keep your clothes on when the serpent attacks and you might survive.'

'How did he get in?'

'Who?'

I summoned an inhuman amount of self-control. 'Þhurs.'

'Last night. I smuggled him in while you were upstairs checking your windows.'

'You said you were bringing help and setting up defences.'

'And so I did.'

I spoke through gritted teeth. 'Bring him up here. Now.'

'I'm not sure how helpful . . .'

'*Now!*'

He disappeared into the cellar. I could hear his voice. Interspersed with a very familiar nasal bubbling.

'Come on, snot-snorter. On your feet. No, put that down. Down. Put it *down*. Now, please. The lady of the house wants to see you. Come along. No, don't pick that up. Just leave it alone, please. Thank you. No, leave that alone as well. Never mind – you can wipe it up later. Don't do that – not in front of ladies. This way. And mind your manners.'

I glanced downwards. The cat was looking up at me. I swear he was smirking. Then he closed his eyes again. I didn't blame him in the slightest. Why on earth hadn't I taken up Dr Bridgeman's offer of free treatment at the government facility?

The cellar door opened and there stood Þhurs in all his glory.

He wouldn't come any further. So tall was he that his head brushed the ceiling. A nightmare seemingly constructed from a beguiling combination of doormats, coat hangers, miscellaneous rocks, teeth, claws and a never-ending supply of snot. And currently living in my cellar.

I turned to Iblis. 'You can't just fill my house with random life forms . . .'

'You already have a dog. And a cat. And me.'

'The dog, the cat – even you – are not going to eat me as soon as my back's turned. You're not going to rip out my spine and use it as a table centrepiece. None of you will cover me in snot or . . .'

'He's the best fighter I know,' said Iblis quietly. 'And you're hurting his feelings.'

'He tried to eat me.'

'Yes, but he knows you now. You've been properly introduced.'

I wrapped my arms around my head. 'Oh God.'

'If it helps, he's a prince among his own people – the Jötnar. And he likes you. And, long ago, he fought Jormungand, the World Serpent.'

'You mean he's an enemy of . . .'

'Sadly, nothing so honourable as that. He just likes a good punch-up. In fact, he'll fight anything, which can be very useful sometimes. Trust me, though – there's no one better. Not that I can get hold of quickly, anyway. If anything nasty turns up, then we can just point old Þurs at it and sit down to tea and scones while he sorts it all out.'

I unwrapped my head.

'See,' said Iblis. 'You're feeling better already.'

I sighed and trudged into the kitchen to prepare the usual Iblis-sized breakfast. And I insisted on cooking a portion for Þhurs on the grounds that if I kept him well fed then he wouldn't find his way to my bedroom in the dead of night and eat me alive. Iblis took him down an enormous plate of eggs, bacon and toast. Cries of appreciation drifted up the stairs. I tried not to wonder what the solicitors on the other side of the wall might be thinking. I knew they had their big photocopiers down in their basement; I could hear the thump of their machines sometimes. And if I could hear that, then they could certainly hear my troll.

I don't know what's happened to my life.

After breakfast I found an old blanket and told Iblis to come with me down to the cellar.

It's not huge – it doesn't run under the whole house – but it was still quite a good size. Big enough to contain my freezer, washing machine, dryer and ironing board. Jones had put up two or three shelves which held all my spare cleaning stuff and a tub of clothes pegs. My recycling boxes were stacked underneath. Mops, sweeping brushes, my clothes prop and the hoover nested in the corner. Two strip lights in the ceiling flickered into life; ventilation was provided by the narrow window at the top of the wall, which was at street level on the other side, but I don't think it opens and I can't reach it to check.

The floor was concrete, with seven brick and concrete steps leading down from the door. A flimsy wooden safety rail might prevent me from plunging to my death. On the other hand, it might not. There were no cobwebs or dust because this was my cellar. In fact, the whole thing was cool and dry and smelled rather pleasantly of fabric conditioner.

The far corner, however, was now home to a rusty-looking troll who, even though he'd been in situ for less than twelve hours, had already surrounded himself with a small heap of miscellaneous items he obviously considered valuable and attractive. A few green and purple laundry pods that hadn't yet gone the way of their fellows, one of my wellingtons, two half-chewed magazines pulled out of the recycling bin, and a stack of plastic food and fruit containers he seemed to have been using as building bricks. I remembered he'd done this with the bones of his victims in his own lair, laying out long bones in a pattern and stacking up the skulls. I suppose pods and plastic containers were a step up from that.

Þhurs was crouching on the bare floor peering up at me.

'He must be cold,' I said.

'He's one of the northern trolls,' said Iblis. 'He doesn't mind the cold.'

'Even so,' I said, and pushed past him. 'Um ... Þhurs, I thought you might like this.' I held out the blanket. 'To keep you warm at night. If you want.'

The old blanket was nothing special – a washed-out pale blue with one of those satin borders. There was a moment's surprised silence and then he half rose off his haunches and reached out his hand for it.

'I ... um ... I hope it's OK,' I said awkwardly because I was a little out of my social depth.

He made a slight sound and held it up. It was impossible to tell whether he was disgusted or delighted. I tensed in case he sprang.

'He likes it,' said Iblis.

'How can you tell?'

'He's not eating us. Come on. We should leave him to it and get back to the cat. It's all go this morning, isn't it?'

He pushed me gently towards the steps.

I leaned around him to see Þurs. 'Will he be all right on his own down here?'

'Oh yes, he prefers it. Trolls are solitary creatures. They really don't like each other very much.'

We left Þurs arranging the blanket around himself and climbed back up the stairs to find the cat struggling to its feet, which, twelve hours ago, I wouldn't have thought possible.

'Just a minute,' I said, and went into the kitchen. I chopped up a little tinned tuna, put it in a saucer for him and tipped some water into a bowl.

Nigel bustled forwards. The cat turned his head slightly. Nigel bustled back again.

I carried the bowls to the cat. He ate unhurriedly and with great delicacy. I mentioned this to Nigel, who pretended to be asleep.

The morning passed very slowly. I busied myself tidying up and trying not to think about what could happen when night fell. I didn't hoover, because of disturbing the cat – and the hoover was currently under troll jurisdiction anyway – but I plumped cushions, nudged Nigel and Iblis outside to do their business, wiped down the kitchen, and wondered how Jones was faring. Was he on his way back yet? Had he even arrived? Had he and Becky somehow been attacked on the way? And then I remembered Melek was with them, drew a breath and finished drying up and putting things away.

At some point, the cat levered himself stiffly to his feet.

I asked him if he was all right – whether he needed help – and was given to understand that he did not. Somewhat unsteadily, he began to wobble his way around the room, sniffing the furniture and investigating the corners. I had a horrible feeling everything smelled quite strongly of Nigel.

His – the cat's, not Nigel's – powers of healing were impressive. At this rate, give him a week and he'd be completely healed. But we didn't have a week. As soon as the sun went down tonight . . .

I spent a couple of minutes trying to envisage life without the sun. How long could we survive without it? Not very long, I suspected.

More to take my mind off things, rather than because I actually wanted to know, I switched on the TV to watch the lunchtime news. We didn't have to wait until noon – all the news channels were full of it. There had been a dreadful catastrophe – preliminary reports indicated a gas main had blown up. The devastation was enormous and widespread. Almost an entire village had been destroyed. The number of dead still wasn't known because the area hadn't yet been made safe, making it impossible to recover all the bodies, but no one was very optimistic about any survivors.

The screen cut to their on-scene reporter.

Such was the devastation that I wouldn't have known where it was if it hadn't been for the updates running across the bottom of the screen. It was Greyston. Or rather – it had been. The camera panned slowly around. The reporter was still talking but I wasn't listening. Most of the village had gone. All of the centre – the village green, the inn, the Travellers' Rest, Alice Chervil's little shop – was gone, just heaps of rubble, along with the village

393

hall and most of the surrounding cottages. The Three Sisters themselves had been almost completely destroyed. Three ugly stumps protruded from the ground like broken teeth, completely surrounded by their own shattered remains. There would be no repairing these stones. Their power was gone for ever.

A great pall of dirty smoke hung over the village.

Iblis came in to stand beside me.

'Look at this,' I said, gesturing at the screen.

He said nothing.

'Is this good news for us or is it bad? Doesn't this mean nothing can happen tonight? The stones are gone and it looks as if most of the women have been killed. What will he have to work with?'

Still Iblis said nothing.

I stared at the TV screen. 'Did we do all that?'

He shook his head. 'No.'

'Then who? And why?'

He didn't bother to answer. Because we both knew who. And we both knew why. He'd finally been successful. Using up women in twos and threes hadn't been enough for him. What we'd witnessed last night had been one final, massive effort. An orgy of destruction, an entire village gone – scores, possibly hundreds of women dead – enough to fulfil even his purposes.

I looked at Iblis. 'He's done it, hasn't he? Whatever it was. He's finally succeeded.'

He didn't answer.

Iblis insisted I cook lunch because it would take my mind off my problems. I thanked him for his concern. The sarcasm went straight over his head. As, very nearly, did a saucepan.

I surveyed the fridge. 'What would you like?'

'This could be our last meal ever,' he said, possibly still not quite up to speed on the precise meaning of comfort and reassurance. 'Let's make it a good one, shall we?'

I regarded him. 'We?'

'Of course. I am Iblis, Man of Cooking Skills Beyond Comprehension, and this is Nigel, Dog of . . .'

We both regarded Nigel, snoring slightly in his favourite patch of sunshine. Whereas the cat slept neatly and tidily, Nigel looked like a toppled compost heap.

'Dog of Sleeping,' finished Iblis.

I sent him down to the freezer for some salmon. He opened his mouth to argue. Apparently, he and Nigel wanted steak.

'For the cat,' I said pointedly. 'Who is injured.'

He disappeared into the cellar. I could hear him arguing with old Þhurs, who, once again, appeared to have discovered something he shouldn't and didn't want to part with it.

'Quite a little nest down there,' Iblis said cheerfully, carefully closing the door behind him so I couldn't see what was going on.

My only consolation was that this time tomorrow I'd be dead and it really wouldn't matter.

We had salmon fillets, new potatoes and salad. I prepared five meals – a normal one for me, one double portion for Iblis, one minus the salad for Nigel, one minus the salad and the potatoes for the cat, and everything that was left for Þhurs. I made several dark remarks concerning mass catering, but no one listened.

I flaked the cat's salmon and gently helped him to his feet to eat.

'Do you think he . . . you know . . . wants to go outside? I'm happy to bring him a dirt box of some kind, although I think he's far too noble to wee inside, don't you?' I looked at the cat. 'Would you like to go out?'

He laid himself down and closed his eyes.

I looked over at Nigel, who also laid himself down and closed his eyes.

I looked over at Iblis, who was preparing to lay himself down on the sofa and close his eyes. I looked at my kitchen, every surface covered in dirty dishes and saucepans.

'Don't you dare.'

CHAPTER TWENTY-EIGHT

The catastrophe began to unfold around mid-afternoon. I think we were all enjoying a post-lunch nap when someone banged on the door. Not knocked. Banged.

My first thought was that Jones was back – although that wasn't his knock. And then they banged on the door again.

'Stay here,' said Iblis, getting up to see who it was.

It was Colonel Barton and he was in a state of some agitation.

'Oh, good,' he said unexpectedly. 'The very person. I'm so sorry to trouble you, but Mrs Barton has had a fall and I can't lift her. She's not injured but neither of us is able to . . . I wonder if you would be kind enough to assist.'

'Of course,' I said, getting up and coming to the door.

'Actually, it was this young man I wanted,' he said, and I could see what an effort that was for him. His colour writhed with a mixture of embarrassment at having to ask for assistance, and shame that he was no longer able, physically, to do what was necessary to help his wife.

I expected Iblis to sweep a grand bow, declare that he, Iblis, Man of Infinite Resource, would resolve the situation instantly. With the aid of his trusty companion, of course. Just to be clear, that would be Nigel, not me.

He didn't, however. 'Of course,' he said quietly. 'I shall be happy to be of assistance. Unless . . .' He looked over at me.

'I'll be fine,' I said. 'You go. Unless the colonel needs me as well?'

'Thank you, no,' he said stiffly. 'I think once Mrs Barton is on her feet, I can get her into a chair and she'll be as right as rain.'

Iblis raised an eyebrow at me. 'Sure?'

He was asking me if the colonel was telling the truth.

'Absolutely,' I said. 'No problem at all.' Because he was.

Iblis nodded and made a gesture. 'After you, sir.'

I think the colonel was a little surprised not to be referred to as Venerable One, but he turned and stumped back down the steps.

'Ten minutes,' said Iblis. 'Do you want Nigel?'

I couldn't imagine any sort of situation where the presence of Nigel would actually improve things, but I wasn't going to hurt either of their feelings by saying so.

'Yes, please.'

Iblis pulled the door to behind him and . . . I don't know why . . . I don't know what put the thought into my head . . . but as it banged shut, I had a sudden and horrible feeling that I'd just made a terrible mistake.

I sat back down again. Nigel lay heavily across my feet, thus ensuring that should mortal danger manifest itself, I'd be completely unable to run away. Or even defend myself. However, for a while, there was a lovely restful silence as I slid in and out of a pleasant afternoon nap.

To wake myself up, I switched on the TV again. Adverts. Some ghastly child was having a meltdown because her pretty top had a stain on it and her whole life was ruined. Fortunately,

Dad had laundry pods on hand. A miracle occurred. The now beaming child was able to attend the party after all. Her doting parents waved her off from the doorstep. Dad was still clutching the miracle pods, carefully ensuring the brand name was clearly visible. The child disappeared to an afternoon of other people's admiration of her party top. Inexplicably, the parents failed to slam the door and move away during her absence. This drama ended with a cheerful ditty extolling the virtues of these particular pods. I wondered idly whether they tasted better or worse than mine.

As if my thoughts had woken him – and that was perfectly possible – there was a sound from Þhurs in the cellar below. I toyed vaguely with the idea of checking whether he was drinking the bleach and decided against it. He was Iblis's responsibility.

That was a point. How long had Iblis been gone? I turned my head to the clock and the sound happened again. I sat up. What was going on down there? Did I perhaps have an infestation of rats and one of them was figuring as a post-lunch snack? I really didn't need rats on top of everything else. And I still fretted about my roof every time it rained. Believe me, there is no end to the number of things you can find to worry about when you're a homeowner.

I didn't know the half of it.

I was just settling back again when something that was neither a scream nor a bellow erupted from the cellar below.

I jumped a mile.

Nigel leaped to his feet barking his head off and I very nearly tripped over him as I ran to the front door. Something was happening and I needed Iblis back here now.

The front door wouldn't open.

You see it in films: the airhead heroine repeatedly tugs at the door – or bangs on it shouting for help – which never comes. I tugged at the handle. The door didn't budge. I thumped on the door, shouting, 'Help, help. I can't get the door open.'

Nothing happened.

I did remember to check the door was actually unbolted and unlocked – I wasn't that far gone – and it was. There was no reason why it shouldn't open.

I grabbed an umbrella and banged on the wall separating me from the Bartons' house. 'Iblis. Iblis – can you hear me? Iblis, I need you now.'

Apparently, he couldn't. Nor could he hear Nigel, who was barking fit to raise the dead.

I ran to the back door. That one wouldn't budge, either.

I was contemplating trying to bash out the kitchen window when there was another roar from the cellar. Followed by the sound of objects falling. Had a shelf collapsed on top of Þhurs? There was another shriek of mingled pain and fury.

I'm ashamed to say it took me a moment. Did I actually want to know what Þhurs was up to down there? It was more than possible that he'd only brought a shelf down on top of himself as he looked for something else to eat. Yes – that was it. It must be. Night had not yet fallen. In fact, it was barely past mid-afternoon. Why would anything happen before night fell?

The answer came immediately. I'd seen the news. There had been that one final, massive effort, which had completely destroyed the village of Greyston, and this time, with the cat too injured to hold it back, they'd been successful.

I stared at the party wall. If that was so, then had Mrs Barton really fallen? Had Iblis been lured away? Were they all dead next door? What was happening?

I banged again. 'Iblis. Get out. Get out of there.'

No response of any kind. Could they even hear me? Whatever was happening – or about to happen – I would be facing it on my own.

OK. Think. Iblis couldn't get in – I couldn't get out. Something was going on down in the cellar. It was all up to me.

I bent down, picked up Nigel and tucked him under one arm. My plan was to open the cellar door just a crack and take a quick peep before committing myself. However, as I knew from previous experiences, Nigel was as brave as a lion, and as soon as I lifted the latch, he'd be in like a small and very misguided missile, so I held him tight.

The cat too was struggling to its feet.

I said, 'Stay here.'

The cellar door was on my left at the foot of the stairs. Even as I hesitated, there was another cry from Þhurs. Stop being a coward, Cage, and check it out. I took a very deep breath and cautiously lifted the latch.

After the bright day outside, the cellar seemed very dark. It wasn't – some light could always get through the little window – so I stood just inside the door, waiting for my eyes to adjust. Nigel was wriggling to get away and I couldn't keep hold of him, so I said, 'Shh,' and set him down just inside the door. Besides, I needed both hands free because, inconveniently, the light switch was behind the door. A genius piece of design on someone's part. I reached around the door. I'd been in here almost daily since I moved in; my hand went straight to the switch.

401

Both the overhead lights came on, went *tink*, flickered and died.

I blinked a few times and slowly, through the darkness, the cellar came into focus.

The floor was moving. Heaving and rolling. For one really stupid moment, I thought I'd had some sort of flood, and black, oily water was surging around the cellar in great waves. I stood and stared while my eyes and brain struggled to come together to work out what on earth was happening. How could the floor be moving like that? And then it clicked. This wasn't water. I was actually looking at coil upon coil of something thick and dark and powerful that writhed and twisted over itself. Mesmerised, I watched one giant loop glide silently over the top of another and disappear into darkness.

Ted and I went to a safari park, once. They had a very good reptile house there, and the crowning feature was a giant glass room – about thirty feet square and ten feet high – filled with bark and wood chippings, with a small pool in the centre and several thick branches artistically arranged to look like trees. Lying half in and half out of the pool was an enormous anaconda. I was so taken up with trying to find its beginning and end that I never noticed a big head drop silently from above, and just for a moment, a second snake and I had gazed silently at each other. Even knowing there was a hefty sheet of glass between us, it had still been an unnerving experience.

Ted had clutched at my hand – to reassure me, he said afterwards – and we'd watched it lower itself from its branch and glide soundlessly across the bark to join the other one in the pool.

For one mad moment I thought that was exactly what was

happening here. That I had a cellar full of snakes, all writhing and twisting around each other. I couldn't see any heads or tails. No beginnings or ends. Just coil upon undulating coil.

But no. There was one end at least. Down at the very bottom of the steps, there was what looked like a tail, looped around my safety rail, gripping it tightly. I could see where the pressure had cracked the wood. Even the tail was thicker than my arm. I stared. I couldn't take my eyes off it. What should I do? I had to do something. But what? The size of it . . .

I will send the serpent. I always send the serpent.

And yes, finally, he had. Another flash of the same memory. A man sitting under a tree. His bare feet in the snow. A face I knew and didn't know. This was his doing. Everything was his doing. Including, I suddenly realised, the illusion at the Sorensen Clinic. When I'd nearly died. Becky had said the sending wasn't working quickly enough. His earthly enemy, the cat, had been holding it back night after night. Failure after failure. Had the episode at the clinic been a shortcut? How costly must that have been in terms of lives and effort? How many Greyston women had he burned through that day? Was that why he'd only tried it once?

I'd survived that day, but now my luck had run out. Jones was gone. Iblis was gone. The cat was upstairs, too badly injured to move far, and finally, the serpent was here. Now. In front of me. In my cellar. And it was huge. Vast. I had no difficulty imagining these coils wrapping themselves around me in thick black loops . . .

I could turn around and flee. I could slam the cellar door behind me, lock it, run up the stairs into the bathroom and lock that door as well. That would buy me a little time. But not much. I could all too easily imagine the speed with which that giant body could slither up the narrow steps, its head smashing through each door as it hunted me down in my own home.

I have no idea how long I stood, rooted to the spot, trying to force my legs to move. I might have stood there for ever, but the silence was broken by Þhurs.

'Ruuuuuuuuun!'

In my own terror – and to my shame – I had forgotten Þhurs.

The light was dim, and it was hard to see who was attacking whom, but it suddenly became clear that there was a titanic battle going on right in front of me. Þhurs appeared to be enveloped in a heavy loop of serpent, but he hadn't surrendered by any means. Both his powerful arms were tightly wrapped around the coil. Almost a lover's embrace, except that his long, wicked claws were raking great gouges in the serpent's body. Grey flesh burst through the black skin, oozing thick, dark blood. So deep were the wounds that I could see the white of exposed bone. Þhurs's eyes were bulging as the grip around his chest tightened, but he was far from finished. Lips drawn back in a vicious snarl, he threw back his head and then embedded his fangs so deeply in the scaly flesh that his face was enveloped in what was either black blood – or pus. I hoped none of it was poisonous. Whether it was or not, he seemed to be doing the serpent a great deal of damage. Flayed skin hung in shreds and black fluid poured from the wounds, but it didn't seem to be having any great impact. Was this thing too big to hurt?

There would be no throwing a blanket over this monster. It was vast and it was here and I was alone. It was right in front of me and I was going to die and so was Þhurs and, probably, so was everyone else.

Something moved. There. Over there. In the shadows. Staring at me from a dark corner. Eyes. Huge eyes. Watching me. Rising slowly from the darkness. Higher and higher . . .

With lightning speed, a giant head lunged at me from the shadows. It was massive. Bigger than my washing machine. I saw its jaws open wide, and then wider, and then wider still. I saw giant fangs, curving backwards. I stared, hypnotised. These could be my last moments . . . and then, faster than my eyes could track the movement, it whipped its head around to deal with a more immediate threat.

I had forgotten Nigel, who pushed past me to hurtle down the steps on his short legs to do battle. He didn't waste time or energy on his usual vocal defiance, either. He launched himself into the air, landed, and sank his terrier teeth deep into the end of its tail. I heard his teeth crunch bone.

That definitely produced some sort of reaction. The serpent convulsed. The giant head swung away from me, looking for this new attacker and, at the same time, Þhurs thrust a powerful arm into one of the serpent's great gaping wounds and twisted.

Every instinct was telling me to run. I'd like to think I stayed because I wouldn't leave Þhurs and Nigel to fight alone, but actually I stayed because my legs wouldn't move as they should.

The head swung back to Þhurs, now identifying him as the main threat.

I saw it sink its teeth into Þhurs's shoulder and arm. He howled with pain, reached up with his free arm and slashed wildly at its eyes, drawing blood and scoring deep wounds.

The serpent's muscles rippled as it reared back and then tightened its grip around Þhurs, who roared and gouged again at the deep wounds he'd inflicted. One last effort. All the way up to his elbows. He must have found some vital spot because a great stream of thick black fluid arced across the cellar to run down the back wall.

It came to me from the depths of my memory. I'd once seen a nature programme. You can sometimes save the victim of a snake attack by unwinding the tail. A woman had once saved her dog that way.

I had no sensation of time passing. I don't think I'd been standing there for more than four or five seconds, but that was long enough for Þhurs to be hoisted off his feet. Still roaring defiance, he disappeared down into the coils.

I took one shaky step downwards and then another and then my legs began to work properly again.

In comparison to the rest of it, this tail end of the snake was not so thick. I shouted to Nigel to get out of the way. He did. I seized the very end and struggled to unwind it from the newel post. It did not want to go. It fought me every inch of the way. And, thanks to Nigel, the tail was slick with blood; I couldn't seem to get a good grip. I wasn't about to give up but it was like grappling with a giant wet muscle, and all the time I was terrified that if I did detach it from the post, it would whip about and fasten itself around me instead.

And then, suddenly, the tail relaxed. I saw no reason why, but there was no time to think about it. I unwound it once, twice, three times, intending to throw it back into the coils, but it whipped itself from my hands, nearly dragging me off the stairs. At the same time, Þhurs was not so much released as hurled across the cellar to crash against the wall, bringing down brushes, mops and the clothes prop. A shelf collapsed at one end and a ton of packets and sprays slid sideways to fall down on top of him.

There was no time to look, because now the snake – the serpent – turned its attention back to me. Suddenly, everything else was secondary. Þhurs was dealt with. Nigel was negligible. I was the target. The focus. The prey. The snake's head whipped back towards me. Cold, flat, merciless eyes regarded me. Its tongue flickered – I thought of Kyle – black and smooth, unrolling from its enormous glottis. Tasting the air. Tasting me. Because I was the one it was here for. Þhurs – Nigel – they were just minor distractions to be brushed aside now that it had located me.

They say don't look into a snake's eyes. That a snake can hypnotise you. Too late for me. I couldn't look away. Those eyes would be the last thing I ever saw.

They were set quite close together under thick brow ridges at the top of its head. Blacker than black. Each deep enough to encompass a world. Two slits for nostrils. And then its mouth was gaping wider than should ever be possible.

I was lost. The world faded. The whole serpent seemed to swell in size. Filling my vision. Filling my world. These black coils were vast. Far too vast for my tiny cellar. The perspective was dizzying. I lost my place in the world where, suddenly, there was no up. No down. No beginning. No end. Just the slow sliding of scales, each the size of a house. I wasn't even a tiny speck. This thing must be lying under the houses next door – the whole street – the whole town – the whole world. This truly was He Who Encircles the World and he had come for me. Nothing could save me from this. Nothing had the power. Even if Iblis had been here, I don't think he could have withstood the Lord of Chaos. The Eater of Souls. This thing would end my days – my life – my very existence. Truly, I was lost.

The serpent reared up to the ceiling and then through it.

407

My house grew pale and transparent around me. Its head rose higher and higher. Its eyes were the size of entire star systems. Its mouth had swallowed the universe and I could see the void. No light. No stars. No suns. Just the endless cold of enduring night. The Eternal Void. The nothingness that will one day engulf us all.

I would have liked my last thoughts to have been of sunlight, or of wind-rippled wheat fields, or of bluebells in dappled beechwoods, or of the crashing sea and the cry of gulls, but all my mind could encompass was the nothingness. Deep, dark nothingness. The huge head hung above me. Stone-cold eyes stared down at me.

A voice filled my head. *I have sent the serpent.*

And then, from the doorway, came a long, blood-curdling yowl that echoed around the cellar. An unearthly, inhuman cry that went on and on. The war cry of a battle-hardened soldier of Bastet challenging his hereditary foe. And he was loud. I felt my ears flinch. Ears flat, eyes narrowed, the cat crouched awkwardly on the top step, shifting his haunches from side to side, preparing to attack.

The snake whipped away from me to face this latest and greatest threat. An old enemy had appeared. An implacable foe. Released from its deadly gaze, my own reality returned. My perspective shifted back and the serpent changed from something galaxy-sized to just huge. I slumped uselessly across the safety rail, rubbed my eyes and tried to see what was happening.

A black streak hurled itself down the steps. Long, lithe and fast.

Black lightning.

He leaped.

The serpent was fast, but the cat was faster. He landed, sure-footed, gathered himself for a moment and began to jump from coil to coil. I have no idea how he managed that with his injuries. How much must it hurt him?

The serpent hissed and lunged again, torn between its legitimate prey and this more immediate threat.

The cat crouched, tail lashing, growling, and gathered himself for his last battle.

He leaped for the serpent's head.

He failed.

Of course he failed. Still not properly healed, his jump lacked power. The serpent writhed and the cat fell, twisting, down into the dark coils below.

CHAPTER TWENTY-NINE

'No!'

I cried out. I couldn't help it. So much courage deserved its own reward, but the world doesn't work like that, and he was gone.

Returning to its true prey, the giant head swung towards me again and now this really was the end. I backed against the wall. I didn't have a weapon. Nothing with which to make even a token defence. Þhurs was gone, the cat was gone, I had no idea where Nigel was. The serpent would return whence it came – with its prey. Me.

And then the cat erupted from nowhere, taking advantage of the serpent's inattention to land squarely on that massive head.

The serpent reared back from me, but that second's distraction had given the cat the time he needed to spread his weight and dig in. Front paws flashed as he clawed at the serpent's eye – the one already damaged by Þhurs. He raked his claws again and again, ripping great lumps of skin and flesh from his ancient enemy.

The serpent writhed and twisted, lashing its head to and fro, trying to dislodge the cat who clung on with everything he had – even his teeth. Such was the force of the serpent's thrashing that I expected to see the cat fly through the air at any moment, smash into the wall and fall, dead, into the coils. But he didn't. He hung on in grim silence. There was no battle cry now.

I could see damage to the serpent's left eye. Some sort of membrane – for protective purposes, perhaps – seemed to have been half torn away and hung limply. Blood and matter bubbled from deep scores across its face. I wondered if it could still see. If the thing was half blind, then there might never be a better opportunity to . . . do something.

I pushed my hair out of my eyes and tried to catch up with what was happening.

At the foot of the steps, Nigel had reappeared and, obeying his terrier instincts, had dug his teeth in again. He'd scraped deep wounds in the serpent's tail. I could see more black and grey flesh through the scales and blood. Most importantly, he was preventing the serpent using its tail to anchor itself to the newel post.

Phurs was face down and struggling feebly to extricate himself from a welter of cleaning supplies and equipment. One or two of the containers must have split. I could smell bleach. Like Nigel, his teeth and claws were thick with black blood.

Since all its attention appeared to be on dislodging the cat, it wasn't clear whether it was deliberate or not, but the great tail lashed suddenly, throwing Nigel to one side and knocking me completely off my feet. I fell further down into the cellar and landed, sprawling, among my own cleaning stuff.

Something burned my hand. I looked down. Oven cleaner. Mr Mighty. The really pungent stuff that makes you cough and sneeze if you're stupid enough to breathe it in, because you forgot to open the kitchen window or the back door, despite the instructions on the can. Protective gear is a good idea, too.

I grabbed two sprays – because my mother always said to have a spare – and turned to face the fight. One spray in each hand.

I ran back up the steps. Unbelievably, the cat was still clinging on for dear life as the serpent swung its great head around. Whether it saw me coming, I don't know, but one extra savage swing whiplashed the cat down into the coils again.

I didn't see where he fell. I was too busy picking my spot.

The head turned my way. For a moment, its one eye bored into mine. I struggled to look away. Bigger and bigger. Darker and darker. Look away. Look away.

In a way, the cat losing his grip had been a good thing. Because now I could deploy my weapons without worrying about hurting him. And if he was down there among the coils, then he was probably dead already.

The head was coming at me. Closer . . . closer . . . not yet . . . Now.

I aimed both sprays directly at its open wounds. The serpent was big. And powerful. But this would hurt.

Spray arced through the air. White foam bubbled in and around its eyes. And that stuff sticks. It doesn't dissolve or run down your oven walls – it sticks. Burning as it goes. The smell seared my nostrils. Foam bubbled over my own hands and arms. Stinging. Then burning. This was evil stuff and I really wasn't using it according to the manufacturer's instructions. Well, it was supposed to dissolve burned-on grease and oven grime. Let's see how it did with sun-swallowing serpents.

The sun-swallowing serpent didn't like it. Not one bit. I'm not saying it was a life-ending moment, but I'd hurt it. It reared back, shaking its head around. I wasn't sure whether it was still able to see or not, but the cat had left deep score marks around its eyes. Open wounds and oven cleaner – probably not a good combination. The foam must be working its way deeper and deeper in its eyes.

Black blood ran freely, turning the white foam a dirty grey. Yes – this was working.

I shouted, 'Come on, you bastard. Let's have another go,' and sprayed again. Not so successfully this time because it had learned to keep its distance.

That was no good. I needed it to come closer. But how?

I don't know where it came from, but it seemed a good idea at the time. I planted my feet, shook the cans again and roared my own challenge. I just opened my mouth and out it came. I hurt my throat quite badly and barely noticed. Hurting myself now wasn't likely to be a long-term problem.

I shouted. I screamed. I yelled. I used bad words. I challenged that motherfucker to face me.

And it did.

It swung its head, good eye towards me, and suddenly the word reptilian – as in cold and emotionless – no longer applied. This thing was almost insane with rage. I could feel wave after wave of blind fury coming at me. It lowered its head for one final attack.

I bent my knees and raised my spray cans – ready to do it all again.

It halted and we looked at each other.

In that moment I felt something brush my ankles. The cat was back. How many lives had he lost this afternoon? The serpent drew back – watching him. I moved to my right. Now the serpent watched me. The cat seized the moment and leaped. The serpent struck. And missed. The cat landed, paused and leaped

413

again, working his way from coil to coil. Always aiming for its head. The serpent struck again. And missed again. It was lightning fast but the cat was even faster. As I said before – black lightning.

Abandoning the cat for the moment, the serpent swung about and came for me. I sprayed again. And missed completely as it swung its head back and up, out of my range.

Which was what the cat had been waiting for. He leaped. Not for the eyes this time, but for its throat, sinking his teeth into its windpipe. The death grip. Like a lion clinging to a wildebeest. The wildebeest has the weight advantage, but if the lion can hold on long enough, then its prey will suffocate.

He was a big cat and hugely powerful, but for how long could he hold on? He hadn't healed. A few hours ago he'd barely been able to stand. Now he hung, claws spread wide and deeply embedded in the snake's throat, his head turned to one side as his jaws locked on. He had his grip and wasn't shifting. The serpent couldn't get to him. With luck it was blinded. I changed my position again, running up a few steps to bring myself closer. Leaning over the safety rail, I sprayed again. I was in the perfect position and I'd keep going until the sprays were exhausted. A lot of black blood was running from the wound in the snake's throat. Not as thick as before. Flowing faster now. The cat turned his head fractionally and gripped even harder. Something told me he would never let go. Not until one or both of them were dead.

The serpent's head was perfectly still now, although its body writhed and twisted. In great pain, I hoped. Its tail slammed into the wooden railing, which shattered on impact. The laundry basket flew through the air. Pegs went everywhere.

My cans felt much lighter now. The spray was nearly gone.

How long before it threw off the cat and attacked again? I blinked to find it had taken advantage of my momentary inattention to get closer. It was inching forwards. Towards me. All ready to . . .

I raised my cans again.

It drew back. Stalemate. Except it could stay here for ever, while sooner or later I would fall asleep or die of hunger. I should find something else with which to hold it off. Surely Iblis would return soon.

Did I have more spray? And should I be careful of the cat? I didn't want to blind him as well. What else could I do? There must be something. We were holding the serpent back, but we weren't winning. Think. I had to think.

Unbidden, a picture sprang into my mind. The goddess Bastet, standing between the sun barque and the serpent, shining like the sun itself and brandishing her gleaming lance.

Lance.

I eased myself to my left. Down one step. Then another. To the bottom.

There it was – half hidden underneath the injured Þhurs, but I grabbed the end and tugged anyway. The movement woke him. He opened his eyes. I shouted for him to move and yanked again.

He rolled away. I seized the clothes prop and set my back to the wall, holding it in front of me like a pole-vaulter.

My plan, such as it was, was to take advantage of the serpent's semi-blindness and batter it around the head. Just keep hitting at it. Distract it from the cat. And Þhurs, who was slowly pulling himself to his feet. I had no idea where Nigel was, and I didn't have time to look, but he was a tough little terrier. I hoped.

415

I took a good grip on the prop, about halfway down. The shorter the pole, the more control I would have. But I'd have to get in close. I waited. Bouncing on my toes. Full of battle fury. Waiting for the right moment . . .

Despite the evil-smelling liquid and foam running down its face and mixing with the blood, I was certain the serpent still had the use of one eye. What weakened it slightly was dividing its attention between the cat and me. I was less threatening and the easier prey. And the target.

I took a firm grip. The cat wasn't going to let go and I wasn't going to leave him to fight alone. I waited for the serpent to swing its head towards me, holding the prop in readiness for a swift backhand blow.

It didn't attack straight away. It actually drew back, arching its neck on high. Preparing to strike. My world stood still. We stared at each other. I barely had time to think *shiiiiiiit – this is it –* when, like lightning, it whipped its head towards me.

Instinctively, I brought up the clothes prop and tried to step back, but I had nowhere to go. My back was literally against the wall. Which was what saved me. The end of the clothes prop wedged itself in the angle between the floor and the wall. The head was coming at me fast and hard. Mouth wide. I saw the curved teeth and the huge glottis. Filling my vision. This was my end. I would have panicked but there wasn't time. And then there was the weight. Huge, heavy weight. I felt the metal hook on the end of the prop pass straight through the serpent's mouth as it impaled itself with a force I could never have hoped to equal. Its own weight and speed rammed the prop straight through its upper palate. I heard the dreadful crunch as it passed through and into the brain pan.

Now there was a terrible scream. A dreadful cry of dying and defeat and failure. I didn't know snakes had vocal chords. This was like nothing I had ever heard before, echoing around my cellar as it flung itself from side to side, seeking to wrench itself free. I just hung on. I couldn't do anything else. Time after time I was slammed back against the wall. Several times I was yanked completely off my feet and heaved, legs kicking, into the air. Muscles tore in my upper arms and shoulders but I dared not let go. It wasn't dead yet. One particularly violent paroxysm smashed my face into the wall. I felt my cheek slide down the bricks. The serpent twisted and turned, seeking to free itself and only embedding the prop even more deeply in its brain.

Don't let go. Whatever you do – don't let go.

Still it screamed. A terrible sound that came not just from the thing in front of me but from the void it inhabited. I remembered the cat and his challenge. And Þhurs. And Nigel, hurling himself into battle.

I opened my mouth and screamed again, 'Die, you bastard. Die. Die, why don't you?' Because now I thought I might have a chance. More than a chance. I was winning. I could do this.

Actually, I don't think I could have let go even if I'd wanted to. My hands were locked around the clothes prop. The serpent's screaming filled my head. Somewhere I could hear Þhurs roaring – I had an idea he was still attacking the other end. And Nigel was still growling and worrying at something.

In one final, desperate attempt to pull itself free, the serpent threw up its head, nearly wrenching my arms from their sockets, and then, seemingly unable to support its own weight, it went limp and collapsed down upon the prop, driving the point straight out through the top of its head via its one remaining eye.

It was dying. It had to be. These were its death throes. It thrashed around. Its whole body convulsed. Coil after coil writhed in agony. Its tail lashed violently, bringing more destruction to my cleaning supplies. I heard the ironing board clatter to the floor. Nigel was in there somewhere. And Þhurs. No time or strength to look. I hung on. Instinct told me it was the safest thing to do. I gripped the prop as hard as I could, set my teeth and *just hung on.*

But it was weakening, its struggles subsiding. Black blood ran from its mouth, its nostrils, its eyes and throat. And from the deep gouges caused by Nigel, Þhurs and the cat. Its tongue hung limply from its mouth. Slowly, that great head began to droop. I forced my fingers to let go of the prop before I was dragged down with it. The tail dropped to the floor. The coils ceased to move. With one final seismic shudder, the thing fell back on to itself, twitched once or twice, and finally, at last, was still.

The weight redoubled. I was falling sideways. Which was just as well because with a really nasty sound that managed to be both liquid and crunching, the head suddenly collapsed down the prop and I was only just in time to throw myself to one side before I was crushed.

There was a long, long silence.

I didn't move. I couldn't. I lay, chest heaving, unable to drag my eyes from this . . . this thing in my cellar.

It was the pain in my hands that snapped me out of my paralysis. I looked down at them. I clenched and unclenched my fists to get some feeling back. My palms were red-raw and bleeding, but in a nice contrast, my fingers were stiff and white where I'd hung on so hard. My forearms were covered in red burns where I'd managed to spray myself with oven cleaner. I got myself to my feet, winced at the soreness in my shoulders and looked around.

Þhurs lay at the bottom of the steps. Face down, but he was still moving. One of his hands scrabbled at the floor as he tried to rise. The cat was half buried underneath the remains of the serpent's head, which, in turn, was held in place by the clothes prop.

Not without massive misgivings in case the thing came back to life and swallowed me whole while I wasn't looking, I struggled across the now inert scaly coils towards the cat. Bracing myself, I got both hands under the serpent's head. Dear God, it was heavy. I couldn't lift it, but somehow I was able to heave it off to one side and pick up the cat.

He gave a faint growl, which I chose to interpret as a growl of victory, rather than a warning he was about to take my arm off.

'Here,' I said, and reaching up, carefully laid him on a step near the top and out of harm's way. Then I picked my way over to Nigel, still with his teeth embedded in the dead serpent. I heaved a thick coil off him – snakes really are exceedingly heavy. He shook his head a couple of times, wrinkling his lips at the taste in his mouth, and made his own way to the stairs to sniff anxiously at the cat.

I disentangled Þhurs from brooms and dustpans. There was a strong smell of Springfresh Fabric Conditioner with Added Softness which was an improvement on his usual something-long-dead aroma. His arm was bleeding sluggishly and – should anyone be interested – troll blood is red. I'd like to say I helped him up, but basically I braced myself while he used me, and the remains of the safety rail, to lever himself to his feet, and we carried out an orderly retreat from the field of battle. Nigel

419

went first, I went next, stooping to pick up the cat, and Þhurs brought up the rear.

Iblis was just letting himself in through the front door as we emerged from the cellar. He actually stopped dead. For the first time ever, I saw him shocked. But not, alas, speechless. 'What on earth . . . ?'

I had to ask. 'Where *were* you?'

'What do you mean, where was I? I was next door. You know I was next door. I've only been gone two or three minutes.'

'No, you haven't.' I glanced at the clock. 'You've been gone for over half an hour.'

'What's happened?'

I struggled to find the words to describe our epic battle and then remembered that a single picture speaks a thousand words. I gestured over my shoulder. 'In the cellar.'

He pushed past us to see for himself. I laid the cat on the rug again. With the air of one who deserved it, Nigel jumped up into the armchair, and who was I to argue. Swallowing down all thoughts of what it might do to my upholstery, I sat Þhurs on the sofa.

He made a sound that I hoped was surprise and delight rather than a prelude to attack, leaned back, and made himself comfortable.

By the time I'd found the first aid kit, Iblis was back, looking, I have to say, slightly stunned. Sometimes – just every now and then – it's nice to render a superhero speechless.

I couldn't decide whether I was relieved the remains were still there or not. The whole thing was so unbelievable – especially with the whole *big enough to swallow the universe* thing – I had worried the corpse might somehow have disappeared, or

420

returned whence it came, and not only would I have no proof, but I'd have been on another one-way trip to the Sorensen Clinic. The downside was that I now had a serious corpse-disposal problem.

I decided to think about that later.

'That,' said Iblis eventually, 'must have been some struggle.'

'It was,' I said, kneeling alongside the cat and opening up my first aid kit, trying to ignore Þhurs, who was peering over my shoulder with great interest. 'It wouldn't give up, even after it was dead. I thought it would never go down.' I set the kit down and looked up. 'What happened to this house being warded?'

'I suspect the wards proved unequal to the task.'

I had to resist an urge to laugh hysterically.

He frowned. 'Why didn't you get out?'

'I couldn't. The door wouldn't open. Neither of them would. I banged on the wall and shouted. Lots of times. You didn't answer.'

'I didn't hear you. We never heard a thing.'

'It is dead, isn't it?' I said, not ashamed of needing some reassurance.

'It is very dead.'

'Did we kill Apep?'

'No – you killed *a* serpent. Not *the* serpent. Apep still lives.'

I looked up sharply. 'Does that mean it will come back?'

'No.'

'You're sure?'

'Absolutely sure. There are rules. The serpent was summoned and failed. You won. Well done. All of you.'

I nodded and wet a dressing in warm water, wrung it out and

carefully wiped the worst of the blood and foam off the cat. He lay still, as uncomplaining as ever.

'Thank you,' I said to him. 'Thank you so much, old soldier. You did your duty. Please thank the goddess for sending you to me.'

He opened his eyes and blinked slowly. Which, I think I read somewhere once, is the way a cat smiles.

Iblis was wiping the worst of the gunge off Nigel, which left me with Þhurs. Not without a great deal of apprehension, I tried to examine his wounds. His upper arm and shoulder had been bitten. I carefully cleaned the punctures and then looked at his forearm, which was badly torn. He made distressed little sounds to himself.

'I'm sorry,' I said. 'I don't mean to hurt you.'

'He's a troll,' said Iblis. 'I don't think you can.'

'He's a very brave troll,' I said firmly. 'He held the serpent in the cellar until we arrived to help.'

It wasn't possible to be absolutely certain, but I was pretty sure he smirked. Þhurs, I mean. And he deserved a smirk. It was quite a nasty wound.

I pulled out a pair of scissors and began, very carefully, to snip away his coarse arm hair. Again, he watched my every move with close attention, which made me nervous.

I used wet wipes to clean the wound and, very gently – because I didn't want to antagonise the seven-foot troll sitting next to me – I laid a gauze dressing over it. I suspected I was wasting my time and that trolls weren't that prone to infections – especially since I'd once been on the receiving end of a quick but involuntary tour of his living quarters – but I bandaged it carefully into place.

The dressing looked very white against the rest of him, and he was obviously extremely impressed, twisting his arm backwards and forwards to view this strange new phenomenon from every angle.

I could only ascribe it to delayed shock, but he was so pleased with his new accessory that I was inspired to pull out a triangular bandage which I draped over him to make a sling, tying a very careful knot.

He made a strange sound that Iblis said was his way of expressing deep joy, and also did I know that the snake must be nearly fifty feet long? And that there was a reward for anyone finding a snake longer than thirty feet? And that he wasn't sure, but he thought it might be quite a lot of money.

'It's all yours,' I said wearily.

'I didn't do anything to deserve it,' he said quietly. 'Honestly, I was next door for less than five minutes. We helped Mrs Barton to a chair. I went and put the kettle on for the pair of them and left at once, their thanks ringing in my ears. You're invited to tea on Sunday, by the way.' He paused thoughtfully. 'It was unclear whether I was included in the invitation.'

'It was a team effort,' I said, because I could see he wasn't happy that he hadn't been here for the battle. 'Þhurs and Nigel went for the tail. The cat went for its eyes, then its jugular, which distracted it long enough for me to hit it with a blast of Mr Mighty oven cleaner, also provided by Þhurs here, which I think temporarily blinded it, which was when it accidentally impaled itself on the clothes prop. They say most accidents happen in the home and that was certainly true today.'

And then, instead of ending on a dry witticism worthy of James Bond at his finest, I burst into tears.

CHAPTER THIRTY

Iblis was wonderful. He cleaned my hands, anointed my burns with something that took the sting away and told me I'd live. He bustled about, put the kettle on, made sure the cat was comfortable and gave him a drink, told Nigel he was the dog equivalent of Iron Man, patted Þhurs, wiped his hand on his T-shirt, and made the tea, pouring a careful drop of something into mine. I've no idea what it was, but it packed a hell of a wallop and, therefore, I should make it clear that many of the subsequent events that evening were Iblis's fault. That's my story, anyway, and I'm sticking to it.

Nigel belched loudly and trotted into the kitchen to see if food was on offer.

'He's hungry,' said Iblis. 'Never let it be said that Iblis, Man of Courage and Resource, would fail his friends. I can see you might possibly be too tired to cook for us all this evening, Elizabeth Cage, and so I, Iblis, will provide a meal fit for champions. Fish and chips?'

'How can you eat at a time like . . . ?'

He gestured at Þhurs. 'He will be hungry.'

'So? I'll do him some toast.'

'No – he will be very hungry.'

'Again – so?'

Iblis gestured downstairs. 'There's good eating down there. Especially one that size.'

I stared in horror. 'What? You mean he'd actually . . .'

'Waste not, want not.'

'But . . .'

'I don't mean he'll drag it up here and chomp it in front of you . . .'

'What?'

'I'll hack him off a bit. Put it on a plate if it makes you feel better.'

'He . . .'

'Do you want some?'

I put my head in my hands. 'I've just vanquished a giant snake. I don't deserve this.'

'So, fish and chips, then? My treat.'

I sighed. 'I suppose so.'

'Shall I take Nigel?'

Nigel, however, preferred to rest and actually, I didn't blame him. My back, shoulders and arms were killing me.

'What if it comes back?' I said nervously.

Iblis shook his head. 'He tried. He failed. You defeated the serpent. There are rules about this sort of thing, you know. For instance . . .'

I was too tired to care.

'Back soon,' he shouted and slammed the door after him.

Wearily, I began to clear away the debris. Bowls of bloody water, bloodstained gauze, scraps of tape, discarded wrappings and so forth. By the time I had everything put away, the cat was struggling to his feet. I watched as he limped towards the door.

He looked back over his shoulder at me and then at the door.

'No,' I said. 'No – you can't go. Not now.'

He looked back at the door again. He'd been sent here for a purpose and that purpose had been fulfilled. He'd return whence he came and I . . . I'd be alone again.

I knelt beside him at the door, suddenly very glad Iblis wasn't here.

'Please don't go,' I said, very quietly. 'You're still hurt. I'm not saying stay for ever – although that would be nice – but stay at least until you're completely healed. You saved me and I should return the favour. And . . . I like having you here. It's . . . sometimes I'm . . .' I swallowed. 'Please – won't you stay? At least a little while longer.'

Two stupid tears ran down my cheeks and plopped on to his head.

He looked at me a while, slowly closed his eyes again, and hobbled back to his place by the fire.

I got up, avoided everyone's eye, and laid the table. By the time I'd finished, the young master had returned, bearing enough fish and chips to satisfy the population of a small town.

I flaked a giant piece of cod for the cat, because he deserved it. I dished up an entire portion for Nigel, because he deserved it. I put a double portion out for Þhurs, because he deserved it as well, but sensibly refrained from providing him with any eating implements. Just in case.

Iblis made more tea – my supplies were really taking a bashing today. My tea tasted a little strange again. I stared at him suspiciously, but he just grinned at me, and after a while I stopped worrying about how to get a dead snake out of my cellar and began to feel much more cheerful about things in

426

general. Being drugged without one's knowledge and consent is probably illegal, but I really didn't care at that moment.

I would regret that.

Finally, we all sat down to eat. Iblis took the armchair and I sat next to Þhurs. Everyone pretended they couldn't hear the noises Nigel was making.

Old Þhurs was delighted with his meal. Initially, there had been a great deal of preliminary investigation – I was guessing salt and vinegar was not a combination that had come his way before – and he was possibly experiencing some disappointment it wasn't giant snake – or even human flesh – but he'd recovered well and was now tucking in with the rest of us.

Silence fell, other than the noise of chomping and the occasional appreciative trill from Þhurs, and then the front door opened – because, once again, no one had thought to lock it – and Michael Jones and Melek walked in.

Both of them stopped dead. As well they might. There was a troll on the sofa – a surprising event in its own right – but this one was eating fish and chips with great enjoyment and wearing a dazzlingly white triangular bandage.

And in front of the fire, a huge black cat daintily nibbled at a piece of cod nearly as big as he was.

And over in the kitchen, Nigel, the JCB of table manners, was making disgusting noises as he hoovered up the contents of his bowl.

And then there was me, on the sofa next to the troll, covered in black snake blood, and dotted with various small wounds.

Iblis, as always, looked as if he'd just emerged from a shampoo commercial.

Jones looked at everyone. I'd like to say we all looked back at him, but we were too busy eating.

Before anyone could start, I swallowed a mouthful and said, 'Go and look in the cellar.'

Jones and Melek disappeared, reappearing rather a long time later and looking rather green around the gills.

'Cage, are you all right? Are you hurt at all?'

'No, I'm fine. A bit battered . . .' Belatedly I realised this was actually a very funny joke although no one else seemed to get it. I pointed at the fish. 'Battered?' Again, no one got it. You can lead people to a joke, but you can't make them laugh. I gestured at the state of me. 'But otherwise fine.'

'The size of that thing,' he said wonderingly.

I nodded.

'The serpent,' said Melek.

I nodded again.

'Actually,' said Jones, 'I think there's a reward for anyone finding a snake longer than . . .'

'We've had that conversation,' I said wearily. 'Anyone clearing that out of my cellar is welcome to it.'

'What happened?' said Melek, carefully closing the cellar door. She turned to Iblis, taking in his pristine appearance. 'And where were you?'

He swallowed a mouthful. 'Next door. Helping Mrs Barton off the floor.'

She narrowed her eyes. 'A diversion?'

He forked in another mouthful and nodded, still chewing. 'Looks like it.'

Þurs had finished his portion, so I gave him what remained

428

of mine. I was too tired to eat. I leaned back and closed my eyes. The discussion took place over my head.

'Is it over?' demanded Jones. 'Is that it? Cage won?'

'For the time being,' said Iblis quietly.

'She can't stay here,' said Melek. 'Not with that thing in the cellar.'

I was in complete agreement. The council's pest control department was going to have a very nasty shock in the morning.

'She can stay with us,' said Melek. 'Just in case.'

I wondered whether I should ask in case of what, but did I really want to know?

'No, she should come to me,' said Jones. 'She already has some stuff there, so no need to pack. We could go now.'

'We have everything she needs,' said Melek. 'And we are closer.'

Their voices were overly polite. We were approaching defcon 1. Or 5. I can never remember whether the scale goes up or down. I just hoped no one was going to ask me to make the decision. That would be a real Solomon's baby moment.

I think at some point I might have dropped off. It was the smell that woke me. Resting your head on a troll's shoulder can do that. I tried not to sit up in too much of a hurry.

Iblis, like me, had withdrawn from the conflict and was washing up at the sink, bless him. I blinked and looked around. The table was cleared, and other than the raging argument, the soldier cat, the unhygienic dog, the bandaged troll and the dead snake in the cellar, order had been restored.

'Becky?' I said suddenly, hoping to distract them.

'Safe and sound,' said Jones, turning to me. 'We had a long talk in the car. She knows virtually nothing. Joanna didn't trust her enough to involve her in anything. It seems no one rated her when Veronica Harlow was alive and Becky skidded even further down the social scale after her death. We arrived at our destination safely, she had a bath and a good meal and was fast asleep when we left.'

'What will happen to her?'

He shrugged. 'She can stay for a few days – longer if she wants – and take the time to decide what she wants to do.'

'Will she be safe?'

'Probably. According to the news bulletins, Greyston's pretty much gone. The stones are destroyed. There's no power there any longer. Whether those who escaped the burnings managed to avoid the dead men in the woods, I've no idea. I'm certainly not going back to check. Now, Cage . . .'

'No,' said Melek, but quietly. 'Please be sensible over this. There has been . . . a serious incident. Everyone needs rest and quiet. There may be some fall-out. Elizabeth Cage's safety should be our prime concern. I can provide that. Perhaps I should make it clear you are included in the invitation. You can provide the reassurance she will undoubtedly need when she has had a chance to reflect on today's . . . events.'

I should say, 'I'm right here, you know,' because they were talking over my head, but I couldn't be bothered. I really didn't care. Getting out of the house was the most important thing. The destination – slightly less so.

'Can we go?' I said. I tried not to sound too pathetic, but suppose that thing suddenly came back to life. In my mind I saw it open its eyes. Lift its head. Look around for me . . . 'Please.'

'Of course.'

I turned to the cat. 'What of you, old soldier?'

'Yes,' said Iblis. 'Warmth and safety tonight, my friend. If you will permit me to carry you.'

I waited for Jones to ask why everyone was talking to a cat. And incidentally, where had he come from? And why was he here? And what exactly was going on? But he didn't. Getting out of the house seemed to be everyone's priority at the moment.

Iblis fetched my coat. I suddenly realised how cold I was. And stiff. And sore. I found my bag and my keys. Jones turned off all the lights and we filed down my front steps. Iblis carried the cat who, despite his injuries, still managed to look regal and noble and completely in control of his own life – which was considerably more than I was managing to do at that moment.

Nigel trotted over to cock his leg on someone's steps.

Þhurs – wearing his blue blanket like a cloak – made a sound.

'He's giving you the troll farewell,' said Iblis. 'He really likes you, you know. And not just because you taste good. And he loves his bandages. You do know he'll wear them until the end of time, don't you?'

'He earned them,' I said. 'If that thing had managed to get past him, out of the cellar, and catch me unawares, then I'd be dead. Or worse. Please tell him thank you from me.'

Þhurs made some sort of gesture.

'He says good luck,' said Iblis, adding helpfully, 'he thinks you'll need it.'

I opened my mouth to ask why, but the seven-foot troll wearing a blue blanket with his arm in a sling was already melting inconspicuously into the night. I saw him go with more affection than I would have thought possible this time yesterday.

The evening air was chilly. I thought so, anyway. We walked very slowly. I had a horrible feeling that tomorrow I wouldn't

431

be able to walk at all. Now that the elation was wearing off, I was realising how incredibly lucky I'd been. How narrow my escape. We could – we should – have died in that cellar. All of us. And I hadn't done anything. I'd just held the clothes prop while the serpent impaled itself upon it. There was no way I had enough strength to thrust the business end up through its skull like that. It had killed itself – it wasn't anything I had done. Really, when I thought about it – I'd been pretty useless. As I always was.

I felt my eyes prick with tears of self-pity. Which didn't help. We were approaching the archway and decision time. Turn right and down the hill to Jones's flat, or left and down the hill for Iblis and Melek. There was about to be another argument.

A tear slid down my cheek. And then another. Oh God, I was going to cry in public. My mother would have been so cross. She'd had a long list of things not to do in public. Eating. Shouting. Smoking. Running. Crying . . .

I couldn't help it. I gave a great sob, leaned forwards as best I could and rested my hands on my thighs. Another sob forced its way out and then I was crying in earnest.

There was massive consternation. Nigel began to sniff around my ankles as if searching for some sort of clue to this extraordinary behaviour.

'Cage, are you hurt? Are you in pain? Should I get you to the hospital?'

I tried to speak. Nothing happened. Just stupid crying all over everyone.

I think Iblis would have put his arms around me, but they were full of cat. I suspected Melek had never hugged anyone in her life, which left . . .

432

Jones put his arms around me. He felt amazingly warm and solid and comfortable.

'It's all right,' he said gently. 'It's all over. You're fine. Everyone's fine. We're on our way to . . .' He chickened out of naming the destination. 'To safety. You can have a bath and a sleep. I'll be there. You'll be safe. I promise.'

I nodded. Words wouldn't come so I clutched at his jacket instead.

'It's all right,' he said again, rubbing my back. 'You're safe. Take your time.'

Of course, as soon as I'd been given permission to stand there sobbing all night if I wanted to, I felt better. I looked up at him looking down at me. Somehow, something happened. I don't know what. He used his thumbs to wipe away my tears. Very gently.

'Elizabeth Cage – will you marry me?'

I continued to disgrace myself in public. My legs gave way and I sat down in shock. Sitting on the ground in public was also on my mother's list.

So – to recap. I was on the ground. Iblis, Melek, the cat and Nigel were all waiting with great interest to see what would happen next. There was still a giant snake in my cellar. A *dead* giant snake. And Jones had just proposed.

Things got even worse. A voice said, 'Is everything all right here?'

I looked up. Police Sgt Bates was standing in the archway, watching us.

I couldn't believe it. We never had the police up here. Rushford is a very law-abiding town – even though it contains Michael Jones – and Castle Close is the most law-abiding area in law-abiding Rushford. I'd *never* seen the police here – ever. But not tonight. Tonight, I was having snakes and proposals and general meltdowns, so yes, of course the police were here. Why wouldn't they be?

I pulled myself together as best I could. 'Yes.'

'That's marvellous,' said Jones, in apparent rapture. 'I am the happiest man in the world. A summer wedding, I think. What's everyone doing the second week in August?'

I stared at him in horror. 'I'm not marrying you.'

'Yes, you are.'

'No, I'm not.'

'You said *yes*.'

'I was talking to the policewoman.'

'Police*man*,' said Iblis, grinning.

'Police officer,' said Sgt Bates. 'What's going on here?'

'This lady has just agreed to marry me.'

'This lady is in tears.'

'You are witnessing the manifestation of her joy at the thought of becoming my wife.'

'She's sprawled on the cobbles.'

'Her extreme joy caused her legs to give way.'

I tried to pull myself together. 'I'm *not* marrying you.'

'You said you would, Cage, and I'm holding you to it.'

'I wasn't talking to you.'

'I asked you to marry me. You said yes.'

'I said yes to Sgt Bates – not to you.'

'That's not the way I heard it.'

'And I'm already married,' said Sgt Bates.

Nigel, obviously under the impression we'd stopped for good, lay down beside me and started to snore.

434

'Again,' said Sgt Bates. 'What is happening here?'

Well, she did ask.

'I've had to leave my house,' I said. 'There's a giant snake in the cellar.'

'Really?'

I could see exactly what she was thinking. There was a tiny snake – possibly not even a snake, probably a large worm – in my cellar and I was being a hysterical homeowner.

She held out her hand. 'May I take a look?'

'Please do.' I fished out my keys and handed them over, saying, 'Please be careful. I spilled some bleach down there.'

She set off for my house.

I looked up to find everyone looking down at me. Even Nigel had opened his eyes.

'What?' I said.

'Cage, you have a fifty-foot-long snake with a clothes prop through its eye and you're wittering on to her about not standing in the bleach.'

'Spilled bleach can be very dangerous,' I said primly, and even Melek snorted with laughter.

Jones pulled himself together. 'Are you going to sprawl there for ever, Cage?'

'Yes.'

'That's twice you've said yes to me in one night. I am the world's luckiest man.'

We all watched Sgt Bates climb my front steps, unlock the door and disappear inside.

'Good job Þurs has gone,' said Iblis. 'A dead snake we can work around. Seven-foot trolls are a bit more difficult. Plus, he's always hungry.'

'You mean he really would have eaten it? He'd be eating a dead snake in my cellar?'

'No, of course not. He would have skinned it and taken it back home to eat.'

'Where's home?' enquired Jones, with interest.

'Under his bridge, I expect.'

'A giant troll sitting under a bridge tucking into a fifty-foot-long snake? That's disgusting.'

'More or less disgusting than eating it in Elizabeth Cage's cellar?'

I buried my face in my hands. 'Oh God.'

Sgt Bates reappeared, paused on my doorstep for a moment to take five or six deep breaths and then spoke into her radio.

'Oh good,' said Jones. 'She'll get the council round to take it away. I confess I wasn't sure whether we should dispose of the remains as ordinary household waste, compost or food waste. Problem solved.'

'Phew,' said Iblis.

'Indeed,' said Jones.

I eyed them all. Speechless.

Sgt Bates returned. Before she could say a word, I said, 'Can you give me a list of crimes which would result in me being banged up for a night? On my own. Absolutely alone. Show me the list and I promise I'll put my hand up to at least five of them and you can arrest me and I can spend the night in a police cell. Did I mention alone?'

'Mrs Cage, did you actually fight off . . .'

'No, no,' I said hastily. 'I just stabbed it with the clothes prop.'

'How on earth did it get in?'

I had no idea what to say.

436

'I expect it crawled in through the little window,' said Iblis helpfully.

'Yes,' said Sgt Bates, with heavy sarcasm. The police do heavy sarcasm really well. 'A fifty-foot-long snake crawled through a tiny window measuring eighteen inches by six.'

'Well, obviously it was much smaller when it crawled in,' said Iblis.

'And lived entirely undetected during the decades it took to achieve that size?'

'Well, it must have,' said Iblis. 'There's no other explanation, is there? It's not like that scene in *Lake Placid* with Betty White feeding all those cows to that alligator.'

'Crocodile,' said Jones.

'No, I don't think so,' said Iblis thoughtfully. 'It's one of my favourite films. I've seen it loads of times.'

'So have I and it's a crocodile. Actually, it's two crocodiles.'

'Hey,' said Iblis. 'Spoiler alert.'

'You said you'd seen it.'

'Elizabeth Cage hasn't.'

'Please lock me away,' I said to Sgt Bates.

'I might have to,' she said. 'Do you have the appropriate snake-keeping licence?'

'I didn't even know I had a snake until it tried to eat me, so no, I do not have a licence. Does this mean you'll lock me up after all?'

'I'll let you off with a warning, since this is your first offence.'

'What have you actually got to do to get yourself banged up around here?'

'Oh, oh, I know the answer to that one,' said Jones, raising his hand and grinning at Sgt Bates.

437

She ignored him. 'I have to ask, Mrs Cage, are there any more snakes on the premises? The pest control people will want to know.'

'If they find any, they can have those too. Otherwise, apart from spiders in the cupboard under the sink – that's it.'

'Just to satisfy my curiosity,' said Jones. 'Will you be calling the council's pest control or the RSPCA?'

'Anyone I can get. I suspect it's going to be a long night.'

'Indeed,' said Melek, entering the fray. 'Mrs Cage obviously can't remain in her own house tonight. She's in a state of shock and is coming home with me and she won't be returning until the remains are safely and responsibly disposed of.'

'She's coming back with me,' said Jones. 'She's my fiancée.'

'No, I'm not.'

'I distinctly heard you say yes.'

'*I said yes to the police officer.*'

'You're marrying the police officer?'

'I'm not marrying anyone.'

'Besides, Sgt Bates is already married,' said Iblis. 'She said so.'

'I'm sorry, Cage, but all I heard is yes. I said, "Will you marry me?" and you said, "Yes." We're talking about an August wedding. Up you get now. You can't sprawl there all night – the sergeant will run you in for being drunk and disorderly.'

'Oh, yes, please,' I said yearningly.

'No, it's all right, Cage. You've already said yes – you don't have to say *please* as well.'

'For the love of God,' I shrieked. 'I was talking to Sgt Bates. Again.'

There was a bit of a silence. I was conscious of my stickiness. 'I just want a hot bath and a nice bed.'

'Well, there's a coincidence,' said Jones. 'Those are exactly my plans for your evening.'

'Mrs Cage, would you like me to run you to a hotel?'

'It's tempting, but no. I'm going with her.' I indicated Melek.

'You shall have a hot bath,' she said. 'And the bed in the spare room is very comfortable.'

'I sleep in the spare room,' said Iblis indignantly.

'You will sleep on the sofa.'

'Nigel sleeps on the sofa.'

'Nigel sleeps on the floor.'

'And I sleep with Cage,' said Jones. 'Lovely. That's everyone settled, then.'

Sgt Bates grinned. 'Mrs Cage, you have only to say.'

'No,' I said wearily. 'It's fine, thank you.'

She nodded at my entourage. 'You're going with them?'

'No, they're coming with me. I'm the Rushford equivalent of the Ancient Mariner, only instead of a dead albatross hanging around my neck, I have this lot.'

'If you're certain . . .'

'I am, Sergeant, thank you.'

'In that case, I'll keep your keys and liaise with the . . . appropriate people regarding the . . . the remains in the cellar. You do know there's a reward for anyone finding a . . . ?'

'I do now,' I said. 'It's yours, if you want it.'

'The snake or the reward?'

'Either. Both.'

'Thank you, but we're not allowed to accept gifts.'

'In what universe is the corpse of a fifty-foot-long snake a gift?'

'You'd be surprised,' she said darkly.

439

'No – I wouldn't. Nothing surprises me any longer.'

'You can collect your keys from the station. Good night.'

We watched her make her way back towards my house.

'Rather her than me,' said Jones. 'Are you going to lie there all night, Cage?'

He pulled me to my feet. Iblis stirred Nigel with his toe and we all set off again. The Ancient Mariner and her dead albatrosses.

We passed through the archway and set off down the hill. Towards Melek's house. I kept my eyes fixed on the pavement ahead because I knew someone would say it. Sooner or later, someone was going to say it. Either Iblis or Jones. Iblis probably. Yes – Iblis.

I was right.

'So,' he said brightly. 'Who wants to watch *Lake Placid* when we get back?'

THE END

MASSIVE ACKNOWLEDGEMENTS AND THANKS TO:

Hazel Cushion – Agent extraordinaire
Julia Turney – Beta reader
Sharon Clint – Beta reader
Phillip Dawson – Advisor on all things illegal, bloody and dubious

Those at Headline:
Jessie Goetzinger-Hall – Editor
Frankie Edwards – Editor
Hannah Sawyer – Marketing
Federica Trogu – Publicity
Ellie Wheeldon – Audio
And everyone else in Sales, Rights, Art and Production.

Not forgetting:
Sharona Selby – Copy-editor
Jill Cole – Proofreader

And Zara Ramm, who reads my books so beautifully.